100
YEARS
SIMON &
SCHUSTER
PAPERBACKS

ALSO BY
ANNA DORN

Exalted
Bad Lawyer
Vagablonde

PERFUME & PAIN

A Novel

ANNA DORN

SIMON & SCHUSTER PAPERBACKS
New York London Toronto
Sydney New Delhi

For Vanessa

ACT I

Many years ago I realized that a book, a novel, is a dream that asks itself to be written in the same way we fall in love with someone: the dream becomes impossible to resist, there's nothing you can do about it, you finally give in and succumb even if your instincts tell you to run the other way because this could be, in the end, a dangerous game—someone will get hurt.

—*Bret Easton Ellis*

one

I meet Ivy on my fading 16-inch MacBook Pro.

Ivy is the newest member of my Zoom writing group, the one I created ten years ago with some dykes I met on Tumblr, the one I stopped attending regularly when my writing career began gathering steam.

On her first day, when Ivy says she's writing about a lesbian love triangle, I know I'm doomed. When she sends me a private message asking me my zodiac sign, it's game over. Ivy is my type. Dark hair, glasses. Chatty but emotionally distant. Refracted attention, definitely hiding something, a sinister side behind a hesitant smile.

Guess, I reply to her query. This is a useful way to ask strangers how you come off. If they say Capricorn, they think you're stuck up and power hungry. If they say Leo, you're talking too much about yourself. If they say Pisces, they think you're weak. People almost always guess me wrong. Aquarius is the rarest sign. Look it up.

Gemini?

Nope. I get Gemini a lot. My mind moves quickly and pivots often. Gemini is an air sign like Aquarius, but the more chaotic one. I promised myself I would stop thinking about astrology after publishing my last book about a cynical internet astrologer. But astrology is the great lesbian elixir!

Taurus?

God no. In her little Zoom rectangle, Ivy stifles a giggle. Taurus is not my favorite sign—stubborn, slow, cocky without much to show for it. But they can be pretty. My name, Astrid, means "divinely beautiful" in Old Norse, but I'm not sure that phrase describes me. However, I activated the Zoom feature to touch up my appearance. Maybe it's working. Gravity's toll on my skin really shows on Zoom. I'm thirty-five. Yesterday I was twenty-five. I blinked and I'm thirty-five. I don't write speculative fiction; I'm being cheeky.

I give up. Ivy says, *I don't want to offend you.*

You already have, I respond. *You aren't a Taurus are you?*

She shuffles in her seat so that I can see the entirety of the *Desert Hearts* poster on the wall behind her. *Nope*, she writes back.

Phew. Tauruses are known for beauty though. Venus-ruled. I hate how much I know about this shit. After this meeting, I'm going to write down the word *astrology* on a piece of paper and then burn it. *I'm an Aquarius.*

Oh! I hardly know any Aquarians.

We're niche, I write.

I'm sure.

I smile.

Want to guess me?

Yeah. I'm very good at guessing people's signs, which is embarrassing. Why can't I be good at guessing something useful like life expectancy or net worth? Ivy's pretty and symmetrical, not a Taurus, so maybe she's the other Venus-ruled sign—Libra. I'm

getting air sign energy. She's talkative but doesn't seem particularly emotionally invested in what she's saying, or what's being
said. She's a little scattered. She has trouble committing to an
opinion, always contradicting herself, offering disclaimers.

Libra?

You are good.

two

Before Ivy asked me my zodiac sign, my haphazard return to my Zoom writing group hadn't sparked much joy. It's sad, because the initial group—named the Lez Brat Pack because we genuinely believed we were the lesbian literary brat pack—was the highlight of my mid-twenties. I had just dropped out of law school and compulsory heterosexuality, and Lez Brat Pack promised a bright future of lesbianism and literary success. We had the vigor and delusion of youth and were convinced we were about to crack open the publishing world.

But at a certain point, the group began to lose steam, feel less cohesive. Writers came and went. Writers fucked each other, nearly ruined each other's lives, got published and cocky, or stopped writing entirely, started working at Google, developed fine lines and cynical attitudes. I've fallen into a few of these categories. Zoom highlights my triangle of sadness, the wrinkles between my brows caused by excessive frowning, and I had a romantic dalliance with Sophie, another founding member and a UCSB PhD student, once the Jay McInerney to my Bret Easton Ellis. Also, I've published three books since the group's founding. The first is essentially dyke fanfic about Kendall Jenner, the second is about a lawyer who wants to be a rapper, and the third is the cynical internet astrologer. Once I started publishing, I felt less need for the writing group. I suppose I was one of the ones who got cocky and disappeared. But I was busy! Writing, revising, and nurturing a light drug problem.

While I was gone, Lez Brat Pack changed its name to Sapphic Scribes. Apparently some of the newer members found the original name "misogynistic," "infantilizing," and "exclusive." They all seem at least ten years younger than me, around the age I was when I joined, too young to realize that Sapphic Scribes is equally infantilizing and that exclusivity is not necessarily a bad thing.

It's not that I have anything against Sappho; obviously, I stan a girl-crazy lesbian poet. And I understand the appeal of sapphic as a vaguely chic euphemism for lesbian. But recently words like *sapphic* and *queer* feel a bit corporate and TikTok-y. I don't use TikTok because it makes me feel like I'm having a seizure, but suddenly I can't open Instagram without being bombarded by some "sapphic bookstagrammer" or "queer radical sex therapist." And, I don't know, maybe I miss when homosexuality was a little less corny? I prefer the word *lesbian* because it conjures a less cringe, more libidinous past.

Anyway, I returned to the group because I was bored, am bored, because I am taking a break from my former extracurriculars—going out, blacking out, doing shit I regret, feeling ill for days. For most of my twenties and early thirties, I got by with the help of a magic cocktail I came to call "the Patricia Highsmith." Alcohol, sativa, Adderall, cigarettes. On the Patricia Highsmith, I could do anything. I published three books, optioned two. I had an active social life; some even called me a "party girl." I dated half of Los Angeles, fell in love more times than any one person has a right to in a lifetime. But like most coping mechanisms, the Patricia Highsmith turned on me. I did some stupid things we don't have to get into, then became what my psychologist called "suicidal." But luckily I'm not in therapy anymore. That lady always had very negative things to say.

The problem is: without the Patricia Highsmith, I haven't exactly been able to write. I'm financially okay for a bit because my astrology novel was recently optioned for a fat sum. The money won't last forever, but the more pressing problem is existential. Without writing books, I have no idea who I am. I'm half dead.

So currently—it's so hard to say this, but: Sapphic Scribes (and more specifically Ivy)—is the emotional focal point of my life, a way to shape my weeks. The time between meetings moves at a glacial pace, especially without the Patricia Highsmith to keep me euphoric. I try to stay busy in the ways I've tried to stay busy since I committed to "getting healthy" at the suggestion of myself and various licensed professionals. I take long walks. I do yoga in my yard. I lie on my bed and listen to audiobooks downloaded for free from the public library app. I FaceTime with Zev, my only friend who is a "good influence." We went to college together, my fag hag years, when I was afraid to be near anyone I wanted to fuck or who wanted to fuck me. Fine, I guess I'm still like that a little bit. Fear is desire's cousin.

: : : :

The night before the next meeting, I can't sleep at all. I toss and turn and listen to an entire audiobook, a thriller a reviewer called "The Talented Mr. Ripoff." The diss is not a diss to me. I worship Patricia Highsmith, obviously, and a book that rips her off is probably better than 99 percent of books, which tend to be very boring.

Growing up, I didn't read much. I preferred television and talking to myself. But when I started trying to write books, I figured I had to read them if I wanted to be good. And I didn't just want to be good: I wanted to be the best. Once I started reading, I realized I liked books about angry, quick-witted women with major interpersonal issues, a genre known on Goodreads as "she's not doing okay at all." I also enjoy deception, glamour, à la *Ripley*. And anything that compares itself to *Single White Female*. I love a stalker, even when I'm the victim—it's flattering!

The group doesn't meet until 3:00 p.m. and until then my body pulses with nervous energy. I make coffee and tend to my Google alerts, which include notifications for my name, Twitter handle, and book titles. When my last book was released, my publisher suggested setting up Google alerts to keep an eye out for promotional opportunities. But recently it's a lot, all the alerts, and now my heart is racing, and not in a fun way. I click Delete All. I don't want to get into it, but I promise you: there are no promotional opportunities.

Afterward, I walk seven miles to kill adrenaline. I eat a big salad and watch Kim and Kourtney eat big salads on a ten-year-old episode of *Keeping Up with the Kardashian*s. I skim the pages we're workshopping today, written by a self-proclaimed sapiosexual named Pia, a Lez Brat Pack OG who tried to kick me out of the group because I hadn't read—I kid you not—*Stone Butch Blues*. She lives in the Bay Area and has that morally superior and covertly filthy rich attitude that constitutes one of the primary reasons I escaped my hometown of San Francisco. Currently she's writing a "cli-fi" novel, a term I just learned, which means speculative fiction about the horrors of climate change. I ask Zev if he knows the term and he says of course and I should be ashamed for not knowing it, especially as an "authoress." Zev is obsessed with the dwindling health of the planet. I never think about her, Mother Earth. Sometimes I feel bad for not thinking about her, and try to read science news, and then I become bored and depressed and think—what did I gain from that? I recycle. I hardly ever fly because planes scare me. Driving on the freeway scares me too. I do my part. I don't need to know all the gory details.

I spend nearly an hour getting ready for Zoom. I try on five different shirts. They're all black and look pretty much the same, but they each do slightly different things to my neckline. I don't have much in the way of breasts, but sometimes on Zoom with the right shirt and proper lighting, I can create the illusion of cleavage. Real movie magic.

My green amethyst necklace draws attention to my fake cleavage. Amethyst is my birthstone, and the name apparently comes from the Ancient Greek word for "intoxicated." Ancient wearers believed the gemstone protected them from drunkenness, which historically I need help with. Except I hate the color purple. It just feels too literal and tragic for a lesbian to wear purple. But then I found a green amethyst, which is made from artificially heating the stone, and is also supposed to protect against negative energy and toxic vibrations, which feels ideal for getting healthy. Mine hangs on a sterling silver cable chain, and it's one of the more expensive things I own.

I consider eyeliner, then decide against it. I don't want to look like I'm trying. Also, eyeliner is risky. My other college friend Otto said I don't have the fine motor skills for eye makeup, and he's probably right. He also said I should stop wearing so much black. "It ages you," he said. "The global You, I mean." He said this when I turned thirty, and I dismissed him as insane. But looking in the mirror now, I think he might be right.

When did I start looking older than twenty-five?

I spritz my forearm and neck with a British cult perfume

named for a lab-created molecule, Iso E Super. I've gotten really into perfume since I stopped feeling twenty-five, when I didn't have to do much to feel sexy, when my skin was smooth and taut and I somehow had abs despite never doing a crunch and drinking twelve PBRs a night. At thirty-five, I'm beginning to feel a bit dusty. I don't want to get Botox like all my fags, and when Otto was in town a while ago, we wandered into a niche perfume store and smelled everything, and I got a sample of a French perfume translated as "queen of night" and described as spellbinding and sensual. I went through the sample quickly and enjoyed how it made me feel, like I was gliding around with this obliquely sexy aura.

Otto said perfume is all about "being someone else," and I write fiction for a reason. So, I began spending a lot of time ordering decants and samples online. This one site has a service where you tell them how you want to smell and they send you a custom sampler pack. I've ordered a bunch because I can't commit to one scent, which is probably a metaphor, but anyway I've told them I want to smell like a Parisian It Girl and sequoia trees at dusk, like Kate Moss in the '90s and a Malibu cloud. I'm dying to find a signature scent, one that transforms me into the perfect version of myself, a scent that people come to associate with me, the new me: who is healthy and lucid and doesn't black out large portions of the evening on a regular basis. It's bizarre to put on perfume for Zoom, where no one can smell me, but Iso E Super does wonders for my mood, eliciting a mild euphoria.

I pour an IPA into a coffee mug and move my laptop to various places in my apartment to test how I look. I pick a spot in the yard, under a big tree, which floods my face in dramatic light, blurring my imperfections. I picked this house in part for the yard. For my first ten years in Los Angeles, I lived in apartments near freeways. Whenever I opened the windows, the surfaces would almost immediately coat in a film of gray exhaust.

Now I live on the top of a hill in Eagle Rock, far from the freeway and surrounded by trees, and when I open the windows, I breathe fresh air. And in the afternoons, I read in the yard or just listen to the birds. This wooded bungalow is crucial to my path to health.

I take a big sip of my beer and click the Sapphic Scribes Zoom link.

:::

Seven faces appear on the screen, but I only notice Ivy. She's wearing a translucent button-down shirt over a pink bra, the left cup visible at the top. Touché, my dear.

I wonder what she smells like. I'm thinking white florals and musk, horny jasmine.

Having mostly abandoned fiction for academia, Sophie is spending the semester in Greece doing research for her dissertation on—drumroll, please—Sappho, so her replacement moderator is a man named Todd. When I found out about Todd, I messaged Sophie, *why the fuck is a man named Todd moderating Sapphic Scribes?* And she said, *how do you know he's cis?* And I said, *too arrogant to be anything but* and Sophie said I was probably right although she didn't know for sure, but that Todd is a successful author of lesbian erotica, which he writes under the pen name Tatiana Moon. I still don't think this qualifies him to lead the group. But I didn't say anything because everyone has been sort of wary of me since I started publishing and stopped showing up, and Sophie's been wary of me since I told her I didn't want to be her girlfriend (I was twenty-seven and struggling with monogamy). I also felt like maybe I could learn from someone who writes lesbian erotica as my writing is tragically cerebral—maybe *cerebral* is too sophisticated a word, *chatty* might be a better one—either way, it's not sexy at all. But Todd never has anything insightful to say, about writing erotica or otherwise.

Todd fumbles through his clumsy opener, and I wait for Ivy to message me. I privately vow to avoid the subject of astrology; I cannot under any circumstances ask her about her rising and moon signs. Astrology is passé. I still need to burn that piece of paper.

As Todd opens the discussion of Pia's cli-fi pages, a mosquito bites my ankle. Then another one, then another. I'm being attacked yet trying to maintain a flirtatious aura. My body itches like crazy. I'm twitchy and hot, not cute at all. A bead of sweat rolls down my arm. This is a disaster. I turn off my camera and move my laptop inside, back to my regular spot in the breakfast nook, where the lighting is just okay. Ivy messages me as soon as I turn my Zoom camera back on. My heart jumps.

What's your rising and moon?

Well, she opened the door. I can bite like a mosquito and then tell her astrology is off-limits, for my mental health. Will that sound crazy? Whatever. Women like crazy. Lesbians love crazy. I'm about to make her guess when she messages me again.

Don't ask me to guess.

Fine, I say. *Leo rising. Leo moon.* People tend to find Leos self-centered and dramatic and, yes, I have been called both of these things.

Ivy responds with a lion emoji.

Before I can ask her hers, Todd addresses me. "Any thoughts from the famous novelist?"

Todd always calls me this, *the famous novelist*, in a lightly condescending tone, like it's not actually true but he's humoring me because my ego is fragile, which it absolutely is. People with healthy egos don't become writers; they become engineers.

I giggle, as I always do—like I'm in on the joke, which I'm not—then open my notes.

"Pia establishes herself as highly qualified to tell this story," I say, avoiding looking at Pia's Zoom square because I assume she is glaring at me, as she always does when I talk. "The voice is confident." I'm bullshitting. I just skimmed the pages. But I keep talking, saying God knows what, stock feedback: *I want your protagonist to be more active, show don't tell, more interiority, but what does your character FEEL, etc., etc., etc.*

When I can't locate any more vacuous bullshit, Ivy starts talking.

"If I could piggyback off what Astrid said," she says, and I immediately imagine her fucking me from behind, the way I like it. A psychologist might say my taste for doggystyle, which avoids eye contact, suggests a fear of intimacy, but luckily I never really told my therapist the truth.

As Ivy monologues with enthusiasm, I slide my green amethyst along its chain and try not to stare at her. I googled Ivy this week and learned that she's a PhD candidate at UCSB, which made sense because she isn't very creative. Also, Sophie's getting her PhD at UCSB and likely brought her into the group. I thought about emailing Sophie, asking what Ivy's deal is, but Sophie would think I'm trying to get with Ivy, which I absolutely am, but I don't need her feedback.

I also learned from Ivy's Instagram page that she has a taste for butch women, and might even be in a relationship with one, a platinum blonde Samantha Ronson derivative, which is often the case with pretty femmes. It worried me, the photo, as I am decidedly not butch. For this reason, it took years to convince people I was a lesbian. Most people thought I was just being an edgelord. I had my first lesbian liaison around the time Lindsay Lohan began dating Sam Ronson, speak of the devil, and everyone thought she was losing her mind, and people thought I was losing my mind, too, and maybe we both were.

Pia's book is so fucking boring, Ivy messages me.

Oh it's torture, I reply. *I skimmed.*

I read the first and last paragraphs, Ivy responds.

You bad, I say, flirting.

We go back and forth like this until the end of the meeting, until she leaves me her number. Success.

I text her before bed. *It's Astrid.*

She doesn't respond.

three

The Pacific Ocean sparkles turquoise in the distance, lightly hypnotizing me.

I'm dining al fresco at Moonshadows, the Malibu restaurant where Mel Gibson went on that antisemitic rant, waiting for my chicken Caesar salad. More than that, I'm waiting for Ivy to text me.

I should probably be "present," focused on spending time with Otto, who is in town from New York to deliver a dress to Zendaya for some movie premiere. I'm not entirely sure what Otto does, but I know it's something involving fashion and celebrities, and sometimes he's like "Last night Anna was cuntier than normal" and I'm like "Anna?" and he's like "Wintour, doll."

Otto went to college with Zev and me, but Zev and Otto weren't friends. They represent opposite edges of my personality. Otto is a bitchy party boy, and Zev is an esoteric nerd. Otto and I went to parties together, and Zev and I met at the graduate student cafe to write scathing remarks on each other's English papers.

"Who is it?" Otto asks.

"Who is who?" I pull my sunglasses closer to my face. We're seated on the deck and the sun beats down on us, causing me to break a sweat.

"The girl?" Otto asks. "You keep looking at your phone. You aren't listening to me at all."

"Yes I am," I say.

"What was I saying?"

"You were talking about Raven." Raven is Otto's dog, a pit bull mix. My gay male friends love their muscular dogs who, unlike the muscular men they date, love them unconditionally and aren't cruising Grindr 24/7. Otto's often talking about Raven, so I figure it's a good guess. He's right, though. I wasn't listening to him.

"Nope," he says. "Who's the girl? I thought you were taking a break from dating."

Otto strongly encouraged me to take time off dating after my ex-girlfriend Devon began lightly stalking me. She was a lot of fun before she became scary. Devon was twenty-seven, the age I was when I started taking the Patricia Highsmith. I've been dating twenty-seven-year-olds since, women in or around their Saturn's Return, women shrouded in chaos. Devon didn't exactly allow me to break up with her. Whenever I tried, she'd become hysterical and a bit violent. (She threw a butternut squash at my car.) I eventually had to block her phone number, her Instagram account, her "finsta," her Twitter account, her "alt" Twitter account, and her Gmail account. For up to a month after the breakup, she would text me from unfamiliar numbers, mostly screaming at me, accusing me of being bipolar or autistic. Sometimes she'd send me flowery and fabricated memories of our time together accompanied by photos of herself crying, mascara running down her cheeks. A few times I saw her car running outside my window, and once I could have sworn I smelled her perfume (she wore *way* too much of it, a cloying gourmand) inside my building lobby. Eventually, the texts stopped. I haven't seen her car in months, and I've moved, so she doesn't know where I live. And I hardly ever think about her. The whole thing really wasn't a big deal; I don't know why Otto took it so seriously. Devon's not the first ex-girlfriend to lightly stalk me, and I assume she won't be the last.

Lesbians have trouble letting go.

The waiter brings our Diet Cokes. This time last year, they would have been margaritas, or Bloody Marys, or champagne. But Otto is sober now, and I'm sober-adjacent. Ever since I turned thirty-five I've felt fifty. Thirty-four was twenty-seven and thirty-five is fifty. Standard mathematical principles can't account for such phenomena.

"It's nothing," I lie. "Just a Tinder date."

He raises his eyebrows at me.

"Has she seen the video?" Otto asks.

"What video?" I ask, even though I know exactly what video.

"Astrid," Otto says. "You know I do PR for a living."

I nod. So that's what Otto does. "Of course, I know that," I lie.

"You need to get on top of this," he says. "Issue a public apology."

"Please," I say. "I'm not Kendall Jenner." I don't tell him my agent also told me to publicly apologize. Instead, I say, "Enough about me, who are you seeing?"

Eagerly, Otto begins to monologue about the various twenty-something models he's fucking. We're both Nordic (his dad is Danish, and my parents are Swedish) and people often think we're siblings, but I think this offends Otto because he's objectively more attractive than me. He has ice-blue eyes and abs for days and conjures a blond James Dean, so men are constantly throwing themselves at him—gay, straight, whatever. Women see him more as a friend. I suspect he's too pretty for women, too threatening. Women just want to feel safe. Women see me as safe because I look less like James Dean and more like Helga Pataki from *Hey Arnold!*

Our salads arrive and Otto is still going. I happily zone out, feel the sun on my face, smell the sea breeze. I think about Ivy, what she's doing, what she's wearing, whether she's twenty-seven, why she's not texting me back, whether she's with that Samantha Ronson derivative from her Instagram. Inhaling marine air through my nostrils, I wish I could bottle it up and spray it on my neck before my next Zoom.

On the drive back, the sun sets over the ocean, but I can't enjoy it, because Ivy hasn't texted me. I become angry, stewing. I decide I don't actually like her at all. I can do better. She isn't shit. She can't write and dates butches like it's 1995. I ask Otto questions about his life with a tinge of hostility.

"You got it bad," Otto says when he drops me off. He always chauffeurs me when he comes to LA, mostly because his work pays for an expensive rental—this time, a shiny white SUV—and Otto gets frustrated with my innately feminine sense of direction. (I don't have one.)

"Shut up," I say, getting out, grateful that I live on the top of a woodsy hill instead of my old apartment where I got attacked by a pit bull right outside my building.

Typically, after Devon would rage out at me, she'd send me elaborate bouquets from overpriced flower shops, signed "Devon the Pit Bull" and begging for forgiveness. And then shortly after she threw the squash at my car and we broke up, I was bitten by a literal pit bull on the street. I was minding my own business, smoking a cigarette and looking at the sky, and next thing I knew—a pit bull was sinking its teeth into my calf. The owner had face tattoos and didn't acknowledge me, just yanked the dog's chain and screamed at it.

Blood ran down my leg and what appeared to be cartilage or muscle emerged from the wound. Inside I texted Zev a photo. He said dogs' mouths are filled with bacteria and I had to go to the hospital. It didn't hurt, but I was annoyed because I had plans to write that evening. Luckily, my twink nurse was polite enough to act incredulous when I said my age. I left with fourteen stitches and two weeks of antibiotics. Later I told my woo woo therapist about "Devon the Pit Bull," how strange it was that I got attacked by a literal pit bull after we broke up. My therapist responded, "As someone who runs in metaphysical circles, I do think it's possible that Devon's consciousness briefly leapt into the pit bull as it bit you, but I'm not sure how useful it would be to 'go there.'"

I quit therapy not long after that.

:::::

In bed I put on a playlist entitled "frequencies for healing and positive transformation" and open my alt Twitter and search Devon, who is blocked on my main account. I'm not supposed to look at her social media for mental reasons, but sometimes I get an itch I simply must scratch, like when I can't help but watch consecutive YouTube videos of Cara Delevingne tweaking on late-night shows. I let myself read nineteen tweets, each of which can be divided into one of three categories: first, incomprehensible strings of words, either inside jokes or early signs of schizophrenia; second, references to her romantic dalliances, with an astrophysicist, a TikTok star, and a "famous writer" (as if that exists); and finally, Hole lyrics. (She always fancied herself a young Courtney Love, although I saw her more as bald Britney Spears attacking a paparazzo with an umbrella.) When I start to feel vaguely ill, I close out of Devon's Twitter account and find

Ivy's, which contains her birth year, which reveals that she is twenty-seven years old.

I close Twitter and open Tinder, begin swiping.

Otto said I should go to a Sex and Love Addicts Anonymous meeting.

But I decide to fall in love instead.

I am hate-messaging three women, messaging because I need attention and with hate because they are not Ivy, and getting ready to put my phone down, when Ivy finally texts me, one quick text after the other. I will later learn this is her style: disappear for a while, then text in rapid succession.

Sorry for the late response

I've been in dissertation hell

I'm so stressed

I almost saved your number in my phone as
Tatiana Moon

Fireflies fill my stomach, flapping madly.

I shut off my phone. I'll respond tomorrow.

I dream of a wolf and a bobcat falling in love.

four

This week we're workshopping Ivy's pages. She turned in a scene introducing the third member of the love triangle, and the main character responds with a hysterical jealousy that reminds me of several ex-girlfriends. I don't love Ivy's writing but I want her to love me, so I read the pages three times and make detailed notes. I flatter her, make jokes, generate ideas and possibilities. My only criticisms—and I must provide some because I want to prove I'm taking her seriously, not just giving empty flattery—are those that seem easy to fix.

Ivy Zooms in front of the *Desert Hearts* poster. She's wearing a shirt tied at the top with a thick ribbon. She looks like a Victorian sexpot, and I fantasize about untying the ribbon. Today I smell something less floral, more leathery and boozy, tobacco and bourbon, a burlesque dive. Like this 1940s perfume I read about on Reddit called Bandit, created by a former model and rumored lesbian. It was purportedly inspired by the scent of models changing their underwear backstage during fashion shows: bitter, green, leathery. In Robert Piguet's 1944 runway show, models dressed as pirates, and one model ended the show by smashing a bottle of Bandit on the runway and stomping it with her stiletto.

I'm imagining Ivy dressed as a pirate and stomping a perfume bottle with her heel when Todd asks me if I have anything to add.

Before I start talking, I check my own Zoom square and am happy to see a tiny sliver of my lace black bra peeking from under my shirt, drawing attention away from my triangle of sadness. When I turned thirty, I stopped wearing bras, which I thought was political. By thirty-three, I found lingerie much sexier. Now, I'm fully trad. I just want a wife.

"These pages are sensual and charming," I begin. I look at Ivy's little Zoom rectangle and it's hard to read her expression, although I'm never good at that anyway, reading facial expressions. I keep talking, falling into the rhythm of flattering speech. At a certain point, a figure passes behind her, a flash of platinum blonde hair, and I'm certain it's the Samantha Ronson doppelgänger, and I'm still talking, but I feel an irrational flare of jealousy, not unlike that experienced by the main character in Ivy's book who I'm currently talking about. At a certain point, Ivy turns around, and her audio is muted but it seems like she's saying something to the butch, and the butch skitters away, and I conclude my remarks.

I'm blushing, Ivy messages me after the meeting.

five

I don't sleep a wink given my new and intense crush, so I take
a long nap in the middle of the day and when I wake up, Zev
is calling me.

"What the fuck?" he says. "I've been waiting for ten minutes."

"Sorry," I say, remembering we had plans to walk. "Be there
in a sec."

I throw on my Sambas, a style of shoe I've been wearing since
I was a ten-year-old soccer star, and head outside to meet Zev,
who looks annoyed, tapping his foot beside his standard poodle,
Jackie-O, named not for Jackie Onassis as everyone suspects, but
rather for Parker Posey's character in the Mark Waters adaptation of the Wendy MacLeod play *The House of Yes*.

It's still light out because it's late May.

As we head up the street, Zev tells me about work—he man-
ages a bookstore where I had the launch party for my most recent
book—and says there is a strange man who comes into the store
every day and calls him "Panda," Zev assumes because he is half-
Asian.

"Do you think it's a hate crime?" Zev asks.

"I don't know anything about hate crimes," I say. It's true, no
one cares if you're gay anymore, not in California, and if they

do, they don't think I am. Even if I am making out with a girl in public, people assume we're European sisters or something.

I worry my response to Zev wasn't sufficiently empathic. "But maybe," I add. Then, "How does it make you feel?"

Zev nearly chokes on his laughter. "I was joking," he says eventually. "I don't give a shit."

For a short period in college, I thought I was in love with Zev, and Zev thought he was in love with me. Then we had sex, or tried to have sex, and it was hysterically bad. We stopped talking for about a year afterward, then started talking again, both pretending the bad sex never happened.

I had sex constantly on the Patricia Highsmith, but I never really remembered it. I was apparently very sexual on it, which puzzled me, because sober I hardly ever think about sex, only about being adored.

I consider telling Zev about my new crush on Ivy, but I know he'll say something rude, like call me "girl crazy." He says this a lot, a lot of people do, but it isn't true. I just happen to think a crush is the best drug there is—and, *trust*, I've tried them all.

Also, I'm an artist. Love is my muse. I'm like Usher.

After the walk, I ask Zev if he wants to come in for an "ironic bong rip." We started calling our bong rips "ironic" when we turned thirty. Five years later, our bong rips could probably most appropriately be called "sad."

· · · ·

As I pack the bong, I remember I have two beers in my fridge. The perfect amount. It's embarrassing that I drink beer, especially as someone who worships femininity, but for some reason it's the only type of alcohol that agrees with me. Well, bourbon and tequila agree with me, too, but I'm off those sauces, unless it's a special occasion. I know where I stand with beer, and I think it's prettier than people give it credit for—golden and effervescent, particularly in an elegant glass. With just two bottles in my fridge, I won't be able to get drunk and text a friend with an Adderall prescription. Zev only drinks expensive wine or liquor, so both beers are for me. I keep a bottle of Tanqueray for Zev. He consumes small amounts, and I find gin nauseating, so I've had the same bottle forever. I hand him the bong—first hit for guests, as an effort to be more other-oriented, part of getting healthy—and then pour him a nip. I pour my beer into a slim pilsner glass I keep in the freezer.

After I hit the bong, Zev starts talking about the customer who calls him Panda again and I suddenly find it very funny. I can't stop laughing. I look at Jackie-O, who appears to be judging me, her snout pointed at the ceiling. Poodles are a very judgmental breed. I silence myself to appease Jackie-O.

Everything feels ominously still.

"Is this earthquake weather?" I ask Zev.

"No," he says.

I gulp my beer.

Zev and I order a pizza and watch *The L Word*. You'd think I, a lesbian, would have to convince Zev, a gay/asexual man, to watch this glossy lesbian melodrama, but it's the other way around. Zev loves *The L Word*. He has more lesbian friends than I do. He identifies as a lesbian and tries to get me to go to Dyke Day LA every summer, which I always decline, I suppose due to internalized homophobia, as well as a fear that I'll run into one of several supremely confrontational ex-girlfriends. I once told Zev when I was feeling spectacularly cunty that the reason he prefers lesbian company is because he gets off on the implicit power imbalance. He retorted that I'm a fag hag for the same reason. I said that fags are men who partner with men and are therefore the most powerful people in society, and I am a woman who partners with women and am therefore the most devalued. Zev said I'm a wealthy white woman so I can't exactly claim to be devalued, and also gay men overcompensate for their shame by laughing too hard at everyone's jokes and I surround myself with them because I'm desperate for a captive audience. And I said "So?"

The next day, I apologized. I told Zev that I really didn't think he hung out with lesbians to feel more powerful. A lot of gay men do that, but Zev isn't one of them. He simply has a feminine energy, which frankly I admire.

Zev didn't take back what he said to me, but I didn't expect him to: he was right.

:::::

Shortly after Zev goes home, when I'm face-deep in the last piece of pizza I was too ashamed to eat while Zev was there, I get a text, and I'm thrilled—thinking it might be Ivy—but instead it's from my landlord, Deedee.

Can we talk?

Ominous.

six

I wake up furious at myself. I ruined the whole day. I shouldn't have eaten all that melted cheese, drank that beer, smoked the bong, ordered those expensive artisan perfume samples from that septuagenarian psychology professor in Oregon, which I'm just now remembering I did. I should have read more, exercised more, done yoga, saved money. I have only one job right now: be healthy. And I can't even do that.

Picking up my phone, I plan to text Zev something accusatory about letting me degrade my body, my temple. But before I can, another text pops up from Deedee. *Are you around this morning? I want to stop by to discuss something with you.*

I recall the text from the previous night and feel sick.

I've lived in this bungalow for roughly two months—the move was meant to kick off my attempt to "get healthy"—but I haven't interacted with Deedee since I moved in, other than to Venmo her my monthly rent payment in a timely manner. Surely I must have done something horribly wrong to receive these texts. My neighbors complained about my loud music or the relentless plumes of marijuana smoke emanating from my windows at all hours. I scratched the neighbor's car when I was parking. I left rotting meat in the trash. A friend left a bag of ecstasy in the driveway, and they think I'm a drug dealer.

Forcing a deep breath, I return the text. *I'm around!*

Letting the coffee brew, I scold Zev to calm my nerves. *I can't believe you let me eat pizza and smoke weed and drink last night.* Zev never seems to care when I lash out at him, which makes him an ideal friend. *I'm supposed to be healthy.*

Deedee needs to hurry up so I can exercise my shame away.

Zev texts me back. *I've said it once and I'll say it again: I'm not your handler.*

He's still typing and I know I'm not going to like what he's going to say.

There is no getting in between Astrid and melted cheese.

I turn my phone off and take some deep breaths. Where the fuck is Deedee? I need to shed the bloat. I get on the carpet and try to do some push-ups and collapse. The most feminine thing about me is my lack of upper body strength.

The doorbell rings.

·····

Deedee is wearing a tropical-patterned muumuu and smiling. She doesn't look like she's going to evict me.

"Hi, Deedee," I say. "Come on in."

"Hi, Astrid," she says, then follows me into the kitchen.

"Can I get you anything? Coffee? Water?"

"Water would be great," she says.

I pour us both glasses, and we take them to the sherbet-colored breakfast nook, my favorite corner of this house. Harsh mid-morning light hits Deedee's face and lights up her green eyes.

"You've been a great tenant, Astrid," Deedee says.

A wave of relief hits. I'm a great tenant. But why is she here?

She sips her water slowly, then opens her mouth to speak. "Don needs back surgery."

Who is Don? "Don?"

"Sorry, my husband," she says. "He's going to be fine, God willing, but the surgery is expensive. We're going to have to sell our house." She pauses, sips again. "And we need to move back in here."

Back in where?

Oh.

She's kicking me out.

I try to locate words, but they're nowhere to be found.

"I'm so sorry, Astrid."

Anger brews inside me. This fucks up my whole plan. I need to get healthy. And I need to do it here. It took me forever to find this place. I hate moving. I loathe logistics. My face reddens, my throat constricts.

"But," Deedee says, grinning, "we have another place for you if you're interested. It's a cute little bungalow just a few blocks away. Very similar property. In the hills, tree-lined street, all new appliances. Dishwasher, AC, hardwood floors. Shared yard."

I exhale.

"It's too small for me and Don, but it's perfect for one person," she says. "And it's cheaper. And to compensate for the inconvenience, we'll cover and coordinate the movers."

Okay. I sip my water again. My throat relaxes. An inconvenience, but ultimately okay.

"Shared yard?" I say. "Shared with whom?" I really don't like to share property, or anything else. I've always lived alone, always preferred to live in a shitty studio than with roommates. I don't like witnesses.

"Oh, yes," Deedee says. "There are two bungalows on the property, almost of equal size. The tenant you'll share a yard with is great, you'll love her. She's an artist. Very free-spirited."

Hmm. I don't like free spirits. I left the Bay Area for a reason. And "artist," to me, reads as "unemployed," which is no good. An office job where she'd be gone during the day would be better. If she's home all the time, that might present a challenge. What if I want to read outside, or I need to really glow on Zoom?

"Is there a bathtub?" I ask.

"Yes!" says Deedee.

"Blinds?" I ask.

"Of course," she says.

"When can I see it?" I ask.

"Today, if you want," she says.

seven

The two bungalows sit at the top of a set of old stone steps, which will be good motivation to not do the Patricia Highsmith because I can imagine myself tripping on a loose stone and becoming seriously disfigured.

The bungalow that would be mine is closer to the road and cute as promised. The bedroom is spacious and tucked in the trees, so I can still open the windows and breathe fresh air. The energy is light and airy, the walls a soft buttercream. Outside of the kitchen is a shaded sitting area. The other bungalow is closer than I'd like, but the yard is lush and has a view of downtown, and who doesn't love a distant cityscape? A city you can see but not hear?

"Let's go see if Penelope is home," Deedee says.

The free spirit, I suppose. Penelope. Like Penelope Cruz, my celebrity crush, and Penelope Disick, my favorite Kardashian child. Not a terrible sign. I'm trying to be positive. This is part of getting healthy. The power of positive thinking.

We knock on the door and I peek through the window. Penelope's bungalow is decorated sort of new-agey, with ornamental crystals and tiny Buddha statues, but also a little goth, with dead roses and velvet furniture the color of period blood. Thick curtains render it a uniquely dark space for relentlessly bright Los Angeles. I hope Penelope is . . . okay.

We wait a few minutes and no one comes to the door. This feels like a good sign. Hopefully, she's one of those extroverted and energetic types who's always out doing things, the opposite of a homebody. Although her living space radiates a reclusive energy.

"I guess she isn't home," says Deedee.

I hope this is common.

"You will like her," says Deedee.

I wonder how she can be so sure of this. Deedee hardly knows me.

"Okay," I say. "When do I need to move in?"

Deedee lights up. "So, you'll take it?"

I sigh. It took fucking forever to find my current place. And I became obsessive, developed an eye twitch staring at Zillow 24/7, carpal tunnel from texting landlords all day. Having a peaceful home is necessary to my getting healthy, my sole task, and Zillow-induced stress will inevitably drive me straight to the Patricia Highsmith. This place seems completely fine, minus the proximity of the mysterious Penelope.

What if she's prettier than me?

"Yeah," I say. "When do I need to move in?"

"Is this weekend too soon?" she asks. I open my Google Calendar on my phone. Without it, I never know what day it is. On the screen, I see that my parents' birthday dinner is this weekend. My parents were born one day apart, so we always celebrate their birthdays together.

"I have to go to San Francisco this weekend," I say. I'm not looking forward to it. "How about next week?" I'll get back on Sunday night, then I'll need at least a day to unwind, preferably two. "Wednesday?"

"We can swing that," says Deedee.

eight

I hate going home, but guilt compels me.

It's not that I hate my family or anything. I just feel very uncomfortable around them and harbor the vague suspicion that they hate me, which isn't entirely unfounded given that while they've been supportive in a material and financial sense, they mostly seem to find my personality, affect, choices, and demeanor to be unpleasant at best.

Nervy and reluctant, I drive through the grapevine, the canyon trail from urban LA to the 5, a flat stretch of highway that terrifies me, until I reach the rolling hills of Salinas. Listening to Bravo recap podcasts, I neurotically steal glances at my phone, waiting for Ivy to text, but she doesn't, even though I sent the last one, a question, and her not answering feels pointed, a subtle *fuck you*, or at the very least a clear: *I'm just not that into you!*

I don't take well to rejection.

Unless I'm the one rejecting.

My parents live in St. Francis Wood, a neighborhood developed as a "garden suburb" a few years after the 1906 earthquake. It was designed by the same architect who designed UC Berkeley's campus, where Zev, Otto, and I went to undergrad, where my parents met in law school, and where I went to law school for one year before dropping out.

When I arrive, both my parents are at work. They refuse to retire despite being in their late sixties and financially comfortable. They work at the same firm and have since the late 1970s. They act more like siblings, or twins, than a married couple.

My younger brother is standing at the kitchen island, digging into a rotisserie chicken with his fingers.

"Astrid," he says between bites. There is chicken skin stuck in his beard.

"Felix," I say back to him.

We hug stiffly, and he smells terrible. I consider asking him if he is wearing deodorant but it will upset him—he's very sensitive. So, I say nothing but privately vow to get him an expensive deodorant and body wash for his birthday, maybe a fragrance, too, something woodsy but sweet enough to counteract the BO.

I go to my childhood bedroom and open the windows to smell the fresh Bay air and listen to the audiobook of *Ripley's Game* until I fall asleep.

I dream I have a sick cat. I go to the mechanic and say, "Do you service cats?" and he says, "No, maybe try tuna fish," and when I get home, my cat is dead.

* * * *

In the morning, I realize my dream is about lesbian bed death. I've experienced it many times, that thing when your girlfriend becomes more like a best friend and then more like a sister. And you love your sister, but you don't want to fuck her.

Speaking of siblings, my parents are at work. They always work on Saturday mornings. They leave a note saying they'll be home for dinner. Whenever I come home, I wonder why I drove six hours for my parents to avoid me, but the gesture—me driving six hours—appears important to them.

Felix and I make coffee and then walk to Mount Davidson, the city's highest peak. Walking caffeinated is one of the only things we enjoy doing together. We don't have much else in common. Felix tends to find my lifestyle frivolous, the fact that I live in Los Angeles and write books about fame. I tend to find his lifestyle obnoxious, the fact that he lives in a van and forages for food, as if he didn't grow up in one of the most expensive neighborhoods in the country. But we can find things to talk about on caffeine and endorphins. Felix is a better listener than me. He works with kids, teaching outdoor education. He's patient.

At the top of Mount Davidson is a big cross shrouded in coastal fog, which looks very sinister and cinematic. I look at the cross and try to feel God's presence. A vague belief in God, of the neo-spiritual Californian variety—informed mostly by Marianne Williamson's *A Return to Love* and Kanye West's Sunday Service—is a crucial component of my path to health. Growing up, I thought it was chic to be an atheist. Now I find nihilism passé, very yawn. At twenty-three, I loved horny-for-nothing Joan Didion as much as the next bitch, but I'm thirty-five now and it's time to believe in something.

Felix walks past the cross and looks over the city. After several minutes of waiting for God's presence and thinking about Ivy, I follow him.

We stare toward the Bay, which glimmers silver. I inhale the fresh scent of a California landscape unadulterated by Los Angeles pollution. San Francisco is filled with a tree called—I kid you not—Victorian Box. Its white flowers produce a fragrant perfume at night, which I smell now even though it's morning.

My phone buzzes with a text from Ivy.

I know I'm sleep deprived because I found myself missing Tatiana.

I giggle. I'll respond later, make her wait a bit.

"What's amusing?" Felix asks, like a grandfather.

"Nothing," I say.

"A girl?" he asks.

"What of it," I say.

It seems like he's going to say something else, and I brace myself for one of his lectures on my "unhealthy reliance on external validation"—as if there's any other kind of validation—but instead he takes a Pax pen out of his flannel pocket, inhales, and blows smoke up toward the trees.

. . . .

At dinner, I make a point to drink LaCroix instead of alcohol, but nobody seems to notice. My parents don't seem to care much about my unhealthy habits as long as I'm thin and successful.

I am therefore thrilled to announce that cringe actress Kat Gold's production company bought the rights to my book. When I first left law school to become a writer, my mom tried to have me committed. My parents were distraught. Felix was a slacker; I was their child with promise. I was the academic superstar. I would follow in their footsteps, work at the same firm.

When I left law school, they lost their minds.

They calmed down a bit when I sold my first book, more when I sold my second, optioned it, then sold my third. But they're still nervous. They still see my career as fickle and unstable. And they aren't entirely wrong.

"Who is Kat Gold?" my dad asks.

"You don't know her?" I'm annoyed because I'm forever desperate to impress my parents, who refuse to be impressed by anything aside from good manners and practical life choices. "She's huge," I say. "She was in a Marvel movie."

"Which one?" my mom asks.

"I don't know," I say. As if I'd watch a Marvel movie. "She played a superhero or something?"

Felix laughs. "That really narrows it down."

"She's also a face of Fenty Beauty," I say, as if anyone in my family knows Rihanna runs a billion-dollar makeup empire. "And her production company is newish, but they're linked to some really cool projects and directors—they're producing a streamer directed by Sofia Coppola." I feel like such a loser spinning my wheels in vain to impress my family, who could not care less about makeup or directors.

"Coppola as in Francis Ford?" my dad asks.

"Sofia is his daughter!" I almost slam my LaCroix on the table with excitement—finally, some recognition—but my dad just nods flatly in response. To be fair, I probably wouldn't be impressed either. Sofia Coppola is a bit over the hill ever since she got semi-canceled for that slavery movie, not that I'm in the position to judge, and Kat Gold is fairly insufferable, not that I've met her—I've only interacted with her minions on Zoom—but my understanding is that she's one of those conventionally hot people desperate to be seen as smart and interesting, à la James Franco. I went with Kat's production company Satchels of Gold for one reason and one reason only: they offered me the most money.

"That's good," my mom says coldly. "Will you be adapting it yourself? I assume there is more money involved that way. You can get royalties."

"I won't be," I said. "I just took the money." I'm sometimes hurt that my parents never ask me what I'm working on or about my process. They don't read my books and never mention the content. Only money, deals. But right now I'm thankful they lack curiosity, that they don't have Google alerts set up for my name, because if they did, I'd have to lie to them, just like I'm lying to myself.

"Why not adapt yourself?" my dad asks.

"Lack of interest," I say. I've done a lot of drugs but I'm not quite brain-dead enough to be writing a screenplay.

"Let her be herself," Felix says.

My parents look at him with confusion.

: : : :

Walking back up to my bedroom after dinner, eager to see if Ivy texted me or at least looked at my Instagram story, my eye catches a photo of myself at twenty-two, propped on a decorative table by the window. In it, I'm standing in front of UC Berkeley Law with my parents. It was my first day of law school and my parents look legitimately thrilled. I look legitimately underdressed, in an American Apparel sweat suit, checkered Vans sneakers, and a very smug expression.

Just seven months later, I called my mom to tell her I was dropping out. I can still feel the chill in her voice, her insistence that there was something wrong with me, that I seemed "unwell." She'd also recently discovered via a childhood friend that I had a girlfriend, my very first, which she believed evidenced some sort of major chemical imbalance.

"I don't understand, Astrid," my mom had said. "You always loved school. You're a gifted debater. You used to be so high achieving."

"I'm still high achieving," I'd said to my mom.

"Novelist is not a career," she said. "I don't understand what your father and I did wrong."

"Danielle Steel has six hundred million dollars," I said. At the time I was really into Danielle, not that I read her or anything, I just loved the idea of her—a California-based romance novelist famous for her massive commercial success and resounding lack of critical acclaim. She'd written 190 books, been divorced five times, and had nine children, including two very chic San Franciscan socialites who I grew up idolizing, the Traina sisters. And she was friends with Rihanna, which at twenty-five rendered her my ego ideal.

"Well, you aren't Danielle Steel," my mom said and then we both hung up and didn't speak for nearly six months, when I got a literary agent and my mom got a psychiatrist who told her I seemed "very ambitious."

I quietly turn over the framed photo on the table, then return to my bedroom.

Skipping to my phone, I'm upset to see no notifications, nothing from Ivy, nothing at all.

nine

Deedee's movers are good. They are careful with my plants, my prized possessions. I have an oversized majesty palm I tell them to put in my bedroom. I like it near my head when I sleep, delivering oxygen to my brain and filling my dreams with lush landscapes.

Sprawled out on the outdoor furniture Deedee left, I listen to Alice Coltrane on my portable Bluetooth speaker, delicate cascading harps at odds with the clomping movers scrambling around me, asking where things go.

I used to make fun of people who listened to jazz—so self-serious—but then this girl I was seeing made me a playlist and one afternoon while I was coming down and watching the afternoon light dance with my plants, "Turiya & Ramakrishna" came on and I felt like I was falling in love, a type of love I hadn't experienced. Later I read that after Alice's husband died, she spent the rest of her life making music for him. Maybe I was hearing that.

A strong whiff of patchouli hits my nostrils. Zev always says I have an overdeveloped sense of smell, like a dog. That's probably why I've become so obsessed with perfume. I always avoid scents featuring patchouli because it reminds me of Golden Gate Park, where I had my first kiss (with a boy) and the scent still triggers a homosexual panic response.

A woman carrying several reusable Trader Joe's grocery bags emerges from the stone steps, weaving around the movers. She seems to struggle with the heavy bags, and I consider offering help, but I'm weak and it would be fruitless. The fact that I thought about it proves I'm a decent person.

"Hi," she says, dropping her bags in front of me.

I force myself to stand up.

"Penelope," she says, sticking her hand out. She's colder than I thought she'd be, giving less free spirit and more frigid bitch. She's also a bit older than I expected, probably late forties or early fifties but still very pretty. Too pretty. Thick dark hair that falls in easy tendrils; big brown eyes lined with lashes that turn toward the sky; smooth, olive-toned skin. Panic wrenches me. This is exactly what I was afraid of.

"Astrid," I respond as Penelope clutches my hand very hard.

"You aren't going to help the movers?" she asks.

"I'm paying them," I say.

"I thought Deedee was paying them," she retorts.

Before I can say anything—and, really, there is nothing to say—she asks me to help her carry her groceries. My throat starts to close. The bitch thinks I work for her.

Penelope picks up two bags, then eyes the other two expectantly. I do as the eyes say. The bags are extremely heavy, filled with clinking glass bottles probably containing kombucha or kefir or kimchi, bougie products for the microbiome.

I struggle with the bags across our small, shared yard. Heaving, I set the bags down for a second.

"Too heavy for you?" Penelope says in an accusatory voice.

"I'm just taking a break to admire the foliage," I lie. Maybe it's not a lie. The yard is pleasant. A few giant lime-green cacti, as tall as trees, and perfectly geometric agave plants. A towering eucalyptus tree hangs overhead and dots patterns of sun on the lawn.

"You should lift weights or do yoga," Penelope says. "Or you'll get osteoporosis."

I feel dizzy, worry there is not enough oxygen getting to my brain. I say nothing, just pick up the bags and follow Penelope into her house. As soon as I step inside, the scent from earlier—patchouli, but also acrylic paint—hits me like a punch in the face. It's everywhere, and ten times more pungent. I drop the bags.

"I have to get back to my place," I say. "I don't feel well." I'm worried I might faint.

"Deedee said you were strange," Penelope says.

I nod, then head toward the door. "Nice meeting you," I mumble, then charge back into the yard. I feel better once I'm out of her space, away from the patchouli and paint fumes. But as I walk across the grass, the phrase *Deedee said you were strange* loops through my brain. It doesn't shock me. I've never really fit in or understood basic social protocol. Things that are easy or even enjoyable for most people—small talk, going out to dinner, having friends in town, weddings, airplanes, amusement parks, "girls' weekends"—are very difficult for me. Things that are difficult for most people—standardized tests, writing books to completion, meeting deadlines, remaining thin—are very easy for me.

But the comment still hurts, I suppose because I'm human. Wanting to be liked is the ickiest sensation.

I text Zev and say I'm coming to the store.

: : : :

I leave the movers to do their thing. I trust them. I don't own anything irreplaceable. Sentimentality is not something I struggle with.

Zev's bookstore is about ten minutes from me, and I drive with blood boiling. When someone tries to cut me off, I honk and scream. I yell "fuck you" at various cars that aren't doing anything ostensibly wrong. I'm angry at myself, for being so strange, for not being able to handle sharing a yard with someone, but I'm projecting it on to other drivers. I finally understand road rage. Normally I drive in a very absentminded and unhurried manner. But today, getting to the bookstore in a short amount of time feels like life or death.

"My life is ruined," I announce inside the store.

Zev doesn't even look up from the book he's shelving. He never really indulges my melodrama, which is part of the reason he's so comforting.

"I thought you said the bungalow was good," Zev says to the spine of a book about spells.

"Penelope treated me like I *worked* for her," I say as someone calls Zev's name. He disappears and I'm left alone in the Occult Wisdom aisle. I fantasize about knocking over the shelf, watching the books fall and scatter over the mud-colored carpet.

My phone lights up in my hand. I'm about to throw the phone against the wooden shelf when I notice Ivy's name. Something shifts in my brain—it starts producing different chemicals or sending them to different places. Rage morphs into euphoria. I haven't touched the Patricia Highsmith in twenty-two days, but now I feel it coursing through me. This is something that I read would happen in the addiction book Zev very rudely copped for me. Angrily skimming, I read that you take a drug to create a feeling, and then you can't create the feeling without the drug, and then you stop taking the drug, and you realize the feeling happens naturally—and it's even better.

I open the text. *Bette Porter is a dyed-in-the-wool Victorian hysteric.* She's still typing.

Please don't tell me you're one of those lesbians who rejects the L Word.

I could respond, *I used to be.* When I was fourteen, our babysitter took Felix and me to Blockbuster and I slyly put an *L Word* DVD in our rental pile. Felix asked, "What's that?" and I said, "It's about love," which wasn't a lie exactly. At home I watched the DVD, the second disc of season 2 because it's all they had available, on my computer with my bedroom door locked. I expected to feel some grand awakening, but all I felt was uncomfortable. These women seemed dumb and looked like catalog models. I'd been more turned on watching *Gilmore Girls*, which was incredibly straight but featured the type of femininity I've always been attracted to: fevered verbosity.

But when Zev finally forced me to watch *The L Word* pilot a few months ago after a massive ironic bong rip, my tune changed slightly. I'm not sure if the weed clouded my judgment or opened my mind, but suddenly these lesbians seemed glamorous. The story is told through the perspective of Jenny Schecter, a writer who moves to California with her boyfriend and ditches him for her lesbian book group. Shane is the heartthrob with the "best nipples in Los Angeles." Alice interrupts Marina's fawning over Anne Carson to tell Jenny where all the celebrities get Botox. All of these things resonated with me on a personal level.

My mind is constantly pulling a 180.

I respond to Ivy, *who says I'm a lesbian?*

I shudder at my use of sarcasm, the lowest form of humor.

Ivy writes back with four smiling laughing emojis, then, *girl I've read your books.*

It's embarrassing to think about Ivy or anyone I know personally reading my books. I write about lesbians, but I don't really talk publicly about my sexuality as my agent says I'm not allowed to do interviews anymore. I become inadvertently hostile when asked about my work. It feels too personal, like I'm being undressed, and next thing I know I'm asking the interviewer if they know how to read. And then there was the time—I guess it wasn't too long ago—that I did a rather important interview on the Patricia Highsmith and said something I thought was totally charming and funny and Twitter did *not* agree, and I guess that's technically why I'm taking a break at the moment, because my agent suggested it, because I am sort of "canceled."

She's still typing.

Zev comes back and says, "You seem fine." Then, "You're smiling."

"What?" I say.

"You came in here raging, saying your life was ruined."

"Oh." I've completely forgotten about Penelope, and time. This was why I took the Patricia Highsmith: to forget about time and all of daily life's mundane irritations. But I'm pleased to have discovered that Ivy has a similar effect. "It's nothing," I say. "Wanna go on a walk later?" I'll need to force some time away from my phone so I'm not overly available with Ivy.

"Sure," he says, and then I leave the store.

.: .: .:

Driving back, I take the same roads, but they feel completely different. The other drivers seem friendly, chill. We're all languidly

floating down a river. I wonder what Ivy's bedroom looks like
and whether she can see the ocean. Santa Barbara is one of the
prettiest places in the world. Maybe we'll fall in love and I'll move
there, and we can share a little bungalow by the beach, spend our
days writing and nights reading and braiding each other's hair.
Maybe Ivy will get me a diamond and get down on one knee at
the beach, at sunset, or maybe sunrise, or golden hour so the rock
really sparkles.

Suddenly I'm almost hitting one of the movers with my car.
I slam the brakes.

"I'm so sorry," I say.

"No worries," he says. He rests his box on the ground.

Penelope stands at the top of the stone staircase, squinting at
me, and my soft rage returns.

She walks past the movers and clicks her olive-green Volvo
unlocked.

My chest tightens.

As she passes my body, I get a strong whiff of patchouli and
have a terrifying vision of being kissed by a man in a Grateful
Dead T-shirt.

At her car, Penelope looks up at me. "I'll be back in a few
hours," she says.

I nod absently and my chest tightens. Why is Penelope
talking to me like her husband she hates? We are neighbors in
a coastal urban city, which is to say we should not be speaking
at all.

As Penelope drives off, my phone lights up again with Ivy's
name, and I start to relax.

I walk up the stairs and through the yard, which looks positively majestic without Penelope's dark energy. Gold light trickles through eucalyptus trees, grand cacti arch toward a cloudless

sky. I take in a deep breath of fresh air and smile. Then a mover almost knocks me over.

"Sorry ma'am," he says. And it's the same mover I almost hit with my car so I forgive him.

"No worries."

I walk inside my new bungalow and am pleased with how it's coming along. My tiny breakfast table that doubles as a writing desk sits in the corner of the kitchen in a pool of light. In the living room, my puffy sectional sits before my big-ass TV I splurged on after my recent windfall. In my bedroom, my bed is pushed up against the wall and my mini palm tree is lit up neon green by the sunlight. I plop on the bed, movers swarming around me, and open my text thread with Ivy.

Also I saw that interview where you called yourself a 'female faggot.'

Shame pulses through me. That interview is the subject of all the Google alerts, the reason I am, I suppose, "canceled." No one really gets canceled anymore. The media cycle is too fast. That's what I tried to explain to my agent. And I showed her all these tweets from suicidal gay men (my audience) calling me an icon. But she didn't seem to agree.

Just before I met Ivy on Zoom, I had an event at Barnes & Noble at The Grove in West Hollywood. I was being interviewed by this sycophantic gay man whose books I'd never read and despite his effusive compliments, I was certain he hadn't read mine either. During the Q&A, he asked me about my sexuality, a question I always hate. Not because I have any doubts or discomfort about my sexuality, but because lesbians make everyone uncomfortable.

With gay men, it's completely different. The sex act is unsettling to people, has been criminalized at various points throughout history, but their partnering is championed, met with parades and rainbow flags and pride. With lesbians, it's the opposite. The sex act is eroticized, drives the entire porn industry (so I've heard!), but our partnering is unnerving to people. So, whenever I'm asked about my sexuality, it triggers a bit of panic. I could just identify as queer and calm everyone down, but when have I ever made anything easy for myself?

Otto happened to be in town for the big Barnes & Noble interview and beforehand we went to the Cheesecake Factory where I chugged skinny margaritas on amphetamines and started joking about how I am a female faggot. I identified as a twink for a while, but I've obviously aged out of that. I've always felt close to gay male culture—uppers and camp and Azealia Banks. Like Camille Paglia said: "When I meet gay men anywhere in the world, there is a spontaneity and a spirit of fun and mischief that lesbians seem incapable of." I suppose in aligning myself with gay men, I was participating in a subconscious form of lesbian erasure. And I was participating in a louder form of lesbian erasure that day when I looked the sycophantic gay man (Tyler? Kyler?) in the eye and said I "don't vibe with dykes" and "identify as a female faggot."

I was expecting raucous laughter, hoots and hollers, wild applause.

But instead, there was silence.

Tyler/Kyler cleared his throat and said he took offense to that word coming out of the mouth of a "pretty girl," someone who had clearly "not been bullied for roller skating down the street singing Britney Spears at the top of his lungs every day in elementary school."

And then came the enthusiastic cheering and laughter I had expected from my own answer, and I cheered along with them simply because Tyler/Kyler called me pretty.

The rest of the interview was stilted, awkward, and afterward, Tyler/Kyler signed a ton of books and laughed with his fans but said nothing to me. I signed only three books and left with thirteen missed calls from my agent. I guess someone in the audience was filming and had uploaded a clip to Twitter and it was going viral, mostly tirades against "privileged white women" (me), written mainly by privileged straight white women.

There was a point at which my politics matched the zeitgeist, and maybe this is just part of aging, but lately my politics feel unfashionable. When I was twenty-eight and published my first book, being a lesbian novelist writing lesbian novels gave me edge and political relevance. Now, the publishing world simply sees me as white and cis and straight-passing, which I am, and was therefore probably unfairly granted political relevance to begin with. And lately it seems like the meanest people online, the biggest bullies with the smallest brains, are obsessed with using misguided political rhetoric as a vehicle for wishing harm upon others. Meanwhile, smart and nuanced thinkers are being called derogative names merely for asking questions. It all makes me feel gaslit and therefore I try my very best to avoid politics, to exist in the frivolous, to make jokes, to ensure I'm branded as fun and not serious, so that I'm overlooked—or at least I was, until that dumb video.

For the record I was on your side, Ivy texts me.

ten

I unpack in one day. I'd say this is a skill to flatter myself, but it's just neurosis. I can't leave things in boxes. My house must be immediately livable. And once I unpack, I won't change anything until I move out. I'm like a shark. I keep moving and don't look back. I texted this to Zev and he responded, *you know sharks are cold-blooded and essentially brain-dead.*

Luckily all my shit fits. There isn't much. I'm the opposite of a hoarder, very unsentimental. I only have about twenty-five books, which isn't much for a writer, but I don't like to keep things around unless they impress me. I don't like to have too much art on the walls because my mind is already very colorful. Ample Himalayan salt lamps compensate for the lack of décor. Lighting is all that matters. It matters that it's dim, soft, and flattering.

There's just the issue of Penelope.

In the morning, I check the mail for the overpriced perfume samples I ordered from the Oregon professor who studies echolocation in bats. Skipping down the stone steps, careful not to trip, I realize my budding perfume obsession feels a lot like being addicted to Beanie Babies as a kid. Beanie Babies were my original addiction. I'd be euphoric to find a new store that sold Beanie Babies I didn't have, much in the way I started to feel when I found out a party friend had ADHD and therefore an amphetamine prescription, the way I now feel when I find out about an obscure fragrance house that might make me smell 13 percent more attractive.

"Yes!" I literally shout out loud when I see the small package inside.

Before I can open it, I smell patchouli, then hear a voice.

"Something exciting?" Penelope asks.

Where the fuck did she come from?

She reaches around me to open the mailbox. I guess we share it, which is tragic. "Nothing for me, I guess," Penelope says. "What did you get?"

I want to say, *How is that any of your business?* But instead, I start to tell her the truth, "Perf—," then stop. I don't need her thinking I'm frivolous or giving me a lecture about toxins. "Vitamins."

"You should be careful," Penelope says. "Supplements aren't regulated by the FDA."

Of course.

"I'm surprised you have so much faith in the federal government," I say, then disappear up the stairs.

. . . .

And then later that afternoon I'm reading—or at the very least pretending to read—when I hear a knock on the door. I jump, grateful I'm clothed. The curtains are drawn but translucent. I put down Jeanette Winterson and my phone and open the door. Penelope is already talking.

"Do you have any cream?"

"Cream?" What is this, *Leave It to Beaver*? "Do people still buy cream?"

Penelope lets herself in and, to my horror, plops down on my couch. "Ugh, I know. I'm vegan, but it's my friend's birthday and she's a carnivore and I'm baking her a cake."

I'm just staring at Penelope sitting on my couch. "A meat cake?"

I expect Penelope to laugh but she doesn't. She just keeps talking. "Tres Leches. It's her favorite." I almost choke when Penelope puts her feet up on my coffee table. I want to say something, but nothing comes out. This is why I must spend so much time alone, be careful with who I let in my space. I have trouble implementing boundaries.

Instead of asking her to move her feet, I ask, "Who is this girl?" and then go into my kitchen and see if the movers moved the beer from my old fridge. I open it and it's empty. Fuckers.

"Well," says Penelope, removing her glasses. "She's a woman."

God. I make a mental note to cyberbully whoever canceled "girl." It's not infantilizing, it's cute. And even if it is infantilizing, who cares? Treat me like a child! Children are attractive and creative and have great skin and hair. I'm constantly fuming with envy over some seven-year-old's hair at the grocery store, so thick and shiny and perfectly sun-kissed even under the fluorescent lights. I bring a photo of myself at six to my colorist.

Penelope is still talking. "She's my ex-girlfriend actually."

I perk up, not at the hypocrisy, that Penelope scolded me for calling her friend a girl not a woman, then calling said woman her ex-*girl*friend in the next sentence, but because Penelope is a lesbian! Well, maybe she's not a lesbian. Nobody is a lesbian anymore. Everyone is queer or pansexual. But Penelope is in her late forties or early fifties, Gen X, meaning she might actually be a lesbian, generationally speaking.

"Oh," I say, which is all I can think of saying. I pour myself a glass of water and one for Penelope. I didn't get a gay vibe from her at all but I have famously terrible gaydar. I thought Deedee said we'd "get along" because we're both "artists"—although fiction and visual art are very different mediums—but maybe she said we'd get along because we're both into women. Of course, that is an even more ridiculous assumption. As I famously told a crowd at Barnes & Noble, I don't vibe with dykes. (Unless I am sleeping with them.) (And even then, it's tenuous.)

I hand Penelope her glass of water and she chugs it in a few big gulps, then puts it down, sans coaster, on my coffee table. She stands up abruptly. "I have to get back to work," she says. "So, you don't have cream, I take it."

"No ma'am," I say, then walk her to the door with perhaps too much enthusiasm.

: : : :

That night in bed, I put my laptop on my belly and google *best opaque curtains for blocking out nosy neighbors*. Then I text Ivy, *turns out my new neighbor is a dyke*.

Ivy responds immediately, which thrills me. I will later learn that Ivy is most likely to respond to sapphic gossip, will learn it's a drug she can't resist. *Omg*, she says. *Age? Occupation? Vibe? (I know every lesbian in Southern California.)*

I don't know much, I write back. *I'd have googled her but I don't know her last name. She's Gen X I think. A visual artist. Her name is Penelope. She's very nosy and self-righteous. A vegan. But she asked for cream to make a cake for her ex-girlfriend. This is absolutely everything I know.*

I'm embarrassed I sent such a long text. Very unchill. But I've never been chill and it's never stopped women from falling in love with me. Chill is the hallmark of a slow and uninteresting brain.

While I wait for Ivy to respond, I google *Penelope artist Los*

Angeles. The results lead me to the Facebook page of someone who is not her, a gallery website also unrelated to her, and the Instagram page of someone who is also not her. I doubt Penelope is on Instagram. I'm sure she thinks the internet catalyzed the demise of society, or something very tired like that.

Adding curtains to my Amazon cart, I wonder if Ivy's claim that she knows every lesbian in Southern California is a "red flag." Otto says I need to be better at identifying red flags.

I open iMessage and text Otto. *If someone you liked told you they knew every gay man in Manhattan would you consider that a red flag?*

He responds, *yes.*

Why? I'm genuinely curious.

Because it means she's a sceney whore, he writes back. *How dreadful. This is the Tinder girl?*

I respond with the zipper mouth emoji.

You're so obvious, Astrid, he writes back. *Btw House of Wax is streaming on Hulu. God is Great.*

I respond with the prayer hands emoji and try not to be hurt that he called me obvious. He's right, though, I am obvious, and it is a red flag.

I'm buying the curtains when Ivy finally replies.

Omg that's a lot of info.

My cheeks heat. I said too much.

She's still typing.

My friend Maribelle dated an artist in LA named Penelope but she was in her 20s. And she was a vegan but the militant type who would never make a non-vegan cake, and certainly not for an ex. Clearly your Penelope has boundary issues. Sounds like my type of bitch!

I know this is a red flag, but I heart the text nonetheless.

eleven

The next day my literary agent, Allison, calls me. She's been my agent for eight years and all three of my books, including two books we shelved, and she's stuck with me for some reason, even after the big Barnes & Noble snafu. Agent Allison initially reached out to me based on a very earnest essay I wrote in my twenties about Andy Cohen's flagrant misogyny. I sent her my gay Kendall Jenner fanfic, and the rest is history.

Watching Agent Allison's name light up on my phone, I worry it's bad news. I recently told her to stop texting me *can you talk?* Because I always assume it's bad news—that she or someone else is going to reject me. Being a writer means being rejected constantly, and that's probably why I like it. Because I'm a masochist. It's probably why I date women too. Hurts so good! Anyway, after I told Allison to stop texting me *can you talk?* she started texting me *can you talk? (it's not bad!).* She asked what she should do if it's bad news, and we decided she should just call, no text.

So, it's bad news.

"Hi," I answer nervously.

"Hiii, how are you?" Agent Allison says in a sort of singsong voice.

"Fine, what is it?" I ask, cutting to the chase.

"I wanted to touch base about Satchels of Gold," she says.

"They want to cancel the deal?" I tend to assume the worst when it comes to my career.

"No, no," Allison says. "They just want to schedule a consultation meeting to make sure you feel heard."

"Oh," I say. "Okay." I pour myself a cup of water. "Why?"

"I don't know," Allison says. "I know you like LA, but these TV people . . ."

The entire publishing industry is centered in New York and tends to look down on LA, which doesn't bother me. Most of their complaints are correct. Angelenos are shallow (I'm one of them) and the traffic is maddening. But I don't romanticize New York the way most brainy Californians do. Maybe I'm not smart enough, because New York stresses me out. I hate rats and networking. I prefer lonely, vapid Los Angeles, where people hardly know what a book is, so my career remains shrouded in mystery.

"They're just very, I don't know . . ." Allison is diplomatic. She won't say what she's actually thinking.

"They're fake," I say for her.

Agent Allison laughs. "It's a lot of hot air."

It's true. When I first moved to LA, I was constantly impressed and intimidated. Everyone was a producer or a director or an actress. Then I realized everyone was lying and delusional and a barista.

"I'm down to smile and nod at a Zoom meeting," I say.

"Good," Agent Allison says. "I'll send you some avails and if there's any sort of agenda, I'll let you know."

"Cool," I say, preparing to hang up. Outside my window, Penelope marches through the yard. She walks with a lot of aggression, stomping almost. She must be going through something.

She can't be in the best place, emotionally, if she's baking a cake for her ex-girlfriend.

"Oh, and Astrid?"

There it is. The slight tone shift. The bad news. It's coming.

"Yes?" My voice cracks a bit.

"I debated whether to bring this up, but I think it's best you know," says Agent Allison.

I gulp some water.

"Someone on the Satchels of Gold team found that video."

I swallow.

"The Barnes & Noble video."

"I know the one," I say.

"I guess the team is just a little nervous," she says. "They don't want the show to have any negative associations."

"Then maybe they shouldn't have optioned my book." I was recently listening to a podcast where an author compared her literary agent to her therapist, which resonated. Agent Allison has seen me at my worst, my most neurotic, my most difficult, and she continues to go to bat for me. But recently I've gotten the impression that I'm running out of chances, that Agent Allison is growing tired of my juvenile antics and would rather spend her energy on clients who make her more money and have a better attitude.

"They love your book!" Agent Allison says, less in her standard hype woman way and more in a noticeably irritated way.

"They don't like me," I say.

Agent Allison exhales. "That's not it," she says. "They just want to make sure you aren't going to do anything unpredictable that might make the show look bad."

"Well," I say. "My artistic process involves having the freedom to speak subversively." I pause, then grin at my reflection on my darkened laptop screen. "I'm like Kanye West."

"Well," says Agent Allison. "Kanye was dropped by the agency." I was thrilled when I learned that Kanye and I were both represented by CAA, but I guess it's no longer true. "I'm surprised you didn't hear. It happened a few weeks ago." I don't really keep up with the news, but vaguely recall Kanye saying something antisemitic in the manner of Mel Gibson at Moonshadows. "I support your creative freedom, Astrid, but you can't just blurt whatever comes to your head publicly. That's just not how the world works."

I'm frustrated even though Agent Allison is right. I've heard this my entire life. That I can't just say whatever I want because people have feelings and people can get hurt. But I'm annoyed because people love my books. Seriously, I have fan mail almost every day. And I can't write these books people love without having the ability to work through some messy opinions. And *opinion* isn't even the right word because *opinion* implies I'm attached to what I say and I'm really not.

"People take me too seriously," I say, then empty the rest of my water into my throat, swallow. "And my characters are rude and unhinged, so why do people always freak out when I act like my characters, who my readers love?"

A door slams in the background. "Readers love *Tampa*, but they wouldn't love it if Alissa Nutting went around preying on underage boys, now would they?" Agent Allison says. "Why can't you just sublimate your dark impulses, keep them on the page and out of your life, like everyone else?"

"Easier said than done," I say.

Agent Allison clears her throat. "How is the drinking?"

I made the mistake of telling Allison about the Patricia Highsmith after my minor cancellation, and now she's very committed to my cutting back on drugs and alcohol. And after realizing

Devon was Tweeting inflammatory things about me—things that, if I were a man, could possibly result in some kind of Me Too situation—she suggested I take a break from women too.

I open my Notes app. "I've gone twenty-four days without the Patricia Highsmith."

"Great," Agent Allison says. "Keep up the good work, Astrid."

When we hang up, I check my bank account to feel comforted. It's the most money that's ever been in there. It won't last forever, and it's a little less than there was when I last looked, but it's still a lot, and right now that feels important.

twelve

My Sapphic Scribes submission is due at midnight.

In hopes that a new location might inspire me, I walk to the coffee shop at the bottom of the hill. It's one of the few coffee shops in Los Angeles that doesn't crank terrible music and that isn't filled with bros talking loudly about their cringe screenplays, often featuring talking lizards.

Today there is only one other patron. He's hunched over a laptop wearing huge headphones, and I'm glad he's here because I really don't want this place to go out of business. I order a cappuccino and open a blank Google document, watch the cursor blink on the white page.

I never thought I'd be one of these people: threatened by the blank page. I used to love the blank page! Pristine and uncorrupted and filled with possibilities. But now all the possibilities seem certain to end in one way: with me embarrassing myself. With people on Goodreads saying I'm dumb. With people online saying I'm homophobic. With white women writing for woke magazines calling me an oppressor. With my parents thinking I'm a disappointment. With Agent Allison regretting signing me. With Satchels of Gold regretting optioning my book. With CAA dropping me like they dropped Kanye.

The Patricia Highsmith allowed me to avoid thinking about

the inevitable backlash. It took me to a place of pure thought-lessness. People say writing is an intellectually rigorous en-deavor, but the Patricia rendered it purely mechanical. *Clack, clack, clack, clack.* I was like an athlete. I was like Michael Phelps swimming laps.

I consider searching my backpack for loose amphetamines, then remember my conversation with Agent Allison. I have to be good and can't just blurt whatever comes to my head. I have to be thoughtful. A person, not a machine. I sip my cappuccino and try to pretend it's champagne. Then I start writing.

In my 20s, I wrote with political urgency. I wanted to give voice to the femme lesbian experience, to write books for funny, feminine, unhinged dykes who didn't see themselves reflected in pop culture or literature. I wanted to make peo-ple laugh and distract them from their mundane or pain-ful lives, to empower them to be themselves. And I thought I was the right person to do it, because I'm obsessive and melodramatic and I come alive on a word processor. But now I think I write simply because I want to be alone, because I want freedom over my time and a socially sanc-tioned way to lie.

When I started writing books, I was so utterly delu-sional. I really thought I had a "point of view." I would walk into a bookstore and feel annoyed that none of the books were mine. I'd open one, read a few sentences, and think: I could do better! Now that I've published three books, I feel like a complete fraud, like everything I think and write has been written, much better, by someone else.

The weird thing about being a writer is that at 25,

you're passionate and eager to share what you consider to be your sui generis perspective, but you haven't practiced enough to be effective, and no one takes you seriously either way. And then ten years later, you've finally written enough to know what you're doing, but you've completely lost the sense of urgency, you're officially middle-aged and shop at the Gap, and you've realized there is nothing remotely political about wanting breasts in your face, that it is in fact the most basic desire there is: ask any baby. Writing books is just your job now and it's just like any other job except you can do it in lingerie.

I stop, horrified. No one needs to know my process. I'm becoming one of those people I used to mock, people who find writing an epic struggle, who compare writing a book to going to war. I used to legitimately love writing and felt like there was no reason to do it unless you loved it. If a doctor hates their job, at least they're saving lives. If an investment banker hates their job, at least they're making loads of money. But if a writer hates writing, maybe they should just stop?

I shut my laptop and leave the coffee shop, rendering the space completely empty except for the baristas.

: : : :

That night I realize I have only a few hours to turn something in. I refuse to let Pia chew me out again like she did the last time my submission was late. Scanning my living room for inspiration, my eyes land on an out-of-print lesbian pulp novel Zev gave me for my birthday: *Perfume and Pain* by Kimberly Kemp. I walk over, pick it up, and admire the cover, which depicts a nude blonde in front of the enlarged face of a seductive brunette, an image that feels autobiographical. I love the concept of lesbian pulp—male gazey sapphic novels from the '50s and '60s, deemed trashy and problematic by more self-serious lesbians and feminists, much in the way my own work is deemed trashy and problematic by more self-serious lesbians and feminists. My favorite lesbian pulp book is of course Patricia Highsmith's *The Price of Salt*, which she published under the pen name Claire Morgan and Todd Haynes adapted in *Carol*, and frankly is more literary fiction, but it's been lumped in the pulp category because no one takes lesbian desire seriously. Maybe my own work has been overlooked for the same reason. Or maybe I'm just untalented. I guess I'll never know.

I bring the book to my desk, flip open to a random page, and begin transcribing. I'd been using the book more as décor, so transcribing it is actually my first time reading it. It's fun and dark and a lot of it resonates, especially now that I'm a perfume addict.

The main character Gail's first lesbian experience is with her aunt (by marriage, but still). I copy the pages in which Gail first smells her aunt Peg's perfume, which "was like a spur inciting her own body to action—the perfumed flesh was a treasure that she had to have." Transcribing it, I think of my elementary school art teacher, my first crush. Although I didn't recognize her as a crush at the time, just saw her as someone I wanted to be close to, and I started to enjoy drawing in a way I hadn't before. I can still conjure her smell, a musky vanilla.

After transcribing seven pages, I run a spelling and grammar check and then upload the Google Doc to the Sapphic Scribes folder.

thirteen

Ivy is the first to weigh in during the workshop. She's Zooming from what looks like a conference room, no *Desert Hearts* poster in sight. Maybe she's at the UCSB library in one of those little side rooms you can rent out for study groups. When Sophie and I had our dalliance, she was always FaceTiming me from those rooms, whispering like a naughty librarian. Today, Ivy looks like a naughty librarian herself—I won't apologize for having a type—in a pink button-down and cat-eye glasses and again, I wonder what she smells like. Again, I imagine white florals. Lily of the valley and creamy magnolia, a dewy morning after a spring rain.

"There is an interesting subversion of the male gaze here," Ivy says. "Rather than being objects of the gaze, the women here are lookers. Voyeurism and surveillance here aren't male inventions inherently hostile to women but rather are powerful tools mutated to serve feminist goals."

Academic language tires me, so I stop listening to her and stare at the place where the buttons of her shirt open, at the tiny line between her breasts. Voyeurism and surveillance, *blah blah*.

Outside my window, Penelope marches by with a big trash bag over her shoulder. She turns her head toward me and for a second, we make eye contact. I quickly turn my head back to my computer and am thrilled to see a message from Ivy. *I LOVE that you handed in pages from Perfume & Pain.* She sends another message: *Gënius.*

I smile. I write back, *you've read it?*

Duh, she writes, *I'm writing my dissertation on lesbian pulp.*

Turned on, I respond, *do you think Tatiana noticed?*

Hell no, she writes back. *She's out to lunch.*

:::::

Ivy and I text until 3:00 a.m., deep in the heavenly mania of lesbian limerence.

Topics we discuss: Bette Porter's terrible taste in art, most fuckable *Real Housewives,* Kris Jenner, our exes, Rachel Weisz, *Carol,* Italian greyhounds, Paris (France and Hilton).

I fall asleep heart racing and wake up smiling. Grabbing my phone, I'm disappointed to see Zev's name instead of Ivy's, telling me to read some book that looks boring as hell. Ignoring Zev, I go to the kitchen and make coffee.

On my laptop sits a fresh email from Agent Allison. She's writing to coordinate a Zoom meeting with the Satchels of Gold team, to make me feel "heard," and I suppose to ensure I'm not going to say anything unpredictable that will sabotage their relatively new company. The email includes a list of eleven times and, like a huge loser, I respond that I am available for every single one. Right after I press Send, another email comes in from Agent Allison. *This just in: Kat Gold herself will be on the Zoom! She loves your book and can't wait to meet you!!!*

I'd assumed that Kat Gold was more of a figurehead and was too busy modeling for makeup brands or pretending to be well-read on TikTok to have an active role in the production company. Agent Allison and I have discussed that people as conventionally hot as Kat Gold should not bother trying to understand Foucault. But Kat Gold wants it all. In fact, she wrote a memoir I haven't read entitled *Kat Gold Wants It All*.

Agent Allison sends a follow-up email suggesting that we should read her memoir before the Zoom meeting.

I type out *kill me*, then delete it, because I must be on my best behavior, and write, *okay!!*

: : : :

When it's 4:00 p.m. and I still haven't heard from Ivy, I start to feel like I'm coming down from MDMA. I sent the last text, a question, *what is your fave season of the L Word?* A very lame question in the light of day.

After my bath, I lie naked on my bed, staring at the ceiling fan. I want to read in the yard, but I don't want Penelope to bother me. I wish Otto were here to hate Penelope with me. I'm afraid Zev will be taken by her morally superior attitude, but Otto will say she's a vile hippie who needs to go back to Santa Cruz.

When are you coming back to LA? I text him. *I need you to put a hex on my new neighbor.*

What's her deal? he texts back.

A dyke, the worst kind. Self-righteous. Nosy as hell.

Otto responds, *do you have a crush on her?*

Gross!!!!!!

: : : :

Later while I'm heating an Amy's frozen meal, my phone lights up with a text. Excitement erupts in my chest, but it's only Felix.

Hey sis, he says, *driving through LA on the way to see some friends in San Diego this weekend. Can I crash with you tomorrow night?*

My brother is always doing this, asking to stay with me with virtually no warning. It was much easier to have visitors when I was hardly conscious. Maybe I can make an exception to my prohibition era, make some calls, disappear into a buzz. But I shouldn't have to procure amphetamines just to stomach hosting my own brother for one night. I can do this sans Patricia. Felix can sleep on the couch. We can smoke weed with Zev and order tacos and listen to Lil Wayne, Felix and my sole shared cultural interest. A lot of people talk about Weezy's public feuds and pro-methazine addiction, but not enough people talk about how he brings families together.

Sure, I write back.

He doesn't respond.

Ivy doesn't text me until 9:00 p.m. that night, when I'm about to block her number.

Hmm, she says. *Season 1 or Season 5. It's a toss-up.*

She's typing.

Hey do you want to FaceTime sometime?

My heart nearly explodes. I want to say, *like right now?* But I can't be too eager.

My brother is coming tomorrow, I write back, *maybe Sunday?*

It's a date.

fourteen

Felix shows up at my door with a massive mountain bike in his arms. He smells like forest and BO. "Hey sis," he says. "Do you mind if I put this inside? I don't want my car to get broken into."

"Sure," I say, but I want to say no. The bike is dirty. Tiny clumps of dried mud fall onto the floor.

I get a broom and performatively start sweeping so he can see what an imposition he's being.

"You didn't text me to say when you're coming," I say as I dump the dirt clumps into the trash.

"My bad," he says. "My phone died. Can I borrow a charger?"

My brother always does this, shows up at my house with demands.

"You don't have one?"

"I left it in the car," he says. "I can get it if you don't want to share yours." He says this with hostility, suggesting I'm ungenerous. He's right, I am not generous, but I'm also offended by his entitlement.

"Give me your phone," I say, then plug it into the charger by my desk.

He plops onto my couch, and I worry he's going to leave dirt stains.

"Beer?" I ask, praying he'll say yes.

"I'm okay for now," he says. "I was hoping I could take a shower."

"Sure," I say. Demands, demands, demands. I'm not the man-hater society assumes lesbians are until Felix shows up. Lesbians don't hate men; straight women hate men. Lesbians are indifferent to men, which everyone else hates. But at this moment, I'm not feeling so indifferent.

I show Felix to the shower. Handing him a towel, I seize up thinking about how muddy my bathroom will be when he's done.

: : : :

While Felix is in the shower, Zev shows up to christen my new place and to see Felix, who he likes for some reason. Zev wants to sit in the yard.

"Hell no," I say. "My dyke neighbor will descend upon us."

I immediately regret saying "dyke," not because it's offensive, but because it's a selling point to Zev. As such, he takes his tiny glass of gin outside.

"I'm meeting Kat Gold," I tell him under the eucalyptus tree. "On Zoom."

"She's the producer lady?" Zev asks, and much like my family members, Zev has no idea that Kat Gold is one of the highest-paid actresses in the world.

I nod. We sit on the rusty chairs that came with the bungalow. Zev removes a joint from his front pocket. Late afternoon trickles through the leaves.

"Miss Hollywood," Zev says flatly and I can't tell if he's talking about me or Kat Gold, but he's definitely mocking the situation. I typically adore Zev's nonchalance, but right now I wish at least one person could be impressed by me.

I'm passing the joint back to Zev for the third time when Penelope shows up like clockwork, barefoot in a teal kimono, taking—I kid you not—the joint from Zev's hand.

She sucks hard. "I didn't know millennials smoked joints," she says on the exhale. "Shouldn't you be vaping or something?"

"Vaping is demonic," Zev says.

Penelope seems charmed, then offers her hand. "I'm Penelope."

"Zev."

I knew these freaks would hit it off.

Penelope plops on the chair beside Zev. Technically this is my furniture, my corner of the yard.

"What were you all talking about?" Penelope asks.

"Kat Gold," I say, assuming Penelope finds Kat Gold lame and vapid and the mere sound of her name will shoo her back to her bungalow.

"Oh, I love her," Penelope says.

"Really?" I say, legitimately surprised. Maybe Penelope is seduced by Kat Gold's pseudo-intellectualism or her supernatural bone structure. "She's adapting my book," I say. "Or her company is. I'm meeting with her next week." I pause. "On Zoom."

"Wow, that's so cool," Penelope says, and I still hate her, but I'm glad at least someone in my life is impressed by my accomplishment. "I loved her memoir," she says.

"Really?" I ask, again surprised. My understanding is that the memoir is mostly Kat flexing the Theory 101 books she probably hasn't read and detailing how she suffers terribly under the male gaze. Not to sound like Megyn Kelly, but I don't think someone who voluntarily models for swimwear can complain about being oppressed by the male gaze. The male gaze probably bought Kat Gold's house.

"Yeah, I find her endearing," Penelope says. "She's very intellectually curious and sincere."

I nod, dubious, but also thinking I can use these adjectives in the Zoom meeting to compliment Kat Gold on her book I certainly will not have read. "What else did you like about it?" I ask, fishing.

"She gives a sort of nuanced perspective of condemning sexism while also using it to her advantage," Penelope says, and I nod, thinking this is kind of Womanhood 101 and there is nothing sophisticated or nuanced about it.

I ask if anyone wants anything from inside and Penelope and Zev shake their heads no in unison, like creepy twins. In my living room, I go to my laptop and type *intellectually curious* and *nuanced* and *the male gaze bought her house* on a Google Doc while the shower runs in the background. Then I text Ivy. *Penelope update: I was smoking a joint with my best friend in the yard and she came over and took the joint from his hand and joined our conversation. The GALL!*

While I wait for her to text back, I take another beer from the fridge and sip it quickly. I crave the Patricia Highsmith. It would put me in a good mood to handle Felix's visit and talk to Penelope. I would be confident and dazzling. Penelope would probably fall in love with me, which would actually be a nightmare. Maybe it's best that I'm my usual grumpy self.

Ivy texts back, *so you're really as unfriendly as the characters in your books?*

I take another big sip to quell my shame.

Taking the joint from your friend's hand is a lot, Ivy continues. *Was he offended?*

I watch them talking through the opening in the curtains. Zev is more animated than normal. They seem taken with each other.

No, I say. *He's a . . . What's the reverse of a fag hag? Like a man who only hangs with lesbians?*

Hmmmm, she writes back. *Lesbi-man?*

I'm annoyed that Zev doesn't even seem to notice I'm missing, and that Felix the self-proclaimed environmentalist is taking the world's longest shower while California is in a drought. Before my conscious mind knows what's happening, I'm texting Jax, an old party friend, *got any AD?* I used to find it significant that my initials, AD (Astrid Dahl), are inscribed onto the pharmaceutical itself, but now I find it pathetic. A lot of people think I'm related to Roald Dahl, probably because we're writers with the same last name, and Roald Dahl has a lesbian socialite granddaughter. But I'm not that granddaughter, although we share at least one ex, and Dahl is a common Swedish last name.

I plop down on the couch with my beer. *They're chatting their brains out and I'm hiding. What are you doing?*

When Ivy doesn't respond right away, I go back outside and Zev is laughing harder than I've ever heard him laugh at something Penelope is saying. I'm shocked because Penelope doesn't seem funny at all.

"What did I miss?" I ask, sitting back in my chair. The yard is fully golden now.

"Penelope was imitating you," Zev says.

"*Pardon?*" I gulp some more of my beer.

"Yeah," says Zev. "She was all, narrowing her eyes, nervous, annoyed at everything, oblivious to the movers, oblivious to everything but her phone."

"Sounds funny." I squeeze my beer hard.

Ivy texts back. *Watching L Word season five and procrastinating. I'm obsessed with Helena's prison romance.* While I'm looking at my phone, Zev and Penelope start laughing again. I look up. Penelope is mocking me, staring intensely at an imaginary phone.

Furious, I go back inside. The shower is still running.

Same and I want to say more on that later, I write back, *but Penelope is messing with the wrong bitch. She's imitating me to my best friend! And that LESBIMAN is laughing his ass off.*

Omg, Ivy writes back, *what is she doing? Just looking beautiful and kinda scary?*

The rage lifts like magic.

‹ ‹ ‹ ›

Back outside, Penelope and Zev emerge from her bungalow, giggling like old friends or—worse—lovers. "Penelope showed me her new piece," Zev tells me when they're back in my corner of the yard. Penelope should have taken a hint and stayed inside. "She made this human heart replica covered in tiny bits of mirror."

"It's about love as projection," Penelope says.

I want to say, *Holy heavy-handed.* But instead, I say, "How interesting" in a tone that reveals I don't find it remotely interesting.

Felix finally comes outside, barefoot, shirtless, water dripping from his beard. The floors of my new bungalow are probably sopping wet. I grip my beer.

"Hey, kiddos," Felix says.

He walks up to Zev and wraps him in a big hug. Zev—I kid you not—*blushes.* All my gay male friends adore Felix and I don't get it at all. Don't they smell his BO? Do they not see the tiny food scraps in his beard?

After hugging Zev for way too long, Felix holds out a hand to Penelope. "I'm Felix," he says. "Astrid's brother."

Penelope stares at him hard, then looks at me, then says, "I don't see the resemblance."

Normally this would flatter me, but it feels like an insult. Most people say Felix and I look similar, we share genes after all. We have the same wavy, white-blond hair and light green eyes sitting under dark, thick brows. We're both lanky, with lean muscle. But Felix wears Tevas and earth tones and sometimes has a carabiner attached to his belt buckle. I wear all black, which I'm transitioning to all white, given the unfortunate fact of my aging, and delicate gold jewelry, which I'm transitioning to larger gold jewelry, to distract from my triangle of sadness.

"Me neither," Zev says.

Felix puts his arm around me, dampening my white T-shirt. He better not be staining it.

"What are you all doing for dinner?" Penelope asks.

Panic wrenches me as I struggle to come up with something.

"No plans," Felix says.

"Me neither," Zev echoes.

I want to hit them both.

"I'm making this new stew recipe, and I'm afraid I've made too much," Penelope says. "Would you all want to eat here?"

"Sounds great," Felix says.

Zev agrees, grinning uncharacteristically.

I try to come up with an excuse but I'm afraid it's too late. My phone lights up with a text. *Beau has some 30s*, Jax replies. Beau is our shady drug dealer friend who I hate but I've always suspected he has a crush on me, so I can probably make him come here. I normally take 10 mg, 20 at the most, so if I buy a 30, it will last me awhile. Or maybe I can split it with Zev or Felix. Felix might want to take it for his drive or something. Procuring Adderall is the sisterly thing to do.

"Astrid?" says Penelope.

"Yeah," I say. "Sounds good." It will be fine. I'll get Beau to drop off an Adderall. I'll pay extra. I have some Marlboro Lights in my bedroom. I'll be adorable and charming and prove to Penelope that I'm not some phone-addicted freak.

I text Beau. *Can you drop off some AD? I'll pay whatever.* I'm rich right now, it's fine. *It's an emergency.*

"Everything okay, Astrid?" Felix asks, squeezing my arm.

"All good," I say. Looking up from my phone, I quote *Jawbreaker*, the black comedy that was popular when I was twelve. "Peachy fucking keen."

fifteen

Beau says he'll drop off the Adderall in thirty minutes if I pay $100 minimum. When he arrives, I tell him I just need one pill, and he says, "That's wildly overpaying" and asks if I want two pills, or a half gram of coke. I tell him, "No, I have a drug problem" and he says, "Sounds like a you problem" and I say, "Yeah, that's what I just said," but he's already driving off. Maybe he doesn't have a crush on me but, whatever: I got the goods.

"Where were you?" Felix asks when I come back up. He's finally wearing a shirt and packing my bong with what I assume is my weed. His entitlement infuriates me, but I'm sure I'll find it charming once the Patricia Highsmith starts swimming through my veins. *Mi casa es su casa.*

"I left something in my car," I say, then go to my bedroom so he doesn't ask any follow-up questions. Under the orange glow of my Himalayan salt lamp, I break the pill in half, then in half again. I crush a quarter of the pill in my molars and taste gasoline. I hope this is really Adderall. For a while I had a prescription, which meant I could get thirty pills for just $3.59 on my insurance, and I'd also know they wouldn't be laced with fentanyl, but I quickly learned I could not be trusted with a prescription.

I sip my beer to get rid of the taste, then put the other quarter of the pill in my jeans pocket. I decide to save the other half rather than offer it to Felix or Zev. It's good to have a half pill for emergencies. I put the remaining pill in my dusty Hello Kitty pillbox and stick it in the back of my underwear drawer. Then I open the "Patricia Highsmith" on my Notes app, and type the date, June 3, so I'm held accountable. Accountability is key. My last slipup was on May 5th at Jax's housewarming party, nearly a month ago, so I'm doing pretty well. I used to do the Patricia Highsmith four times a week.

"You ready to go to Penelope's?" Felix calls into my room. I go out into the living room, where weed smoke hangs in the air. Zev hands me the bong. I take a small hit and text Ivy, *the dyke is forcing us to eat stew*.

She texts back immediately: *Omg I can't wait to hear about it on our big call*. I smile, feeling the amphetamines. Everything is good. I put the phone in my charger in the kitchen and decide I'll leave it here, prove to Penelope that I can be "present."

I grab some beers from the fridge. "Here, help carry some," I say to Felix.

"Are there more people coming?" Felix asks. "Why do we need this many beers?"

I eyeball them, count four in Felix's hands, four in mine. I've already had two. Felix will probably drink three at most (he's annoyingly moderate) and he's already had one. On the Patricia Highsmith, I can drink up to ten beers, which is part of the reason I had to stop. I grab two more just in case.

"It's polite to bring more than we can possibly drink," I say. "Didn't your mother teach you anything?"

Zev raises an eyebrow at me. He always knows when I'm on the Patricia Highsmith. Luckily, he's not a fiend like so many of my friends, meaning he won't ask for any Adderall. I remember

the cigarettes in my bedroom—the final component, then hand
Zev the beers.

"Hold these," I say. "I'll meet you all over there."

Grabbing the pack of Marlboro Lights, I realize Penelope
will likely frown upon the cigarettes and possibly won't let me
smoke them on her side of the property. I'll take two hits of the
cig at my place before I walk over. Passing through the kitchen,
I'm tempted to text Ivy again, then decide against it. I need to
make her wait a bit. In the doorway, I almost run into Zev.

"You got Adderall," he says rather than asks. Zev's persistently
flat affect is immensely comforting to me. He might be judging
me, but he doesn't sound like he's judging me, and that is all I
need.

"Extenuating circumstances," I say. "Split a cig with me before we walk over?"

Zev smokes cigarettes very occasionally.

"Why not wait?" he asks. He pours a splash of gin into a cup
with ice. "Why are you so rushed?"

"Don't you think Penelope will judge? Or forbid?"

"I can't say, I just met her. Let's enjoy a drink first."

I hate when Zev makes me slow down, but I know it's good
for me.

"Fine," I say. I grab a final beer and we walk over.

. . . .

"I put your beers in the fridge," Penelope says when we're in her
corner of the yard, which is lit up by string lights and the moon.
"You didn't need to bring so many, but I appreciate the generos-
ity." I eye Felix when she says this to highlight that people think
I'm generous, and he looks back at me like I have three heads.

Penelope is wearing a bright red sundress, red lipstick, red espadrilles, turquoise earrings. For a second she looks hot, then I remember I have amphetamine taste at the moment. Everyone looks hot. If not for the incest taboo, I'd probably think Felix looks hot too.

"I appreciate you sharing your stew with us," I say with what I hope is a charming and not creepy smile. The goal tonight is to charm Penelope, get her to like me, then back off.

"I'm glad you all are hungry," she says. "I couldn't possibly finish it myself. It's heating up now and should be ready in about thirty minutes. I made some baba ghanoush to snack on in the meantime." She gestures toward the table, where a bowl of beige goop sits beside some pita chips. I watch Felix dig in with vague curiosity, a tinge of disgust. The Patricia Highsmith renders food perplexing. Why would one eat? So messy. So charmless. And I'd have to stop talking.

"Looks delicious," I lie. "You made it yourself?"

"Yep," says Penelope. "Does anyone want wine?" She pops open a bottle of red. There are some glasses on the table.

"I'd love some," says Felix.

Zev lifts his glass of gin. "After this."

"I'm good with beer," I say, lifting mine.

"Just us, then," Penelope says to Felix with what looks like a wink. God, I hope she isn't bisexual. I hope she isn't attracted to my loser brother. How tragic.

We sit in wicker chairs after Penelope pours the wine. I crave a cigarette, but I'm trying to slow down like Zev said.

"So, Felix and Astrid," Penelope asks, "where did you all grow up?"

"The Bay," says Felix, and I try to conceal my disgust. Felix always does this, says he's from "the Bay" to avoid revealing he's from the most expensive city in the country. He loves to cosplay as a "regular guy," rather than what he is: a spoiled rich kid.

I'm sure to Felix's delight, Penelope doesn't ask where in the Bay.

"What about you?" I ask and while I wait for her to answer, I try to guess in my head. I'm thinking Portland, somewhere in the Pacific Northwest. Maybe Northern California. Outside of California they say San Francisco is Northern California, but it's actually right smack in the middle of the state. Penelope could be from *actual* Northern California, like Humboldt County.

"Massachusetts," she says, and I'm ashamed of how dead wrong I was. "I escaped." Then she winks again. All the winking is an interesting choice. "Zev, you're from here, right?"

God, they're best friends. I hope they didn't get matching tattoos already.

"Yeah."

"Jealous," Penelope says.

"Astrid is the only other person who has ever said that to me," Zev says.

Most San Franciscans detest Los Angeles, most people most places do, but I'm rebellious. When people hate something, I love it. When people love it, I hate it. It's not the best quality, being an insufferable contrarian, but much like Paglia, "I positively glory in homosexuality's oppositional character." And is there anything more contrarian than dating women? As a difficult woman, I've always been drawn to LA: its cotton candy–colored smog and pre-apocalyptic climate, sunning lizards, lazy diction, palm trees, strip malls, bad values. It's a goal-oriented town but pretends not to be, and I live for artifice. I want to be around people who are as concerned as I am that Brittany Murphy and her weird husband died within months of each other of the same mysterious cause, people who want to spend their evenings guessing what happened. (Mold poisoning or murder?) People so dissociated that it doesn't even occur to us that it's a spectacularly dark way to pass time, until hours later, when our high starts to dip, and we're alone in the bathroom, and we realize that we're mortal and one day Brittany will be us, six feet under, and hopefully people are speculating about it.

But why does Penelope love Los Angeles? It feels like she'd be more at home in, I don't know, North Carolina? I've heard people are very pretty there. The rest of the country has it all wrong. They say, "I'm not hot enough to live in Los Angeles." But just because we're looks-obsessed doesn't mean we're attractive.

We prefer to work for it, and our taste is abject.

"Most people tell me they hate Los Angeles," Zev says, and I realize I'm slightly uncalibrated. Too jittery but also tired. I could feel better.

"I have to use the bathroom," I say, and turn toward my house.

"You can use mine," Penelope says to my back.

I turn around and whisper, "Period issues."

I don't want her to think I'm doing drugs, which I am, and also smoking a cigarette.

Penelope nods knowingly.

Inside I crunch the other quarter Adderall in my teeth, taste gasoline, open a beer to wash it down. I eye my phone, think about texting Ivy. I shouldn't, but I have very little self-control at this moment. I hate losing control, but it's probably good for me, which is how I justify the Patricia Highsmith. It's good to be pure id occasionally. It makes the skin glow.

I pick up my phone and text Ivy. *We should talk tonight if you're still free*, I write. *Circumstances have changed. I have too much to say. And I suspect I'll have a headache in the morning.*

I put the phone down and sip more beer and watch the screen as though it's a grenade about to go off. Nicotine calls my name, but Penelope will surely smell it, know I've been up to no good. Maybe I can smoke out of my bedroom window and if she says something I can blame the neighbors or people passing on the street below. I can just take two puffs and save the rest for later. I grab my phone and open the window, light the cigarette, inhale, and stare at my screen. No response. Oh well. The amphetamines are mixing with the nicotine in my blood and I'm feeling very positive. I put my phone in my charger and walk back to Penelope's, where she's serving the stew.

"Everything okay, Astrid?" Penelope asks.

I pretend not to hear, look up at the pinkening sky.

She hands me a bowl of stew and it smells nice, like coconut and turmeric, more of a perfume than a food. I can't imagine eating, but I take a bite to be polite and it tastes delightful.

"I smell cigarette smoke," says Penelope.

"There were some kids on the street smoking," I say perhaps a little too quickly.

"Damn," she says. "I was hoping it was you. I'd love a post-meal cig."

I'm speechless.

"I'm always trying to quit, but my current rule is I'm not buying them," Penelope continues, "but I'm allowed to bum."

"I have some," I say. "Back in my room. I'll grab them after dinner. This stew is delicious, by the way."

"It really is," Zev says.

"Totally bomb," says Felix.

"Thanks, guys," she says. "You're making me blush."

Taking in the scene—my brother and my best friend and my new neighbor eating a sensual stew under a eucalyptus tree and a pink sky—a perhaps chemically induced wave of wholesome bliss washes over me.

"Penelope," I say in between bites. "Did your ex-girlfriend like the cake? Did you find cream?"

She nods to register the question and points to her mouth to indicate it's full of food. Zev and Felix lack context, and now we're all silent while Penelope finishes chewing. I sip my beer and wonder if Ivy texted me back.

"I made it without cream," Penelope says when she finally finishes chewing. "I used soy yogurt. It was okay? It wasn't my best work." She looks at the boys. "I asked Astrid for cream the other day to make a cake for my ex . . . Very lesbian behavior, I know." She laughs at herself and my stomach spasms slightly.

"You asked Astrid for cream?" Zev laughs. "Clearly you don't know her very well."

"She's kind of impenetrable," Penelope says. Why is she talking about me like I'm not here?

"She likes to think so," Zev says.

"Otto always says I'm very obvious," I say, then feel embarrassed that I'm talking about someone not everyone knows again, making very alienating conversation. I should be doing better, but Penelope makes me uneasy. The problem with drugs is that they can turn on you just as easily as they facilitate things. "Otto is my other good friend from college," I say. "Zev being the first."

"Otto's a cool dude," Felix says. I've suspected that Felix and Otto have hooked up. One night a few years ago Felix and Otto were both staying with me in my tiny one-bedroom apartment in Echo Park and we stayed up all night doing coke, and I went to bed and expected to wake up with Otto beside me, but he was on the pull-out couch with Felix in the morning. Felix has told me he's hooked up with guys. Actually, I believe his exact words were

"Sucking dick is really hard" and I said, "Honey, who are you telling?" I assume most men, gay or straight, have fooled around with other men, and that most men have the dignity not to tell their sisters about it.

"So, the three of you hung out a lot?" Penelope asks, referring, I suppose, to Zev and Otto and me.

"God no," Zev says. "Otto was Astrid's genetically privileged party friend." Zev has a wonderful appearance, but he's very insecure because I suppose he doesn't have "the look" that gay men cherish, meaning he does cardio instead of lifting his vanity muscles.

"I'm sort of like that too," Penelope says. "Lots of scattered friends rather than having a group. I've never been much of a joiner."

"Me neither," says Felix.

"Same," says Zev.

"Look at us," I say. "A bunch of loners sharing a meal. Life is magical."

"It really is," says Penelope, and she gets up and takes Felix's empty bowl from his hand, stacks it on top of her own.

"Don't let her do that," I say, getting up, taking both bowls. "You cooked, I'll clean," I say. I love cleaning on Adderall. And weed. And nicotine. And alcohol.

"Oh, don't worry about it, Astrid," Penelope says.

"I insist," I say, then head inside. The scent hits me again, patchouli and glue, but it doesn't bother me so much this time. Instead, I get excited about the glue smell, acidic and intoxicating. The kitchen is filled with vases of dead roses. Various spices and cutlery litter the countertops. I find a sponge and some organic dish soap and get at it. I clean both bowls, dry them, then the knives and some spoons. I clean the counter with some organic wipes and my mind floats to pleasant places, fantasies of Ivy and me on a boat in the Pacific, drinking champagne, laughing, crunching amphetamines in our molars. She's a PhD student, which suggests she has access to the good stuff.

"Astrid," Penelope says, appearing out of nowhere with another empty bowl. "This is not necessary at all. Go finish your stew and enjoy yourself."

"The stew is incredible," I say. "But I have terrible cramps and I can't eat any more."

"Maybe you shouldn't be drinking," Penelope says.

"Oh no," I say. "Alcohol is fine. I'm Irish. It's like water to me." My lies are harmless. It's just my fiction brain having fun.

"Your brother said your parents are Swedish," Penelope says.

"He says a lot of things," I say. "Let's go have that cigarette!"

∴ ∴

Outside, the sky is navy blue. I take a deep breath and taste eucalyptus in my lungs.

"Who wants a cig?" I ask the boys.

Felix looks at Zev. "You want to share one? I don't want a whole."

God, they're flirting.

"Sure," says Zev.

"I'll just bring the whole pack," I spit with disgust. Then I remember my phone in my kitchen and excitement surges through me. I charge across the lawn feeling like a forest fawn, playful and in my element, prancing on the grass on a summer night. I go to my room to get the Marlboros first, saving the phone for last, a little treat. But back in the kitchen, I'm devastated to see no notifications. My stomach sinks. I feel like collapsing. The world is turning on me. I'm no longer a forest fawn but rather a sea urchin clawing onto the depths of the ocean floor, dark and icky and about to get eaten by a shark.

Then I remember the other half of the Adderall in my Hello Kitty pill box in my room. I was supposed to save it, but this is an unusual night. I must charm Penelope. I might talk to Ivy later. I have to entertain my brother and be on my game. I must be a deer again, not a sea urchin. My id takes me into the bedroom, where I break off another quarter, smaller than a quarter, and crunch it in my teeth. I do some quick math. The entire pill was 30 mg. I've had roughly 70 percent of it, maybe 65 percent. According to my iPhone, 65 percent of 30 is 19.5 mg. That's fine. My limit is 20 mg and I'm well within it. I check my messages again and see nada. Ivy's probably working on her dissertation, having very brilliant thoughts about the lesbian experience. All is good.

I return to Penelope's side of the yard, prancing like a forest fawn under the darkening sky, then dole out the cigarettes like Oprah giving out free cars.

"God bless," Penelope says. "Laura hated when I smoked. All my exes did, except for one, but she was a bad influence." She lights eagerly.

I'm thrilled Penelope is talking about her exes. God forbid people talk about their jobs or their diets. Relationships, crushes, falling in love and out of it, breakups, heartbreak, these are the only conversation topics I recognize.

"Laura is the girl you made the cake for?" I ask.

"Woman, yes," she says and I'm thankful for the amphetamines because I don't even begin to roll my eyes.

"When did you break up with this woman?" I ask.

"Well, she broke up with me," Penelope says.

"*Astrid*," Felix hisses at me.

I shrug. "Sorry," I say. "I figured it was the other way around, given you baked the girl a cake." I light my cigarette, inhale. "Sorry, baked the *woman* a cake."

"It's okay," Penelope says. "I'm pathologically forgiving."

"God, same," I say, dragging again.

"You are?" Zev asks.

"Yeah," Felix says. "I wouldn't describe you that way."

Why does it feel like everyone is conspiring against me? That Felix and Zev are a couple in limerence, high off the idea of bringing me down? As the nicotine enters my bloodstream, I try to steer myself back to the airy fawn, away from the sea urchin. I look up at the now nearly black sky and see, for the very first time since I've lived in Los Angeles, the faint hint of the Big Dipper. I had completely forgotten about stars.

"Devon threw a butternut squash at my car and I didn't press charges," I say. "I had to replace the window."

"*Pardon?*" Penelope laughs. Her teeth are very white for someone who doesn't have a dishwasher. "I need to hear more about that."

"Please God, no," Zev says. Zev has stressed on numerous occasions that he finds my love life very tedious. "I don't typically wish real life was more like the internet but I'm dying to put the mute function on the name 'Devon' so I never have to hear about that girl again." He clears his throat. "Sorry, *woman*."

Felix giggles.

"I'm going to refresh my drink," Zev says, lifting his glass.

"I'll go with you," Felix says.

Penelope is just laughing. "This is how my friends were about Laura for a while," she says. "I'm new to Devon so I don't need to mute her yet."

"Okay," I say, trying to think about what I want to reveal to Penelope, if I want to reveal anything at all. I'm nervous now that it's just the two of us. I'm scared if I say something, she'll follow up tomorrow, when I'm not on the Patricia Highsmith, and it will be torture. "Is it just me, or are they flirting?" I ask, eyeing Felix and Zev as they disappear into my bungalow.

"I'm not sure," Penelope says. "I only just met them. Your brother seems naturally flirtatious."

"Ew," I say.

Penelope laughs. She drags her cigarette and exhales rings.

"Wow," I say, impressed by the rings floating up into the night sky.

"So, Devon?"

"There's not much to say . . . We had great sex, fought constantly." I drag, exhale. "I dumped her and she threw a squash at my car."

Penelope bursts out laughing, flashing straight white teeth at me. "Deedee was right, you really are a strange one."

I look over at the bungalow, hoping the boys come back soon.

"Did Laura ever throw anything at your car?" I ask.

"No," Penelope says. "Not at my car. She did throw my phone against the wall once."

"Saw something she didn't like?"

Penelope nods. It feels like we're getting along, but it's probably just the drugs. I recall her making me carry her heavy-ass groceries, putting her nasty feet on my coffee table, lecturing me about vitamins. She seems like a different person now, but the Patricia Highsmith can cloud things, making what's objectively ugly seem beautiful. In the morning, I'll no longer be a fawn, light and airy, but I'll be the sea urchin, dark and sad. And Penelope will be a pain in my ass once again. I hope Ivy and I can talk tonight. I'll be in no state to have any sort of conversation tomorrow.

The boys return with two small glasses of gin.

I sip my beer and realize I'm turning, entering that gray zone, where I might start repeating myself, have trouble following conversation, when my words become slushy. This is what I like to call "the point of no return." I need water, but I won't touch it. I'll just keep drinking and drinking until I'm asleep.

sixteen

It's dark in my room, but I can tell by the taste of hot gasoline in my mouth that it's morning. I try to piece together the rest of the night. Penelope gave me a glass of water, I remember that, and forced me to eat more stew. I remember excusing myself shortly thereafter to drink more beer in peace.

Shame rushes over me like a hot shower.

Did I FaceTime Ivy last night? I have a vague memory of FaceTiming Ivy. She was wearing a hot pink dress, which I complimented effusively. What did we talk about? Maybe I dreamt it? I pick up my phone and check my call log. I didn't dream it. God!

What did I say to her?

I need water but don't want to see Felix. Heaven forbid he confronts me about my actions last night, actions I can't possibly defend because I hardly remember them.

I scroll through my texts for clues. Nothing to Ivy, thank God.

My texts seem okay. I didn't text anything incomprehensible to anyone.

Holding my breath, I open Instagram to ensure I didn't post a blurry photo I mistook for "art" or worse, a nude I mistakenly found "tasteful," both things I once did regularly. Otto says I'm an "internet exhibitionist." I exhale when I see I posted neither.

I also check my bank statement to make sure I didn't order any overpriced perfumes or body lotions or candles or any other indulgent personal items. Luckily, I only see the $100 I sent to Beau on Venmo accompanied by the dolphin emoji.

But the intensity of my shame makes me feel like I did something absolutely horrible, like I murdered someone or committed an act of pedophilia.

I return to my call log. Holy shit, I was on FaceTime with Ivy for two hours and forty-three minutes. No wonder I didn't post anything or text anyone. I'm terrified thinking about what I did or said. I hadn't used the Patricia Highsmith in twenty-nine days, meaning I'd forgotten why I'd stopped. For this feeling. The hot shame. The taste of acrid chemicals in my throat. Vague nausea that will have no relief. I never vomit. I keep the toxins inside, poisoning me.

Afraid I might die of dehydration, I make my way to the kitchen, terrified to confront Felix. I'm thrilled to see his bike is gone. The blanket he used is folded on the couch.

There's a note on the fridge that says, *Thnx for hosting, sis.* *<3, Felix.*

I don't even mind all the dirt he's left behind.

I text him, *Drive safe, bro! Love you!*

I really do love him in this moment, for giving me what I need for once—space. While the Patricia Highsmith makes me social, the comedown renders me more isolated than ever.

Sprawling on the couch, I scroll through photos of Italian greyhounds—such elegant creatures—and consider whether I should text Ivy. Outside the window, Penelope is walking through the yard with a petite blonde woman. She's laughing, grazing the woman's arm, *flirting*. Repulsive.

Turning my head back toward my phone, I open my text

thread with Ivy and there is nothing since the desperate text in which I demanded I needed to speak to her. The shame burns and I chug vitamin water, hoping it will neutralize me.

I look out the window and the yard is empty minus a squirrel. I wonder who the blonde was, whether it was Penelope's ex Laura and they're getting back together, or whether it's a new girl and Penelope is trying to find her next Laura. Whoever it is, I fantasize the girl, woman, whatever, will take Penelope away from our shared yard, that they will hang at her house instead.

Feeling slightly energized by this fantasy and maybe also the vitamins, I gather the strength to text Ivy. *Sorry if I was demented last night . . . I was overserved . . . by myself.*

She replies quickly, *Omg stop you were so fun! Excited to meet up for real this week.*

Shit, I guess we made plans. Her text conveys the two major problems with the Patricia Highsmith. One, I'm *fun*. That's why I kept doing it. Rave reviews. Rave! I would black out and people would fall in love with me. Even Felix told me he loved me. Given the terrible reviews of my sober personality—rigid, hostile, strange—it makes it very hard to quit.

Problem two, I make plans I don't remember. Sometimes, this works out. I've blacked out and pitched articles to editors, then they follow up and offer me money to write them. I make plans to go hiking, go to the beach, I even made plans to go to Paris. I guess that's part of the fun of the Patricia Highsmith, the idea that the future is filled with promise and possibility, instead of fear and anxiety. But the problem is in the not remembering. When I have to tell the editor to "refresh my memory" on the details of the pitch because "I'm very scattered haha!" Or when an angry friend calls me from the car, furious I'm not already on my way to Malibu.

I'm happy I made plans with Ivy but sad I don't know when they are. I open my laptop and scan my Google Calendar for the upcoming week. No evidence.

Another text pops up. *Cabo seafood grill in Oxnard on Wednesday at 6*, Ivy writes. *In case your memory was hazy. I was pretty lit myself but not quite on your level. Hopefully I'll get there on Wednesday.*

God is good. Well, God is okay. I'm glad she told me so I didn't have to ask. I'm not happy she noticed I was blacked out. I'm happy we're meeting Wednesday, so I have time to recover, but not happy it's in Oxnard. Why in God's name are we meeting in Oxnard?

A memory floats back, us looking up the halfway point between Los Angeles and Santa Barbara, finding this shitty Mexican restaurant and thinking it looked like "good fun." But how are we going to get fucked up if we both have to drive over an hour? Ideally, we'd meet at one of our houses and sleep over so we can drink freely. I'm not supposed to be getting drunk to the point I can't drive, but first dates are an exception. How else are you supposed to get to know someone?

ACT II

NICK: Wow, that's interesting. You've fallen in love with a woman.

JENNY: No, no, no. I don't know if it's love. It might be sort of, like, this, you know, [smiling] fantastic, sort of, like, demon possession sort of thing.

—*The L Word*

one

I fill a kombucha bottle with an IPA for my drive to Oxnard. Frankly, I'm a better driver with a little alcohol in my system. I'm probably low femme but I drive like a high femme—absentminded, skittish, always missing my exit due to chatting. I'm not just drinking and driving for myself, but for the other drivers on the road.

And when a Dodge Ram nearly runs me over as soon as I merge onto the 101, I'm thankful for my naughty kombucha bottle. I take a big gulp as the Ram cruises off. Its bumper sticker says: CAUTION: THIS VEHICLE MAKES SUDDEN STOPS AT YOUR MOM'S HOUSE.

I take another gulp and hear a siren. Frantically, I put the bottle in the cup holder, pop a piece of Trident Ice in my mouth, begin chewing hungrily. The cop flies past me and I make my way to the right lane, where I won't piss off anyone. Google Maps said the drive would take one hour and thirty-six minutes, but I leave two hours because I tend to get lost.

I drive a black Subaru, which is embarrassing, being a lesbian who drives a Subaru. But I know almost nothing about cars and when my Saab died a year ago, I simply googled "low maintenance practical cars" and Subaru Impreza was at the top of the list so I bought one used off the internet. I didn't even have to talk to anyone! And, well, so far so good.

In Thousand Oaks, I finish the dregs of my "kombucha" and feel slightly less invincible. Google says I have forty-two minutes remaining. And no alcohol left. Without thinking very hard, I take the one-third Adderall I have in my pocket and crunch it in my molars. The plan was to wait, take it after my first drink at dinner, but plans are merely a blueprint, they aren't written in ink.

Now I'm just driving past office parks and outlet malls, feeling excited and oddly patriotic. Lana Del Rey plays on the speakers and I see beauty everywhere. There's that line in *Grey Gardens* when Little Edie is digging through a pile of what looks like garbage and mutters, *This is all art*. She says it quietly and it doesn't appear on the transcript PDF of the film I've read over a hundred times on my laptop, but I'm positive she says it. And now I'm repeating *This is all art* to myself like a schizophrenic mantra while watching an American flag wave perkily above a P.F. Chang's.

I smell my forearm. I've abandoned Iso E Super, which has started to smell chemically and sour. This afternoon I tested many sections of my arms and sniffed for hours like a damn bloodhound, eventually landing on a woodsy peachy scent created by a married couple in Brooklyn. I fantasize, briefly, about being married to Ivy and writing books together, a dream. Sniffing now, I'm confident I picked the right one. It smells spicy and creamy, as one should smell on a date.

I hope I'm not too confident to see Ivy. It's best to be a little shy on a first date. Society overvalues extroversion. That's why I became seduced by the Patricia Highsmith. Society had fooled me into thinking confidence was something to be aspired to. To get healthy, I just have to keep reminding myself: confidence is tacky.

I light a cigarette and smoke out the window.

:::::

Oxnard is creepy as hell—flat, sparse, decrepit. Dusty colors from another era. I smell the ocean, but I don't see it.

The restaurant has a plastic awning with miniature wooden fish hanging from it. The sign, which just says Cabo, is sun-bleached blue.

Parking my car, I remember I'm about to meet Ivy and feel something, I'm not sure what. My feelings have always been a mystery. Thoughts are much easier, more fun.

I pull down my sun visor and begin to check my reflection in the mirror, then shut it. I'm sure I look fine. It doesn't matter. The nice thing about dating women is that we aren't men. Men are much more visual. And youth obsessed. My thirtysomething gay male friends will front, like, *Check out this twenty-two-year-old model I'm fucking* and show me a picture of his cut triangular body in a Speedo. My thirtysomething lesbian friends will front, like, *I'm exchanging very long text messages with this forty-six-year-old academic.* Men love young tight bodies and women love words and power. The gender binary has been canceled, but I can still think these things privately. I guess this is what Agent Allison wants me to do. Think don't speak the cancelable thoughts.

The clock on my dashboard says 5:56. Perfect. It took me nearly half an hour longer than Google thought it would and I'm only a tiny bit early. I'll have time to order a drink.

The inside is dim, concealing that it's summer and therefore still oppressively bright out. And Ivy, to my surprise, is already seated at a booth in the corner. She's wearing a bright pink shirt that matches the pink plastic chairs at the bar, almost like she planned it.

"You have legs!" I shout playfully when Ivy stands. I'm hamming it up, classic Patricia Highsmith behavior.

Ivy laughs and looks down, seeming shy. She's wearing low-waisted boot-cut jeans and pink ballet flats. I imagine Otto would say something snarky, ask why I'm going out with someone dressed like Lauren Conrad in 2006. But I'm charmed by Ivy's dated attire. It has me feeling nostalgic: 2006 was a good year for me. I bought my first bong and enjoyed how weed made everything sound better—music, birdsong, and most importantly: people talking. I was deep in the "indie sleaze" movement, going to Diplo and M.I.A. shows and trying to be a dissociated white girl rapper like Uffie, which all ended up in my second novel.

"I got you a margarita," she says sort of quietly, sitting down. "I hope that's okay."

I sit beside her in the booth and slyly try to smell her, but I just smell the restaurant, tortilla flour and lime.

"It's more than okay." I gulp my margarita. "Harsh chemical perfection," I say, then my heart speeds up. I'm with Ivy. Ivy! The girl over whom I've been obsessing digitally for months. And now we're sharing air space.

"I know, right," she says, loosening a bit. "It's like Pine-Sol plus high fructose corn syrup and it's totally incredible."

"Was the drive okay?" Ivy asks, making small talk, how adorable. I vow not to hit my vape pen until we're on our second round.

"It was haunting and spiritual," I say. "I always start to believe in God around Calabasas."

"Oh right," Ivy says. "You're a big Kardashian gal."

The waiter comes and takes our orders. We both order the fish tacos and then laugh at ourselves. Dyke 101.

"How's school?" I ask. I miss being in school all the time. I even enjoyed law school, I just dropped out because I knew I didn't want to practice law and it felt like a waste of my parents' money, which would become my money if I dropped out. I used the money to support myself in Los Angeles while I wrote my first book, the one about the Kardashians, and boom, suddenly I was making a living. I've been insanely lucky. I make a mental note to remember this feeling of gratitude when I'm coming down off the Patricia and inevitably feel bleak.

"Ugh," Ivy says. "My dissertation will be the death of me."

I try to nod sympathetically, but I really don't understand when PhD students complain. It's like when people complain about writing books. Like "Oh my God, my editor gave me this deadline, I'm losing my mind." Why? Writing is just typing, and typing is much easier than most things.

"At least you picked a fun subject," I say.

"Did I?" she says. "Did I?? I worry that by writing about lesbian pulp, I am enacting tragic stories in my romantic life."

This, I know, is a red flag.

Seemingly reading my mind, Ivy says, "I guess that's a weird thing to say on a date."

"It's not," I say. "Well, maybe it is. But I don't mind. I've felt similarly about my own writing. I sit down wanting to write the great lesbian love story, but wacko bitches just keep coming out." I guess God is using me as a vessel to capture the hysterical female experience.

Ivy laughs. "We're doomed."

"Our lives are rich," I say.

two

After we order our second drinks, I excuse myself to the bathroom to vape sativa on the toilet. This is something I've been doing for years. It's silly, because I was born and raised in California, where weed was de facto legal even before it was officially legal. But I've always been embarrassed by stoner culture, which I associate with outdoorsy boys with low IQs, boys with "happy to be here" energy, boys like Felix, with Phish and hacky sacks and dreadlocks and patchouli and staring into space with nothing to say. I pride myself on my quick mind and on never listening to jam bands.

I smoke weed for the five minutes of euphoria.

When I return to the table, our drinks and tacos have arrived. For a second, I'm stressed by the challenge of eating a taco in a cute way. I have a small mouth and shaky hands. I sip my beer, pick up my fork, and announce to Ivy that I'm taking a break from writing.

"I haven't written in—" I pause, thinking. I put some fish on my fork. "Nearly six months. The longest I've ever gone. Ever."

"Maybe you need a break," Ivy says. "Some time to recharge. You're disturbingly prolific."

People say that a lot and it always feels like an insult. They don't tell me I'm a good writer, they say I'm prolific.

But she's right that I need a break. Recently when I think about writing a novel, it just seems so hard. And I *never* used to feel that way. The idea of writing a novel used to seem so fun, a treat, a fantastical world where I got to be God. But I suppose that was all before I had "an audience." Before I had thousands of people calling me vapid and cringe and an oppressor on the internet and, on a few unfortunate occasions, to my face.

"Maybe," I say. "It doesn't matter."

We take bites in silence for a second, me with my fork and Ivy with her hands.

"So, have you heard from Penelope since the Patricia High-smith night?" Ivy asks and my heart jumps. I don't remember telling her about the Patricia Highsmith. I've only used that sequence of words to a select few. Zev knows it. Otto knows it. Agent Allison knows it. A few other party friends here and there. But I don't normally tell potential lovers. Maybe I do. It kills my memory.

"God," I say flatly, trying not to show my hand, nonplussed that she knows my secret. "She came over the next day with Alka-Seltzer. Alka-Seltzer! Like she's my grandmother? She was all, 'You must have a headache,' and I was all, 'I don't know what you're talking about, I feel great!' Then I got into downward facing dog to show her I was not only fine but also busy. If there is one thing hippie dippy Gen Xers understand, it's that yoga is sacred. It worked—she skedaddled."

Ivy laughs hard, which intensifies the euphoria whipping through me.

When she finally stops laughing, she takes the last bite of her taco, then reaches into her Coach purse. She puts a blue pill on the table, then says, "I brought dessert."

And it's the most gorgeous red flag I've ever seen.

⁝ ⁝ ⁝ ⁝

We're in a dark bar and I'm not sure how we got here.

Ivy is holding my waist hard. She's more of a top than she seems. I must have sensed something. My dream is a femme-presenting woman who can take charge, dominate me, slap me, objectify me, turn me into a little shiny object to be adored then punished. Forever a little girl in trouble.

"You're a dream," I whisper into her ear. Drake is blasting from the ceiling. Mild panic suddenly appears in my stomach. "I didn't drive here, did I?"

"I did, honey," Ivy says. Top energy, I knew it.

"I can't drive home tonight," I say.

"Oh, yeah, that won't be happening," Ivy says, grabbing my waist tighter.

"You can't possibly drive me all the way to Los Angeles," I say.

"I can't, no," she says. Then she kisses me. It's hot, but I'm still concerned about getting home, about where I'm going to sleep.

"We'll sleep at your place?"

Ivy's energy changes, she moves away from me and sips her cocktail. At first I think she's rejecting me, but then I realize she's ashamed.

"So," she says. "I still live with my ex."

A less beautiful red flag. I recall the Samantha Ronson derivative from her Instagram and from her Zoom square.

"It's not what it seems. We only recently broke up and we're both looking for other places, but the Santa Barbara rental market is totally insane."

I nod and move away from her instinctively.

"Ugh," she says. "I know it sounds bad, but I promise there is *nothing* between us anymore."

"The lady doth protest," I say.

She puts a finger over my lips and grabs my waist again, pulls me close, then whispers in my ear, "I'll get us a hotel."

three

I awake under stiff white sheets that reek of bleach. Ivy's arm is wrapped around my waist just as it was for most of last night. I vaguely remember us booking a room on Hotel Tonight, then her riding me, me thinking, *Knew it, a top.*

I don't feel hungover at all. I am still drunk, high, all of it. The hangover will hit tonight or tomorrow. Maybe I will want to die. But if there is one thing that can defeat a hangover, aside from benzodiazepines, of course, it is limerence.

A half-empty Aquafina bottle sits on the bedside table and I chug its remains. Ivy stirs but does not wake. I tiptoe across the electric blue carpet to the window. Just shifting the curtain floods the room in sharp lines of glowing yellow. Ivy makes a noise and turns over.

Returning my gaze to the sliver of window, I'm thrilled to notice sand dunes and sparkling turquoise water behind it. The beach! Ivy got us a hotel on the beach! I'm definitely still a bit fucked up. I try to find my phone, and Ivy groans again. I find it on the floor at the foot of the bed, and it's nearly out of juice, which never happens to me unless I've been bendering. Sober, I pride myself on just a few things: svelte figure, a lot to say, and a fully charged iPhone.

I attach my phone to the charger.

My clothes are strewn across the carpet. I gather them and go to the bathroom, careful to avert my gaze from the mirror to avoid being confronted with the likely horrors of my reflection. Once dressed, I creep out of the room and into the hallway.

Spots of red and yellow flood my vision as my eyes adjust to the bright morning light. I forgot to look at the time on my phone, but it doesn't matter. I feel untethered to time these days. I have no real obligations, other than to be healthy, at which I am clearly failing. But I feel fine. *I feel great*, I tell myself in a loop as I walk outside.

It's chillier than I expected, but the morning fog is just beginning to burn off. Without thinking, I'm running toward the ocean. I stop and sit just before the line of wet sand, then stare at the waves crashing, anesthetized by the sight and sound.

. . . .

I'm not sure how much time has passed when there's a tap on my shoulder. Ivy is carrying two steaming cups of coffee. What a perfect morning. Oh, sweet limerence.

I take a sip, then put my coffee into the sand. Ivy pulls my phone from her bra.

"It's been ringing off the hook," she says, handing it to me.

Panic rises from my gut. Did someone die? On the screen are four missed calls from Agent Allison.

"Why is my agent calling me on a Saturday?"

Ivy laughs. "It's Thursday."

I shrug. "She shouldn't be calling me. I'm taking a break! I'm on sabbatical. I'm having my year of rest and relaxation. The only thing I'm really on the hook for is the occasional 'consulting' meeting for my adapta—OH."

Ivy laughs, but I'm not laughing. This was the big meeting. The one with Kat Gold herself.

I open the text thread with my agent, Allison. The first text says, *Astrid, can you confirm you're still on for the meeting with the Satchels of Gold team at 9amPT?*

Agent Allison always sends me these little reminder texts before meetings because I have a tendency to forget. I'm an artist. I can't be bothered to maintain a schedule. Also, ever since my big Barnes & Noble snafu, I suspect Agent Allison likes to get my head right before I talk to anyone about my work, taming me like an unruly dog. I keep reading. *I assume you're still sleeping given the time difference and that you will be there for the meeting.* Another one. *Astrid, we're all here, including Kat!! I'm stalling.* Another one. *Okay, I made a little white lie about you having a medical emergency. Please call me.*

Ugh. I don't want to talk on the phone with Allison. I want to sit on the beach with Ivy drinking coffee and talking about Bette Porter. I text her instead of calling.

I'm so sorry, I write, trying to think of a little white lie of my own. I'm not feeling very creative. I look out at the water. Several big ships bob in the distance, a mass of gray air hovering above them. *Your white lie has some truth to it. Sorry I overslept; I am having a terrible reaction to the LA pollution. I read online that its symptoms mimic that of heart disease. The supply chain issues are causing pollution levels like the 80s here.* I saw something about this on Twitter. Oxnard isn't exactly Los Angeles, but I'm looking right at a heap of polluted air.

As soon as I click Send, Agent Allison is calling me.

"Astrid," she says. "Are you on drugs?"

"No," I lie, or maybe it's not a lie. I haven't consumed any drugs since the previous night, but I'm definitely still high. "I've been having a lot of problems with time."

Ivy giggles, and I slap her leg.

"You sound like you're on drugs," Agent Allison says flatly. "I told the team that we can reschedule for tomorrow at nine a.m. If you have a conflict, move it. And please don't make me lie to Kat Gold again."

I know for certain that I will be hungover as hell tomorrow morning. I will feel like death at nine a.m. I'll do the meeting and fall back asleep. I don't have to do much at these meetings anyway. They say things and I nod. Occasionally they ask me my opinion and if I can't think of anything to say, Allison steps in for me. Kat Gold will probably be zoned out looking at TikTok the whole time.

"Astrid?" Allison asks, impatient.

"I'll be there," I say.

"Great." *Click.*

"Everything okay?" Ivy asks.

"Peachy fucking keen," I say.

four

When my alarm sounds the next morning, I'm sure I'm dreaming it. I'm convinced it's the middle of the night. I yell, "Siri, snooze!" When it goes off the next time, I feel the same, maybe worse. My body is heavy, like it was hit by a truck. This is a medical emergency, like Agent Allison told the "team" I had yesterday. But I must make the meeting. I have no choice. Satchels of Gold could cancel the contract and Allison could drop me and I'll have to query agents again. I'll have to move back in with my parents where they'll inevitably make me go back to law school, or—worse—work for them.

I slap myself in the face. Not too hard, just hard enough to perk myself up. I throw on the white button-down shirt with magnetic buttons I bought on Amazon for thirteen dollars and head to the kitchen to make coffee.

While the coffee brews, I chug a glass of water, then do a few jumping jacks. As I do, I catch Penelope walking by my window. We make eye contact, and I keep jumping. She approaches my door.

I walk over, annoyed as hell. "Important meeting," I hiss through the cracked-open window. "Can't talk."

"Okay," Penelope says, looking down at my pantless legs. Perv. "I heard screaming, so I wanted to make sure you were okay."

"I was just yelling at Siri," I say. "You heard that?"

"I think your bedroom windows are open."

I make a mental note to never, ever, leave my bedroom windows open again. "Meeting with Kat Gold," I say, pointing to my laptop. "I really can't talk." Penelope nods and, thankfully, walks away.

My iPhone says 8:58 a.m. Perfect. Just suffer the meeting, then back to bed. I take a few big sips of coffee and look at my phone. I have a text from Agent Allison. *Astrid, meeting in 5—be there and be sober! For the love of god!!*

I open my laptop at my desk. Ready to rock.

I click the Zoom link.

Squares of heads pop up, way more than seem necessary. I recognize Agent Allison, and Maude, the producer I met with last time, and then a few people whose names I don't remember, and a few people I've never seen before. Roughly seven boxes total. I wave at no one in particular, and a new rectangle appears. It's Kat Gold, in a bright room surrounded by very healthy-looking plants, much healthier than mine, which tend to be brown on the edges of the leaves due to overwatering, i.e., smothering. Kat Gold's skin also looks very healthy, much healthier than mine, and I'm sure she doesn't even have to use the Zoom feature to touch up her appearance. I slyly google Kat Gold's age. The internet says twenty-nine, which probably means she's thirty-three. She has deep brown, almond-shaped eyes and wispy chestnut hair, and when she adjusts in her seat, I notice she is wearing a T-shirt with Joan Didion's face on it and I try my absolute hardest to maintain a positive facial expression.

"Astrid," Maude says. She's in an office made of glass with views obscured by haze. "Thanks so much for joining us. We hope you're feeling better."

"Thanks," I say. "I'm so sorry about yesterday. I had a very dramatic reaction to the elevated pollution levels from the breakdown in the supply chain."

"It's a shit show, right?" Maude says. "I get a migraine just walking to my car."

I eye Allison to prove I wasn't lying about the heightened pollution. She eyes me back as if to say *They're in Los Angeles, too, Astrid, and they all made the meeting.*

"It's like the eighties," says someone I've never seen before.

"So, Astrid," Maude says, "we're thrilled to finally introduce you to our fearless leader, Kat Gold."

"Hi, Astrid," Kat Gold says. Her voice is soft and fluffy. "I'm *sooo* glad to meet you. I'm such a huge fan of your books, and you generally, and I'm beyond grateful you chose to work with our kooky little company on this adaptation. We're going to take great care of your baby."

I check my Zoom square to ensure I'm not scowling. I hate when people compare writing a novel to giving birth; it's more like an exorcism, *Rosemary's Baby* at best. "Thanks," I say.

"I adore the way you explore fame and femininity," Kat continues. "Themes close to my heart." She presses her hands on her chest. "And the way you handle the interplay of craving the male gaze while also resenting it," she says, "it's just so dexterously done." I nod and wonder what Kat Gold is referring to, whether she's mistaking my book for her own book, which I still haven't read, but I remember Penelope's description and writing down *the male gaze bought her house.*

"I like that about your memoir," I say, eyeing Agent Allison to show I've done my homework. "Your nuanced take on condemning sexism while also profiting off it." I think these were Penelope's exact words.

Agent Allison nods, seeming proud, or maybe just relieved.

I smile to myself, thinking: *The cat's in the bag*.

"Oh my gosh, thank you so much," Kat Gold says, putting her hands together in a prayer motion, and the way she keeps moving her hands as she speaks reminds me of someone doing sign language. "That means a lot coming from you. I always assumed you'd find my writing kind of simplistic and, well, cringe." She laughs, and I try my very hardest to make a disbelieving expression. I'm a terrible actress.

"Of course not," I say. "You're very intellectually curious."

"Curiosity killed the cat," she says, and laughs ripple around the Zoom, and I realize she's making a pun. *Curiosity killed the Kat*.

The Kat's in the bag.

"Anyway, your writing is much braver than mine, Astrid," she says. I get this a lot, *brave*, and it always cracks me up because I am the weakest bitch I know. I don't write because I'm brave; I write because I'm afraid of leaving my house.

"I love how you're a little subversive," she continues. Basic women love to tell me I'm subversive. I'm the basic woman's edgy. That's my market, and I must respect it. "I didn't even think that whole thing at Barnes & Noble was such a big deal," she says.

Someone on the screen with blue hair and a solitary dangling earring appears to shudder.

"Not that I condone hate speech," she says, seemingly to appease the blue-haired person. "But literally everyone gets canceled these days, and it's never really a big deal anymore."

I nod and look at Agent Allison, as if to say *I told you this*, and she just blinks at me.

"Maude, remember when people found out about my original nose?" Kat says, and Maude nods. I found this story on Google not long after Agent Allison told me Satchels of Gold was interested in adapting my book. The internet was exasperated that Kat Gold the self-proclaimed feminist got plastic surgery at sixteen, back when her name was Katie Goldstein.

"People acted like I was a member of ISIS," Kat says, and this time I legitimately laugh, maybe too hard, because Agent Allison glares at me a little.

"Okay, so I've established I'm a big fan of yours," Kat says. She twirls a lock of hair between her fingers. "And I was wondering what you thought of my playing the lead character in the adaptation?"

I consider this for a second. Kat Gold isn't remotely how I imagined the character, or any character I would write. My characters are messy and charismatic and *jolie laide*, and Kat is tidy and soulless and just plain *jolie*. When I wrote this book, I was imagining my former party friend Emily, who has pale blue eyes like a husky and radiates hostility. She's hot.

A private message pops up from Agent Allison. *Act excited!*

"I love that," I say. My voice emerges flat and unenthusiastic. I often struggle with conveying the appropriate emotional response, but excitement is always the hardest to muster. I suspect my blasé affect is a carefully calculated defense mechanism. And my defense mechanisms—it's becoming increasingly clear—are no longer defending me. Maybe they never were.

Kat laughs. "You seem thrilled." She looks almost hurt for a second. "We could also go with someone else. It was just an idea."

"No, no," I say. "You'll kill it." Again, it sounds really flat, or maudlin, like she's actually going to commit murder.

"Curiosity kills the Kat," Kat says again, then pauses, looks down. "We'll come up with a list of other actresses to see if any-one else seems more exciting to you," she says. "We really want you to feel heard in this process."

"Thank you," I say. "But I think you'll be fantastic." I know I don't sound believable.

"I'd try," Kat says. "Maude, you had one other thing you wanted to address, right?"

"Yeah," Maude says. She shuffles a stack of papers and clears her throat, and I brace myself. "So, we were thinking of ways to maybe, like, queerize the adaptation a bit. We love your voice and the story, but we think the older lesbian character is maybe a bit . . . dated?"

Before I can really process what Maude is saying, blood rises in my chest. Allison looks at me with the most threatening eyes.

"Rye had some interesting thoughts about this," Maude says. "I'll hand it over to them."

The person with blue hair who shuddered earlier starts talking. "Yeah, so, like Maude said, I was feeling a little alienated by the lesbian character, who felt maybe almost offensive to me? I know you're being satirical, but I'm not sure it will translate that way on the screen."

I have a new private message from Allison. *Take a deep breath. Think before you speak. Or let me speak for you.*

"I was thinking we could maybe get rid of her, or combine the two main characters," Rye continues. "That they could be one main character, maybe nonbinary to modernize it a bit, which we all know Kat would totally slay." Rye pauses, and yasses ripple around the Zoom.

"I've always wanted to play nonbinary," Kat Gold says. "I feel super oppressed by the gender binary all the time."

Blood continues to rise. Another message from Agent Allison. *Breathe.*

"And their love interest could be queer or pansexual?" Rye

continues, "I just feel like lesbians these days have a kind of alienating connotation, like I don't want to use the word *TERF*, but—"

"This is so dumb, I'm sorry." I'm speaking, and Allison's eyes are begging me to stop and she's messaging me, but I am at the point of no return, a tea kettle reaching a boil. "You know they sell 'Nonbinary Legend' T-shirts at Target? Nike hands out 'They/ Them athlete' pins at the door. There is nothing subversive or hip or progressive about making this adaptation nonbinary. It's positively corporate!—"

"Astrid," Allison cuts me off.

"I'm not done," I say, feeling mildly possessed. "If you're interested in me, in my book, in my writing, a big part of that is its femininity. I care about women, our stories, our experiences." I'm not sure this is even true. I mostly write to make myself laugh. "And writing about lesbians does not make me a TERF."

I'm scared to look at the incoming messages from Agent Allison.

Rye's little Zoom square disappears.

"Well," Maude says. "Now seems like a good time as any to wrap it up. You've certainly given us a lot to think about, Astrid."

"Amen to that," says Kat Gold with an unreadable tone.

The Zoom meeting evaporates like mist.

Agent Allison is calling and I press Ignore. She calls again and I press Ignore again. She calls a third time, and this time I answer.

She's speaking before I can say hello.

"Astrid WHAT. THE. FUCK?"

"I refuse to compromise my values!" I yell.

"What about making money?" she says.

My heart is still beating fast, and Agent Allison is right. I need money, and Agent Allison has been so supportive and patient with me, I want to make her money too. Since when do I have values? My primary value is not having to move back to San Francisco.

"Fuck fuck fuck," Agent Allison says. "Maude is calling. I'll call you back. FUCK!"

I pace my apartment while I wait for Agent Allison to call back, thinking about calling my former therapist to discuss my impulse control issues. I had one job: show up and not offend anyone. Exhibiting said impulse control issues, I go into the fridge and crack open a beer and without thinking, start chugging.

Penelope passes by my window with a brimming trash bag—I wonder how the woman generates so much garbage—and we make brief eye contact while I'm chugging the beer at 9:33 a.m. I shrug and mouth "tough meeting." She raises an eyebrow and keeps walking.

Agent Allison is calling again.

"Okay," she says. "I saved your ass, *once again*! I told Maude you're going through some upsetting family trauma."

"Isn't that bad karma?"

"I don't give a fuck about karma, Astrid! Maude says she and her team have 'concerns' about you. They love your book, they love your writing, but they have concerns about *you*. Are you hearing me?"

Oh God, she's going to drop me.

"I'm really sorry." I'm crying. Why do I only cry when my career is on the line? I cried in school when I got any grade lower than a 95, never at breakups or loss or anything normal people cry about, although I suppose gay shame compels a person to overprioritize academic achievement. "I really fucked up. And I don't blame you for hating me. And wanting to drop me."

"Astrid, I don't hate you," Agent Allison says. "I love your quirky personality." She swallows. "But CAA has expressed concerns as well."

"Please!" I wail. Haunting images fill my head: moving back in with my parents, reviewing documents at their firm, dying a slow and painful death in my childhood bedroom. "Please, I'll do anything. I'll go back to therapy. I'm doing really well. I'm working on a new book that you'll love and, more importantly, will make us both rich." The lies flow almost too freely.

"Calm down," Agent Allison says. "I'm not going to drop you. And Satchels of Gold hasn't canceled the contract. I think I put out the fires, for now. But I really need to see a change in you. I can't keep doing this forever."

"Understood," I say. "I'll change. I promise."

"I don't want you to just say it," Agent Allison says. "I want to see it."

She hangs up and I pour the dregs of my beer down my throat.

five

I'm drunk and looking for a loose Adderall in my underwear drawer when Otto calls to tell me he's coming to LA next weekend to deliver another dress, this time to Lil Nas X.

"I got a room at the Petit Ermitage for the weekend, but I was thinking maybe I could stay with you on Thursday?"

"Fabulosity!" I shout, knowing that sober Astrid will hate having a houseguest and would never use this word. But I find half a blue pill in the back corner of the cabinet, and I crunch it in my teeth and feel optimistic and hopeful, like the universe is abundant and benevolent. Satchels of Gold didn't cancel the contract, and I'm pretty sure the Petit Ermitage has a pool.

"Cool, I gotta run, but enjoy . . . whatever is happening over there," Otto says vaguely, but I know exactly what he is referring to: my apparent buzz, my rummaging. But I'm too lit to experience shame.

"You too!"

Near seconds after we hang up, Ivy calls. Butterflies flap in my belly.

"Hi dear," she says, and suddenly we're here, in this intimate space, longtime lovers, an old married couple, although we've just hung out once in person, twice if you count the following day, during which we drank coffee on the beach, then Coronas, then fucked until we had to check out and she drove me to my car. Ivy drives a vintage baby pink Fiat, a fact I didn't notice on the Patricia Highsmith, therefore constituting a glorious revelation in the light of day. She told me she bought the car used from an Instagram psychic and that Barbie drives the same one. The inside smelled like tangy orchids and glitter, if glitter had a smell. And now I imagine her sitting inside of it, breathing in my lingering pheromones with her bare feet on the dashboard. Lesbians grow familiar at the speed of light. We chat relentlessly as if we have nothing else to do and soon we're calling each other "dear," and it hasn't even been two weeks.

"Hi dear," I say.

"When can I see you next?" she asks. Then: "I need more."

"Same," I say. "My best friend Otto is coming Thursday. Why don't you come then? I'll have a little soiree. He's lots of fun." This is classic Astrid, introducing a relatively new lover to an old friend who is seeking quality time, planning to do drugs to smooth out the awkward edges. This is exactly the type of thing I'm not supposed to be doing now, but in my buzzed state it sounds like the best and frankly the only idea.

"See you then," says Ivy. "Actually," she says, "I guess I'll see you on Zoom before that."

"Right!" I say. "You, me, and Todd."

"Our third." Ivy laughs.

"The greatest love triangle of all time."

We go back and forth like this and then finally hang up, and all the bad stuff in my life—the Satchels of Gold meeting, my impulse control issues, the fact that Agent Allison might drop me and I might have to become a godforsaken paralegal—don't matter at all.

My problems evaporate like mist.

Outside, I smoke a cigarette in the golden hour light. Inhaling, my lungs fill with a tingly warmth that radiates to the rest of my body, down my fingers and toes. Exhaling, the smoke turns neon orange in the light, floats toward the trees. Not even Penelope could ruin this feeling. This bliss.

On my third drag, it occurs to me I could write. That I *should* write. That I *must* write! Lack of Patricia Highsmith was the only thing stopping me from writing, and Patricia is back, baby! I need to write the nonexistent book I told Agent Allison I was writing, the novel I said would get us rich. I could write an original adaptation of *Perfume and Pain*, a lesbian pulp revival, a delicious campy delight.

I throw my cigarette on the ground, stomp it theatrically, then storm inside and open my laptop, feeling like Carrie Fucking Bradshaw.

A blank Google Doc stares at me.

The blinking cursor taunts me.

It's so silent in here. The only sounds are birds and distant cars.

Music, I need music! I turn on Azealia Banks, then Rihanna. Soon I'm dancing and singing in my closet, trying on dresses tucked in corners, finding clothes I forgot I had, like the baby tank that says "indie darling" I bought from Hollywood Gifts 99 while extremely drunk, putting on trashy dramatic eyeliner, getting my Carrie Bradshaw on. If I'm going to write, it has to be *fashion*.

And then I hear a knock on the door, and everything sort of turns gray.

: : : :

In a bizarre turn of events, I dream of Penelope.

She's wearing that red dress, the only one she seems to own, and she's onstage at an intimate jazz club, looking right at me. She's singing Rihanna's "Stay," the song Rihanna performed inside a floating glass walkway when I saw her live at the Forum. But now Penelope's singing it to me, and she has a fucking incredible voice—better than Rihanna, honestly—and she's bathed in the yellow glow of the stage lights, and for some reason I don't hate her. Instead, I'm kind of attracted to her? She's curving a red-nailed finger in my direction, a come-hither motion, and I walk to her, toward the stage, but once I'm in the yellow glow of the lights, I can't see anything. I'm totally blinded and I can't find Penelope anywhere and my eyes are burning. And then I wake up. Next to a pint of melted ice cream.

:::;

I'm coming down and watching a butterfly float past my window when my phone buzzes. It's Agent Allison. I answer with trepidation.

"They canceled the deal?" I say instead of hello.

"Quite the opposite," Agent Allison says, her voice cheery. "Kat Gold thinks you're a 'firecracker.'"

I laugh. "I love being the basic woman's subversive." I'm relieved, even though I don't respect Kat Gold at all. I just don't want to have to move back home.

"So, they sent over a list of other actresses given your apparent lack of enthusiasm," she says. "But Kat still really wants to play the role."

"Then she should!" I say, finally able to convey excitement now that it doesn't matter. "She's the one shelling out the funds." I'm not precious about this adaptation at all. I don't need it to be high art. My books are hardly low art. I just need money. And health insurance.

"Well, you should tell her yourself," she says. "She asked for your phone number. She wants to get coffee with you."

"Really?" I say. "Why?"

"She admires you, Astrid," Agent Allison says. "I know you think she's a little corny, but she's a powerful woman in Hollywood and her book was a bestseller. She can be useful to you. If I were you, I'd take advantage of her interest."

The absolute last thing in the world I want to do is get coffee with Kat Gold. But I need to stay on Agent Allison's good side. I need Satchels of Gold to give me, well, satchels of gold. I keep wondering if the production company's name is a *Real Housewives* reference, as possibly psychotic cast member Kelly Bensimon utters the phrase during the iconic episode "Scary Island," seemingly in response to nothing.

"Okay," I say. "Give her my number."

"Great!" Agent Allison says.

six

I spend twenty minutes trying to figure out what perfume to wear for the next Zoom workshop and decide on one that at first smells sexy—a smoky leather—but ultimately makes me nauseous during the meeting. Perfume—like people, alcohol, my coping mechanisms—frequently turns on me.

Now I'm drinking beer from a coffee mug and trying not to throw up. My eyes dart around the laptop screen, avoiding Ivy's little rectangle because I'm feeling shy, a middle school girl with a crush, wondering whether my fellow Sapphic Scribers can tell what's up. But ladies have been hooking up off screen in this group since its inception, and in fact off-screen hookups are part of its appeal.

We're workshopping the pages of a Gen Z queer named Charli who Zooms from her parents' basement in Albuquerque. She seems at least a decade younger than me, but I haven't been active enough to know whether she's a recent recruit or what. She's writing about a girl trapped in a video game, which I find to be among the hardest genres to read, up there with cli-fi, sci-fi, unicorns, dragons, and dystopias. The world is uncanny enough as it is.

About halfway through my beer, I gather the courage to speak and tell Charli she's really excelled at "world building" but could stand to slow down a bit for readers less versed in STEM, at which point Ivy chuckles, my heart skips a beat, and Charli butts in, despite that she is supposed to remain silent during her own workshop.

"My work is intended for people already literate in this space," she says. "Maybe those who aren't can hold their commentary in this workshop."

Music to my ears! It's not like I wanted to engage with this dumb video game book to begin with. "Understood," I say, then perform zipping my lips shut.

My Zoom chat lights up.

How deranged, Ivy says.

These video game people are really just astoundingly cocky, I write back.

I finish my beer and finally get the courage to look at Ivy's Zoom rectangle. She's wearing a salmon-colored cardigan and her hair is tied up in a black bow and my heart throbs. She's in front of the *Desert Hearts* poster, and I remember that she still lives with her ex and wonder who bought the poster, who will get it when they move out, whether they'll share joint custody over the poster.

I forgot to ask: how was the big TV meeting? Ivy asks.

Next subject please! I write back.

LOL, Ivy says.

I'm typing *I looked cute and alienated everyone* when a platinum blonde head appears in the background of Ivy's rectangle. The Samantha Ronson derivative is wearing a black hoodie and approaching Ivy. Ivy's audio is muted, but it seems like the butch is yelling at her. Ivy turns around and seems to yell back. They yell for a few seconds while Charli drones on about the sociopolitical potential of video game literature. Charli is getting heated about something called *Fortnite* when the butch approaches Ivy's laptop and slams it shut.

And—poof—Ivy's Zoom rectangle is gone.

:::::

I expect to hear from Ivy after the meeting—some explanation of the recent drama, the slammed laptop—but my phone is silent. Hours later, when I do finally have a notification while I'm heating up an Amy's frozen meal, I expect it to be from Ivy, but instead it's from Kat Gold.

Hey girlie, she says. *You free to grab coffee next week?*

I'll respond to Kat later. No one has probably ever made the bitch wait before. It'll be good for her.

After I've eaten and watched two vintage episodes of *Keeping Up with the Kardashians* and I can't wait for Ivy any longer, I text her a simple *everything okay?*

She responds quickly with a GIF of Natalie Portman holding a gun to her head from *The Professional*.

I respond, *So sorry bb, let me know if I can do anything.*

She doesn't respond after five minutes, after ten, after thirty, after an hour.

To busy myself, I do seven mini crossword puzzles, make AI art of baby foxes, practice French on Duolingo, then look at my calendar and text Kat Gold with some "avails" as we say in showbiz.

Fabulosity!! Kat Gold responds when we nail down a date and time. *Can't wait to chill with you, chica!*

Wishful thinking, chica. I've never chilled in my life. But in an effort to be good, I put a heart on the text.

Preparing for bed, I think of the slammed laptop, of Ivy's Zoom square abruptly disappearing. I become convinced that

Ivy is done with me, that she's back with her ex, she won't come over Thursday and I'll never see her again, she'll leave Sapphic Scribes, and our brief romance will fade into a distant memory.

Just when I decide I'm over her too and open Tinder, Ivy sends me an artful nude, which turns into artful sexting, artful orgasms, and suddenly: it's as though the laptop was never slammed.

seven

Ivy arrives before Otto, which is ideal. I've always felt more comfortable with a new lover than with an old friend. That's probably the type of thing I should explore in therapy if I ever go back.

Ivy is wearing pink again, this time a dress with black boots and thigh-high stockings. The look is very Hot Topic, especially emerging from her vintage pink Fiat. She greets me by pushing me against the door and jamming her tongue down my throat, and I'm partially turned on and partially thinking about Ivy's butch ex slamming her laptop in the last Zoom meeting.

Kissing Ivy now, I breathe in those metallic orchids I smelled in her car. Normally I would need to be warmed up for this sort of thing, but Ivy doesn't give me a choice, and in fact I'm pinned against the wall, a little crushed, physically, but also turned on. When Ivy unpins me, she reaches into her purse and pulls out a bottle of pink rosé that matches her dress. Then she opens her wallet and unearths a little blue pill, pinched between glittery pink fingernails. She splits the pill in half and puts one half on her tongue, the other on mine. As I crunch the blue pill between my teeth, I try to push away the nagging thought, the one I'm trying my very hardest to avoid but that's persistent, that this situation with Ivy is "not good," that it is in fact the precise situation I've committed myself to avoiding.

Ivy has already poured herself a glass and is peeking through the curtains. "Is Penelope here? I'm dying to meet this dyke in the flesh."

"Oh, I'm sure she'll show up at some point," I say. "She bothers me pretty much every day. Yesterday she knocked on my door to tell me she saw a microwave meal box in my recycling that looked highly carcinogenic. She also told me that beer causes Alzheimer's." I don't tell Ivy that a few times I've lied to Penelope about having people over to justify how many beer bottles she's finding in my recycling. I've been feeling extra annoyed by her since she appeared in my dream the other night, like she even crashed my subconscious, literally stealing the show and blinding me with those dumb lights.

"Holy shit," she says. "She looks through your trash." Ivy turns toward me, sips her wine. "Do you think she's in love with you?"

:::::

When Otto arrives, he's visibly annoyed that I've invited a lover, and that I've been drinking.

Ivy seems annoyed by him, too, I'm not sure why.

When I introduce them, they greet each other with icy tones.

A horrible thought enters my head, a slight desire that Otto might relapse. Things would be so much easier if he would just drink. Sure, he might get drunk and say something completely offensive to Ivy's face, but at least we could laugh it off afterward.

I walk Otto into my bedroom to show him where to put his stuff. With Ivy out of sight, he says, "I didn't realize you were having guests."

"I think you'll get along well," I say. "She's a lot of fun."

"She's wearing a lot of pink," says Otto.

We're interrupted by voices coming from the other room. Not just Ivy's, but another. Penelope. Of course.

Before we return to the main room, I whisper to Otto, "The nosy dyke" and he nods in understanding.

In the living room, Ivy is pouring Penelope a glass of rosé.

"Penelope came over to let us know there is a full moon to-night," Ivy says, and raises an eyebrow at me.

"We should have a séance," says Otto.

I grab him a Diet Coke from the fridge. Ever since he's been sober, Otto mainlines Diet Coke and iced coffee the way he used to do with vodka and white wine.

"I was planning on having a fire out back," says Penelope. "And letting go of some negative patterns by writing them on pieces of paper and throwing them in the fire."

"Sounds fun," says Otto, surprising me. This is the type of thing I'd expect him to mock.

"I think Zev is going to come over soon," says Penelope. "Laura too."

"Your ex-girlfriend?" I ask.

"Zev as in our friend from college?" Otto asks.

Penelope nods. I remember seeing Penelope flirt with the blonde woman in the yard before I went to Oxnard. I guess it was Laura.

"We're friends," Penelope says, and I can't tell if she's talking about Zev or Laura or both.

Ivy clinks Penelope's wineglass. "Cheers!"

eight

The orange flames of the fire dance in the reflection of Ivy's irises. I steal a glance at Laura, who sits across from me in the circle and looks different from what I expected. Younger, less bohemian, more suburban, with salon-blonde highlights and wearing what appears to be head-to-toe Madewell. I think she's the woman I saw flirting with Penelope in the yard, but I can't be sure. She's extremely generic looking. "She kind of looks like you," Otto whispered in my ear when she first arrived, and I stuck my tongue out at him in return. She brought vegan cookies, and she and Penelope briefly disappeared to put them away.

Penelope hands out pieces of paper to write down what we want to let go. Lots of things come to mind. Ivy and I split a second half-Adderall while Penelope was showing Otto her art—somehow, he seems to be under her spell as well—so I'm ready to start writing. I haven't written in a while, so the words jump off my pen.

Talking about astrology

The Patricia Highsmith

Microwave meals

Attitude toward authority figures

Binge drinking

Cigarettes

Vaping on the toilet

Women who hurt me

Edgelord behavior

Being a contrarian

Melted cheese

Otto looks over at me, writing furiously, and says, "Damn, Astrid, are you getting rid of your entire personality?"

Zev giggles.

"I have a lot to let go of," I say, looking at Penelope, hoping she sees that I'm taking her exercise seriously, but she is looking at Laura, and I'm confident they are fucking. I'm not sure why I'm so eager to impress Penelope right now. I shouldn't care what she thinks. But I feel like she's my mom or something, and while I've accepted that I'll never get my own mother's approval, maybe I can get hers.

Otto steals a glance at my paper.

"Melted cheese?"

Zev laughs again.

"Hey," I say. "This is supposed to be sacred."

Penelope nods in agreement.

Ivy squeezes my hand.

. . . .

A movie flickers in front of me on a big screen. We're in a room I don't recognize, which I assume must be in Penelope's house given the vague odors of patchouli and paint. My legs are tangled in Ivy's under a blanket. A glass of water sits in front of me, and I assume Penelope put it there. There is a can of beer in my hand, almost empty. Ivy squeezes my waist. Lindsay Lohan appears on the screen with just one leg. Oh my gosh, it's *I Know Who Killed Me*. Otto and I have watched this movie hundreds of times, so I'm sure he suggested it.

"This film is totally insane," Penelope says. I know she's Gen X because she calls it a "film."

"It's high art," Otto says.

"Criterion Collection," says Zev.

"Are we watching the same movie?" asks Laura, apparently unappreciative of camp. Laura is sitting on a chair by herself and we briefly make eye contact. Her eyes are saying something to me, but I can't quite tell what.

I sip my beer.

· · · ·

Ivy is on top of me, riding me, a vibrator in between our clits.

Usher plays from my Bluetooth speaker.

"Do you think Otto can hear us?" I ask.

"It's fine," Ivy says, then wraps her hand around my neck.

She squeezes.

Hard.

nine

Ivy, Otto, and I sit in my yard drinking coffee in the sun.

Otto spreads his arms up toward the bright blue sky. "I feel cleansed," he says. "I let go of so much last night."

"Same," I say.

"I don't know, Astrid," Otto says. "You wrote down microwave meals and melted cheese, then took a frozen mac and cheese to the face when we got back from Penelope's."

Ivy laughs and I feel ashamed.

"You weren't supposed to look at my paper," I say.

Otto ignores me. "I think we really blew Penelope's mind with *I Know Who Killed Me*."

"I think we did," I say.

"You know, I like her, Astrid," he says. "She's much better than you made her sound." A slight pause. "She's sweet."

Ivy glares at him a bit.

Otto keeps talking, oblivious to Ivy's radiating hostility, or maybe just ignoring it. "I'm not sure about her ex-girlfriend, though," Otto says. "She seemed a bit . . . smooth-brained."

Ivy cackles.

"I like Penelope, though. You know she had a piece in the Whitney Biennial?"

"Who cares?" I say.

"Um, like the entire art world," says Otto. "And—well, this might be of more interest to you, Astrid—Penelope is currently living off a lawsuit settlement. Urban Outfitters stole one of her designs for a T-shirt." Otto smirks. "Astrid, remember how you worshiped Urban in college? Like your entire wardrobe was from there, and weren't you even caught shoplifting?"

"None of this needs to be said out loud," I say. But I do think it's kind of cool that Penelope is living off Urban Outfitters settlement money.

Ivy rotates her torso toward the sun. "Can you put sunscreen on my back?" Ivy asks me, and Otto gets up to go to the bathroom, making a very quiet gagging noise on the way.

:::

After Otto leaves for the Petit Ermitage, Ivy and I laze around in bed. We order Chipotle burrito bowls and watch season 5 of *The L Word*, when Jenny makes *Les Girls*, a film inside a show. Otto invites us to the pool, but we don't go. Penelope knocks on the door, probably with Alka-Seltzer, and we pretend not to hear her.

"Where did you grow up?" I ask when I hear Penelope walk away. I'm embarrassed I don't already know this, then realize that it's possible that Ivy told me this and I just don't remember. "Forgive me if you've already told me this," I add.

"I definitely didn't," Ivy says. "I don't advertise it. I grew up in Santa Cruz. Raised by dirty hippies."

"Wow," I say. "Penelope vibes."

"She wishes," Ivy says. "Didn't she say she's from Boston? I'm from a farm. All of our food came from our yard. We didn't even have electricity for a while. My mom taught yoga—she's dead now—and my dad teaches metaphysics." Ivy tugs at her pink nightgown. "Why do you think I dress like a Barbie doll? Rebellion, baby!"

I giggle. I grew up not far from Santa Cruz, but my parents are the opposite of hippies, rigid and logic obsessed. But I was surrounded by hippie culture—burning sage and jam bands and nostalgia for a version of the '70s that probably never existed.

I'm shocked by the flippancy with which Ivy announced her mom's death.

"I didn't want to come out to my mom, but not for the reason everyone thinks," Ivy continues. "I wasn't scared she would reject me. I was scared she would be too excited! Half my mom's friends growing up were lesbians. And in fact, I had my first lesbian experience with one of them—"

"Hold the phone, that's hot!" I think of Gail's first lesbian experience with her aunt Pam in *Perfume and Pain*.

"It was," Ivy says. "But also traumatic, like most hot things."

I nod vigorously at this red flag.

"I actually met her at my mom's funeral." She smiles in a vaguely demonic way. "Any other biographical questions for me, Terry Gross?"

"Sure," I say, affecting my best NPR voice. I briefly consider asking more about her mom—how she died, how old Ivy was, if she misses her—but decide against it because I don't want to make her sad. "How did you decide to study lesbian pulp?"

"Well, Terry," she says, spinning some black hair in her fingers. "I always felt pretty alienated by lesbian culture. Softball and Home Depot and all that. Benevolent butches like Ellen DeGeneres. Hippie freaks like my mom. It wasn't sexy."

I nod. I've also struggled with the disconnect between women—sensual, complex, intuitive—and lesbian culture—moralistic, corny, sexless.

"And then I was nineteen and sifting through the fifty-cent bin at a used bookstore in Santa Cruz, and I came across Vin Packer's *Spring Fire*. I know with the benefit of hindsight that these mid-century lesbian pulp books are problematic. It was the McCarthy era, and the postal service wouldn't even deliver them unless the characters were punished for their sexuality."

I remember reading this when I first came across lesbian pulp at around age twenty-three, in the bathroom of a girl I'd hooked up with in Crown Heights while I was visiting Otto in New York. The cover depicted a MILF type gazing lustily at a teenage blonde and I remember being envious of the blonde, wanting to be looked at that way by a sexy brunette woman twice my age. I still remember the quote on the book's cover: "She was pink and gold, soft and sweet . . . too strong a temptation to resist." I wanted to be a pink and gold temptation. I thought about asking my hookup about the book, but I was embarrassed it was the type of thing all lesbians should know, and I would out myself as a bad lesbian for asking. So I memorized the title—*When Lights Are Low*, by Dallas Mayo—and looked it up on my phone when I left. It was my very first smartphone, and I was still kind of amazed to have the internet in the palm of my hand. On the train back to Manhattan, I read the Wikipedia article for "lesbian pulp" and was totally captivated. How did this entire genre exist without my knowing?

"But in a weird way," Ivy continues, "reading it made me feel seen for the first time. I wanted to be punished for my sexuality, which felt sinful and unnatural. And, sure, these books were male gazey, but at least they were *hot* and *femme*, unlike most lesbian representation. They reminded me of Mischa Barton and Olivia Wilde's relationship on *The O.C.*, which was formative to my sexual awakening."

I put my hands together in a prayer motion. Marissa Cooper and Alex Kelly were important to my sexual awakening as well, mostly because it was the first lesbian romance I'd seen on television where both women were femme, similar to the pulps. And as in the pulps, Marissa acted a fool and left Alex for a man.

Ivy keeps talking. "This is all to say, my interest was initially more emotional. And frankly a little sexual. Not academic at all. I decided to study lesbian pulp simply because I wanted to keep reading it. So, I found a way to make it academic."

"I get it," I say. "That's how I feel about the Kardashians. My writing has been likened to satire and cultural criticism, but it didn't start out that way. I have a genuine fondness for those women, their sisterhood, and their feminine supremacy. They're like the March sisters but way less cringe."

"Right!" says Ivy. "That's why I love your work. It's very sincere."

My cheeks heat a little.

"So, what's your thesis?" I ask, changing the subject. "About lesbian pulp?"

"Oh God," she says. "It's always changing. And my thesis adviser says it's a difficult position to take. But I'm basically trying to say that lesbian pulp has been unfairly overlooked. That it has merit. That while it's been dismissed as homophobic, maybe our dismissal is even more homophobic, because it lacks an understanding that lesbian relationships are not straight relationships. That they have their own specific set of rules and expectations, and that melodrama is part of their special power, not something to be avoided."

Before I can respond, Ivy kisses me, and when I kiss back, she flips me over, melodramatically, almost violently, and soon she is inside of me, and afterward, we tangle our bodies and begin to drift off, despite that it's still light out.

Waking up in the middle of the night, I sniff Ivy's neck, hoping to get a little high off her pheromones. But I smell something sour, like the orchids have wilted and the metallic tinge isn't glitter but instead a nuclear arms factory. I roll over and clutch my green amethyst, which is ice cold in my fingers.

ten

My body feels evacuated, empty, hollow. After Ivy leaves, I drink coffee in the yard and hope the sunshine will heal me. It normally does. In California, we pay higher taxes in exchange for the healing powers of the sun.

"Hi, neighbor," Penelope says not long after I start to feel myself wake up.

For a brief second, I imagine throwing my hot coffee at her. And just the thought cheers me up a bit. The amount of Patricia Highsmith I consumed two nights ago would typically have me feeling suicidal around now, but my phone keeps lighting up with texts from Ivy, even though she just left, which keeps me happy to stay alive.

Penelope is still talking.

"How do you feel?" she asks.

"Great," I say. She wants me to say I'm hungover, that I'm sick and need her help. I'm not biting. "How about you?"

"Oh, I'm fine," she says, and for the first time, I see some major sadness in her eyes. I wonder if she got in a fight with Laura, if they couldn't make it work, or if it's something else, whether the Urban Outfitters money is drying up. "Otto invited me to the pool. He said he texted you but hasn't heard back, so I thought I'd check on you. I figured you might be tired from the other night."

Ugh, she's so exhausting. Also, wait, what? Otto invited her to the pool? Literally what is going on? I was counting on Otto to hate her with me, to make fun of her earnest Gen X attitude and fedora-adjacent fashion, but instead he's inviting her to the pool?

I look at my phone to see several unanswered texts from Otto, starting last night. The first one: *Pool tomorrow?* Then: *Lil Nas X hit on me.* Then one from this morning, a photo of Otto's tanned thighs in front of the shining pool, and: *Cum bitch.* Then, finally: *If you don't respond I'm inviting Penelope I swear to God.*

The last text relieves me a bit. He only invited Penelope to fuck with me. But he really did invite her. I curse myself for not looking at my phone earlier. But maybe it's not so bad. Penelope can drive and I can have a few drinks at the pool.

"Let me grab my suit," I say.

.: : : .

Penelope's Volvo smells like palo santo. There's a half-burned stick of the fragrant wood in the center console. A dream catcher hangs from the rearview window and Patti Smith plays from the shitty stereo. I recall Penelope singing to me in my dream.

Before she starts driving, Penelope hands me a coconut water, which I appreciate, especially because it's the pink kind, even though she says, "You're probably dehydrated" in a very judgmental tone when she hands it to me.

I text Ivy, *you won't guess where I am.*

She replies, *???*

Penelope's car(!), I write, *I'm looking at a dream catcher.*

Ivy replies with just a bunch of dots, consecutive ellipses.

"You're smitten," Penelope says.

"Maybe," I say.

We ride in silence along the edge of Griffith Park, surrounded by green.

"What's going on with the TV show?" Penelope asks finally.

I forgot I told Penelope about the TV show, mostly so she'd be impressed with me, so someone would care about my career in the way I wish my parents did.

"It's good," I say. "I'm getting coffee with Kat next week."

"Wow, great," Penelope says. "So, you were worried for no reason."

I'm a little confused. I don't remember telling Penelope I was worried they'd cancel the contract. Maybe I said something to her when I was out of it.

"I'm actually kind of nervous," I admit. "About the coffee date." It's true. I hate getting coffee with people, having to sit across from them and look into their eyes and make normal, appropriate conversation. Zoom is fine, but in person just freaks me out, unless we're drinking heavily, and Kat Gold strikes me as sober, or at the very least, sober-curious.

"Why?" she asks.

"I don't know," I say. "Kat Gold is very extra. And she kind of annoys me. She's very obsequious with me. It creeps me out." I don't want to admit to Penelope just how uncomfortable I feel in my own skin, or that I'm afraid of blurting out something offensive that will cause her to cancel the contract and I'll have to move back home with my parents.

"She seems sweet," Penelope says. "It's nice that you have such a devoted and influential fan." This is the kind of very diplomatic thing Agent Allison would say.

"I don't like to be around women who are prettier than me," I respond.

Penelope laughs harder than I expected.

I don't say what immediately comes to mind, which is *Why do you think I'm always avoiding you?* Instead, I just stare at the green expanse. I read that a mountain lion crossed the 405 freeway from the Santa Monica mountains and now roams Griffith Park. Alone, no mate. Living the single life. People are always posting videos on Twitter of run-ins with the mountain lion in the surrounding neighborhood, and I'm always shocked by how huge it is—like this legitimate lion roaming around this banal yuppie neighborhood, looking in vain for a partner like everyone else.

Then there is another text from Ivy. *The woman is legit in love with you. I'm starting to find this less funny.* More ellipses.

"How was it seeing Laura?" I ask Penelope to avoid the ellipses.

"Oh," Penelope says. "It was good. We're friends."

"Did she sleep over?" I ask, recalling how they kept looking at each other flirtatiously around the fire, how I saw Penelope flirting with that woman in the yard who was likely Laura a few weeks ago. Maybe they're getting back together. Maybe this was an inappropriate thing to ask.

"God no." Penelope laughs and I relax a little. I don't know why. I should want her to have a girlfriend so she leaves me and my friends alone. But Laura has bad vibes. I don't want another annoying dyke in the yard all the time. "It's not like that. She's lonely. She has trouble making friends."

"I can see why," I say without thinking.

"What do you mean?" Penelope asks defensively.

"Oh," I say. "She's pretty. It's hard for pretty girls to make friends. People are jealous. And accuse them of being bitches when they aren't over-the-top friendly." It's a decent save and not entirely a lie. Laura is pretty, but I don't think her looks are holding her back from making friends. Rather, I suspect it is her personality, which evokes the faint hum of a refrigerator.

Penelope says nothing, just turns up "Redondo Beach." I remember what Ivy said, that Penelope's one of those East Coast girls who grew up idolizing California, thinking it was some paradisiacal dreamland instead of an environmentally precarious spiritual wasteland.

I look out the window and my gaze meets a palm tree, arched and dying.

:::

Otto is wearing tiny red swim trunks that show off muscular legs. Several guests and employees of various gender presentations stare at him as he stands to greet us.

He holds up his nearly empty iced coffee. "I'm getting another one of these," he says.

"Gay water," I say.

"Exactly," he says. "What can I get you all?"

"Gay water sounds good to me," Penelope says. Annoyance runs through my veins. I want it to be just Otto and me. I want to talk shit.

"Margarita," I say.

"You sure?" Penelope asks. I want to hit her.

"I'm sure, Mom," I say.

Otto disappears, and Penelope and I set our things on lounge chairs. Penelope removes her linen dress. Underneath is a green one-piece bathing suit, the same color as her Volvo, but in a surprisingly sexy cut, her breasts cupped with precision. Her body is annoyingly toned, probably from yoga, and her skin is lightly tan and speckled with large freckles or tiny moles. Her eyes meet mine and I quickly look away, take off my T-shirt and Adidas shorts. I'm wearing a black one-piece, the only bathing suit I own.

Otto returns and I snatch the margarita from his hands. Penelope takes her iced coffee and we all sit on lounge chairs.

"This is really weak," I say after my first sip.

"Yeah," says Otto. "Because it's virgin." He runs his fingers through his blond hair. "A gift for all of us."

Penelope laughs, and I want to throw my virgin margarita on her head.

"Tell us about Lil Nas X," I say to Otto.

He lights up. "Oh my god, he was basically trying to suck my dick at the fitting."

"Were you into it?" Penelope asks. "Some of his stuff is pretty innovative."

I'm shocked Penelope knows who Lil Nas X is. I *hardly* know who he is. I know he wore an incredible gold Versace bodysuit at the most recent Met Gala, but I couldn't name one of his songs.

"He was thirsty," Otto says. "It was tacky." He sips his drink and looks at me. "Speaking of thirsty, Astrid, that chick wants to skin you and wear you like last season's Versace. What's her name? Poison Ivy?"

Penelope giggles. I suck my virgin marg, hoping I can trick my brain into believing it's alcohol.

"What do you mean?" I ask.

"Are you kidding? She was all over you with that deranged look in her eyes. The chick is unhinged. Don't come complaining to me when she tries to *Single White Female* you."

"Or *Fatal Attraction*," Penelope adds. "You don't have a bunny, do you?"

They both laugh, and I dive into the pool.

⁝ ⁝ ⁝ ⁝

When Penelope and Otto are both swimming, I announce to no one that I'm going to the bathroom and instead walk over to the bar, slip the bartender a ten-dollar bill, and ask him to pour a double shot of tequila into my once-virgin margarita. He cocks his head at me and says, "You aren't in rehab, are you?" I say, "No, but my friend just got out," and point my head toward Otto, who is swimming freestyle from one end of the pool to the other. "He's on his high horse."

The bartender nods in understanding, then shakes his head. "Sober people suck," he says as he dumps the double shot into my margarita. "I only ask because we recently had this group of friends from rehab staying here and one of them fell off the wagon and I was scolded for pouring tequila into his virgin margarita, as if I was somehow responsible for his alcoholism, as if I neglected him in his formative years."

I tell him, "That's bullshit," and wonder how he knows I'm not bullshitting myself, that I'm not that rogue alcoholic friend right now.

On my way back to my chair, I sip my drink and feel slightly less annoyed about Penelope's presence, about Ivy's hostile ellipses, about the fact that my best friend and my enemy are getting along swimmingly and are in fact swimming right now in front of me like two childhood besties.

I sip my drink and instinctively reach for my phone, then remember the hostile ellipses and put my phone in my purse. When I look up, Penelope is drying off her toned yoga body and I look away, toward Otto getting out of the pool with an even more toned body, and I wonder if I need to be doing exercise other than stomping angrily up a hill.

A figure blocks the sun above me and I worry it's the bartender about to blow my cover. But it's a tiny gay man I don't recognize, a sinister-looking twink wearing a puka shell necklace and a tank top that says Bottoms for Hillary. I clutch my green amethyst, hoping it will protect me from the twink's toxic energy.

"Astrid Dahl?" says the sinister twink, who I realize given the Hillary Clinton tank is probably too old to be a proper twink, that he's had work done, expensive work. He smiles and unnaturally white teeth glint in the sunlight.

"Yeah?" I say nervously.

Penelope is looking at me, and Otto eyes the twink with suspicion. I probably met him on the Patricia Highsmith. Maybe I met him with Otto, and he's intimidated by Otto, so he's approaching me instead. Lots of gays go through me to get to Otto. I've been approached in public for my writing only a few times in my life, and it is normally by gay men, but this twink isn't the correct breed of gay. The gays who approach me don't whiten their teeth and they don't vote.

"You did a book event with my friend Kyler," he says, and takes a sip of his hot pink frozen drink I didn't notice before. "At Barnes & Noble."

I gulp my no-longer-virgin margarita.

Apparently sensing my discomfort and the twink's innately nefarious nature, Otto comes over and puts an arm around me. "What's up?" Otto says.

The twink glares, impervious to Otto's eight-pack and piercing blue eyes. He's out for blood.

"You know your friend here"—he looks right at me and lowers his voice to a whisper—"said faggot." He sips his drink again. "In a Barnes & Noble."

Otto rolls his eyes. "God, this again," Otto says. "She *is* a faggot! She watches Bravo nonstop, counts calories excessively, and she's Azealia Banks's biggest fan. All her friends are gay men, and she can't even look at a woman without trying to lick her pussy."

Penelope stifles a laugh, and I glare at her, then glare at Otto, shuddering at his crude and masculine reduction of lesbian behavior.

"Astrid can say faggot," Otto says.

The bartender who slipped me the alcohol looks over at us.

Otto lowers his voice. "It's old news, queen," he hisses at the twink.

"She's a Karen," the twink says.

Otto rolls his eyes again, this time more theatrically. "She's not a Karen, she's a feral faggot with little to no impulse control."

Penelope unleashes a laugh this time.

"Why don't you get lost?" Otto says. "Go bottom for Hillary."

The twink spits in my direction, then skips off to a gaggle of similarly corny, triangularly shaped men who are all saying *yasss*.

"Did that twink really spit at you?" Otto asks me, puffing his chest in a way that reminds me of something I typically forget: that Otto is a man. "Did it get on you? I will go over there, I swear . . ."

I check my body and don't see anything. It seems the spit was mostly gesture. I've never been spit at. I feel oddly exhilarated. Otto protected me.

"He didn't get me," I say, and take another sip of my drink. "Don't go over there." The twinks are still cackling. They sound like witches, and not the fun kind. "It's so tragic."

Otto turns toward the twink coven and raises his eyebrows, lowers his voice. "How dreadful."

Penelope, who I'd forgotten was even here, comes over and puts her hand on my shoulder and asks me if I want to go.

eleven

On the drive back to Eagle Rock, Penelope asks me how I'm feeling.

"I think I'm okay?" We ride along the Sunset Strip, past the Pink Taco—a garish Mexican restaurant whose founder Lindsay Lohan dated before he died of a likely overdose. "I don't really care what some corny twink thinks of me." This is true enough. I have relatively thick skin when it comes to people I don't know, and very thin, nearly anorexic skin when it comes to people I do know. I recall Penelope laughing while Otto called me feral and horny. "You seemed to find it pretty funny."

"Sorry," Penelope says as we pass the Chateau Marmont, the hotel where Lindsay Lohan lived for two years before being permanently banned for racking up an unpaid balance of $46,000. "I laugh when I'm uncomfortable."

We ride in silence past oversized billboards for action movies.

"You know I googled you," Penelope says after a few minutes. "When Deedee said you were moving in." She pauses to switch lanes. As she looks in her blind spot, I watch the veins on her neck extend and retract. When she turns back toward the road, I look away. "That interview came up."

I wish Penelope wasn't telling me this. This is the hard part of being a writer for me, that idea that people can google me, that they might have a preconceived notion of me based on the things I type or say when I'm extremely caffeinated or very fucked up. And, of course, my brief cancellation only made things worse. Agent Allison worked hard to ensure the *Gawker* story on the viral video of me calling myself a faggot in a Barnes & Noble is not the first thing that pops up when one googles me, but I think it's still in the top five. I don't know. I don't google myself.

"I didn't get why people thought it was such a big deal," Penelope says. "You're a gay woman." She pauses. "Well, I don't know how you identify, but you clearly have lesbian leanings at the very least."

I laugh. "I identify as a lesbian," I say. "I'm not a Gold Star, but I would be if I weren't blacked out for most of my early twenties." I smile, then realize that this is perhaps a very dark thing to say, that it suggests I was having sex with men against my will. But the line between having sex by choice and against one's will, I've always thought, is impossibly thin. Especially when you're a petite lush, when you're a drunk and impossibly thin yourself.

Penelope is silent for a few seconds, perhaps due to my dark confession.

"We live in such punitive times," she says finally.

"Yeah," I say. "And it's always the ACAB bitches who are most desperate to punish you."

Penelope laughs. "Bottoms for Hillary."

I laugh too. "Right," I say, then stop laughing. "As if the Clintons didn't spearhead the prison industrial complex. God forbid anyone knows what they're talking about." I don't really know what I'm talking about. I'm just repeating something I saw on Twitter.

"People just want their moral superiority," Penelope says, then laughs, "written on their tank tops," and I say, "Amen."

We glide in silence for a while, down the 101, up the 2.

"Do you really think Ivy is toxic?" I ask Penelope as we pass Forest Lawn Cemetery.

As if Ivy knew I said her name, my phone lights up with a text from her. *And now you aren't responding?? Sus!!*

I respond, *Sorry I had a triggering altercation with a twink in a "bottoms for hillary" t-shirt. He quite literally spit at me.*

She writes back, *Ew*.

"I'm not sure," Penelope says. "I don't really know the girl. And I'm not always the best judge of that sort of thing."

I want to know more about this. "Is Laura toxic? Or was she when you dated?"

"Oh yeah," Penelope says. "It's better now that we're friends. But she was controlling. She would lash out at me for things she did herself, like she was projecting all the bad stuff about her onto me. She hated that I smoked, but she would smoke when she drank, and she drank a lot. She was super jealous even though she was cheating, and I was loyal as a dog."

"Been there," I say, and it's true, although I really have the loyalty of a cat. Laura doesn't seem sharp enough to be capable of any real psychosexual damage. "What did you like about her?"

We stop at a red light and watch a homeless person push a shopping cart in front of the Volvo.

"My therapist says I have a savior complex," Penelope says.

The light turns green and Penelope presses the gas, and maybe due to nosiness or simply a desire to fill the silence, I ask, "Are you saving anyone right now?"

Penelope inhales sharply, then looks at me. There is mascara smudged under her right eye. "I'm taking a break from saving people," she says.

"I'm supposed to be taking a break from dating too."

Penelope laughs and so do I, but then I worry she's laughing at me like she was at the pool, so I stop.

"Why are you trying to take a break?" she asks.

"I wanted to ask you the same thing."

Penelope turns her head back again before changing lanes, and again I watch the veins pop from her neck. "I'm trying to figure out how to focus on myself," she says.

I consider this for a second. I've heard people say this type of thing before. "I need to date myself right now" is something Pia once said in a Lez Brat Pack meeting after a breakup and I'd tried really hard not to laugh, because Pia is a malignant narcissist who has always and forever prioritized herself. At least I'm self-aware enough to know I'm self-centered, to know I would be better off prioritizing others, seeing them for who they are instead of who I write them to be in my head.

"What about you?" Penelope asks.

I twirl a lock of hair in between my fingers. "I think I have problems with projection."

Penelope says, "Who doesn't?" and turns onto our street.

∴ ∴ ∴ ∴

At home I text Ivy that I'm sorry. I'm not totally sure what I'm sorry for, but I know it's important to say I'm sorry.

I'm the one who should be apologizing, Ivy responds, and I'm relieved. She isn't toxic. She's a reasonable and nice person. *I'm PMSing and stressed about school and coming down from our VERY MAGICAL bender and I took it out on you and it wasn't cool at all.*

Suddenly and without warning, I want to tell her I love her. This always happens to me. I have an intense urge to declare my love far before it's appropriate. A lot of lesbians feel this way, and maybe there is an alchemical explanation, too much estrogen or something. Sometimes I can't tell if I love someone or if I just want to up the stakes of the relationship or if there is a difference.

I write back, *It WAS magical, maybe we should do it again soon?*

Then I google the appropriate amount of time to tell someone you love them. The results vary, but two months appears to be the agreed-upon mean. I can't decide whether to calculate from the time I first met Ivy on Zoom or from the time we first kissed. If I count from Zoom, I've known her for six weeks, meaning I have to wait two more weeks to tell her I love her. If the timer starts when we first kissed, it's been just over a week, meaning I have to wait just under another seven.

Ivy writes back, *yes, Thursday? Camarillo outlets? Amphetamines at Johnny Rockets then shop till we drop?*

I check my calendar. Today is Saturday. So, I have five days to recover and catch up with Zev and get coffee with Kat Gold and be healthy. I open Apple Maps. The Camarillo outlets are closer to me than Oxnard, right by Thousand Oaks, not far from Calabasas.

Perfect, I reply.

twelve

Kat Gold invites me to her house in Echo Park because "the paps have been crazy lately." She lives on a quiet street beside Elysian Park, at least a mile from the raucous section of the neighborhood where I lived in my twenties. Her house isn't visible from the street. I arrive at a tall gate and text her. *Here.*

The gate opens and Kat Gold appears in the yard wearing almost nothing, her tan skin gleaming in angelic light filtered through tall bamboo. The gates close quickly behind me, and I'm suddenly claustrophobic, trapped in this compound where everything is prettier than me.

"Astrid Dahl," Kat Gold says, her voice velvety. She opens her arms like she wants to hug me, which I immediately dread.

Reluctantly, I walk toward her and let her wrap me in her arms, try hard to hug her back in a normal way. Finding the American social practice a bit barbaric, I prefer the French air kiss, which involves no skin-to-skin contact, or even the Swedish handshake, which is cold and businesslike. I prefer not to hug someone unless I am fucking them.

"You look fab," Kat says, unleashing me from her freakishly petite body. I always think I'm skinny until I'm around Hollywood people and then suddenly I'm convinced I'm bloated and misshapen. I definitely don't feel fab, although I did put some effort into my appearance today, as I always do. I'm wearing my softest white T-shirt, Issey Miyake knockoff plissé pants, Sambas, a dab of mascara, and my most niche perfume. My hair is behaving, looking more lioness than mental patient—it often toes this line.

"You too," I say because I feel compelled. But also it's true, she looks good, her skin even more radiant in real life than it was on Zoom. The shape of Kat's face recalls a deer, or the deer filter on Instagram. She's wearing a crop top that says Valley of the Dolls, which is honestly very cool, and her stomach looks rock-hard, like if I hit my head on it I'd get a concussion. Kat Gold is so algorithmically hot it's uncanny, approaching satirical. Whatever she has, I don't envy it, because it looks very uncomfortable, which in turn puts me at ease. "I'm obsessed with that shirt—where did you get it?"

"Oh," Kat says, looking down at her chest as if she forgot what she was wearing. "My friend made it. I haven't read the book, but I love the shirt."

"You've never read *Valley of the Dolls*?" I ask with faux shock. Of course, Kat Gold hasn't read *Valley of the Dolls* because Jacqueline Susann isn't an esoteric European philosopher. She probably hasn't even read my book, just like I haven't read hers, hence why we basically repeated the same vague and abstract flattery about our books to each other.

"No!" she says. "Should I? I've heard it's kind of trashy."

"You should like trashy," I say. "You bought the rights to my book."

"Oh, please," she says. "You're a genius." She motions for me to follow her on a stone path through her lush yard, significantly more manicured than my own and surely violating water restrictions. I smell wet dirt and also Kat's perfume, which I'm certain is Santal 33, the scent of the nouveau bourgeoisie.

"You always bring out the book T-shirts for me," I say as we walk, unable to tolerate the silence.

Kat stops and turns toward me, tilts her head.

"On Zoom," I say. "You were wearing a Joan Didion shirt."

"Oh right," Kat says. "Good memory."

"I'm kind of autistic," I say. God. It's been two minutes and I've already called my book trashy and said something ableist.

Thankfully, Kat laughs and says, "I love you." Then, "Let's go inside."

Kat's living room revolves around a mint green wraparound sofa and eclectic mismatched rugs. Big windows provide ample light for healthy pothos and monstera plants of the variety I saw in the Zoom call, and there is also a giant fig tree, almost big enough to belong in the yard. Incense wafts through the air and smells like juniper. Kat Gold asks me if I want coffee or tea, and I say coffee, and she says cappuccino or pour-over, and I say whichever's easiest. She tells me to take a seat and disappears.

Sinking into her sofa, I covertly snap a photo and decide to send it to no one. Zev wouldn't care. Otto would say Kat Gold is cringe. Agent Allison would say I'm disrespecting her privacy. Penelope would care, but I don't have her number. And for some reason, I haven't told Ivy about Kat Gold.

Scanning the room, I am shocked to see not a single book. Not even a coffee table book. There are pink tulips on the coffee table, a record player on the credenza, but no bookshelf and no books. Where are all these philosophy books Kat is holding up on TikTok? Maybe she Photoshops them in.

Music floats into the room, some generic psychedelic rock,

and Kat Gold reappears with two steaming mugs. She hands me a cappuccino, and I'm happy because that's what I wanted. Her cup contains something dark green and resembling sludge.

She sits and we sip. In the brief silence, I blurt out, "Hey, question—is Satchels of Gold a *RHONY* reference?"

Kat Gold tilts her head. "Rhony?"

"*Real Housewives of New York*," I say. "What, you're too busy reading Deleuze to watch the housewives?" I scan the room again. Maybe the books are in her bedroom, or in an office upstairs. There isn't a TV either. Maybe Kat Gold uses her living room for what living rooms are actually designed for: living, talking to people, not hiding behind a book or a screen.

Kat laughs. "I'm not a big reality TV person," she says. "I grew up in a very dramatic household. I've experienced enough personality disordered behavior for a lifetime." She pauses, sips. "But I appreciate your sort of anthropological take on the genre."

Her flattery is so creepy. I'm not an anthropologist, I'm a voyeur, and probably a sadist. I sip my cappuccino, which is rich and velvety and, frankly, perfect.

"Satchels of Gold is a reference to my name," she says. "Obviously. And, like, a gold pot at the end of a rainbow. My birthday is March seventeenth—Saint Patrick's Day—and my mom is Irish, so I've always been drawn to Irish lore."

"I thought your name was Katie Goldstein," I say, then immediately curse myself. Strike three, Astrid. Why can't I just be normal, say *Cool name, love the Irish*, like a normal fucking person? Although Kat Gold doesn't look Irish, more Italian or Spanish.

Kat laughs. "You really don't hold back, do you, Astrid?"

"It's a major problem," I say. "It's ruining my career."

"I admire it," Kat says. "You could probably benefit from

some media training"—she pauses, sips—"but part of me thinks you should stay the way you are. Everyone is so freakishly polished these days, like walking PR machines. We don't let anyone be messy anymore."

I shrug. "The other day a twink spat at me." I pause. "At the pool."

Kat looks confused, her eyes wide like a baby deer's.

"He said he was friends with the guy who interviewed me at Barnes & Noble," I explain. "And he was super angry. He called me a Karen and he spit at me."

Surprising me, Kat laughs. "I'm sorry," she says, still laughing. "That's so fucking funny. You have to put that in your next book."

"It was kind of traumatic!" I say, feigning offense. But she's right. With the benefit of a little distance, it's pretty funny. "He was wearing a Bottoms for Hillary tank top."

Kat laughs so hard she hunches over, her chestnut hair cascading over her head. I appreciate that she lets herself laugh. I figured she'd be one of those girls who flatly says *I'm dead* instead of laughing. Kat gasps for air. "This is too fucking good."

"I'm glad my trauma is so hilarious to you!" I say, playing up the bit, now enjoying it—oddly, enjoying myself.

When Kat finally catches her breath, she says, "This sort of brings me to something I wanted to ask you."

"Something twink-related?" I ask.

"Not twink-related," Kat says. "Well, only insofar as you are a twink, which you are a little, no? Is that off base?"

"I'm too old," I say, "but thank you."

"Well, you don't look a day over twenty-nine," she says, and suddenly I'm starting to like Kat Gold. "I was hoping I could shadow you."

"Shadow me?"

"Yeah," she says. "I know this is kind of corny, but I'm a Lee Strasberg gal."

Devon (of the butternut squash incident) was an aspiring actress so I know that Lee Strasberg is the long-deceased theater director and acting teacher all the It Girls love now. He's the father of Method or something.

"You're Method," I say, and wonder how one goes Method for a Marvel movie.

"Exactly," she says.

"You know the character in my book is not me," I say.

Kat narrows her eyes at me, disbelieving. "Right," she says.

"She's not!" I say. "I'm not an astrologer. I don't have black hair." I try to think of other differences between myself and the character, but I'm not coming up with much. "I'm not a Scorpio."

"Well, you wrote the book," Kat says, and I'm relieved she doesn't ask me my actual zodiac sign, because I burned that obsession with the full moon, hence why I haven't glommed on to the fact that Kat Gold told me her birthday, that she's a Pisces, and that is why she is so desperate to be liked. "I want to get in your head a little more."

"I really like to be alone," I say. "Like I need to be alone most of the time or I go a bit mad. Just thinking about being around people for an extended period, like going on a group trip or having my own family member stay with me, makes me insanely nervous and basically drives me to binge drink and do drugs."

Kat nods with a serious expression. "I get that," she says. "I'm not saying I'd move in with you or anything. I just want a little more access."

"Can it be over text message?" I say. "Or email? I'm great digitally."

"I want to get your mannerisms," she says.

"We can Zoom," I say.

Kat laughs. "You're so funny, Astrid," she says, placing her mug on the coffee table. "You know I have thirty million followers on Instagram. Rihanna invited me to a Lakers game tonight. Courtside. And I can't get you to hang out with me."

"I'm here now," I say.

"I need a little more," she says.

A burly man with a blond beard appears in the doorframe and I jump a little.

"Did I hear you announce to this poor girl how many followers you have on Instagram?"

Surprising me, the blond man has a British accent.

"Astrid," Kat says. "Meet Eli, my dick husband."

"Hi, Astrid," he says. "I hope you're enjoying my narcissist wife."

"What a weird banter you all have," I say.

Eli disappears, mumbling something about basketball.

"I think he's a little jealous," Kat says, then winks.

"Of?"

"He knows I'm queer," she says, and I try not to gag. "And a little obsessed with you."

"You aren't going to murder me, are you?"

Kat laughs. "Not unless you want me to." She winks.

My phone buzzes with a text from Ivy.

"Hey, I have a question," I say to Kat, "since you're married and all." I pause. "And *queer*," I add, to humor her. "What do you think is the appropriate amount of time to wait before you tell someone you love them?"

"Oh my gosh," Kat says. "Now you're making *me* jealous!"

I'm annoyed by Kat Gold's performative interest in women,

in me. I can tell by the look of Kat Gold's mouth that she isn't into women. Lesbians have thin lips and tend to scowl, as if their mouths were designed to preclude any possibility of fellatio. Personally, I have trouble getting my mouth around a sandwich. Bisexuals have slightly poutier mouths, but Kat Gold's pillowy lips, slightly parted into an expression of eagerness and confusion, seem optimized for seducing men. It's the straightest mouth I've ever seen.

"Who is the lucky girl?" Kat asks, carrying on the charade.

"I'm asking for a friend," I say.

"Right," she says. "Tell your friend—" Kat pauses, bites her lip. "That there are no rules in matters of the heart."

A black cat appears out of nowhere and rubs up against my shins.

thirteen

I vy tells me she loves me over rum-spiked strawberry milk-shakes at Johnny Rockets.

A chalky blue Adderall sits uncomfortably on my tongue when she says it and I clutch my spiked milkshake to swallow it down before I reply.

"I love you too," I say, then nuzzle up to her, wondering whether I mean it or it's just the excitement of saying it, the rum, or the proximity to the amphetamine high. "I was trying to wait to say it." A brief pause, then, "The internet says two months is appropriate."

"Yeah," Ivy says. "The internet says a lot of things."

Kat Gold said there are no rules in matters of the heart.

I try to remember if someone has ever told me they love me first. I typically say it first, but the other person always says it back. I can tell when someone is in love with me. And while I'm not the most likable, I'm somehow very lovable, despite looking like Helga Pataki, despite having a face no one has ever called beautiful, not even my parents, despite having no breasts to speak of, and despite a personality that has been described, by many, as "very abrasive."

Otto told me people don't tell me they love me first because I am scary.

But Ivy isn't afraid of me.

Ivy pulls me close to her and kisses me.

"Let's shop till we drop," she says when she pulls away.

Ivy takes my hand and walks us straight to Victoria's Secret, a store I haven't been inside since I was thirteen and all the cool girls in my class who I idolized and in retrospect probably had crushes on wanted to go. I remember feeling embarrassed that my breasts were so small and straining to look for triple A bras, which they rarely had in stock. Back then, I associated Victoria's Secret with a type of female sexuality to which I was not entitled, from which I had been unjustly excluded. But now, today, here with Ivy, my crush who just confessed her love, trying on lingerie we will surely fuck in, after Victoria's Secret has been canceled for promoting unrealistic body ideals and generating low self-esteem, and perhaps some kind of tenuous connection to Jeffrey Epstein, on the Patricia Highsmith, feels perfect. Ivy, in her pink dress and pink cowboy boots, matches the store, its walls, its energy. Everything she picks for herself is pink—pink silk shorts, pink lace bralettes, a pink silk kimono—and she picks the same items for me in black and a smaller size. There is something spectacularly hot about this experience, about Ivy taking charge inside this glittery pink dreamscape, about co-opting an aesthetic experience that's been targeted toward the male gaze for our lesbian purposes, from which men are entirely excluded.

It's my turn to exclude, and it feels marvelous.

In the dressing room, I take a whiff and realize this store is Ivy's scent, the one I smelled in her car: blooming orchids and metal. The metal scent, I've realized from my time spent in fragrance Reddit forums, is likely aldehydes—an organic compound popularized by its use in Chanel No. 5 in 1921 and that smells champagne-like, sparkly, fizzy, metallic.

We leave the store with $470 worth of lingerie that Ivy puts on her card. I wonder where her money comes from, given she's a PhD student and her sole parent is a teacher, then decide it doesn't matter. The point is she paid for me and we're high and in love and I'm about to do a striptease for her in the nearest Marriott.

:::

When I first switched from sleeping with men to sleeping with women, the thing that shocked me the most was the time differential. The zeitgeist is wrong about nearly everything, but lesbian sexuality is at the top of that list. For some reason, no one can figure out how it happens, which is insane because over half of the human population has a clitoris. People imagine lesbians as sexless creatures busy rearing cats and doing home improvement, but every woman I've dated prefers dogs to cats and not a single one has a power drill. Sexual intimacy is our primary preoccupation. Sex with a man is child's play. Heterosexual sex is quick. Twenty minutes max. Lesbians will fuck for hours. And hours. And hours. The sorest I've been in my life is from lesbian sex, and I've done Barry's Bootcamp. And when you add amphetamines into the mix, it can approach medically dangerous territory.

When we finally stop fucking, it's dark out, and Ivy suggests taking another Adderall and going to a martini bar and bistro called Oasis. Ivy seems to really know this area and I wonder if she's taken other lovers here. I wonder how long she's lived with her ex, and when we're on our first drink and shrimp cocktail at the tawdry Camarillo bistro, I ask her about it.

"How's the apartment search going?" I dip a shrimp into cocktail sauce and pop it in my mouth.

"What do you mean?" Ivy sips her drink, which is bright red and called "the naughty strawberry."

"You're living with your ex, right?" I ask between bites of shrimp. "And you said you're looking for new places."

"Oh, right, right," Ivy says, her eyes flitting about the room. I read online that this type of eye movement signals deceit, but as Ivy said, the internet says a lot of things. "Yes, it's slow going. The rental market is crazy, and we haven't had much time to look with school."

Ivy's use of "we" sounds like they're looking together, as a couple. But maybe she just means they're both looking, separately. Dopamine flooding through me, I choose to believe the latter. "What's the vibe in the apartment like? Is it tense? Do you still share a bedroom?" I'm hit with an uneasy awareness that these amphetamine-fueled questions under the harsh lights above us make it sound a bit like a custodial interrogation. Recalling my one year of law school, I wonder if I should read Ivy her Miranda rights.

"It's tense," she says, then clears her throat. "She sleeps on the couch."

"What's she like?" I ask.

"I really don't feel like talking about her."

I want to know more. I want to know her name. I want to know if she's anything like me. I want to know if she knows about me. But Ivy is clearly uncomfortable, so I change the subject. I consider mentioning my weird hang with Kat Gold, but I have a feeling Ivy won't like that, so instead I ask, "Is Victoria's Secret lesbian pulp?"

"Absolutely," she says. Then she sticks her hot tongue in my ear and I remember a Camille Paglia quote I saw on Twitter earlier:

"Lesbian lust is supercondensed female sexuality, all smooth, soft, shiny surfaces, evoking [. . .] a subliminal memory of the lost paradise of the maternal body, where they blissfully floated in the warm, sensuous bath of the womb."

In the middle of the night, I wake up to go to the bathroom and have trouble falling back asleep due to the stimulants. I wrap my arm around Ivy and with my free arm, I hold my phone, go on Twitter, find the Camille Paglia quote, and retweet it.

fourteen

Back home I feel hollow and miss Ivy, so I pick up *Perfume and Pain* and go into the yard. For a second I'm worried about Penelope bothering me, but my need for the sun overrides that concern. I lie on a towel on the grass and sprawl out, then flip to a random page.

Gail and her crush Wanda go biking, and when they stop to take a break, Wanda reaches into her carrier basket and pulls out a perfume atomizer. She hands it to Gail and says, "Spray me. All over . . ." Gail gasps, and so do I.

My phone buzzes, interrupting my thoughts. Zev is Face-Timing me.

"I saw you texted," he says. "But I couldn't read it." He sighs. "My eyes are going."

Zev has terrible vision but finds glasses uncomfortable and contacts nightmarish. I don't remember texting him anything in particular, but I'm firing off texts at all hours of the day and can't be expected to remember every one of them.

I flip over on my back and hold my phone toward the sky, blocking the sun.

Zev is also lying on his back, with his poodle Jackie-O nestled into his rib cage.

"What's up, weirdo?" I say.

"You get so testy when you're in love."

"How did you know I'm in love?"

"I was joking," he says. "But you seemed into that girl the other night." He pauses to give Jackie-O a kiss on the head. "You're really in love?"

"Ivy said it first" is all I say.

"That's good," Zev says in a sort of fatherly tone. His unease around intimacy comforts me immensely. "Penelope texted me about going to see Cat Power at the Lodge Room next week. If you want to come."

Zev and I worshiped Chan Marshall in college. *The Greatest* came out when we were sophomores and we would hit his baby blue bong and play it over and over. We saw her live and she had a bit of a breakdown onstage, for which she is apparently well known. She kept screaming at the sound guy midsong, changing songs without warning, and then at one point began throwing unidentifiable objects into the audience.

We loved it, loved her. "Great energy," Zev said afterward.

I'm sad that Penelope is interfering with something special I have with Zev.

But I'll go to the concert, because if I don't, they'll go without me, just the two of them, a visual that makes my organs sink.

"Sounds fun," I say in a forced voice. "I'll get a ticket."

When we hang up, I look over at Penelope's bungalow and wonder if she's inside texting my best friend right now. I glare at her window for a few seconds, anger bubbling, and then return to the sexy scene to calm down.

Wanda's body revolves in the mist. "All over," Wanda keeps telling Gail. "Keep on spraying until it's all used up." Gail objects that the bottle is almost half full, and Wanda tells her to keep spraying. As she moistens Wanda's body, Gail finds it "maddening to have all that delectable flesh so close and still not touch it," then wonders if she's in love. I wonder if I'm in love. Zev's reaction reminded me that it might be premature.

I hear a noise and jump. Penelope's front door is opening. She laughs. "Sorry, I didn't mean to startle you." She's walking toward me. I hope she isn't planning to stop and chat. I stare at the page to appear busy.

"Zev says you're coming to the Cat Power show?" Penelope says, her voice closer. She's standing over me, silhouetted by the sun. She's wearing jean cutoff shorts and, for an unfortunate second, I can see that she isn't wearing underwear. I look up at the trees and say, "Yeah."

"Someone is texting you," Penelope says. I can't totally make out the features of her face but it seems like she's grinning. "I wonder who."

I redirect my focus to my phone. I have a new notification from Ivy. My stomach flutters. Opening the text, I briefly fantasize about Penelope moving to France and Ivy taking her bungalow, which we'll convert into our writing studio.

I look back up at Penelope and say, "See you at the concert," hoping this will signal to her that from my perspective, our conversation is over. Penelope seems to get the hint and says, "See you," then walks off toward the stone steps.

Once she's gone, I open the text from Ivy and am let down to see: *Is your IG private?*

No, I write back, *why?*

Can you take down that photo of me?

I don't recall posting a photo of her. I must have put it on my story. I tend to do this—post blurry and disorienting photos on my Instagram story I don't remember. I open my Instagram to find I did in fact post such a photo: Ivy in a pink kimono, mostly silhouetted by the yellow hotel lamp. I assume it was taken after the bistro, the portion of the night of which I have no memory but knowing myself I likely did some sort of clumsy striptease to Lana Del Rey.

Right after I click Delete, another text from Ivy pops up. *My ex is kind of unstable*, she writes back, *just trying to make my living situation tolerable.* Then, *I know it's totally weird and I'm sorry and I'll make it up to you once I move out I promise.*

Already deleted, I write back, and then shut my phone off.

Seconds later, Penelope is coming back up the steps. Irritated, I say, "Back already?" Another figure appears behind her, and at first I think it's Laura, but it's a different woman who looks a little bit like her.

"I was getting Nadia," Penelope says, gesturing to the woman. Nadia. Sounds Russian. The woman looks vaguely Slavic. Prettier than Laura. Ash blonde hair and wide-set eyes, a haunted icy green. I wonder if this is the girl from the yard a few weeks ago. Or maybe that was someone else. Why is Penelope always surrounded by these birdlike blondes? "Nadia, this is Astrid."

"Hi," I say, then pick up my book and disappear back inside.

The last thing I need right now is to make small talk with this suspiciously attractive Russian.

fifteen

For Method purposes, I agree to let Kat Gold go on a walk with me. She wants to see my house, but I tell her I'll meet her on the street. We do a version of the walk I do with Zev, in the late afternoon, when everything is golden.

"I love your neighborhood," she says, spreading her arms into the sky. For once she isn't wearing a literary T-shirt. Instead, she's wearing a red bodysuit and her skin glistens and I feel so bloated and frumpy in my big T-shirt and Sambas.

"Did you tell the girl you love her?" Kat asks.

"I don't kiss and tell," I say. Then, "She said it first."

Kat squeals. "Lucky bitch! Can you please tell me about this chica? Name, age, occupation?"

I shake my head, pull a phantom zipper over my mouth.

Kat frowns and says, "I'm so bored in my marriage."

Unsure what to say, "I'm sorry" is all I can come up with.

"It's okay," she says. "Eli just doesn't get it. He thinks I'm vapid for being on social media. He's a finance guy, he doesn't get that people look up to me, that I'm influential, and I'm not like telling people to drink tummy tea—I'm getting them to read and think critically about themselves and their bodies."

"Right," I say. I haven't looked at Kat Gold's Instagram much, but I can't imagine it's contributing anything significant to society. The last thing young people need is to think more about themselves and their bodies. I, for one, could stand to think about someone else.

"It's so boring," she says. "Marriage." She turns toward me. "Should I have an affair?"

I shrug. "Probably." Then, "But with a man."

"Why? I'm so over men, I hate them!"

"You only hate them because you love them," I say.

"You're so old-fashioned, Astrid," Kat says. "You know sexuality is a spectrum. It's fluid. We've known this for decades."

"Yeah, yeah," I say. "The Kinsey Scale was invented in the fifties, I think, so it should be overturned by now. Every scientific finding is overturned. The coastal elite loves 'science' and hates 'capitalism,' but every major scientific study is funded by a major corporation so science changes when the CEOs change. Remember when scientists said veganism was the world's healthiest diet and would save the planet? And now they say veganism is unsustainable and fake meat will kill you. Real meat is murder, but fake meat, as it turns out, is suicide."

"Well," Kat Gold says, stopping, turning toward me, and it annoys me how she keeps doing this—stopping, looking into my eyes—when we're supposed to be in motion, looking forward, avoiding eye contact. "According to the Lindy theorem, the longer something has existed, the longer it will continue to exist. Scientists only heralded veganism for a few years, so they could easily stop. Kinsey's been around for seventy years, so I think it's safe to assume it will stay."

"Didn't scientists believe the Earth was flat for, like, thousands of years?" I say, marching forward. I heard a podcast on Lindy and think it's kind of common sense and doesn't need to call itself a *theorem*. "That was obviously overturned. Maybe we just need to wait a little longer on Kinsey. It will be overturned, and we'll all laugh at how ridiculous it was that we ever believed it. Then maybe it will come back. People think the Earth is flat again, or at least 'flat Earther' is always trending on Twitter. I saw a headline that said flat Earthers think Australia doesn't exist and people who live there are actors paid by NASA." My parents would be so disappointed to know their daughter who attended a top ten law school is playing devil's advocate with an actress and model who didn't finish high school.

"Fuck!" Kat shouts, and for a second I think she has really strong opinions about flat Earthers, but then she hunches down and covers her face, like we're being attacked, and I hear what at first I think are gunshots but then notice elongated camera lenses emerging from a black SUV.

Kat gives the cameras two middle fingers and turns around.

"Let's go back to your house," she says, holding her face in her arms.

"Fine," I say, covering my face with my T-shirt. "But you aren't coming inside."

I follow Kat, and the SUV follows both of us. We walk in silence, covering our faces, cameras clicking at us. Kat screams at the paps, begging for a "moment of fucking peace" until they finally disappear. This must be annoying for her. But Kat asked to be famous; I didn't. These photos might be published some-where, and I look like shit. What did I do to deserve to be photo-graphed next to Kat Gold, a literal swimsuit model and the face of fucking Fenty?

Making matters worse, Penelope and the Russian are emerg-ing from Penelope's Volvo as we approach the bungalows. From roughly twenty feet away, Penelope waves and I wave back.

"Is this the chick you're in love with?" Kat whispers. "She's a fox."

"No," I whisper back. "She's my annoying neighbor, and I'm pretty sure she's fucking that hot Russian."

"Hi, I'm Kat," Kat introduces herself when we get closer. "I'm playing Astrid in the TV adaptation of her book."

"The character is not me," I mumble.

Penelope introduces herself to Kat, then says, "I loved your book."

"Aw, that's so sweet." Kat puts up prayer hands.

"This is Nadia," Penelope says, gesturing toward her lover.

Nadia looks at Kat rudely, or maybe that's just her natural expression: resting hostile Russian face. "Hi," Nadia says, then disappears toward the stairs, and I'm thankful she has no apparent interest in small talk. "Nice to meet you," she calls over her shoulder.

"Nice to meet you, Kat," Penelope says.

"I hope to see you around," Kat says.

Penelope smiles. "Me too." She trails behind Nadia.

Once Nadia and Penelope are out of eyesight, Kat jabs my rib cage.

"You're blushing, Astrid," she hisses. "That's totally your girl."

"I can't stand her," I say. "And obviously she's with that Russian."

"God, that woman was really rude, right?" Kat says. "Also, you seem a little jealous?"

"I'm definitely not," I say. "Did you get enough of my mannerisms, Ms. Strasberg?"

"There's never enough," Kat says mysteriously, then disappears toward her car. "I'll text you! Sorry about the paparazzi."

:::::

I wake up to a lot of texts. From Otto. From Agent Allison. From Kat Gold. From Ivy. Ivy texted me twelve times.

I open Otto's text first. *Saw you in the Daily Mail girl! *NeNe Leakes voice* You have arrived!*

Fuck. I don't want to see myself next to Kat Gold. I probably look like a troll.

I open Agent Allison's text. *So glad to see you're getting along with Kat! You look great in the photos!*

I open my Google search engine, begin to type my name, then realize the *Daily Mail* will probably list me as "friend" or "frumpy friend" or "mentally ill companion." I begin to type "Kat Gold" and then close the search engine, open Kat's texts.

Sorry the paps got us babe, she says. *We look so cute together though.*

God.

I want to see the photos, but I also really don't.

I waver between opening Ivy's texts and opening the *Daily Mail*.

I go for the *Daily Mail*, ripping the Band-Aid.

I'm shocked to see I look totally fine. Not gorgeous or perfect but fine. My legs appear long and my hair is behaving, and I look like someone who could be hanging out with Kat Gold, who looks freakishly perfect per usual. And the way she's walking, strutting almost, as though on a runway, in her bright red bodysuit and cat-eye sunglasses, she certainly knew the paparazzi would be there. The bitch probably called them. I should have known when I saw her in a bodycon outfit instead of an ill-fitting literary T-shirt.

Taking a deep breath, I open the texts from Ivy.

What the fuck are these photos of you and Kat Gold?

You are so sketchy Astrid, I swear to god . . .

You know that chick is a predator, right?

She preys on tragic dykes all the time, strings them along, tells them she's queer.

It's really sad, Astrid.

I'm mostly just worried about you. It's not a good look.

Are you okay? Like, did you hit your head?

It's just so weird you wouldn't even tell me you were hanging out with her?

Like how did you even meet? You never leave your house.

You know what, never mind, I'm going to assume there is a logical explanation.

I'm sorry for overreacting.

I hope you have a great day!

sixteen

The night of the concert, it's raining, which is nearly unheard of this time of year. We were planning to have a drink in the yard beforehand, but instead we meet in Penelope's living room. I have no Adderall, but Chan Marshall doesn't exactly make amphetamine music, and I figure it will be good for me to practice going to an event without it. I buy a five-hour energy shot from the liquor store down the street and put it in my purse just in case.

Rain hits the windows and echoes through Penelope's humid living room. She is wearing the red dress she wore on stew night and red lipstick, her thick brown hair hanging in loose waves on her shoulders, her eyes lined in brown. She greets me with a kiss on the cheek and my face heats a bit when she does. Zev just holds up his glass of gin in my direction. I clink it with my already open beer. I have another in my purse just in case.

We listen to *Moon Pix* on Penelope's record player. When "I Don't Blame You" comes on, sweet nostalgia fills my belly. Zev and I used to play this all the time when taking breaks from writing our papers, and when the chorus arrives, we start to sway and sing in faux-operetta voices. Penelope joins in, annoyingly melodic and on-key. I can't help but think of my dream, when she sang to me and had a similarly good voice. I wonder if Penelope sang for Laura, if she sings for the Russian.

Ivy texts me, *you excited for the concert darling?*

We've made up since the Kat Gold incident. I told Ivy that Kat is adapting my book, and that I didn't tell her because it wasn't public yet, even though it totally was, but she seemed to buy it and apologized again for overreacting and for calling me tragic. But I'm still feeling a little weird about Ivy, about Kat Gold, about everything really.

Yeah, I reply. Then, to appease her, I write: *I wish Penelope wasn't here.*

Me too, Ivy says.

Ivy became a little aggressive when I told her I was going to the concert with Penelope, an aggression that felt so familiar—of past girlfriends and recent Ivy—that it almost felt safe.

I wish it was you instead, I write back. But I'm not sure I mean it.

Ivy responds with seven pink heart emojis.

:::::

Sitting on the toilet while the opener plays, I open my throat and pour down the five-hour energy shot and wonder at which age I'll stop covertly getting high on toilet seats. Penelope is in the stall next to me. The first chords of "Fool" start to play through the bathroom speakers and Penelope lets out a little squeal. I flush the toilet and go to wash my hands and she intercepts me.

"Germs are good for the gut," she says, grabbing my hand. She pulls me out of the bathroom and toward the concert hall. Her hand is warm and oddly comforting, but that might be the 200 mg of syrupy caffeine I just dumped down my throat mixed with the 2.5 IPAs in my blood.

Inside the concert hall, Penelope doesn't let go of my hand and I don't let go of hers. I hear my phone vibrate in my purse. I don't look at it, first because I have a strict no-phone rule during concerts, and second because—for reasons that are entirely obscure to me—I don't want to let go of Penelope's hand. We find Zev alone in the corner, where one can always find Zev.

"Should we go closer?" Penelope asks him.

Zev shakes his head. "I don't like people."

Penelope doesn't respond, just pulls my hand toward the front, pushing and weaving through bodies until we're right at the edge of the stage, right below Chan, who kind of looks like Penelope, with the same uncombed auburn hair, smudged eyeliner, sharp cheekbones, middle-aged bohemian aesthetic.

My purse continues to vibrate and with my free hand, I switch the phone to silent without looking at it. In the process, my hand grazes my now nearly warm beer. I remove the bottle from my purse and whisper to Penelope, "We can share."

I realize I don't have a bottle opener. I could open it with a lighter, but that would require letting go of Penelope's hand.

Penelope takes the bottle with her free hand and places the top in her mouth, hinging the cap between her teeth. The cap pops right off.

"Hell, yes," Chan says right at Penelope, in between lyrics.

Penelope raises the beer bottle and people around us clap.

:·:·:

Soon it's the encore and the beer is done and Penelope is still holding my hand while Chan sings about the moon. I recall throwing the words *melted cheese* into a fire on the full moon and giggle to myself.

"What's funny?" Penelope whispers into my ear and her warm breath sends a shiver down my spine. I'm tripping a bit, or under a spell. Maybe Penelope drugged me. Maybe she casts legitimate spells and that's why she's always bringing these modelesque and vaguely Slavic women to the yard, why even Kat Gold found her attractive. Although Ivy said Kat Gold is attracted to tragic dykes, and I've since been unable to see Kat's name on my phone without feeling a hint of shame.

"Nothing," I whisper back.

The song ends and the lights turn on and Penelope drops my hand. The spell is over.

"Chan must be on mood stabilizers," Zev says to me when we finally find him. "She didn't yell once."

"Probably," I say, and feel sad or something similar.

In the back of Penelope's Volvo, I remove my phone from my purse to find seven missed calls and thirty-two texts from Ivy.

I shut my phone off.

. . . .

I want the spell to come back, so I ask Zev to come over so we can all watch a movie. He says he's tired and Penelope drops him off. When he gets out of the car, I move to the front, and my heart starts to race. I'm so confused as to what's happening, as to why Penelope is suddenly making me very nervous, and not nervous in the same *I hope she doesn't bother me* way like before, but more like I'm nervous I'm not pretty enough to be in the front seat of her car.

Cat Power's cover of Rihanna's "Stay" comes on the speakers and I remember my dream, when Penelope was singing the original version, and I wonder if I'm psychic. Maybe I'm the witch. Riding in silence, I try to use my newfound clairvoyance to psychically will Penelope to suggest that just the two of us watch a movie, that it culminates in us tangling our bodies under warm covers. But no such suggestion comes.

Instead, she asks, "What are you smiling about?" Then, "Ivy texting you?"

I sigh and say, "She texted me thirty-two times."

"She likes you," Penelope says, nonchalant. Only a true lesbian would be unfazed by thirty-two texts in a row. Before I ghosted her, my therapist told me, "Lesbians are very verbal." Yeah, no shit. Although I suppose I wasn't being very verbal when I stopped responding to my therapist's emails.

"It's a little alarming," I say.

"Yeah?" she says, turning toward me, looking into me with her lined brown eyes.

"Yeah," I say, and then, because I can't help myself, "Is the Russian girl texting you?"

Penelope tilts her head at me, then turns back toward the dark road. "Oh, Nadia?"

"Whatever her name is." I don't know why my voice comes out hostile.

"I don't know," Penelope says. "I left my phone at home."

"How old-fashioned," I say. Discomfort swirls inside me as I imagine Penelope returning to her phone and having an appropriate number of text message notifications from Nadia. Penelope will likely text her, *I'm still wide awake from the concert*, and Nadia will respond, *I'll come over with a bottle of red*. And then they'll fuck and fuck and fuck and Penelope will completely forget about holding my hand.

"You okay?" Penelope asks.

"I'm great," I say, realizing I'm squeezing my phone really hard. "Just thinking about calling Ivy," I lie. "Can't wait to talk to her." My heart is beating out of its chest, and I curse myself for drinking the five-hour energy. I will need to drink some alcohol to get to sleep. Normally I'd FaceTime Ivy while I drink, but that doesn't feel like an option right now.

"Yeah?" Penelope says, obviously not buying it. Or maybe she's just distracted. She's probably thinking about Nadia naked. I'm sure that bitch does Pilates. Her body probably belongs on a calendar.

As Penelope pulls into her parking spot, I say, "Thanks for driving. That was fun." I open my car door and get out before she responds.

"My pleasure," she calls to my back as I head up the stone steps toward our bungalows.

"Good night," I call without turning around. "Have fun with the Russian," I mumble at the stones beneath me.

"What?" Penelope calls after me.

I turn around. "Nothing." A gust of wind whips through my hair.

"Oh," Penelope says, and for a second it seems like she's going to say something else. But she says nothing. And I say nothing.

I turn back around and march up to my bungalow.

seventeen

I wake up to the sound of my phone ringing.

Still in dreamland, I answer without thinking.

The person on the other end is screaming.

"DID YOU FUCK HER?"

Maybe I'm still asleep. I say nothing, hoping it's a nightmare from which I'll soon awake.

"ASTRID I CAN HEAR YOU BREATHING," Ivy is shouting. *"DID YOU FUCK HER?"*

"No," I say, although I'm still unsure what she's talking about. Fuck who? Why is she yelling? My curtain blows in the breeze and bright light hits my face, jolting me into reality. Ivy is mad at me because I didn't respond to her last night. She texted me thirty-two times.

"Bullshit," she says. "You went to that weird concert with her and went AWOL."

Memories of last night flood back to me, Penelope holding my hand while Chan sang to us, the strange spell. Penelope leaving me to fuck her hot Russian lover.

"I turned my phone off at the show," I say. True enough.

"Bullshit," she says. "You're being sus, Astrid."

"I understand why you're upset." It feels important to validate her feelings. "I turned off my phone and then I was super tired when I got home and went straight to bed." This is all basically true. I plugged my phone in and listened to Cat Power loudly, maybe hoping that Penelope might come over, leave her Russian, and tell me to turn it down. I didn't look at my phone because I wanted to avoid this, what is happening now, Ivy screaming at me. But I should have known that it would be worse the longer I waited. That I exacerbated things per usual.

"I have to go," I say, and I hang up.

eighteen

Later that morning I receive a Google Calendar notification indicating a journalist from a queer literary journal will be calling me in twenty-three minutes. I don't remember agreeing to this, and I'm confused, given Agent Allison has strictly forbidden me from doing interviews.

I should probably call Agent Allison and ask her if she wants me to cancel the interview, but right now I'm thrilled to have a distraction from Ivy. A wiser and more stable person might say, *My love interest just screamed at me and my interview skills are terrible under even the most favorable conditions and my agent has in fact forbidden me from doing interviews and has also vaguely alluded to dropping me if I fuck up again so I should probably cancel,* but no one has ever accused me of being wise or stable. So, I chug three glasses of water and sit at my desk, and soon the journalist is calling me.

After exchanging pleasantries, the journalist asks me "how my queerness informs my writing."

I told myself before the interview that I would try my very best to think before I speak, but of course that doesn't happen. "I don't really identify as queer," I say. "I used to, before the term was co-opted by straight academics and woke big box stores." Allison would absolutely kill me for saying this, and I have a feeling it's only going to get worse. "All the self-identified queers these days are straight women with boyfriends, i.e., 'partners,' privileged white women who resent their normativity. Or social justice bros who think hating the government gives them a stripe on the Pride flag." I know I need to stop, but I keep going. "Or Southern California lesbians desperate to be aligned with the New York intelligentsia. I heard one such Southern California author refer to Disneyland as a 'queer space.' Disneyland is not a queer space. There are no queers at Disney. There are no queers south of the I-10 freeway. Queers are getting their PhDs and shopping at Target. Disneyland is Gay, Gay, Gay!" I take a sip of water. "Wait, what was the question?"

"I asked how your queer identity informs your work," the journalist says. "But you've certainly given me a lot to work with."

Oh God. I have to undo this all somehow. Agent Allison will drop my ass. Satchels of Gold will convince Kat Gold I'm not worth it.

"Can I strike my previous answer from the record?" I ask. I learned a thing or two from my one year of law school.

"Sure," the journalist says. "I want you to feel comfortable with what's printed. We're big fans of yours at our website."

"Thank you so much," I say, feeling bad for being so aggressive to someone who just wants to promote my work on her website. "I just had a big fight with my girlfriend, and I'm a bit scattered." I hope this makes me more sympathetic, even though I don't think Ivy is my girlfriend—we've never discussed it—and she might in fact have a girlfriend who isn't me.

Taking a deep breath like Agent Allison always recommends, I try again.

"I'm primarily concerned with writing stories that make women proud to love women instead of ashamed, like I used to be. I want to speak to young women who are afraid to come out because they don't see themselves reflected in"—I swallow—"queer culture. Because they are feminine. Because they wear dresses and ribbons"—I think of Ivy for a second, then continue—"and have zero interest in home improvement. And because they're attracted to femininity too. And when they hear the word *lesbian*, they imagine a volleyball coach or a woman in unflattering cargo shorts."

The journalist giggles.

"Or a femme woman with a butch dyke, which looks identical to heterosexuality, to their parents, to the sexless partnership they're dying to avoid. And for feminine-presenting out"— swallow—"queers, who hear wildly homophobic statements in their presence because they don't look the way society has been told gay women look. I want to remind lesbians it's okay to revel in the feminine, to be frivolous, submissive, a brat. That we can be sexy and glamorous, and in fact, we've always been sexy and glamorous. That Sappho, and Marie Antoinette, and Virginia Woolf, and Patricia Highsmith were all dimes. That the word *lesbian*, unlike the word *gay* or *queer* or *fag* or *dyke*, has glamorous and not derogatory origins, of an idyllic Greek island where feminine women loved feminine women and truly lived it the fuck up! And that by identifying as lesbians rather than queer, we honor this legendary history." I clutch my green amethyst, confident that I landed upon an answer that feels both inoffensive and also authentic, something I didn't think possible.

"Does that work?"

"That's great, Astrid," the journalist says. "Thank you."

nineteen

I spend the afternoon wandering the neighborhood and ignoring texts from Ivy, which begin mean and accusatory—*you're a sleaze and everyone knows it*—and eventually become apologetic and effusive—*you're my dream woman and I have trust issues from my ex and I'm so sorry . . . how can I make it up to you?*

These texts are a bit intense from a person I've only hung out with thrice in person, six times if you include the following days in bed as separate hangs, but lesbians move quick. And Ivy told me she had boundary issues. Almost everything she's told me about herself is a red flag. And Otto and Penelope said she was trying to *Single White Female* me. What's the Maya Angelou quote? When someone shows you who they are, ignore them entirely and project whatever you want?

I turn my phone off and think about my interview, feeling concerned that the writer will use the first, angry portion but feeling proud of the more positive answer I eventually landed on. I've always been a bit "slow to warm." I hated Penelope at first and now I can't stop thinking about her. I wonder if she's thinking about me, about the concert, about holding hands, whether she regrets it, whether I regret it, whether Ivy was right to be jealous, or whether she's wrong, that Penelope has no interest in me, that she's forgotten about holding hands, that she's currently in bed with a Russian woman who is much prettier than me.

Walking up the hill to my bungalow, I recall how at twenty-seven I wrote out a list of things I wanted to accomplish by forty: (1) publish a *New York Times* bestseller; (2) sell book rights to a major production company; (3) appear as a guest on a Bravo-related podcast; (4) romantically reject Kristen Stewart; and (5) diamond.

The diamond represents marriage, but I have some qualms about marriage as a legal institution and I'm sort of embarrassed by how desperate I am to marry, so I wrote "diamond" as code. I also do want a diamond, or maybe a sapphire. Just a big-ass rock on my finger that represents a compelling woman's undying need to possess me forever.

So far, I've only accomplished (2) and (3), but I have plenty of time. And one time when I was on the Patricia Highsmith, I got very close to (4). I saw Kristen Stewart at Akbar, the East Side gay bar, and she undressed me with her eyes. But I need more. All Los Angeles lesbians have a story about dating or almost dating Kristen Stewart. I want a story about how Kristen Stewart tried to kiss me and I ducked.

For a while I related to Kristen Stewart, her stiff movements and difficulty making eye contact, the fact that she's always touching her hair in interviews. Then I saw her on *Howard Stern* and her hair was all spiked up like a '90s boy band member, and she was jerky, twitching, using phrases like "dude" and "bro" and "rocked up to the party." She reminded me of the type of straight man I used to be forced into conversations with at 3:00 a.m. when I did a lot of cocaine. I've had suspicions that she isn't even gay, that so many dykes projected lesbian narratives onto her tomboyish unease that she had no choice but to play the role.

She's a fabulous actress. Zev and I have probably watched *Clouds of Sils Maria* a thousand times.

At the top of the hill, a hummingbird briefly lands on my hand. And it feels like a bigger accomplishment than anything on my list.

The light is starting to dim. I try to guess what time it is and land on 6:35 p.m. I was gone for hours. When I see Penelope's Volvo parked beside my Subaru, my heart does a confusing little jump. I climb the steps and spend a few moments in the yard, watching the eucalyptus trees sway and the sky turn a darker blue, maybe hoping Penelope might come out to ask me if I'm okay.

I put my key in the door, but it's already unlocked. I'm constantly forgetting to lock my door. Zev always scolds me for it, says I conduct my life like someone begging to get robbed or kidnapped or murdered, and I say he's been brainwashed by the true crime–industrial complex, and strangers really aren't that dangerous.

I walk inside and realize my bedroom light is on, which I also sometimes forget to turn off. But then a familiar smell hits me, one that's foreign to my apartment, a perfume I know but don't own. I hear a boot hit the floor and I jump. Someone is inside my apartment. I'm about to run when I identify the smell: tangy metallic orchids. Ivy emerges from my bedroom. I'm relieved at first, it's just Ivy, but remember that danger mostly comes from the people we know, the people we love.

"Why the fuck didn't you answer me?" she says, stomping toward me, her pink dress shaking with fury. "Did your phone break? I thought you were dead."

"I left it here," I say. "It's turned off." She's still walking at me. I instinctively back up.

"Let me see it," Ivy says.

"See what?" I back toward the door as she continues to charge at me.

"Your phone," she says, reaching for my pockets. "I know you have it on you. You never leave without it."

Suddenly there is a hand on mine and a body in front of me. I jump, planning to run, then hear another voice behind me.

"Everything okay in here?" Penelope asks, stepping in between Ivy and me.

"No," Ivy says. "Why the fuck are you always barging into my girlfriend's apartment?"

This is the first time Ivy has used the word *girlfriend* to describe me.

"Let's calm down," Penelope says, but Ivy is charging at her. I move to the side and wonder if Ivy is actually dangerous.

"Don't tell me to calm down," Ivy says, shaking. Ivy doesn't look like she is going to hurt Penelope. She doesn't have a weapon. She's just angry.

"If you can't calm down," Penelope says, "I'm going to have to ask you to leave."

"And what authority do you have?" Ivy says. "You know Astrid hates you. She's constantly making fun of you and saying you're the bane of her existence. She's clueless and can't see your pathetic crush."

I'm reddening, embarrassed. Penelope looks over at me, also seeming embarrassed. I want to go back to wandering the neighborhood alone and letting my thoughts wander with me, no phone or human to interrupt their path.

Ivy looks at me. "Astrid, what the fuck is wrong with you? Too fucked up to speak?"

I'm completely sober, but I wish I was blacked out. I'd love to not remember this.

"I'm going to ask you to leave one more time," Penelope says.

Ivy looks at me again. "I'll leave if Astrid tells me to leave. This is her house that she pays rent on, not you."

My throat is dry. Ivy is shaking and furious, a composite of so many past girlfriends. Penelope appears tall and strong and safe in her red dress.

"Ivy," I say, and her expression softens slightly. "I want you to leave."

Ivy leaves screaming. She calls me an alcoholic and a narcissist and bad in bed. She calls Penelope a nosy cunt and a cultural appropriator. I laugh, unsure what culture Penelope is appropriating.

"Everything is a fucking joke when you're high 24/7," she yells at me.

I say nothing but look at Penelope, who is also giggling.

"You two are sick," Ivy shouts. "I hope you have bad sex together." Ivy clicks the fob on her pink Fiat, which is parked behind a truck so I didn't see it earlier. She's yelling up from the street. "Enjoy Astrid, Penelope, she's like fucking a ragdoll." A few neighbors turn on their lights.

"You all will regret this," Ivy shouts. "I promise you. This is not a threat; it is a promise."

"That's a line from *Real Housewives*," I whisper to Penelope. "A very pulp text."

Across the street, a neighbor in a nightgown comes outside and stands at the top of her steps.

"Don't worry, ma'am," Ivy shouts at the neighbor. "I'm leaving. But watch out for your lesbo neighbors. They're real sickos."

Ivy revs the car in reverse and nearly hits a palm tree, but slams the brakes just in time, then zooms off down the street.

"Loser dykes!" Ivy shouts out her window as she zooms off.

The neighbor frowns and walks inside, and Penelope and I don't stop laughing until we can no longer see Ivy's Fiat. In the sudden silence, I experience that post-adrenaline crash, that organ-sinking feeling, and I assume Penelope does, too, because she says, "I should get back to my painting," and I'm crushed. I want to process what just happened. I want to tell Penelope that Ivy was writing her thesis on lesbian pulp and that she tried to write us into her own anti-lesbian propaganda tonight. I want to tell her that Ivy probably has a girlfriend. I want to FaceTime Otto with Penelope and tell him everything that happened, for them to laugh and say "I told you so."

"Good night," Penelope says, probably eager to get back to the Russian.

I want to grab her hand and bring her into my bungalow, but instead I just say, "Thanks for saving me."

"Anytime." She smiles and my heart flutters a bit, and she lingers a second, as if waiting for me to say something, but I can't manage anything, so I smile back and then go inside, taking care to lock the door behind me.

twenty

I have no fucking idea why I show up to the next Sapphic Scribes workshop, but I do.

Spritzing my wrists with a silky musk, I'm confident that Ivy will not show.

She hates me. She called me a loser dyke. She has zero interest in seeing me ever.

When I click the Zoom link, I gulp some IPA from my coffee mug, confident her rectangle will be absent.

But I'm wrong.

It's there.

Ivy Parker. She's outside somewhere, somewhere green, maybe a park, maybe her ex kicked her out and she's living on the streets now. She's holding a book, which partially obscures her face.

The book is: *Perfume and Pain.*

"Whatcha reading, Ivy?" Todd asks.

"Oh, it's this lesbian pulp book I got for my thesis." Ivy bites her lip, looks right into the camera, right into my eyes. "Let me read you a few paragraphs."

"I'd love that," Todd says. "I always welcome an impromptu reading."

I consider shutting my laptop, but instead I move my arm only to empty the contents of my mug into my throat.

Ivy begins reading. "The perfume—" Ivy clears her throat. "The perfume in her nostrils. Aunt Peg's hands and lips were marvelous, but the perfume was like a spur inciting her own body to action—the perfumed flesh was a treasure that she had to have. The dark negligee was gone now and the defenseless flesh, pale and perfumed, was hers for the taking. The heaving breasts, the trembling thighs—did she need words to tell her what to do?"

Ivy stops and looks around, then says, "Sound familiar?"

"It does," Todd says. "Where have I heard that before?"

"Astrid plagiarized it!" Ivy beams.

Todd looks like he's been shot.

"Wow," he says. "Wow, okay. This is really catching me off guard. I want to get to Pia's pages, but I'd be an irresponsible moderator if I didn't take some time to address this very serious news."

I know I can shut my laptop, but I don't. A part of me must want to be punished.

"As a published author of countless works," Todd begins, "I take plagiarism very, *very* seriously. I'm beyond hurt, Astrid, that you would disrespect all of us by handing in someone else's writing."

He pauses, perhaps waiting for me to say something, but I'm silent.

"You know, Astrid," Todd says, "I actually wasn't familiar with your work until my wife looked at my roster and informed me she's a fan of yours."

Oh my God. Todd has a wife. He's not even a fag! Jesus, what a freak.

"I checked out your book about the reality television star from our local library and I must say"—he pauses—"it struck me as very vapid and unpleasant."

Flinching a bit, I beg God to put another sip of alcohol into my mug. But it remains empty.

"For this reason, I was blown away by the pages you handed in for your workshop. They were pulsing with life and energy and desire; a far cry from the trendy nihilism of your first book." He adjusts his glasses, then looks right into his camera. "I'm devastated to learn you didn't write these pages."

Again, I say nothing.

"And as a lesbian scholar in this oft-discarded genre," Ivy says as a fly crosses her face, "I'm especially offended."

"I can't imagine how crushed you must feel, Ivy," Todd says. "As a fierce ally of the LGBTQIA+ community, I must say I'm also crushed that you would do this, Astrid Dahl." Todd rubs the bridge of his nose. "And I'm certain your grandfather Roald would be very, *very* disappointed." He pauses again. "I think we should take a five-minute break and regroup from this shock."

Before people start turning off their cameras, I blurt out, "It's not plagiarism; it's pastiche! It's *homage*!" I remember from my one year of law school that plagiarism only warrants legal action if it infringes upon the original author's copyright, and I'm pretty sure the copyright on this out-of-print book from 1962 has lapsed, and either way I presented the pages to a Zoom writing workshop, not the public marketplace, but it's not worth getting into it with these morons. Instead of defending myself further, I look right at Todd's little Zoom square and say, "Give your wife my number!" Then I throw up a peace sign and shut my laptop.

twenty-one

In bed that night I try to open Ivy's Instagram, but she's already blocked me. Shame pulses through me in waves.

A soft, warm wind blows through the trees and into my room, fills it with the smell of eucalyptus. It's a pleasant, peaceful environment I've set up for myself, my little bungalow at the top of the hill, surrounded by fluttering eucalyptus leaves, in the glow of Himalayan salt lamps and lesbian nesting music, a far cry from the dusty neon-lit apartments of my early thirties from which party rap was always blasting. And yet, my emotional landscape remains the same. I continue to fall too quickly for women who are bad for me. I continue to take the Patricia Highsmith and put my foot in my mouth. I continue to offend people, to disappoint, to attract controversy.

I try to remember the name of Ivy's ex, the platinum blonde Samantha Ronson derivative. I want to say her name was Romy, or Ryan, or Sam, or Zoe, meaning I lack sufficient information to find her on social media.

Then I remember Sophie, my Lez Brat Pack cofounder and ex-flame, is in the same department as Ivy.

Hi doll, I text her. *I hope you're lezzing it up in lezbos. Q: What's up with Ivy Parker?* Sending this, I realize the name Ivy Parker is eerily similar to Vin Packer, the pseudonym of Marijane

Meaker, Patricia Highsmith's partner and writer of *Spring Fire*, credited as the very first lesbian pulp and the book that Ivy told me got her interested in the genre. *Is that even her real name?*

She responds almost immediately. *I was waiting for you to ask, Astrid Dahl.* Sophie always calls me by my first and last name. She might also think I'm related to Roald Dahl. *I don't know her well, but she's sort of infamous in my program. She was *very* adamant about getting into Sapphic Scribes. I had a feeling she had her eye on you and a feeling you'd be into her as she's hot and nutty and, yes, I suspect Ivy Parker is a pseudonym.*

Sophie's still typing.

Don't tell me you already slept with her.

I respond with an upside-down smiley face emoji.

God, Astrid! Sophie replies. *Well she's sexy, I'll give you that. But she's a famous woman-eater in our program. We call her Poison Ivy. Always has a girlfriend, always cheats.*

My stomach drops. *Does she have a girlfriend now?*

Last I checked she was dating Joey Silva. Sweet girl, really. Totally harmless and wrapped up in Ivy's sick games.

Do you know if they're still together?

Hold plz, Sophie writes.

God bless you lesbian yenta, I reply.

Waiting for Sophie to respond, I text Otto that he was right about Poison Ivy. It's nearly 3:00 a.m. in New York so I don't expect a response. I sip my beer and turn up the music, hoping Penelope will hear it and come tell me to turn it down, catch a glimpse of me in my black silk nightgown Ivy bought me in Camarillo, and think I look irresistible.

Ok yeah, Sophie responds, *my sources say she's still with Joey although its v tumultuous and Ivy cheats constantly . . . same shit diff dyke.*

While I'm thinking of what to type back, Sophie shoots off another text.

Sorry if that's not what you wanted to hear, babe . . . Prob for the best to get out sooner rather than later though.

The fact that Sophie is warning me about Ivy probably signifies Poison Ivy is particularly toxic. After I told Sophie I couldn't be exclusive with her—I liked her, just not enough to stop dating other people—she told me I was a sex and love addict. I'm pretty sure she called me a narcissist too. Eventually, we became cordial, but I don't think I'm someone she'd recommend to her friends. And yet, Ivy is even worse than me.

Blocking her number now, I say, then I do it.

Good girl, Sophie says, like I'm a rowdy dog. *Also! I'm back in like . . . a week. I never thought I'd miss America but here we are. I want a matcha latte. Buy me one when I'm back? I'm going to be subletting my cousin's place in Los Feliz.*

I know she just wants gossip, to hear about my experience with Poison Ivy, and maybe I'd like to meet up with her for the same reason. And, I suppose, I'm single now. Maybe Sophie and I will have a spark again. Maybe I can show her I'm a changed woman. I need to occupy my time somehow. Los Feliz is only a fifteen-minute drive from Eagle Rock, much closer than Santa Barbara.

Would love, I say.

twenty-two

Penelope's Volvo isn't in the driveway.

Drinking coffee and texting my friends, I periodically peek out the window. But the Volvo doesn't return. I go for a walk, and when I get back, the Volvo still isn't there. It isn't there that evening either, when I peek out of the window in between bites of Amy's, or the next morning, while I sip my coffee. I guess Penelope went out of town. Over the next few days, I continue to go on long walks to my Cat Power playlist and think about Penelope holding my hand. Whenever I get back, I look for the Volvo and every time it isn't there, I imagine her face between the Russian's legs. Maybe they went on a romantic getaway. Maybe they eloped to Vegas.

Have you talked to Penelope? I text Zev on day three.

She's in the desert, he replies.

I knew it. She's on a romantic getaway with the Russian. They're probably fucking in a hot tub that overlooks the San Jacinto mountains, picturesque and perfect.

For how long? I ask.

Why are you so interested all of a sudden? I thought you couldn't stand her.

I start to lie, type out *wondering how long I'll have the place to myself,* then delete it, decide to be honest. *She grew on me at the show.*

Oh yeah? Zev replies. I didn't tell Zev about Ivy's intrusion, about Penelope saving me, and I'm not sure if he saw us holding hands. If he were anyone else, I would say it was impossible to miss. But Zev is very oblivious to this sort of thing. *I think she'll be back on Friday.*

I check my calendar app. It's Tuesday. Three days. I can do this. I suppose I could ask Zev for her number and text her, but I'm not sure what I would say. I don't exactly know why I'm so desperate for her to be back either. All I know is I want to see her Volvo in the driveway. Actually, it feels like less of a want and more of a need.

:::::

That night in bed, I google *Penelope Greek mythology.* Apparently, Penelope was Odysseus's wife, famously faithful and extremely patient. She waited twenty years for him to return from the Trojan War. I try to channel that energy as I wait for the Volvo, which has been gone for a few days.

Before I go to bed, I FaceTime Otto and tell him what happened with Ivy.

"Normally it feels great to be right," Otto says. He's wearing a Versace robe and surrounded by flickering Diptyque candles. "But honestly? I wish I was wrong. I just want you to be happy, Astrid. We're too old for this shit."

When we hang up, I ask Sophie if she wants to get coffee on Wednesday.

twenty-three

Sophie wants to meet at a place called Go Get Em Tiger. She says it's where all the great "queer girl gossip" happens. Hearing both these things make me feel a bit nauseous, as does trying to find parking in Los Feliz. I'm grateful that I left the part of the city with metered parking.

Sophie is already seated with an iced matcha latte that matches her green sweater. She wears tortoiseshell glasses and a green ribbon in her hair, a precocious little brat. She looks up and says, "If it isn't Astrid Dahl."

"If it isn't the lesbian yenta of Southern Californian academia," I say.

We kiss cheeks, *faire la bise*, and I go to grab a cappuccino, remembering on the way that I was supposed to buy her matcha, so I grab her a cookie with green icing to match her outfit.

"Did you just think of someone other than yourself?" Sophie asks when I hand her the cookie. She takes a dainty nibble. "Also, you look great. Healthy."

"Is that a euphemism for fat?"

"It's a euphemism for . . ." Sophie pauses, sips her matcha, looks at the ceiling. "Less of a drunk?" She's a Twelve-Stepper, thinks everyone has a problem.

"I haven't had a drink in . . ." It was the concert and thinking about it makes my stomach swirl. "Six days." Two days until Penelope is back from the desert.

Sophie shakes her head. "So, Astrid Dahl and Poison Ivy."

"Seven weeks in hell," I say.

"Wow," Sophie says. "How did you last so long?"

I tell her about the Zoom flirtation, about our dates in Oxnard and Camarillo, the hotels and the lingerie. I leave out a few things, like the *I love you* exchange at Johnny Rockets on our third date and the great plagiarism snafu, but Sophie seems nonetheless concerned.

"You know, Astrid," Sophie says. "When you're dating someone who doesn't let you post pictures of them on the internet or go to the place they live, you might consider backing off."

"Yeah, yeah," I say. Sophie is right. "It's like I go blind."

"You need to go to a SLAA meeting," she says.

"Tell me about your love life," I say. "Since you're such an expert."

"Oh, honey." She bites her lip. "Those who can't do teach."

I consider asking Sophie about Penelope, if she knows her, but decide against it. I'm sure Penelope went to grad school, probably art school, probably CalArts or maybe somewhere in Boston, Emerson or something. But Sophie would inevitably return the subject to SLAA if I told her I'm not even thinking about Ivy anymore, that instead I'm thinking about a woman who, when I first met her, was baking a cake for her ex-girlfriend.

Instead, I ask Sophie about her dissertation. She shows me a photo of a painting on her phone from 1811 called *Sappho Recalled to Life by the Charm of Music*. In it, Sappho is passed out on a fainting couch while some old guy holds her head, and these young nymph-like women play harps and shit. Sophie tells me Sappho's allegedly melancholic over being rejected by this dude Phaon.

"*Pardon?*" I say. "Dude?"

"Well," says Sophie. "I have theories about that." Sophie tells me that in Greek mythology, Phaon was a mythical boatman in Lesbos. He was old and ugly but gave a free boat ride to Aphrodite, who rewarded him with an ointment that made him young and beautiful. Sophie read this to mean it made him into a woman. Enter Sappho. She fell madly in love with Phaon and was so distraught by Phaon's rejection that she threw herself in the sea.

"Damn," I say. "Lesbian pulp."

Sophie laughs. "Exactly."

I laugh, too, but then become uneasy, mentally aligning my own romantic tragedies with those of Sappho, being recalled to life by the charm of Cat Power.

"Why did Phaon reject her?" I ask, nervous that Phaon left Sappho for a prettier Russian.

"I think he just got bored," Sophie says. "Sappho was very extra."

I sip my cappuccino and it burns my tongue.

:::

On the street outside the coffee shop, Sophie again tells me to go to a SLAA meeting, and I tell her we should get drinks instead. She smiles and she says I'm "bad news." She also tells me I may think Ivy is gone, but she's not. She'll be back. She doesn't give up. "Taurus moon," she says, and I want to get into that, Taurus girls, Taurus exes, their undying persistence, the most stalkerish sign, but I burned my interest in astrology with the full moon. Sophie also says Ivy has an anonymous Tumblr on which she documents her sexploits, which everyone knows is her except, miraculously, her girlfriends. It's called *The Demons That Tempt*

Me, which is, of course, an *L Word* reference, the name of Jenny Schecter's short story collection.

I tell Sophie about how Ivy said lesbian relationships are inherently histrionic and that is in fact the thesis of her dissertation.

"Oh, I know," Sophie says. "The girl is deranged." She clicks open her Prius. "I'll let you know when you're up."

"What do you mean?"

"On Ivy's Tumblr!" she says.

"No thanks," I say, then, in a Valerie Cherish voice, "I don't want to see that."

"I do," says Sophie.

"Hey," I say, over Ivy as a subject, "now that you're back, can we change the group name back to Lez Brat Pack? Sapphic Scribes is corny as hell."

Sophie scrunches her nose. "So is Lez Brat Pack."

I look up, thinking. She isn't wrong.

"And the bisexuals don't like it," Sophie continues.

"What bisexuals?" I ask.

"Everyone is fluid now," Sophie says. "And Sappho is hot." I frown as Sophie gets in her car and says, "Bye Astrid." I wave good-bye and walk over to my Subaru.

Tucked under my windshield wiper is a parking ticket for $75.

twenty-four

Back home I'm paying my parking ticket online when I notice a missed call from Agent Allison. No text. I'm really not in the mood for bad news, especially not after the parking ticket.

As I plug in my credit card information, I become convinced Agent Allison is calling about that interview I did with the queer literary journal, convinced the journal quoted the slightly offensive answer I told them to strike, convinced Satchels of Gold found out about the interview and they want to rescind the deal.

A text pops up on my MacBook. *Do you have a second to chat?*

I call her back. "I told them to strike it from the record," I say when she answers.

"Wait," Agent Allison says. "Strike what from the record?"

"What are you calling about?" I ask.

"Satchels of Gold update," Agent Allison says. "But you're scaring me. Strike what?"

"Oh, that queer literary journal interview," I say. "I said something I told them to strike."

"Jesus, Astrid," Agent Allison says. "I told you, no interviews. You're supposed to be laying low right now. No interviews, no women, no drugs!"

"I'm trying my best," I say. But I'm not sure that's true.

Agent Allison says she was calling to tell me production is

starting, so I should get my second option check soon. I don't know why she didn't just email me. I'm such an idiot. Why did I have to tell her I fucked up? Why can't I keep literally anything to myself?

"How bad is it?" Agent Allison asks. "The interview."

"It's not bad," I say. "I told them to strike it from the record."

"Okay," Agent Allison says with hesitance.

We hang up, and I am certain my writing career is over.

I make a Pinterest board to brainstorm how I'll redecorate my childhood bedroom.

:::::

Zev and I walk through the neighborhood as the sun sets. I try to focus on the pretty sky instead of my dead writing career or Penelope stroking the Russian. On a particularly steep hill that invigorates me, pumping endorphins to my brain, I notice Zev's poodle Jackie-O has a limp.

"Is she okay?" I ask.

"She hurt her paw," Zev says. "I told you this."

"What happened?"

"I'm not sure," Zev says. "The vet couldn't figure it out, so he did some tests."

"I'm sorry," I say. I can tell Zev is scared. He's rarely scared, but he loves Jackie-O in a way he doesn't love humans. He puts all his human need for attention and affection into that dog. I often worry about what will happen to Zev when he inevitably outlives her. "Let me know if there is anything I can do," I say.

"It's fine," Zev says. He seems a little pissed at me, probably because I didn't remember that he already told me this. "Penelope drove us to the vet before she left."

That familiar mini rage swirls inside me, then quickly dissipates. I'm not angry at Penelope. It's very sweet she drove Jackie-O to the vet. Zev has a lot of driving anxiety.

"Do you know what she's doing in the desert?" Again, I imagine Penelope licking the inside of the Russian's thigh.

"Some artist retreat," Zev says, and I'm relieved. But what if Penelope and the Russian are at the artist retreat together? Maybe with the journalist who threw me under the bus and ruined my career. And they're all fucking in a weird orgy designed to ruin my life.

Then I remember that article hasn't even come out. That the journalist didn't necessarily throw me under the bus. That I don't even know if Penelope is fucking the Russian or even likes her. That my career isn't necessarily over. That Agent Allison was just calling to tell me I'm about to get a check. That I'm paranoid.

"I have to get Jackie-O home," Zev says as soon as we reach his car. He leaves in a hurry, and I'm left alone with my freaky thoughts.

: : : :

Penelope has no social media presence, which makes my obsession difficult to nurture. But I find photos of her art on various gallery websites. I almost think of buying a piece—a self-portrait combining Penelope's face and the body of Penelope the Greek queen—but decide against it.

Sophie was right; Ivy pops up again. I blocked her number and she blocked me on Instagram, but Google makes blocking email annoyingly difficult. I imagine the feature was installed by an incel with zero experience being stalked, only stalking, hence why the application favors the latter.

The subject line says: *I'm sorry.*

I'm tempted to open it. With Penelope's Volvo gone, I'm desperate for some interpersonal drama, for the push and pull of a toxic romance. I want to forgive Ivy, to have makeup sex. To forget myself in someone else's pheromones, in her metallic orchid perfume.

I screengrab the subject line and send Ivy's email to Sophie. Then I delete the email.

Sophie responds, *Told you she'd be back!* Then, *Waiting with bated breath for the Tumblr post.*

You seem to be enjoying this, I write back to Sophie.

I am, she replies with a dancing girl emoji.

I know I need to figure out how to be alone with myself, with my feelings, without a target or audience. But that feels impossible. Transferring my romantic energy onto Sophie is not entirely innocent, but it feels marginally better than reengaging with Ivy.

Well, it's better for me. And maybe it's better for Sophie too. Maybe Sophie is using me the same way I'm using her. Aren't we all using each other? As a distraction? From death?

Sophie and I spend the night texting, about girls, about *The L Word*, about novels we've recently loved.

We text until I fall asleep.

I wake up in the middle of the night cradling my iPhone like a baby.

twenty-five

All day Thursday, my body trembles with anticipation. One more day. I'm not sure what I'm expecting when Penelope comes home. I just know I need to see her Volvo in the driveway. I feel like the Greek Penelope, symbol of fidelity, waiting for Odysseus to return from the Trojan War.

To kill the hours, I drive to the niche perfume store that sparked my obsession. It's on Beverly Boulevard in Fairfax, the historic center of the city's Jewish community, home to LA's Holocaust museum and Canter's Deli, but also lots of streetwear stores and the iconic outdoor mall, The Grove. It's nearly a forty-minute drive from my house, which seems like a nice opportunity to listen to roughly thirteen Cat Power songs. *Sappho Recalled to Life by the Charm of Music.*

I haven't been to the perfume store in a few months, but upon entering, I immediately vow to come more often. The vibes are impeccable. Philip Glass is playing and both employees are hot—a woman with silver hair that hangs below her tits and a streetwear twink with cheekbones that rival Otto's—and the shoppers are also hot—a blonde and a redhead, both imperceptible ages due to expensive poreless skin, and I'm pretty sure I've seen them both on television. Everyone in the store is chatting, animated, high, and handing each other little tester strips to sniff, like we're in the bathroom at the Chateau Marmont and someone has exceptionally pure cocaine.

"Here," says the blonde suspected television actress when I walk through the door. She hands me a test strip. "It smells like a buttery croissant from the streets of Paris."

I take it in my hand, sniff, and she's right, I could eat the paper. "I'm not sure I want to smell like a croissant," I say.

"Me neither," she says. "But isn't it amazing?"

And it is, and it's probably the Philip Glass, but I'm convinced I've stepped into *The Hours* or—better yet—*Mrs. Dalloway*.

"Smell this," says the redheaded suspected actress, who I now think looks exactly like Julianne Moore in *The Hours*. I take the test strip and sniff, and it smells so chic, the world's rarest rose.

"Decadent," I say.

"Right?"

The silver-haired employee asks me what I'm into, and I almost tell her to buy me dinner first, but instead I say I want to smell "enigmatic."

"Of course," the blonde suspected actress says, not in a rude way.

"Who doesn't," says the redhead.

"I like to smell like sex," says the twink.

"Oh, me too," says the redhead, and we all agree that we want to smell like elusive fucking.

The twink and the silver fox retrieve a bunch of perfumes in ornate bottles, each more inventive than the next. We all try each scent and, based on the redheaded actress's encouragement, I get free samples of a niche amber and a spicy rose. When I leave, I'm shocked that the redhead hugs me. I drive home upset that I'll never see her again, but happy to have found such a nice community, a place where I felt warm and accepted and didn't once think about Penelope or Ivy or the Patricia Highsmith or my dead career.

When I get home, I take a bath and read Anne Boyer's *Garments Against Women*, a book of lyric essays Zev gave me a while ago. I read online that Boyer was one of seven queer Whiting Award winners in 2018. Queer women, Sophie told me recently, dominate literature. She cited me as one of them and I laughed. I've never won any award.

"You know, Astrid," she said. "You might be happier if you accepted your success."

I said, "I'm not queer." Then, "I don't have a PhD or a boyfriend. And I don't shop at Target."

She told me to stop being difficult, and I told her that was easier said than done.

Coated in bubbles, I read this one Anne Boyer paragraph over and over. I take a picture and send it to Zev and also Sophie.

After the bath, I click around on the fragrance subreddits and make a Google Doc organizing all the perfume samples I've tried, which houses and notes and accords I love—amber, musk, black tea—and despise—tuberose, powder, gourmands (why people want to smell like food is beyond me). I fantasize about starting my own perfume line, a thought that excites me in the way the thought of writing a novel once did, back when I didn't realize how hard it would be, in the early days of the Lez Brat Pack when the publishing world felt like a code I was about to crack. I start brainstorming names and notes.

patricia highsmith: tobacco, bourbon, pine

lunar palm: sand and the moon

acrylic nails on breasts: plastic and milk

twink: sunscreen and poppers

los angeles: marine layer and car exhaust

penelope: patchouli and pheromones

I imagine the bottles, tinted blue or green glass, adorned with minimalist sans serif font, blankish slates on which to project.

I'll call the brand something like: Please God Let Me Be Anyone But Myself.

: : : :

At midnight, I'm still buzzing. So, I light a chamomile candle and take a ZzzQuil.

In bed, I screen *The Favourite* on my laptop and realize Penelope looks a bit like Rachel Weisz, my top celebrity crush along with Penelope Cruz and Sonja Morgan and, fine, Kris Jenner.

As the ZzzQuil hits, I imagine Penelope in a corset, fucking me from behind, then start googling SLAA meetings on my phone.

I text Sophie a photo of Rachel Weisz shooting a rifle and Sophie responds with a drooling face emoji. Then she says, *Is it the Unisom or did I just see photos of you and Kat Gold on lesbian Instagram?*

Old news, I respond. It was like three weeks ago, I think. Time is elusive. Kat Gold and I have texted some since, but Ivy's words wormed their way into my brain, that Kat Gold loves attaching herself to tragic dykes, and I'm the most tragic dyke of all.

Astrid!!!! Sophie responds, *When you hang out with an extremely hot queer-identifying celebrity who's well-versed in Foucault, you absolutely must tell me. I'm the first person you should tell. Do you understand? This is serious.*

You think she's hot? I respond.

Oh my god Astrid were you dropped on your head? Of course she's hot! She's like universally recognized as the hottest person alive!!!

Zev finally responds to my text from the tub. *I've been trying to get you to read that book for six years.*

He's angry with me.

When the ZzzQuil starts to make my head pleasantly fuzzy, I receive a text from an unknown number.

Did you get my email? I'm sorry, Astrid.

Poison Ivy. I'm very tempted to respond. Penelope's Volvo is still gone and I'm buzzing on diphenhydramine and I need to fill the void. I used to get off on fighting. I went to law school for one year for a reason.

I know I should delete the text, disengage. But my thumb hovers over the reply box. I type out: *Are you texting me from your girlfriend's phone?* Just as I'm about to hit Send, another text floats in from a different unknown number that my phone thinks "might be Penelope Paladino."

My veins throb.

What a great name. Alliterative. Rhythmic. Lyrical. Perfect.

I open the text.

Hi Astrid, the text says, *I've been meaning to check in, but this is a wireless retreat. I'm breaking the rules. But I've been thinking about you and wishing for your safety. I'll be back tomorrow. I hope you're well.* —Penelope

My palms are sweating all over my phone and it almost slips from my hand.

I compose and delete several texts.

Finally, I send, simply: *Thnx for checking. I'm safe.*

Penelope puts a thumbs-up on the text. Platonic. The Russian is probably between her legs right this second.

Another text floats in. My cells flutter.

Also do you mind bringing in my mail?

It's as if someone popped a water balloon on my head. I must have been dreaming when I saw Penelope as anything other than an entitled bitch who thinks I work for her.

I put a thumbs-up on her text.

twenty-six

I wake just a few hours after finally dozing off at around 4:00 a.m. I downloaded the audiobook of Donna Tartt's *The Secret History*, which Sophie recommended because Donna Tartt herself reads the audio version. I tell Sophie I typically prefer voice actors for audiobooks, and it's true—I would never pay to hear myself read my own book—but Sophie says this is an exception. She's right. Donna has this syrupy Mississippi accent that is completely hypnotizing. The novel stars a Californian who's a fish out of water at an elite New England college, which I assume is based on Bennington College, where Tartt herself went with Bret Easton Ellis. Listening, I'm grateful I didn't go to school in New England like my college counselor wanted me to. Also, I fall in love with Donna's voice.

Unable to go back asleep, I walk through the hills and watch the sky turn different shades of pink and purple and listen to Donna. Under the shade of a tree, I google photos of Donna looking unbearably sexy in her black bob and men's suits. Apparently she dated a lot of gay men, Bret included, and I can see why—she's a bit of a twink. I text Sophie, *any chance Donna is one of us?* Then, *I'm in love.*

Sophie responds quickly, *I've heard rumors.* Then, *Did you find a SLAA meeting?*

Donna would make a perfect wife. We'd live in the country and read each other's drafts and I'd become a much better writer. She would read to me every night, and I would have the most perfect sleep. I'm blissed out in the daydream until I get back home and the Volvo still isn't there.

I open our shared mailbox and it's empty.

. . . .

It's only 9:00 a.m., but I open a beer and sip it in silence while texting Sophie and Zev and Otto. Zev doesn't respond, but Otto and Sophie do. Otto and I text about the *Real Housewives of Miami* reboot. Sophie and I text about Judy Poovey, our agreed-upon favorite character in *The Secret History*, a California girl with "wild clothes, frosted hair, a red Fiat with California plates bearing the legend JUDY P."

Ivy has a Fiat, I text Sophie. *Barbie pink.*

Sophie writes back, *you think I don't know about the Bitchmobile?*

When I finish my beer, I put on some BB cream and mascara, and my favorite white T-shirt, my most flattering Levi's, Levi's that would make Kristen Stewart jealous. While I vehemently reject Kristen Stewart as a sex icon (because why her and not me?), I do like her personal style. She's a delicate tomboy, which is always how I've seen myself. She isn't afraid to show off her legs and her abs, and she'll wear Chanel with Sambas at Cannes. She's blonde right now to promote *Spencer*, and she's dressing more femme, in pinks and baby blues, ribbons, too, an elegant bottom, aspirational.

I spritz myself with a sample of a niche French perfume that's supposed to smell like tattooed women smoking cigarillos. Fragrantica—essentially Rotten Tomatoes for perfume—identifies its primary notes as woody, aromatic, and fresh spicy, and reviews say it's a knockoff of Santal 33, the cherished scent of Kat Gold and most people who claim to be gluten intolerant. But a few weeks ago, I went on the r/fragrance subreddit and asked if anyone had recommendations, writing something along the lines of: *elusive fragrance for an aspiring it girl?* I got samples of most of the recs, unless they were made by mainstream luxury brands, or if the person recommending seemed insane or had an anime avatar. I like this one, even if it's a Le Labo knockoff. At least it's actually French, as opposed to knockoff French like Le Labo, which is based in New York and smells like new money.

Smelling exquisite, I lie on the couch with my phone above my head and click around with manic fingers. Somehow I end up inside a *Marie Claire* article from 2014, in which Kristen Stewart is asked about a poem she wrote called "My Heart Is a Wiffle Ball/Freedom Pole." She tells the interviewer, "I don't want to sound so fucking utterly pretentious, but after I write something, I go, 'Holy fuck, that's crazy.'" To my iPhone screen I say, "You and me both, sis."

. . . .

By the time the Volvo finally arrives at around 11:15, I've read Kristen Stewart's poem eleven times and am starting to think it's good, particularly the line "I'll suck the bones pretty," which is probably a reference to the vampire franchise that made her famous. I'm also a little drunk.

Looking out the window, I worry the Volvo is a mirage. I dart outside with *Garments Against Women*, try to look as though I've been out there reading for hours, not inside drinking beer and staring at Kristen Stewart's bad poetry on my iPhone. I'd prefer to be listening to *The Secret History*, but an audiobook has no aesthetic.

"I love that book," Penelope says to my copy of Anne Boyer when she arrives at the top of the stone steps, slightly out of breath in a way that turns me on. I want to suck her bones pretty.

"Oh," I say, pretending I didn't know she was coming, pretending I haven't been rabidly awaiting her, that I've been enjoying the time to myself, that I'm chill and haven't been imagining her in bed with another woman. "Welcome home."

Penelope drops her leather duffel beside the chair across from me and sits down. She's wearing a paint-stained Joy Division T-shirt, cutoff jean shorts that reveal legs darkened by the desert sun.

"Thanks," she says.

"How was the retreat?" My heart thrashes in my chest. I wish I had more alcohol. Beads of sweat develop under my arms.

"It was great," Penelope says. "So beautiful. Really magical. Great people, great energy." She flicks a tiny leaf off her T-shirt. "But I was a little distracted."

"Yeah?" I dig a fingernail into my palm. She was certainly there with Nadia. Maybe Laura too. Maybe it was just some bird-like femme fuck fest.

"I was worried about you," she says. "That was really intense the other night."

My heart jumps. She wasn't distracted by Nadia or Laura. She was distracted by me.

"Eh," I say, cool as a cucumber, not shaken by the reveal that she was thinking about me, not trembling and sweating profusely, not desperate for alcohol to calm my nerves. "It wasn't the first time a girlfriend has gone loco on me."

I laugh, but Penelope doesn't. I guess it isn't funny. Historically, I play these things off as humor, as a show, as "material." I think I can keep the hysteria at a distance, that it won't affect me, that I can take the good—the mania, the spontaneity, the laughs—without the bad—the neediness, the aggression, the cruelty. And maybe people put up with me for the same reason.

"But I really appreciate you helping me," I say. I mean it. "It would have taken much longer without you."

"No problem," she says. "I know what it's like."

She picks up her duffel and my heart sinks. She can't leave. Not now. I need her. But I can't think of anything to say. And soon she's walking away.

When she's gone, I go inside and pour another beer into a mug, then return to my reading spot. I figure if I stay out here all day, she'll come back. I stay and read and periodically go inside to get more beer. I text Sophie and Otto and watch the light move around the yard, illuminating different plants as the sun moves. The sky changes from bright blue to harsh whitish blue to warm orange blue to purple blue to salmon blue to gray blue to navy blue. And Penelope doesn't return.

By the time the sky is dark, I am cold and drunk and desperate. Everything feels very unfair. A month ago, all I wanted was for Penelope to leave me alone. And now I finally want her to bother me, and she's suddenly as elusive as a clouded leopard.

I realize I haven't eaten all day and heat up an Amy's frozen meal, the kind that Penelope told me to stop eating. Hopefully, she smells it and comes over to scold me.

But she doesn't.

I watch the *Kardashians* episode where Caitlyn comes out as trans while shoving melted cheese into my mouth.

I burn my tongue.

When Khloe starts crying, Sophie texts: *the post is up.*

twenty-seven

I tell Sophie I'm not going to read the post, so Sophie sends me screenshots. I tell her I'm turning off my phone. But instead of doing that, I text Penelope, almost automatically. *Ivy wrote about me on her dumb Tumblr.*

You okay? she writes back. *You want me to come over?*

I do want her to come over. But I don't want to tell her I want her to come over.

I'm okay, I write back, hand shaking slightly, then get in the shower.

While I'm toweling off, there's a knock on my door. I put on the black silk kimono Ivy bought me at Victoria's Secret, and—now my whole body shaking, a light vibration, not entirely unpleasant—go open it.

Penelope is wearing an oversized cashmere sweater over what appears to be a nightgown. She's holding a bottle of red wine.

"This is for me," she says, holding up the wine. "It was a sober retreat, and I know you only have beer."

"I know it's very masc of me to drink beer," I say. "Embarrassing."

Penelope is already scanning my cabinets. I didn't invite her in, and just a week ago this would have bothered me, her entitlement to my space, but at this moment it feels intimate, an act of love not aggression. Penelope pours herself a glass of wine and pours a beer for me. She hands me my glass and I admire the golden bubbles.

"Women dominated the beer industry for most of history," she tells me, sitting down. "In the seventeenth century, women brewers were accused of witchcraft. And drinking beer increases estrogen, so some could argue it's the most femme thing you could drink."

"How do you know all that?" I ask, turned on. I've always been drawn to women who sound like encyclopedias.

Penelope just shrugs. I put on my Cat Power playlist and turn on two Himalayan salt lamps, so the room is bathed in a warm, orange glow. Womblike. I sip my witches' brew.

Penelope puts her feet up on my coffee table, like she did the first time she came over, when I was disgusted by her presence and desperate for her to leave, but this time I imagine putting her toes in my mouth.

I consider sitting next to her on the couch, then decide to sit in the millennial pink shell chair across from her instead.

"So, what did Poison Ivy write?" Penelope asks, curling her lip a bit to signify she's in on the joke. She takes a big sip of her wine.

"I didn't read it," I say.

"What!"

"No interest."

"How can you resist?" Penelope asks. "And how do you know about it?"

"My friend Sophie told me." I sip my beer.

Penelope raises her eyebrow at me.

"She knows Ivy, she's getting her PhD at UCSB."

"Sophie who?"

"Lyonne," I say. "Like Natasha."

Penelope presses her lips together. "I think I've met her."

My heart sinks a bit. How did they meet? Tinder? Did they go on a date? Did they fuck? I sip some beer.

"So, Sophie told me Ivy is infamous at UCSB for being—as you and Otto predicted—very toxic. She has an anonymous Tumblr called *The Demons That Tempt Me* about her sexual exploits and I guess everyone knows it's her." I sip my beer. "And OH, she has a girlfriend."

Penelope is silent. She sips her wine, looks at her lap. "I sensed that," she says.

"Pardon?"

"I just got the feeling that she was hiding something." Penelope flips her hair to the other side. "And then when we were watching that movie. You were pretty gone."

I slide my green amethyst along its chain.

"She said she had to go to the bathroom and I heard her on the phone. It definitely sounded like some sort of lover's quarrel," she says. "Otto and I debated telling you but decided against it because we didn't have definitive proof, and also you seemed so smitten."

I put my hands over my face, embarrassed.

Penelope reaches over the coffee table and taps my arm playfully.

The contact of her skin against my skin sends a sharp electrical current throughout my body.

"Don't be embarrassed," she says. "Especially not with me. I'm the queen of ignoring red flags. The *queen*."

"I find that hard to believe," I say.

She shakes her head.

"You seem like you have your shit together," I say.

"You should have seen me when I was your age." Penelope smirks. "Let me read the post," she says. "I'll read it for you."

"Fuck no," I say. "You've seen enough of me."

"Come on." She reaches over and jabs my ribs.

"Stop," I squeal, wildly ticklish under normal circumstances, but at the moment it's unbearable.

"Let me read it," she says.

"Fine," I say. "Fine!"

I send her the link that Sophie sent me. All I saw was the title of the post: *Perfume & Pain*.

"Let me guess," I say while Penelope focuses on her phone. "She calls me an alcoholic. A narcissist. A sex and love addict."

"Check, check," Penelope says, her eyes flitting over the screen. "*And* check."

"Cluster B personality disorder? More than one?"

"She says you have all of them," Penelope says. Then, "This makes her seem way worse than you. She's clearly unhinged. Also, she gave you a fake name."

"Ooh," I say. "Who am I?" I suppose I mean this literally and metaphorically.

"Asterix Doll," she says. "D-o-l-l."

"Oooh," I say. "I love it. The Kardashians all call each other 'doll.'"

"I asked Otto if you were related to Roald," Penelope says.

"And let me guess, he said"—I pause to locate my best fag voice—"'*She wishes.*'"

Penelope laughs. "You seem fine."

I tilt my head at her.

"When you texted, I thought you were upset."

"You thought I wanted you to hold me while I cried?" Of course, that is exactly what I want.

"I would never expect that from you." Penelope corks her wine, then stands up. My stomach sinks. She can't be leaving. Not now.

Tell her you're sad, my inner voice screams. *Tell her you need her!*

"I should go to bed," Penelope says. "I hardly slept at that retreat."

My stomach tightens. The Russian was at the retreat. Penelope was busy pleasing her, braiding her hair, whispering sweet nothings in her ear, not sleeping at all. Nadia is probably waiting in her apartment right now, legs agape, spread-eagle.

Penelope doesn't like me; she's worried about me. I'm like a sick, stray cat she's nursing to health out of pity.

"Okay," I say, and Penelope disappears.

twenty-eight

I spend the entire next day in the yard and somehow never once see Penelope. She must be holed up working, or maybe she's avoiding me. I could go over there, invent a lie about how I need sugar, or text her that I'm suddenly upset about Ivy's Tumblr post, but I want her to come to me. With no writing to occupy me, no Ivy, I spend most of my time texting Sophie, pretending she's Penelope. I finish *Garments Against Women* (it's short) and then listen to *The Secret History* (it's long) on my headphones until it's too cold to be outside and return first thing the next morning.

. . . .

Zev asks me to go on a walk and I invite him over instead, not wanting to leave the grounds and perhaps miss an opportunity to see Penelope. Plus, Zev is a Penelope magnet.

Right after Zev texts me to say he's on his way, Otto texts me, *you okay?*

I'm fine, I say. *Zev is coming over.*

You know I'm sort of a PR genius, he writes back, *if you need my help.*

Now I'm confused. *Huh?*

He calls me. "People are talking about you on Twitter," he says. "You didn't see?"

"No," I say. I've opened Twitter roughly five times today, but I'm not demented enough to search my own name, and I muted Google alerts a long time ago.

"Yeah," he says. "Poison Ivy wrote some Tumblr post, and someone else posted it, saying 'Asterix Doll' is clearly you. Some people are weighing in."

I'm annoyed at Otto for telling me this. What people are saying about me online is none of my business. I'm also surprised that Otto's Twitter feed, surely filled with bitchy fashion gays and campy D-list celebrities, picked up this literary lesbian gossip.

"How did you even find this?" I ask.

"A lesbian in my office sent the thread to me," Otto says. I consider asking her name, to see if I've ever seen her on Tinder on one of my visits to New York, and if not, to see if she's single—I love a fashion lesbian. Otto worked for Diane von Furstenberg and said she was always preying on young female interns, a titillating visual.

My phone lights up with another call. It's Allison.

"My agent is calling," I tell him.

"Text me," he says, and we hang up.

Agent Allison is already talking. "You should write something to get on top of it. Maybe a Medium post."

"Is that necessary?" I ask. Across the yard, Penelope peeks through her blinds, then disappears so quickly I wonder if I imagined it.

"Yes, Astrid," she says. "And you really need to cut the shit. You said you were taking a break from women."

Suddenly Zev is hovering above me, and I tell Allison I have to go, partially because I don't want to be rude to Zev but also I'm convinced she's going to drop me if I stay on the phone.

"Everything okay?" Zev asks.

A text from Kat Gold pops up. *Heartbreaker!!!*

"Yeah," I say to Zev. "Poison Ivy wrote about me. Doesn't matter."

Zev says nothing for a few seconds. "Jackie-O's paw is worse," Zev says finally. "I knew you weren't going to ask."

"I'm sorry," I say. "Do you want some gin?"

"Please," he says.

When I return with a beer for myself and gin for Zev, Penelope—as expected—is in my portion of the yard, chatting with Zev. I wonder why it took Zev coming over for her to leave her bungalow. Is she afraid of me alone?

She's wearing a T-shirt as a dress and paint-splattered Birkenstocks. Her hair is tangled and her eyeliner smudged. I know this look. She is positively postcoital.

I gulp my beer.

Penelope looks right into my eyes. "How are you holding up?"

"What were *you* just doing?" I ask with a wink I immediately regret. Otto told me that when I try to wink it looks like I'm having a stroke.

"Painting," Penelope says, but I don't believe her. "My lesbian group chat is popping off. You're the talk of the town. This is what you wanted, right?"

"Wrong," I say. While I have on occasion, and perhaps on the internet at this precise moment, been labeled an "attention whore," I would prefer to go unnoticed. I would prefer to write things no one reads, at least not my loved ones, only a faceless, nameless audience that derives immense pleasure from my books, quiet people without Goodreads accounts, ideally without internet connections entirely.

"Poison Ivy is really the only one who looks bad," Penelope says.

"I have to go," says Zev suddenly. He's pissed. "Jackie-O is sick and I don't have time for Astrid's never-ending cycle of self-created melodrama. It's boring."

He storms off.

And, surprising myself, I start to cry.

Penelope rubs my back and then I cry harder. I'm unsure exactly why I'm crying. But it feels incredible. I read online once that crying releases a chemical compound akin to morphine. I hardly ever cry so I'd forgotten how good it feels. Then I remember what triggered the tears, my being a bad friend to Zev, him hurting my feelings, and also people are talking about me online, saying horrible things, so bad that my agent thinks I need to write a Medium post to address them.

"I'm a horrible person," I say.

"You aren't," Penelope says, and I realize this is all I wanted when I kept waiting for her Volvo to appear. I wanted her to rub my back while I cry.

My gaze meets her almond-shaped eyes, and I become self-conscious.

"I should call him," I say. "Or should we bring something for Jackie-O?"

"That's a good idea," Penelope says.

. . . .

Penelope drives me to a fancy pet store. I pick out a "doggy get well" package, and Penelope says I should pick a different one because Jackie-O prefers bones to biscuits. I'm ashamed that Penelope, who's only known Jackie-O for roughly a month, knows this and I, who's known Jackie-O since she was a puppy, don't. But I trust her and buy the bone-abundant package.

When Zev answers the door, he looks tired and sad. Jackie-O, who is normally peppy and alert, is asleep on the rug.

I hand Zev the care package, and he apologizes. "I'm sorry for snapping at you," he says. "I'm just really stressed about Jackie-O."

Penelope walks over to the dog and rubs her head. "Is she eating?"

I wish I had Penelope's natural knack for caretaking. I wish I was more feminine in this way: more nurturing, less cavalier.

"Not really," Zev says. "I called the doctor and the tests aren't back yet. I have a bad feeling it's cancer."

"I don't think so," Penelope says. "She probably has an infection. She just needs antibiotics. She'll be better soon."

I can tell Zev is comforted by Penelope's words, although I doubt she knows what she's talking about. Maybe she does. I hope she's right.

"Do you want to watch *Real Housewives of Atlanta*?" I ask Zev, my best attempt at emotional support. It's his favorite franchise.

"That's okay," he says. "I think I just need to be alone for a bit."

"Let us know if you need anything," Penelope says. "Jackie-O will be okay." Penelope kisses Jackie-O's forehead, and it seems as though she's transferring some kind of positive healing energy, like when she petted my back while I cried. I don't fuck with astrology anymore but I am positive Penelope is a water sign—intuitive, witchy, the most womanly.

"Feel better, Jackie-O," I say to the dog without touching her.

. . . .

Back in the Volvo without a task to occupy me, I'm nervous, edgy.

I hope Jackie-O is okay.

I hope Penelope doesn't ditch me again.

I hope the blue-haired person at Satchels of Gold doesn't convince Kat I'm bad news.

"My agent wants me to write a response to Poison Ivy," I say when Penelope turns onto our street.

"Don't," Penelope says. She parks her car. "It's more powerful to say nothing. Be the bigger person. If anyone asks, say you didn't read it."

"That's my instinct too," I say. "Also, it's the truth."

Penelope is wise.

I'm shaking.

Should I ask her to come inside for a glass of wine?

Should I invent a crisis?

"Good night, Astrid," Penelope says at my door, and my body melts.

I spend the night texting Sophie, my emotional support animal, my Jackie-O.

* * *

How's Jackie-O, I text Zev in the morning.

The doctor said it isn't cancer, thank God, he replies, *Penelope was right. He prescribed antibiotics.*

I respond with the prayer hands emoji.

Jackie-O likes her bone from the care package, Zev says. Then: *I'm glad you're getting along with Penelope. She seems like a good influence on you.*

I feel weird, like Zev is my dad and Penelope is my mom and I'm their angsty teenager they don't deserve. My own parents never told me someone was a good influence on me. They never encouraged me to hang around people with good values. They encouraged me to achieve. To win.

I text Felix, who I haven't heard from since he left for San Diego.

Do you think our parents gave us bad values?

He responds, quickly, *no doubt*.

. . . .

Growing up, my parents—my mom especially—always wanted me to be friends with blonde and athletic girls, girls with round faces and Swedish coloring, girls they could pretend were their own daughter, a superior version of myself. An Astrid who was equally high achieving but also agreeable and pleasant. An Astrid who would attract a nice boyfriend in law or finance, who would one day raise blond children and have a stable career and say all the right things at cocktail parties. An algorithmic Astrid without messy feelings or unpopular opinions or lesbian leanings.

In seventh grade, I became friends with this girl named Dalia who my parents hated, not least of all because she was a brunette. In retrospect, I probably had a crush on Dalia, who wore thick black eyeliner and plaid skirts with Doc Martens. She was broody and snarky but really sweet once you got to know her—she was always feeding bits of her lunch to squirrels, and once she even saved a baby bird that crashed into our school atrium window, nursing it back to health for weeks. We had art class together but no other classes or extracurriculars, as Dalia never did her homework and hated sports. But she was incredible at drawing and had the most inventive ideas. We would spend all class talking about how we wanted to escape San Francisco. Dalia wanted to go to New York and show her paintings at MoMA. I wanted to move to Hollywood and be a pop star—this was back when I was insecure enough to actually want to be famous, when I wanted the world to validate me in the way my parents never did, when I wanted to look back and say, *Told ya, I'm special!* But Dalia made me consider moving to New York, and I would fantasize about us sharing a penthouse overlooking Central Park.

I was beyond thrilled when Dalia invited me to her parents' house in Oregon that summer, but my parents said I couldn't go because it would "interfere with my soccer training," which was bullshit because I had six weeks of soccer camp scheduled that summer and nothing scheduled that particular week. Dalia was either in Oregon or at art camp all summer, so I didn't get to see her at all. We exchanged a few messages on AIM, during which my heart would race, but they also left much to be desired, as Dalia was always running to some camp dinner or to watch an auteur horror film with her architect father.

When I got back to school for the first day of eighth grade, I practically raced to art class. But Dalia wasn't there. I figured she signed up for a different class, and that maybe she'd outgrown me that summer with her cool art camp friends and all the critically acclaimed horror films she'd watched. But after a few days, when I hadn't seen her once, I figured something was up—my class was small enough that I should have run into her by then. I asked my parent-approved friend Margot, a blonde on my soccer team, who said Dalia was in "the looney bin." Then she made a very gauche cutting motion on her wrists.

twenty-nine

Kat Gold texts me, *hey heartbreaker, what are you doing today?*

I hover over the reply box, not knowing what to say. Do I tell her I'm just sitting around waiting for the woman she correctly thought I was interested in to give me attention, that I have literally nothing else going on?

Just some revisions, I lie.

Play hooky, she says. *Let's go on a drive. I got a new car and the paps don't recognize it yet.* Then, *tinted windows.*

I try to think of an excuse but can't come up with anything.

I'll pick you up in 30, she says.

Forty-five minutes later, I hear bass rumbling. Outside my window, a matte black G-Wagen shakes on the street.

"Look at you," I say when I get in. "So Kardashian." I breathe in that pleasing, antiseptic new car smell.

"Right?" she says. "It's my divorce vehicle."

British grime is playing so loudly I can hardly hear her. I feel old when I ask her to turn it down a little.

"It's my divorce vehicle!" she says again, this time yelling, which is unnecessary since she's turned down the volume. She looks different, like she got a haircut or Botox or some Hollywood beautifying procedure I've never even heard of. If it's possible, Kat Gold is somehow even more beautiful, and even more uncomfortable looking. And again I realize I'm uniquely at ease around Kat Gold because she's hardly a human being at this point, mostly microplastics, and it's like hanging out with brunette Barbie who's taking a Philosophy 101 course. "Don't you love it?"

"You got a divorce?" I say. "I'm so sorry."

"Oh, it's fine," she says. "I'm a free bird!" She grins maniacally. "How are you? I saw all those Tweets about you being mental or something?"

Kat starts driving down the hill, and I remember I have to tell Sophie first if I hang out with a hot queer-identifying celebrity who reads theory. If the paparazzi have figured out this car and photos come out, Sophie will be furious.

"Can you pull over for a sec?" I ask Kat Gold.

She rolls the G-Wagen under an oak tree.

"My friend has a massive lesbian crush on you," I say. "Can we send her a quick selfie and completely make her day?"

Kat lights up. The woman loves a selfie. "Of course! Is your friend hot? I need a rebound."

"I'll tell her to send a selfie back," I say. "You can judge for yourself."

I hold up my camera and try to make my face not look like a gremlin next to Kat. I don't notice until I see the photo that Kat's crop top has a graphic of the cover of Foucault's *The History of Sexuality*. Sophie is going to lose it.

Sophie responds almost immediately with roughly thirteen exclamation points.

Then, *is that a Foucault shirt? Fuck!!!* She follows up with a drooling emoji.

"She's losing her mind," I tell Kat.

"I wanna see this bitch," Kat says.

She wants a selfie back, I write. *She's single and ready to rebound.*

I can see Sophie is typing, stopping, the little dots appearing and disappearing.

"I'm worried she's going into shock," I say.

"FaceTime her," Kat says to me.

I do as told, and Sophie's cute little face—to me, much cuter than Kat Gold's freaky algorithmic deer face—appears on the screen. Sophie quickly covers her face with her hands.

"Hi, Sophie," Kat Gold says. "Astrid has told me all about you!"

"I'm freaking out," Sophie says through her hands on her face.

"Don't freak out," I say. "Kat is such an epic dork. And I've told her almost nothing about you."

"You know I love dorks, Astrid," Sophie says.

"But Kat Gold is like a dumb dork," I say, then remember Kat is paying my bills at the moment, but Kat seems to like it when I neg her a bit. "Kat, have you even read *The History of Sexuality*?"

"Of course!" Kat says, putting a hand on her chest with faux offense.

"What's the thesis, kitten?" I ask her.

"My ex-husband called me that," Kat says, then briefly appears sad in a very artificial way. She straightens up in her seat. "Well, it's four fucking volumes, Astrid, but I'll try to be brief. Foucault basically argues that the idea of sexuality as a separate object from procreation is a relatively recent invention of the Western world, and that it emerged from certain power structures. And it basically contradicted the idea that came before it, that we're all sexually repressed due to the rise of the bourgeoisie in the seventeenth century."

Sophie starts clapping, finally removing her hands from her face.

"So, you've read Wikipedia," I say to Kat.

"You're gorgeous, doll," Kat Gold tells Sophie, ignoring me. I'm actually sort of impressed with Kat's response, even as someone with incredible phrase recall, who can easily memorize strings of words and who often reads Wikipedia as opposed to the source text. Maybe it's her actress training. Maybe it's Lee Strasberg.

"I think I might pass out," Sophie says.

"Go drink some water, doll," Kat says. "I'm going to cruise around with your asshole friend. Hopefully I see you around!"

"Bye, Sophie," I say.

Kat hangs up and puts the car in drive. "Is that your girl?"

"No," I say. "Well, at one point, I guess."

"She's adorable," Kat says, and drives down the hill. "So, do you want to talk about what happened? Maude was a bit alarmed, but I told her to chill out."

I swallow.

"I was like," Kat continues, "'Who hasn't been in love with a psycho who's said horrible things about you on the internet?' And Maude was all 'I haven't' and I was all 'You're a prude.' And she said Rye—remember the blue-haired person who got all aggressive with you on that first meeting? Well, Maude said Rye would quit if we didn't drop your book and I said, 'Let them quit' and—don't repeat any of this—but Rye left the company."

I nod, uncomfortable but grateful that Kat Gold took my side over her own employee's, also a little guilty. "It's all just so embarrassing," I tell Kat. "I don't know why I can't just be normal."

"Who wants to be normal?" Kat drives up another hill. "Be completely lame?" She pauses the car, stopping abruptly the way she did when we went walking, looking at me with her weird deer face. "Astrid, your strangeness is a gift." Kat pulls a small crystal out of her bra and hands it to me.

It's yellowish gold and warm in my hand.

"It's citrine," Kat says. "You can't have it—it's important to me. But you should hold it while we drive. It helps eliminate the fear of being judged."

"I'm not afraid of being judged," I say, rubbing the smooth surface of the crystal with my thumb.

"Right," Kat says. "Just hold it for a second. I assume you're into crystals, given your book and everything. I'm surprised you haven't asked me my sign."

"You're a Pisces," I say, embarrassed to know this. "And the book is kind of cynical about astrology." I still suspect that Kat Gold has not read my book, which doesn't bother me as long as I get paid. But I feel bad that Rye lost their job because of me. I'm not too concerned about this adaptation being good or accurate, and a nonbinary character is not a hill I need to die on. "I like crystals," I tell Kat, "but I'm not convinced they really have any healing powers."

"Right," Kat repeats as she rounds a curve.

With my hand that isn't holding the citrine, I clutch my green amethyst and slide it along its chain.

"Are you still hung up on the chick who wrote the blog post?" Kat asks.

"Not at all," I say, still rubbing the citrine. "It was an amphetamine-fueled relationship." I slide the amethyst back and forth.

"Been there, sis," Kat says. Then, "So what are you down about?"

I inhale deeply, clutch both crystals. "Remember when we went on our walk and we came back and saw those two women, the hostile Russian and—"

"The sexy art teacher lady you totally had the hots for!"

Maybe Kat Gold is smarter than I give her credit for.

As we wind up and down hills and the light turns orange and gold, stopping occasionally to take pictures of a For Sale sign—Kat needs a new place to live postdivorce—I tell Kat Gold all about Penelope, about hating her at first, about things shifting mysteriously at the concert, about Nadia the hostile Russian, and about how now Penelope appears to be avoiding me. Kat is a surprisingly good listener, asking questions at appropriate times and letting me talk when I need to.

When I finally let it all out, she says, "This is really great."

"It is?" I say. "I'm pretty sure Penelope hates me, or is too busy with the hostile Russian to even think about me?"

"No, no," Kat says. "She doesn't hate you. I saw how she looked at you." Kat crests a hill and the sky explodes with color. "Just be patient, Astrid. The universe has a plan." She eyes the citrine in my hand. "Keep rubbing," she says, and I do. I clutch my green amethyst too. Both crystals seem to vibrate on my fingers.

When Kat stops in front of my house, I worry she's going to ask to come in. Instead, she says she has a gift for me. She reaches into her purse and pulls out a *Valley of the Dolls* crop top, holds it up, and gives it a shimmy. I'm legitimately excited, and immediately start brainstorming when and where I'll wear it, then worry I'm too old to wear a crop top.

"Thank you so much, Kat," I say. "This is amazing."

"I also read the book," she says. "Because you were so judgmental."

I'm surprised and embarrassed, thinking now would be a very bad time to admit I haven't even read the book myself, that I was just being a little shit.

"It was actually pretty fun," she says. "I can see why it's one of the bestselling books of all time."

"Right!" I say. "And Jacqueline Susann was an actress. An actress and a bestseller, like you." I haven't read the book, but I have read Jacqueline Susann's Wikipedia page. On it, I also learned that after days of lapsing in and out of a coma, Susann's final words to her husband were: *Hey, doll, let's get the hell out of here.*

"Exactly like me," Kat says, then winks. "Okay, I have a dinner date with Sofia Coppola—give me my crystal and get out of my car!"

"Happily," I say, handing back the citrine and exiting her divorce vehicle, "thanks for the T-shirt, and for listening."

"Anytime, sis," she says, then drives off.

Her bass seems to shake the trees on the street even after she's gone.

thirty

Sophie invites me to drinks to thank me for introducing her via FaceTime to Kat Gold. To get excited, I imagine I am going on a date with Penelope. The best thing about having a crush is feeling like you're on a stage that your crush is always watching, compelling you to be your best, most interesting, most entertaining self.

I wear a thin white T-shirt that drapes perfectly on my collarbones over a black lace bra. I put on Levi's and Sambas and baby blue eyeliner for some color. I spritz my forearm and neck with a Polish perfume that smells of sparkling citrus and gauzy white florals. Light, fresh, flirty, fun.

Getting dressed, I imagine Penelope and I are cohabitating on the top of a hill, a spot I suppose not unlike our current bungalows, but they're one bungalow and it's covered in bougainvillea. And as I put on my necklace, Penelope comes up behind me and clasps it for me, sending shivers down my spine and causing the amethyst to throb on my chest.

On the drive over, I imagine that Nadia is back in Russia. Or prison. Not dead, but out of the picture permanently.

Sophie is already seated at the bar. She dressed up for me in a cute, collared dress. Green is her color, and she looks like a sexy little plant. "Okay," Sophie says when I sit beside her. "Is my Unisom playing tricks on me again or did you FaceTime me today with Kat Gold and did she summarize the thesis of *The History of Sexuality*?"

"It happened, babe," I say. "What did you think of her summary?"

"Oh, definitely a crude and bastardized understanding of the text but, honey, with that face? I just love that she tried."

"She's grown on me," I say. I don't trust a goddamn word Kat says, but she's entertaining and filling my bank account, which is more than I can say for most people. "Maybe cringe is cooler than I realized." I think of that meme: *I am cringe, but I am free.*

"Spoken like a true Sapphic Scribe," Sophie says.

I came planning to flirt, but I find myself unable to return Sophie's playful grazings of my arm, her teasing. I try to see myself on the stage, the one Penelope is watching intently, but Sophie's warm green eyes keep taking me out of the moment, reminding me she's a person, not a game.

When she tries to talk about the Ivy shitstorm, I change the subject and ask Sophie about herself. I ask her what she's reading and how her dissertation is going. I ask her what TV she's watching, if *The Goldfinch* is as good as *The Secret History*, what she thinks Judy Poovey would be doing right now if she were not a fictional character. I ask her about herself and I listen to the answers. I don't perform.

After two drinks, I tell her I've had a nice time, but I need to get back. I have an early morning, the whitest of lies.

Sophie says, "You're a new woman, Astrid Dahl."

:::

At home, I turn on all my lights and play my music loud, hoping once again that Penelope will come over and tell me to turn it down, that she'll leave the Russian and come to me. I am not a new woman. I am acting out. I am the exact same bitch.

I text Sophie, *Do you know a Russian/LA dyke named Nadia?*

Typing bubbles appear, then disappear, then reappear.

I wish I could unsend the text. Why am I bothering Sophie with this bullshit?

Yeah, Nadia Kotov, Sophie responds. *She's a dime.*

I squeeze my phone hard and turn up the music.

Is she? Then, *I guess if you're into that sort of generic symmetrical thing.*

Everyone is into facial symmetry, Astrid, Sophie responds. *Ivy is symmetrical.* Then, *so are you.*

I open my window a little more. *She seems kind of dumb*, I write back.

Wind ruffles the curtains.

She's, like, kind of a genius? Sophie writes back. *Like legit got a perfect score on her GRE?*

I turn up the music and write, *that's a very narrow and dated measure of intelligence.* I recall taking the LSAT, how I took it twice, how I cried when I received my first score as it was so very average, how the second score was acceptably above average but not remotely impressive.

Hmm, Sophie writes, *you sound a little jealous.*

I turn up the music one more notch.

Penelope doesn't come by, nor does she text. It's probably hard to hear my music over Nadia Kotov's ecstatic moans. I google *Nadia Kotov* and find her website, which announces herself as "an interdisciplinary artist and academic focused on the queer topography of eighteenth-century Slavic knots." Okay.

I compose and delete a few texts to Sophie. *I have no desire to be an esoteric academic.* Delete. *The academy is for children.*

Delete. *I'd rather be Nora Ephron.* Delete. Sophie's an academic. No need to offend her. No need to insult this Russian woman I met once for twelve seconds.

In vain, I google *Penelope Paladino Nadia Kotov* to see if I can find a photo of them together. Only photos of Penelope's art come up. Then I google *Paladino surname meaning.* I learn *Paladino* is Italian for *paladin,* which means "defender." My stomach tightens into a knot of the variety the Russian studies.

Desperate to feel close to her, I reread our previous exchange over and over, mostly the text she sent me from the desert retreat. The way an iPhone alarm continues to rattle through your brain long after you've turned it off, I hear strings of words from the text for the remainder of the night. *Meaning to check in. Wireless retreat. Breaking the rules. Wireless retreat. Back tomorrow. Breaking the rules. Hope you're well. I've been thinking about you. Breaking the rules. Thinking about you.*

I've been thinking about you.

I've been thinking.

About.

You.

I fall asleep to Donna's syrupy drawl.

⋮⋮⋮⋮

The following afternoon I'm reading in the yard when Penelope walks over, wearing a linen sundress that reveals hard nipples, and asks me if I want to come over for dinner that evening.

I nearly fall out of my chair, then whisper, "Yes."

thirty-one

I spend nearly four hours preparing for dinner.

First, I go to the fancy wine store at the bottom of the hill and buy vegan cheese and Marcona almonds and three bottles of Delirium Tremens, a fancy Belgian beer, a "strong blond" much like myself. Actually, I'm a weak blonde, but the label is baby blue with a pink elephant, very cute, elegant shit, a beer for bottoms. I plan to drink just these three bottles of beer this evening, nothing special for a normal, well-adjusted adult, but a big deal for me, an adult baby recovering from light alcoholism. I won't bring my vape pen or cigarettes or five-hour energy or any other stimulant. I will be moderate and normal!

Back at home, I put on my Cat Power playlist and begin testing perfume samples. For almost an hour, I spritz various sections of my arms, sniffing, moving into different rooms, sniffing, moving outside, sniffing, seeing how they smell after one minute, after fifteen minutes, after thirty. I eventually land on a Swedish perfume described not as a fragrance but rather as "moon milk." It's supposed to smell like creamy black tea and soft woods and smooth leather, and also a Scandinavian cave at night. (The moon apparently makes stalactites drip white liquid puddles on the rock floor.) Of the many samples I try, moon milk works the best with my skin chemistry, smells the best over time, has the best "sillage"—the trail created by the perfume—and I eventually become certain that 'moon milk' is a poetic euphemism for female cum.

I also like that it's Swedish, an ode to my roots.

Confident I've picked the right perfume, I run the bath, adding a few drops of chamomile oil and a sprinkling of sweet birch and magnesium bath flakes, a birthday present from Zev, because he knows I love my baths. I can tell they're expensive so I'm savoring them, only using a few pinches per month.

When "Fool" comes on the speakers, I get in the bath and remove the mask. I wash my face with a French green clay and Madonna lily scrub. Then I massage rosehip seed oil into my face and décolletage in soft circles. I scrub my arms thoroughly to ensure all the lingering competing perfume scents are gone. I shave my legs and my bikini line and then rub rosehip seed oil into both.

After the bath, I spend a few minutes just breathing in the steamy spearmint air as "Good Woman" plays. I rub argan oil moisturizer and pumpkin serum into my face. I cover my body in manuka honey moisturizer and then more rosehip seed oil. In the chance event this evening ends the way I want it to, I need my skin to be so soft it's alarming. I want Penelope to realize I'm twelve, maybe fifteen years younger than her. I want her to know that I have something she doesn't—fewer years on Earth.

Maybe I don't need to be so competitive.

There is something very nice about engaging in these beautifying rituals. For most of my life, I've existed entirely within my brain. Little miss straight-A student goes to law school, quits to publish novels. Words, words, words. When I believed in therapy, my therapist said I had a good intellectual grasp of my problem areas but had "a world of work to do in the realm of the somatic." She started asking me where I felt certain emotions in my body, how I knew I was angry or afraid. These exercises made me feel exceptionally dumb, like I suddenly knew what it was like to be bad at school and I did *not* like it. But the universe eventually gets you where you need to go. That's probably why I got into perfume. It's pure sense, wordless, a brain break.

While I'm deciding what to wear, Sophie texts me and asks if I'd like to get drinks again soon. I remember Penelope saying she knew Sophie and feel a flicker of jealousy. I tell Sophie I'd like to, but as friends, because I'm not ready for anything more post–Poison Ivy, the latter portion a partial lie to maybe spare her feelings.

Who said I wanted anything more? she writes back with a winky face emoji. Then, *I'd love to be friends with the new Astrid Dahl.*

I heart the text.

I debate FaceTiming Otto, asking him what I should wear. Fashion is his job, after all. But I fear his judgment. He likes Penelope, but I'm not sure if he'll like the idea of me dating anyone right now. He's always telling me to take a break from romance. And who knows if this is a date, but I'm preparing for it like it is, and Otto will probably tell me to chill.

Dressing for a first date often feels like an impossible task.

My biggest fear is showing people just how much effort I'm putting into things. The goal is to downplay the effort, to look accidentally sexy. The thought of Penelope learning or even sensing I spent four hours preparing for this maybe-date renders me red hot with shame.

Instead of calling Otto, I try to pretend he is in my head. I imagine him telling me I look awkward in dresses. Skirts are flattering but would convey effort, so they're out. Black is aging and makes me look mean. I need to soften my look, he says, not harden it.

His voice ultimately encourages me to land on a slight variation of my typical uniform. Levi's and a drapey thin white T-shirt. Lace green bra. Deep green loafers, nearly the same shade of

Penelope's Volvo, which hopefully don't show effort but rather convey respect.

After dressing, I apply BB cream to even my skin tone without concealing the light splattering of freckles on my nose. I pick up my light blue eyeliner then put it down, decide to go with something more natural, a smudge of brown on the edges of my eyes. Brown mascara. I use a lip-plumping balm that burns my lips.

I spritz the moon milk, hopefully the perfect amount, nearly undetectable but subtly irresistible.

I check the clock on my phone. Twelve minutes until I'm expected at Penelope's, but I should arrive five to seven minutes late to give her time in case she's running late.

This is when I would normally open a beer.

Actually, normally, I would have opened one before this, and one before that.

I write down a list of conversation topics on my Notes app:

Grad school

Favorite visual artists

Working on anything new?

Celebrity crushes

Favorite bar in LA

Fave movies

Have we ever dated anyone in common?

I highlight the last one and click Delete.

Then I open *Perfume and Pain* to a random page, for luck. My eye hits the following line, which feels fortuitous:

"Nude, the little blonde whore was quite attractive."

thirty-two

The patchouli smell that once repulsed me now fills me with a warm, serene feeling.

Penelope is wearing that same red dress from the concert, no shoes. She's done a sort of '70s cat eye with chalky brown liner.

"I like your eyeliner," I say.

"Really?" she says. "I feel like I messed it up. Luckily, the lighting is low."

Only one lamp is on in the living room and candles provide the rest of the light—a soft, flickering yellow.

I smile. This is date lighting.

I hand Penelope the vegan cheese and the almonds and she says, "Wow, I love this brand. Thank you." I'm not sure if she's talking about the vegan cheese brand or the almond brand and her hands are shaking ever so slightly when she takes them.

She heads into the kitchen and I start to follow her, but she stops me and says, "The kitchen is a mess, just make yourself at home in the living room."

I sit on a green velvet couch that matches my loafers and remove the Delirium Tremens bottles from my purse. I'll wait for her to get a drink before I open one. I want to put the rest in the fridge, but she told me to stay here.

Inhaling through my nose, I recall an article I read recently about how patchouli is a scent with "a lot of misconceptions." While now associated with hacky sacks and jam bands, early European traders valued patchouli as highly as gold, and Egyptian pharaoh Tutankhamun was buried with forty liters of patchouli oil. I ordered a few patchouli-based perfume samples, pulling a 180 on my beliefs per usual.

Cat Power is playing, *The Greatest*, the album Zev and I loved in college. I sing softly to "Lived in Bars" and open my phone.

I have a text from Sophie. *This just in: Poison Ivy's gf found out about the demons that tempt me and dumped her.*

I turn off my phone.

. . . .

Penelope returns with a cheese board, with the vegan cheese and almonds I brought, but also pickled vegetables and jams and seeded crackers.

She sees the beers I put on the table and says, "Oh, I bought you some beer. I was about to grab it." She picks up my beers. "Would you prefer one of yours? I got something called Pliny the Elder? I don't really know anything about beer, but I asked my friend who is a bit of a beer snob, and she recommended it. Although I suspect you aren't a snob."

She's right. I legitimately love Bud Light. But part of being thirty-five means pretending to love expensive alcohol, and I know from my beer snob friends, and from growing up in the Bay Area, that Pliny the Elder is a very nice beer brewed just north of the Bay in Russian River Valley.

"I'd love a Pliny the Elder," I say. "That's a really nice beer."

Penelope smiles and disappears back into the kitchen.

She returns with a glass of red wine for herself and a frosted glass of beer for me.

The first sip is so delicious and refreshing, like I'm tasting beer for the first time. I remember what Penelope told me about women dominating the beer industry for centuries, then being ousted as witches. And how beer increases estrogen. Sipping, I imagine my breasts getting bigger.

Penelope sits on the burgundy couch adjacent to mine.

We're silent for a moment. Nervous tension ripples through the room.

Chan croons.

"I'm sorry I've been kind of weird the past few days," Penelope says finally.

I'm glad she's acknowledging it. I thought I was imagining it. Just inventing melodramas like Zev said.

"I felt like you were avoiding me?" I say, and cringe at my own uptalk.

"I was," Penelope says, and I feel slightly less crazy, but also hurt. Penelope was avoiding me.

She cuts a piece of vegan cheese and puts it on a cracker.

I follow suit.

We both bite into the cheese crackers, apparently thinking the other would fill the silence while we ate.

Instead, we crunch, and we laugh.

"Avoiding me why?" I say when I swallow.

Penelope sighs, then washes down her cracker with a big sip of wine.

"I'm a bit nervous," she says.

I slide my green amethyst along its chain. "Me too," I say. "We can talk about something else."

Penelope smiles.

thirty-three

I drink just one beer before dinner and eat three crackers with vegan cheese in between sips to line my stomach and keep me alert.

We get to two of my listed conversation topics before dinner. First, grad school. Penelope moved to LA to get her master's at CalArts, as I suspected. There, she met her first girlfriend. It was the '90s, so there was more pushback around being gay. Her family tried to disown her, but now they're relatively supportive, although they wish she was married. I tell her my parents tried to have me committed when I started dating women, particularly because I dropped out of law school at around the same time, and that now they aren't supportive, but they aren't actively hostile, just disinterested.

I ask Penelope what she's working on, and she walks me into her studio and shows me a painting of a woman's décolletage, collaged with photographs of what appear to be eucalyptus leaves. But I'm focused on the woman's hair.

"A *blonde*!" I squeal, and Penelope looks down, and then I remember Nadia Kotov, the knot scholar, is blonde. Laura, the smooth-brained carnivore for whom Penelope baked a cake, is blonde. The painting is obviously not of me.

Penelope disappears into the kitchen, leaving me alone

to look at her art for a few minutes, then calls out, "Dinner is served." She brings two colorful plates to a small table in the breakfast nook lit by a candle in the center. She brings me another beer and another glass of wine for herself. She made olive oil flatbread and braised cauliflower and arugula salad.

"This looks great," I say.

"You said your favorite food was pizza, so."

I laugh, embarrassed. "I have the palate of a child." I bite into the flatbread, and it's gooey and delicious. "This is incredible."

"Thanks." Penelope picks at her cauliflower.

I was going to ask her about ignoring me but decide to wait.

Instead, we talk about our celebrity crushes. Mine: Penelope Cruz, Rachel Weisz. (I don't say Kris Jenner.) Penelope's: Jemima Kirke, Cara Delevingne. (I wonder who she doesn't say.)

"You kind of look like Cara," Penelope says. I've heard this before. I find Cara obnoxious, another casting call queer like Kristen Stewart. But there is no denying the girl is pretty, not that I look like her at all. I think I get the comparison because we're both gangly, dark-browed blondes. Both a little feral. I recall that video that circulated of Cara Delevingne after Burning Man. She was covered in dirt and sand, shoeless, jittery, shaking her tangled hair and chain-smoking. People speculated she was on meth. I suspected the Patricia Highsmith.

"You kind of look like Rachel Weisz," I say.

: : : :

After dinner, we return to the living room, and Penelope puts on the Smiths, another band I loved in college, a band I listened to constantly when I studied abroad in London. I desperately want Penelope to sit beside me on the couch, but she sits across from me again.

Opening my third beer, right on track, I feel emboldened. "So, why were you avoiding me?"

Penelope bites her lip.

I sip my beer.

"Is it the Russian?" I ask.

Penelope tilts her head, looks at me. "Nadia?"

I nod.

"What about her?"

"You're dating her?" I say, unable to hold back the hostility in my voice. "You were too busy with her to see me?"

Penelope smiles a little, then shakes her head. "She was a distraction," she says.

I dig a nail into my palm. A distraction. They fucked. Why do I care? I don't own Penelope; she can fuck who she pleases. "A distraction from?"

Penelope blinks at me, then sips her wine.

Morrissey sings and I sip my beer.

Penelope sips more.

We both breathe.

"You," Penelope says finally. "A distraction from you."

She looks at the ceiling, then back at me.

"I like you, Astrid. I'm sure you know that."

My heart starts flapping. I gulp my drink to steady myself.

"I don't know that," I say. "I mean, I hoped."

"You hoped? I thought you hated me. Poison Ivy said so."

"Poison Ivy is deranged," I say. "And I thought you hated *me*."

"Hate you?" she says. "Astrid, I make any excuse to go to your house. Do you know how many times I've pretended to take out the trash just hoping I'd run into you?"

"I was wondering how you generated so much garbage," I say. "I figured it was just an artist thing."

"Nope," Penelope says. "It was an Astrid thing." She grins. "I befriended your two best friends. I even text your brother."

"I hardly even text my brother," I say quietly. My gaze floats to the lamp between us. I'm under the strange spell again, like at the concert. Maybe I've been under the strange spell this entire time.

"When did this all start?" I ask.

"Oh." Penelope shrugs. "Probably when I first saw you." She leans back on her couch, away from me. I'm confused. She's telling me she likes me, but her body language is saying something else. "I sort of have a type."

I pause. "Demented?"

Penelope laughs. "Blonde."

"I thought only gentlemen preferred blondes," I say.

Penelope smiles. "I guess not."

"Your therapist said you have a savior complex," I say, recalling that afternoon in the car on the way back from the Petit Ermitage. When we first met, she immediately started bossing me around and told me to lift weights or I'd get osteoporosis. She liked me because she thought I needed help.

She looks at her lap. "I don't think you need saving, Astrid," Penelope says. "I think you're hot."

Euphoria pumps through my veins. "The Russian is hot," I say. "I'm average." I don't know why I'm still talking about the Russian.

"What is your obsession with Nadia?" Penelope asks. "Do you want her number?" She smirks. "I can set you up."

"God no," I say, mad at myself for ruining the moment. "I was jealous."

Penelope looks at the ceiling, takes a breath. "You have nothing to be jealous of," she says. "I saw her to stop thinking about you. It was immature."

Morrissey sings.

"I'm sure she's fine," I say, convinced no one with such delicate bone structure can have a complex inner life, that no one capable of severe mental anguish would choose to study knots for a living. It's too literal.

Penelope laughs, briefly flashing her very white teeth, then stops. "So yeah," she continues. "At first I just thought you were hot." It's refreshing how Penelope is honest about her basic desires. Lesbians rarely cop to objectifying women. We always claim there is something spiritual or intellectual or psychosexual involved. Maybe by the time I'm forty-seven, or fifty-one, however old Penelope is, I can finally like a woman simply because I find her hot, and not because she's likely to ruin my life. "And then there was that night you were so open with me, and I felt like I finally saw the real Astrid beneath all the defenses."

"At Cat Power?"

"No, no," Penelope says. "That night after your TV meeting?"

I think. The Satchels of Gold meeting. I started drinking heavily after it, depressed, ashamed, and I found some Adderall in a secret stash, and soon I was shopping my closet blasting Rihanna, waking up in a puddle of melted ice cream. And that was the night I had that weird dream. Where Penelope was singing to me. Shit. That's why I dreamt about her.

She was there.

"I was afraid you might not remember," Penelope says.

Shame stabs my chest. "I remember having a dream about you," I say quietly.

Penelope's eyes meet mine and I'm not sure what they're saying. "I'd seen you drinking early in the day when I was taking out the trash"—she pauses—"*pretending* to take out the trash, and then later I heard music blasting, so I came by."

I slide the green amethyst back and forth.

"You greeted me so kindly, so unlike before when you always seemed irritated by my presence. You were wearing this baby tank that said 'indie darling' and dramatic eyeliner and you offered me some gin."

"Wow," I say. "How fun am I?"

"You were fun. You started dancing with me."

A sharp craving hits, a pang for the Patricia Highsmith. I want to be loose and fun. I want to dance. I stop myself. What's the point of being loose and fun if I don't remember it? If I wake up with a pit of dread in my stomach in a puddle of melted ice cream.

"Was I a good dancer?" I ask.

"Totally," Penelope says. "A little unsteady at times, but...it's all about attitude."

I sip my beer slowly. "Did we fuck?"

Penelope reddens a sliver, but it might be the lighting. "No," she says. "I couldn't possibly, with you in that state."

"Did I try?" I ask, shame compelling me.

"Not really." My cheeks heat. "I mean, I don't know. We mostly just talked. And at certain points you sort of curled up on me, like a cat. It was . . ." She looks at the ceiling, then at me. " . . . Very cute."

"Maybe Poison Ivy wasn't paranoid after all," I say.

"Maybe not," Penelope says, and my heart flickers.

"What did we talk about?" I ask.

"Art and money, mostly," she says. "You got a little upset about the meeting. And you asked me all these questions about my career, and I told you how at your age, I'd just been in the Whitney Biennial and had a solo show at MOCA and felt like I was on top of the art world. And how in the past few years, I've suddenly felt untouchable. And if it weren't for the Urban Outfitters settlement, I'd probably have to move in with my sister in Santa Ana."

"I constantly feel like I'm on the verge of having to move back home," I say.

"You said that that night." Penelope laughs. "We talked about how we're both living off these dwindling pots of money."

"Sounds like we really bonded," I say.

"I thought so," Penelope said. "It scared me, though."

"Why?" I ask.

"You aren't good for me, Astrid." She looks at her lap. "I saw you and my heart did its thing. I found myself becoming obsessive, thinking about you constantly, about what was good for you and excuses to talk to you. And I was like, I've seen this movie before, so many times, and I know how it ends."

Penelope's explaining exactly how I felt about Ivy.

"And I told myself it was fine because you clearly weren't interested," she says. "You were in Poison Ivy land and I knew nothing was going to happen. So, I could just get a little high on you, knowing it would never be anything more."

I can't really imagine someone getting high on me, but I suppose we're all just getting high on ourselves, using other people as vessels.

"But then the concert happened," she continues.

In a flash of boldness, I get up and sit beside her. Her body radiates warmth.

Penelope backs up a bit.

"And then I felt you wanting more," she says. She swallows some wine. "I felt you wanting me."

I scoot a tiny bit closer to Penelope and she backs away again.

"I was freaking out a bit the night of the show," she says. "My friend texted me about a last-minute opening at her retreat and I figured while I was gone, you'd develop a new crush and forget about me."

I slide the green amethyst, thinking about Sophie, and also Donna Tartt.

"I can go five days without a crush," I say, but it isn't true.

Penelope sips her wine. "Then I get home, and you're in the yard every second," she says. "Wearing basically nothing."

"I'll put a towel over my body next time." I laugh, but Penelope doesn't.

"You're dangerous to me," she says.

"You know today I walked into a wall while texting," I say.

Penelope smiles, then twists her mouth into something more despondent.

"Did you invite me over here to tell me I'm dangerous?" I scoot closer to her and this time she doesn't back away.

"Sorta," she says. "For me."

And then she kisses me.

: : : :

Penelope has the most beautiful body I've ever seen. Olive skin, an artful smattering of moles. Perfectly proportioned, her nipples are ripe berries that harden on my tongue.

She's more dominant than I imagined.

A thrilling surprise.

I can't remember being this present in someone else's bed, maybe ever.

I finally understand why people don't black out.

Sometimes life is worth catching.

Our bodies writhe under a lamp shaped like a cloud.

When she slides into me, I feel her everywhere, our cells entangled and on fire.

She rides me with her fingers inside me, her breasts dancing on my chest.

I come quickly, and when I do: I scream.

thirty-four

I awake blissful and warm, like a baby.

The warmth evaporates when I roll over to find Penelope isn't there.

Maybe she's in the bathroom.

I grab my phone from the bedside table and busy myself with responding to texts from Otto, Zev, Sophie.

When Penelope isn't back after fifteen minutes, I look for her.

She isn't in the bathroom or the kitchen.

I put on my jeans and walk across the sunny lawn.

Her Volvo isn't there.

My stomach sinks.

I return to her bungalow to get my purse.

And I linger there for a bit.

I pour myself a glass of water and take deep breaths, inhaling the scent of her living space, what she eats.

From the fridge, I grab a piece of leftover flatbread from the previous night. I chew it slowly, looking out the window, watching a hummingbird float around a tree branch.

In her bedroom, I smell her pillow and understand why the pharaoh wanted to be buried with patchouli. I touch myself, and soon I'm coming again in her bed.

And then I hear the door open.

She returns to the bedroom with lidded coffee cups emitting steam.

I'm relieved, then embarrassed.

Does she know I just touched myself in her bed?

If so, does she think it's hot or unbearably pathetic?

Penelope puts down the coffees on the rattan bedside table.

"Stop thinking so hard," she says, then kisses me, hard and wet, and my body lights up, and soon her weight is on me, pressing me down, and I can't breathe, but not in a scary way like when Ivy grabbed my neck and squeezed. I feel excited, but also safe.

"You're trembling," Penelope says.

* * * *

Penelope and I don't leave the bungalow that day or night.

We take our coffees to the living room and sit on her velvet couch with our legs entangled and listen to Patsy Cline. Halfway through the coffees, a quarter of the way through *Showcase*, Penelope kisses me and I kiss her back and slowly remove her nightgown and her underwear and soon she's coming in my mouth.

After we brush our teeth, Penelope makes us tofu scrambles with spinach and vegan cheese and we eat them on the couch, feeding bits to each other. We talk throughout the day, but the content is neither important nor memorable. The focal point is the connection between our bodies, the energy that is both exciting and safe, a foreign experience, at least for me—for whom sexual attraction, at least historically, revolves primarily around words. Nice words, but also mean words. Words, words, words.

We nap and somehow wake up fucking and then we eat and we fuck and we rest and soon it is morning and I am alone in her bed once again.

∴ ∴

I assume Penelope is getting us coffee again and become excited thinking about the imminent caffeine high, about the high of her touch and her pheromones, about having another day like yesterday, about never leaving this bungalow again. I text Otto and Zev and Sophie but don't tell them where I am, because I want what's between Penelope and me to be private and only for us, protected from the harsh world. I periodically sniff Penelope's pillows and feel dizzy with desire. I brush my teeth and try to remember what day it is, and whether there are any important emails or meetings I'm missing. After rinsing my mouth, I answer these questions by looking at my phone: It's Sunday, no meetings, emails only from Urban Outfitters. I'm surprised I still get emails from Urban Outfitters after I shoplifted from them. I wonder if Penelope still gets emails from Urban Outfitters after she sued them.

I go to the kitchen, chug a glass of water, watch another hummingbird float delicately outside the window, and wonder if it's the same hummingbird from yesterday, or if Penelope's window attracts a posse of neighborhood hummingbirds. I remember my seventh-grade crush Dalia, how she nursed that bird to health, then disappeared.

I get back in bed and touch myself and come and then look at Instagram, mostly photos of Italian greyhound puppies, my eyes glazed over in a haze.

After an hour, I start to worry a little.

I text Penelope, *you ok?* And the text is green, which suggests her phone is off.

I take a long shower, enjoying her body wash that smells like roses and also her. I consider searching her cabinets for perfume or essential oils, whatever she uses to smell so divine, but opening a closed compartment feels like a violation.

I'm thrilled to see a pair of black lacy underwear strewn on the floor, and I'm sort of turned on by the idea that Penelope didn't bother to remove it, like she wanted me to see it, and I think about Bandit—that 1940s perfume inspired by the smell of models changing their underwear—and pick up the underwear and take a sniff, inhale deeply, feel dizzy. Sitting on the ledge of the tub, I coat my body in shea butter and then sprawl on the velvet couch naked, ready for her to top me when she returns, which I assume will be soon.

After waiting this way for roughly twenty minutes, watching the door like a hawk, I get cold, and put on a T-shirt and get my phone and do several mini crosswords.

Another hour passes, then another.

I hook up my iPhone to Penelope's speakers and make a playlist called *Perfume and Pain*, filled with songs of romantic anguish and lesbian pining, songs by Lana Del Rey and Patsy Cline and Usher and of course Cat Power.

And then I become sad.

Time continues to pass and I continue to become sadder.

I want to wait until Penelope returns, to never leave, to stay in our little patchouli-scented bungalow forever, safe and cocooned from the cruel outside world, from judgments and pain and mundane obligations like "making a living." But then I remember this is real life, not a dream, and I've only just become intimate with Penelope a day ago, and she clearly left because she doesn't want to be around me, because she's likely back with Nadia Kotov the knot scholar, a smarter and less feral distraction, and I should respect her boundaries and go home and pretend this never happened.

But I'm not sure how I could possibly forget or move on.

Back at home, my heart aches.

I look out the window for Penelope's Volvo, but it does not come.

I touch myself and come. Again and again. Until I'm raw.

: : : :

Have you heard from Penelope? I text Zev the next day.

Her Volvo still isn't here.

I could text her, but her disappearance is its own message, loud and clear.

She doesn't want anything to do with me.

I'm toxic.

I'm her Poison Ivy.

Nope, texts Zev.

: : : :

The next morning, I awake to a din in the yard.

Men yelling. Heavy objects dropping.

I go outside and see movers.

Someone is carrying a blonde woman's décolletage across the yard.

No, no. This can't be happening.

I text Deedee, *Is Penelope moving?*

Yes, she replies, *she was a great tenant. At least you'll have the place to yourself for a bit. It will take me a while to find someone to fill her shoes.*

ACT III

It would be Carol, in a thousand cities, a thousand houses, in foreign lands where they would go together, in heaven and in hell.

—*Patricia Highsmith*

one

I need to get my hands on the Patricia Highsmith.

To be fully dissociated, hardly alive.

I text Beau and offer him $300 to drive amphetamines and whatever other uppers he has to my house.

I plan to bender.

I hate Beau, but I ask him to hang out with me because I can't be alone and he's the only person who will drink and do drugs with me on a Tuesday morning.

I let him control the music because I know he won't play anything with guitars or feelings. Only nihilistic beats.

We do blow to Lil Peep.

"I heard people were talking about you online," he says. "Saying you're some kind of femme fatale."

I don't ask how he found out.

Instead, I do another line and smile, thinking of myself as a femme fatale. Femme fatale is good. Femme fatale is great.

I invite Zev over and some friends from my party days.

I drink and smoke and snort and crunch and press Repeat while the light moves through the yard, the sky changes colors.

· · · ·

I wake up with Sophie in my bed, my breath smelling of pizza.

The post–Patricia Highsmith suicidality is back.

More Patricia is the only cure.

For breakfast I crunch an Adderall and chug half a beer, then smoke a cigarette out the window, femme fatale shit.

I look at my phone and see that I texted both Penelope and Poison Ivy last night.

To Poison Ivy, I wrote, *cum over.*

To Penelope, I wrote, simply, *please.*

Poison Ivy replied, *you need help.* Then, *but maybe :).*

Penelope said nothing, and my text is green. Her phone isn't off: she blocked my number.

"The old Astrid is back," Sophie says as she walks past the kitchen to find me sipping my morning beer, hovered over my phone.

Sophie heads toward the door. "Bye, Asterix," she says on the way out.

I'm left alone in my own filth.

....

I spend the next few days in and out of consciousness.

Different bodies come and go, sentient slates on which to project.

At one point I see Poison Ivy, but I'm not sure if it's real or a dream or a hallucination. I also think I see Kat Gold.

I put on my *Valley of the Dolls* crop top, and don't take it off for days.

I continue to text Penelope, fevered messages she won't get, because they're green—I remain blocked.

I buy more Adderall and try to write, to unblock myself. I

crunch blue pills in my molars and sip carbonated alcoholic beverages and type and the words flow.

Fevered and unthinking, I text Ivy. *I think I'm writing the great lesbian pulp novel.*

"That's already been written, babe." I jump. Ivy is emerging from my bedroom, wearing the pink lingerie she bought from Victoria's Secret the day she told me she loved me, the day I told her I loved her. And now she's here. And I'm texting her. And when did she get here? And what day is it? Is it day or night? I blink and look outside, the sky a sort of soft periwinkle, but is it dusk or dawn?

"What's the great lesbian pulp novel?" I ask Ivy, trying to conceal my shock that she's in my home, and my confusion as to where we are in space and time as she makes her way to my kitchen and pours herself a glass of water as though she lives here.

"*Price of Salt*," Ivy says. She's so comfortable in my kitchen that I start to wonder if this is her home and I'm the interloper. Ivy is skilled at making me question my reality. I'm wondering if she's even really here when she adds, "Duh."

Ivy sips her water and I nod, then ask if she wants to go smoke a cigarette. She shrugs and follows me. Outside, I squint at the sky. I carry my cigarette to the top of the stone steps, where I crane my neck and look for the sun or the moon. Ivy sprawls out on the grass, which must be wet with dew. Or maybe not if it's nighttime.

Lighting my cigarette, I take a step forward and there must be a loose stone because the weight of my body pulls toward the steps, and I start to tumble, and there's a sharp burning sensation on my neck—must be my cigarette—and soon I'm halfway down the steps, peering upwards, thinking it must be dawn because the sky looks clearer, and realizing I could have just looked at my phone or asked Ivy for the time. I look around me for blood, feel my arms and legs and head, and see no red. Miraculously, I am bloodless, other than a tiny bit from where my cigarette burned my neck. But I imagine it looks very cool. Femme fatale shit.

I'm positive, even in this moment, that my blasé attitude is fully the product of the Patricia Highsmith. I've fallen before on it, and the pain never comes until later. I get up slowly and wait for Ivy to be concerned, maybe judge me, or scream at me as she loves to do. I'm more concerned about Ivy yelling at me than I am about the burn on my neck. I crawl up the steps, limping slightly, wondering what good deed I did to deserve Ivy's silence. Maybe she didn't hear me fall.

At the top of the steps, I look at the grass.

The grass appears moist—it's definitely morning—but Ivy is gone.

:::::

I wake up on the couch covered in blood. It's thick and bright and definitely looks unhealthy. My neck burns and my knee throbs. I must be dying, or maybe already dead? Maybe I died on those steps and now I'm in hell, trapped in this bungalow of misery forever. But then I smell something sort of sweet and lick a little blood on my arm and am slightly relieved but also disappointed to learn it's tomato sauce.

I'm alive.

Locating my phone on the sticky floor, I am scared to look at the screen. But I look anyway, mostly to punish myself. Beneath a thin layer of tomato sauce, I see that I sent many more texts to Penelope, which move from cute—*I think my favorite Chan song is Metal Heart what's yours? We should go to another* concert together! *Do you think Lana Del Rey is vapid?*—to needy—*Do you think I'm vapid? Do you know Chan Marshall and I are both Aquarius suns with Leo risings? Do you think I have a metal heart?*—to unhinged—*Do YOU have a metal heart? You MUST have something wrong with you to leave me like this!! For a RUSSIAN KNOT SCHOLAR no less!! HOW COULD YOU DO THIS TO ME I'M DYING?????*

They're all green and unanswered.

I apparently texted Agent Allison: *I'm writing the great lesbian pulp novel.*

She responded politely: *Always love to hear that you're writing, girlie!* (Star emoji.)

My last text to Ivy is nearly identical to the one I sent Agent Allison and remains unanswered. I wonder if Ivy was ever even here. I've never fully hallucinated on the Patricia Highsmith, just not remembered things, but having psychotic delusions under my belt could be chic. It might even qualify me to publish a memoir. I open a blank Google Doc and write: *if psychotic, then write memoir.* Around the time I decided to get healthy, I read Marijane Meaker's memoir about dating Patricia Highsmith. Apparently at the end of Pat's life, she was so drunk and dissociated she often mistook her own backyard for Paris. Maybe I'm already there. For a second I panic that I'm not even in Eagle Rock, that I never left San Francisco, that I'm in my childhood bedroom.

A text from Kat Gold floats in. *Sick party, girl!*

⋮ ⋮ ⋮

That afternoon (or is it morning?), Zev comes over and gives me an intervention of sorts.

"Cut the shit," he says. "What's on your neck?"

"Burned myself with a cigarette," I tell Zev, feeling like Amy Winehouse, "while falling down the stairs." I touch the burn and it stings.

"That's so dark, Astrid," Zev says.

I tell him about Penelope, about sleeping with her, the best sex of my life, and her leaving me, blocking my number, all without warning.

"You told me this," Zev says. "This is the third time you're telling me this."

"I don't know if I'll be able to go on." I put a hand on my forehead.

"Buck up, bitch," Zev says. "You hated Penelope."

"And then I loved her," I say.

"You hardly knew her."

two

When Zev leaves, I sleep for probably twenty-four hours, maybe longer, to the point I diagnose myself with bed sores and hypersomnia.

When I finally get the energy to open my eyes, I'm more tired than I was before. More tired than I've felt ever.

In the kitchen, I drink some water, then stumble over to my laptop and look at the pages I tried to write the other day, or was it yesterday? I quickly learn that I was not in fact writing the great lesbian pulp novel. I was writing nonsensical trash. Hardly English. If someone handed in these pages in Sapphic Scribes, I'd tell them to try another medium, like painting or basket-weaving, then try to 51-50 them.

I started taking the Patricia Highsmith because I thought all the greats wrote on a speedball. I thought it made me write faster and better. But I'm now remembering that while it feels genius and revelatory at the time, my speedball writing is muddled and chaotic in the light of day and takes forever to edit—it is in fact slowing me down.

I also started taking it to help me socially, but the other night Ivy emerged from my bedroom and I have no memory of what came before that or if she was even there at all. And if she was, I'm terrified I'm going to end up on another Tumblr post or worse. If people start attacking me online again, Agent Allison will surely drop me and then I'll have to move back to San Francisco and work for my parents and I'll surely die in my childhood bedroom.

High off shame and self-loathing, I take my laptop to my bed, put it on my belly, open Twitter, and search my own name.

My eyes glaze over the results.

@uglyadjacent Asterix Doll = Astrid Dahl = Pathetic Plagiarist! #NotMyDyke

@sassybottom astrid dahl spat a homophobic slur in a barnes & noble, we already know she's demonic . . . why are we still giving her airtime?

@cybersapphic my friend went on a date with astrid dahl and said she was a nightmare . . . poor demons that tempt me . . .

@bookishgalpal An author takes a terrible risk writing a vapid, foolish, superficial protagonist in first person and Astrid Dahl has fallen into this trap headfirst. Three times!!!

@readingyou can we talk about writers with talent instead of edgelord astrid dahl? literally the only reason she gets press is because she's hot and obnoxious and probably a nepo baby???

@killmeplease astrid dahl did nothing wrong, you people are so dumb and moralistic. is your high horse uncomfortable or do you love it up there? great artists steal, nerds.

@thekatgold Astrid Dahl is The Shit!!!!!

@pollypocket i actually feel sad for astrid dahl because she's obvi going to die alone

The last Tweet includes a link to Ivy's Tumblr post.
Without much thought, I open it.
And I read.

three

THE DEMONS THAT TEMPT ME

Home Archive Random RSS Search

PERFUME & PAIN

Greetings Ladies and Lesbimen!

When asked about writing her iconic 1957 novel *Odd Girl Out*, Ann Bannon said, "you had to be young, dumb, and determined, and I was!"

There are only a handful of authors today writing in the spirit of the lesbian pulp of the 50's and 60's, which is to say campy and sapphic and not the slightest bit literary, and this post is about one such writer in particular. Let's call her "Asterix Doll." Bannon's selling herself short above, but Doll is nothing if not young, dumb, and determined. Although I suppose she isn't really young anymore. . . . But she was just 28 when she published her first novel about a lesbian reality TV star desperate to escape television and her family. It's sort of fanfic about Kendall Jenner, who most of us sapphics suspect is one of us due to her boyish swagger and general air of unease. And then there was that *Vogue* article where the interviewer asked Kendall about her sexuality and Kendall said, "I don't think I have a bisexual or gay bone in my body, but I don't know! Who knows?" and then a bunch of chaotic rambling, concluding with, "I'm not gay. I literally have nothing to hide."

The lady doth protest!

I was excited to see someone was writing a novel loosely inspired by Kendall-the-closet-case, and it had a very fun cover. I was a baby dyke and developed a little crush on Asterix, tinged with a healthy dose of professional jealousy. Lesbian pulp was *my* thing, so how dare she reinvigorate the genre before me??

Then I read the book and it was utter shit. It made me so depressed about the state of publishing that this trite word vomit made a splash. So lazy and uninspired. It's, like, just typing? And not sexy AT ALL. No libido. And then I hear from various friends that Asterix is a lesbian about town, that she's fucked half of Los Angeles. And I'm like . . . her? I looked her up on Instagram and I couldn't say she was a looker. Nice legs, sure. Knows her angles. But a bit equine for my taste. Homely is another word that comes to mind. And she was always quoting sociopathic racist Patricia Highsmith and corny neocon Camille Paglia. And then she did that interview where she was clearly fucked up and called herself a "female faggot," and I was like oh, she's one of those tragic self-hating lesbians, a boomer essentially, your tone-deaf dyke Aunt. Out of morbid curiosity, I always wanted to run into Asterix but I never did. Apparently by the time I started going out in LA, she was deep in the throes of alcoholism and never really left the house.

Fast forward to my first semester at UCSB. My classmate brags that she's in Asterix's Zoom writing group, but that Asterix never really shows, that she's too cool for school. I emailed the moderator begging for a placement in the off chance Asterix might show and I could seduce her for sport. And even if Asterix didn't show, it would be a good opportunity to work on my lesbian pulp novel, to do what Asterix does better. In fact, Ann Bannon started writing lesbian pulp after reading Vin Packer's *Spring Fire* and thinking *she* could do better.

And then when I opened the first Zoom link, my jaw dropped. In one of the little rectangles appeared: Asterix Doll! Bloated and catatonic with a brittle blonde ponytail! A gift from Goddess! I was expecting a fun little challenge, but unfortunately Asterix threw herself at me. I've never seen someone so thirsty! Homegirl needs some electrolytes. She messaged me incessantly, asked for my number, FaceTimed me BLACKED OUT and told me she had a major crush on me. It was all very easy. And honestly . . . boring!

But at some point something shifted. I found myself developing feelings towards Asterix. I don't know what it was. Something about her desperation. Her discomfort in her own skin. She was like Kendall! Except not modelesque or rich or famous. She was your standard East LA narcissist—she'd been inside me like 12 times before she even bothered to ask me where I was from—with an addictive personality and an insatiable hunger for melodrama. But also so awkward and tragic and really living in her own world, like completely oblivious to anything outside herself, and it was kind of fun to hang out in that world for a bit, to escape myself and my dissertation and our dismal political landscape. And she wanted me so badly. And suddenly I found myself thinking about her a lot.

Do yourself a favor and never develop feelings toward Asterix: as soon as she senses your bite, she begins to turn. She lovebombs and then once she has you, she pulls away, shifts her attention toward someone else. In my case, she transferred her feelings onto this Gen X VEGAN LOSER, and I'm pretty sure she had a weird thing with tragic dyke magnet Kat Gold. Pretty soon she was treating me like yesterday's trash. It was just so classic cluster B addict, I cannot believe I fell for that shit once again! And I'm embarrassed I actually liked her!

Do yourself another favor: don't read her books. They're garbage. And not in a fun way. She's not an artist, she's just persistent. Same goes with her love life.

And Asterix, if you happen to come across this, do *yourself* a favor: Try having a friend who isn't a gay man who laughs way too hard at your jokes(?) thereby giving you a wildly distorted self-worth. Get in a 12-step program ASAP and try Pilates? Skinny fat doesn't age well. And maybe stop writing and go back to law school? Desperation and no creativity a great lawyer make!

Oh and one last thing: That book you love so much that you PLAGIARIZED it in your workshop, *Perfume and Pain* by Kimberly Kemp? KIMBERLY KEMP IS A MAN!!! His name is Gilbert Fox and he was an Air Force lieutenant in WWII. He's also Dallas Mayo, the other pulp you said you liked. Very fitting of you to pick the absolute SLEAZIEST of lesbian pulp to latch onto. At least my girl Vin Packer is a woman—Marijane Meaker, i.e., Patricia Highsmith's lover. The best of the best. Meanwhile, you're drawn to a lurking army dude drawing the most cartoonish portrayal of womanhood.

Classic Asterix!!!

four

I dream I'm trapped in a dungeon, and someone is pounding on the door. But I'm not dreaming. Or the dungeon part is a dream, but someone is really knocking at my door. I get up and stumble, sun in my eyes. Why is LA so fucking bright all the time?

Opening my front door, I'm first hit with a scent. Orchids and metal. I look down to avoid the sun and see pink cowboy boots. Looking up, I see dark hair, eager eyes.

"Hi, Astrid."

Ivy's back. She's looking right into my eyes. And she's holding a diamond ring.

. . . . .

We're sitting on my couch and Ivy is trying to shove the ring on my finger. It looks like a real diamond. And it's so shiny.

"Forgive me, Astrid," she's saying, and I must still be dreaming, but the ring is glinting in the sunlight, and it's absolutely mesmerizing. The diamond is huge and makes my finger look so slender. And I feel so rich, loved, admired, taken care of, safe.

"You said I was a psychopath on your Tumblr," I say.

"I was upset, Astrid," she says. "I didn't mean any of that."

I know I should tell her to leave. But without Penelope here to back me up, and no one to witness how dumb this is, I look into her frenzied eyes and say, "I forgive you." Then, "The ring is beautiful." Finally, "I love you."

* * * *

Waking up alone in my bed, I look at my finger. It's bare. No ring. It was a dream. And I'm relieved but also sad. I wish someone wanted to claim me. I wish the last three women I'd been with hadn't thrown a squash at my car, said I was a psycho on her blog, and moved to get away from me.

I'm vile, repulsive, a pariah.

I grab *Perfume and Pain* from my desk and flip to the end. Gail is all alone. Wanda is gone, in bed with her husband. Aunt Peg is married to some dude named Harold. Gail takes a handful of sleeping pills. The last line of the book is Gail wondering how long the pills will take to work.

How long until she'll be dead.

I touch the burn on my neck and revel in its sting.

five

After another twenty-four hours of intermittent sleep, getting up periodically for water or snacks, I start to feel semi-human again. I'm depressed, but I put the depressive energy into cleaning my apartment. Whenever I have a negative or sad or self-defeating thought, I put it into cleaning.

And when my apartment is clean, I write.

I write sober, fueled only by caffeine and sparkling water.

I abandon my lesbian pulp novel.

I decide to write something more earnest, less campy, something where the protagonist doesn't kill herself at the end.

I decide to write "from the heart."

I write about a girl trying to change, like every other book.

The words come easily. I guess I don't need the Patricia Highsmith to write. Maybe I just needed to feel something. Maybe Penelope ditching me was the best thing to ever happen to me.

When a romantic urge pops up, a need for attention, I put it on the page.

When my knee heals, I go on long walks. I do yoga. I finish *The Secret History*, then *The Goldfinch*, which is even better, and when it ends, I cry—at the story, because it's over, and also because Donna only releases a book every ten years, meaning I'll have to wait a few years until her next one.

I stop eating microwave foods.

I eat black beans and eggs and fresh spinach and tinned fish.

I stop drinking and smoking.

My skin starts to glow and my brain expands.

I tell Sophie about the Penelope fiasco, and she says I already told her, that I told her several times. She reminds me that she knows Penelope's ex Laura from grad school. The famous, smooth-brained Laura. The Laura I have in darker moments thought about harming, simply because she was able to capture Penelope's heart in a way I wasn't—not only becoming her girlfriend but also receiving home-baked cakes from her after they broke up. "You kind of look like her," Sophie says, and instead of being offended like I was when Otto said the same thing, I ache.

When I ache, I write, and transfer my emotional experience onto the page, where I am every character.

I feel what my characters are feeling, and sometimes when I write, my heart races.

six

I'm writing when I hear a knock on the door and my chest flutters thinking of how Penelope would bother me. Except she never knocked, she just barged in, and I hated it, and now she's gone. And I can't put the feeling on the page because the knocking continues and I have a feeling it won't stop until I answer it, so I get up and my foot is asleep—I write cross-legged—and hop to the door.

Gazing through the peephole, I at first think I'm looking at Samantha Ronson from 2009 and wonder if someone put LSD in my Brita filter. Then I remember Ivy's ex-girlfriend, or actual girlfriend, or maybe ex again: the Samantha Ronson derivative from her Instagram. Joey. Joey Silva.

Wondering if she's lost, I answer the door. "WeHo is like thirteen miles away," I say.

Joey's face is sullen, wan, and I wonder if she, too, has a drinking problem. "Hi," she says, ignoring my rude WeHo comment, which makes me respect her a little. Maybe we'll fall in love. "We haven't met—I'm Joey."

"Astrid," I say. "I recognize you from Instagram." The sun burns my eyes just like it did in my dream, when Ivy was at my door with a diamond ring.

"You too," Joey says. "Can I come in?" I wonder how she got my address.

Instead of asking, I follow Joey into my own home, still hopping because my foot is still asleep. She sits on the couch and I offer her some water. She shakes her head no and starts talking. "I'm sorry for barging in on you like this, but I didn't know where else to go."

I sit on the shell chair across from the sofa and feel shaken by Joey's unrestrained eye contact and the predictability of her uniform—the Dickies, the Vans classics, the muscle tee advertising what I can only assume is a skateboard company. She has three visible tattoos: a palm tree, a lion, and—oh my god, is that Taylor Swift's face? But I'm wearing a nightgown midday and have been hopping around my apartment like a freak and am in absolutely no position to judge.

"I can't find Ivy," Joey says.

"I thought you broke up." I twist my ankle in a circle to get the blood flowing.

"We did," she says. "But I still care about her."

"Why?" I say without thinking.

"No one can find her, Astrid," Joey says. "Her family is concerned. Her mom called me. And she has reason to believe Ivy was with you."

"Oh my god, are you accusing me of murder?" I've been watching a lot of true crime for a drug-free adrenaline rush and suddenly I'm one of those brain-dead murder-obsessed bitches I've always made fun of. Somehow I always end up becoming the type of person I once made fun of. Maybe one day I, too, will have Taylor Swift's face tattooed on my forearm.

"Of course not," Joey says just as something hits me: Joey said Ivy's mom called her. Ivy said her mom was dead.

"Wait, who called you?" I ask. Maybe I misheard. Maybe she said *dad* and I heard *mom*. I have a tendency to unconsciously feminize.

"Her mom, why?"

I shiver.

I consider telling Joey what Ivy told me—that her mom is dead, that she had her first fling with a woman at her mom's funeral—then decide against it. Joey seems good-natured, and it will likely alarm her. Ivy probably needs someone like Joey, someone calm and sincere to balance out Ivy's chemical imbalance, as opposed to someone like me, someone equally imbalanced if not an even bigger candidate for mood stabilizers, but at least I'm not crazy enough to fake my own mom's death.

"Have you seen her?" Joey asks when I say nothing. "Was she here?"

I twist my ankle again, finally getting the feeling back. I recall Ivy emerging from my bedroom and not remembering how she got there. She lay on the grass while I fell down the stairs and then she was gone.

"I'm not sure," I say, the truth.

"What do you mean you aren't sure?" Joey's right eyelid twitches and for the first time I remember her slamming Ivy's laptop. I'm not worried about Ivy—psychopaths always land on their feet—but right now I'm worried about myself, worried about Joey slamming me like she slammed the laptop. Maybe it could be hot.

"I went, um." I swallow, gather my words. "I went on a little bender. I have a vague memory of Ivy being here. I'm not sure if it's true."

"Okay," Joey says and her eyelid twitches again. My heart races. Maybe Joey is just as crazy as I am, as crazy as Ivy, crazier than both of us combined. Maybe there is a way I can get on her good side. Maybe I'll charm her and we'll fall in love. Maybe she'll ruin my life. Maybe she'll murder me. But first: we'll get matching Taylor Swift tattoos.

"I was ghosted," I tell her. "By this woman I was, um, sort of in love with? And I went a little loco." Joey cocks her head at me. I need to use lesbian speak. "I didn't cope well. I had bad boundaries. I'm working on it in therapy. I'm in love with my therapist too." Obviously I am not in therapy, but lesbians love transference.

Joey nods. "I get it," she says.

Told you.

Joey clears her throat. "Ivy always thought you were using her."

I squint at Joey, grip the arm of my chair. Me, using Ivy? How rich. But I won't say anything. Joey is worried.

"I'm sure she's okay," I tell Joey. And I mean this. Psychopaths have nine lives. I recall falling down the stairs, being fine.

"I hope so," Joey says, then gets up.

I see her out and for the rest of the day, I feel very weird. To externalize those weird feelings, I watch a Netflix docuseries about a family of murderous redheads in small-town South Carolina, and by the end I can't stop mimicking their accents. *I didn't kill that faggot*, the redhead named Buster said about a young man he absolutely did kill, which I'm now saying to myself in the mirror. I text Otto, *I didn't kill that faggot*, knowing he'll get the reference because if it is on Netflix, Otto has seen it. He responds quickly: *Prince Harry should play Buster in the Lifetime version.*

seven

Sophie asks me to apologize to Sapphic Scribes. At first I tell her hell no, my Sapphic Scribes days are over, they ended when it stopped being called the Lez Brat Pack and I should have never gone back. She tells me to bite my tongue, that I'm full of shit and I owe them an apology. Plus, she reminds me, Ivy is missing. (Sophie also speculated that Ivy fabricated her mom's death to conform to lesbian pulp tropes, in which the main character often seeks a mother figure in an older love interest, à la Gail and Aunt Peg.) And Todd left the group to focus on his new Tatiana Moon book. So, I agree to the apology.

I sit under the eucalyptus tree and fire up Zoom. Today my coffee mug is filled with coffee, and I take a sip as the faces load. Sophie's hair is down, falling in thick curls. Pia is wearing a sweatshirt that says Queers at Google. Charli is in a very dark room that looks like a dungeon. There is also a new girl, a brunette Zooming in front of a poster of Rita kissing Camilla Rhodes in *Mulholland Drive*. She's wearing thick-rimmed glasses and before my mind can go anywhere untoward, I see a message from Sophie.

Don't think about it, Sophie writes. *Also she has a boyfriend smh. Bisexuals...*

You have so little faith in me, I write back. *Does she call him her "partner"?*

Sophie is somehow talking to the group in a polished manner and messaging me at the same time. She's infinitely more natural than Todd, asking the group about their week and responding warmly. When she finishes her opener, she addresses the elephant in the room: me.

"I know there was an incident a few months ago involving Astrid and a former member of our group," Sophie says. "Astrid is here to say a few words about that if everyone is okay with it."

Reluctant nods ripple around the Zoom. The new girl, whose name is Teresa, seems confused. I imagine Sophie messaging her privately to inform her of the "situation."

I open the script I'd written the previous night after googling "successful celebrity apologies." The internet stressed to be direct, take accountability, and not make excuses. "Hi," I say, my voice froggy because I haven't used it all day. I clear my throat and sip my coffee, then take a deep breath. "I want to sincerely apologize for plagiarizing my pages to this group, which was unethical and made you all feel unsafe. I was going through a rough time and feeling very insecure about my writing and my personality, and that isn't an excuse, but I felt too vulnerable to show my writing to others. And I should have just said that. But I made a stupid decision that tarnished the group's integrity, and for that I am deeply regretful." I'm using words lesbians love: *feel*, *unsafe*, *vulnerable*, *integrity*.

I look up at Sophie to see if I'm on the right track, and her eyes encourage me. Pia looks bored, picking at her nail. I can hardly see Charli; her dungeon is so dark. It seems Teresa has left the room. I realize I am just apologizing to Sophie. And that's okay.

"The Lez Bra—sorry, *Sapphic Scribes*—has been invaluable to my growth as a writer and a person," I say, looking right at

Sophie. "I've learned that good writing is not a purely solitary endeavor, that it takes good friends and confidants to push through the billion drafts required to write something worthwhile." Sophie smiles. "Through Sapphic Scribes, I've met some of my best friends and the smartest bitches I've ever known." I'm really just talking about Sophie, which she knows. "Without it, I'd probably be a miserable lawyer in the Bay Area. I might even be straight."

Sophie laughs. No one else does. Teresa has returned to her Zoom rectangle with a green apple, which she's eating on mute.

"So, I just want to say thank you to everyone for hearing me out and for letting me return to the group," I say. "I promise to be honest and upfront with you all in the future, and never again act in a way that makes you feel disrespected."

"Thank you, Astrid," Sophie says.

"We never agreed to let her back in the group," Pia says. This is not the first time Pia has tried to oust me. If we ever meet in person, I imagine trying to seduce Pia onto my side. No, that's the old Astrid. The new Astrid will let it go.

"If you have an objection to Astrid's return to the group she cofounded," Sophie says in her most professorial voice, "you can email me."

Pia frowns, and Sophie leads us into workshopping Charli's video game pages.

I message Sophie while Pia monologues. *I wish Charli would stop writing about being trapped in a video game and start writing about being trapped in her parents' basement in Albuquerque.*

Same, Sophie responds. *And thank you for doing that.*

I meant every word, I write back.

: : : :

At dusk I'm trying—and failing—to do a cartwheel in the yard when my phone vibrates in the grass. An unknown number flashes across the screen. I'd normally send it to voicemail but for some reason, today, I answer.

"It's Joey." Her voice is more feminine over the phone, although I can't really remember what her voice sounded like in person, only her 2009 aesthetic and Taylor Swift's face on her arm. I don't ask how she got my number. I don't ask anything. "Ivy texted," Joey says.

I say nothing. I was never worried about Ivy, but I'm a little worried about how out of breath I am from trying—and failing—to do that cartwheel. Joey keeps talking.

"She was camping, and her phone was off."

This, I'm absolutely certain, is a lie. But Joey seems committed to believing it. So, with great effort, I say, "Phew."

"I figured you'd want to know," Joey says. "There will be no murder investigation."

I grin. "Excellent news. I'll let my lawyer know."

Joey laughs. "Take care, Astrid."

With a click, she's gone.

. . . .

In a penitent mood that night while watching a vintage *Keeping Up with the Kardashians* episode—"Kris auditions to become a cheerleader but is quickly overwhelmed"—I text Kat Gold.

Hey, I write. *I feel bad about Rye losing their job because of me. Maybe they should be in the writers' room? It might be nice to have a nonbinary perspective, especially given most people find me abrasive and old-fashioned and I'm famously uninformed. Just an idea!*

That is a fabulous idea, Mx Dahl! Kat responds quickly. *I will talk to Maude about it in the morning! Also: I think Kristen Stewart is flirting with me? Stay tuned!*

On the screen, Khloe dips a tampon in a glass of water to teach Kendall about puberty.

eight

I think about Penelope every single day, until one day: I don't.
This is roughly six months after she walks away, the day I
hit 50,000 words on my draft, at which point I call it a book. Poison Ivy's Tumblr post and the resulting discourse has blown over,
and Agent Allison admits that in retrospect I was right to not
engage. She also tells me she's "very impressed" with my quote
in the queer literary journal and thinks I'm ready to start doing
more interviews and to "get my queer writer girl on."

And that afternoon, Zev comes over with a letter. To me,
from Penelope.

"Here," he says flatly, handing me the envelope.

"You saw her?" I ask, heart racing, transported back to three
months ago, when I felt things related to people as opposed to
characters in my book.

"She stopped by," he says. "She brought bones for Jackie-O."

"Where the fuck has she been?"

"She's renting a place in Joshua Tree."

I nod. I've never really understood the hype about Joshua
Tree, or the desert generally. There's no shade. No trees. It's too
dusty. Too dead.

"She got this residency," Zev says. "It's super prestigious, I
think. She seemed happy about it."

For a second, I'm annoyed. But then I'm happy too. I recall that conversation we had, the one I didn't remember the first time, about how Penelope's career was popping off at my age, how it had dwindled and felt dead, how she was living off the Urban Outfitters money that wouldn't last forever. Getting this residency might mean she's back on top. I'm happy for her, but I'm also happy for me. I don't have to dwindle. I can get back on top too. I might be doing it now. We both are, which connects us in some way.

Zev says he has to run to the store, and I'm thankful for the opportunity to read the letter in private.

I go into my room and set the vibe. The lighting (candles), the music (Chan). I get a glass of water with ice. I put on my black silk kimono. And then I open the letter.

Hi Astrid,

I don't know where to begin. It's intimidating to write a letter to a famous author, and I know I began in the most cliché place imaginable. I'm not great with words. I'm better with images. And feelings. And acts of service. Never mind, this isn't my Hinge profile.

I first want to say I'm sorry. It feels empty and meaningless to say. I know I hurt you. But I genuinely believe in my heart of hearts that I did the best thing for both of us. If I hadn't, we would have dated. We would have fallen in love. I would have fallen for your quick mind, your youthful energy, your soft skin. And you would have fallen for my maturity, my experience, my willingness to care for you. But then we would have fallen out of love. You would have found me nagging and out of touch, and I would have found you immature and bratty. We would have inevitably hurt each other. I know because I've been in this relation-ship before, and I've been working on staying out of it.

I normally choose to do what I think others want, ig-noring my own needs. When I got the call about that res-idency, I knew I had to take it. The old me would have stayed for you or brought you with me. For the first time, I chose myself. And I hurt you in the process. And that isn't fair. But I promise you will be better off in the long run. You will have some time to yourself. You will write. You will get healthy, like you planned. You will sell another book. And when you're ready to date, you will be introduc-ing the world to the best version of you. You will dazzle. And you will meet the love you've been waiting for.

I signed a year-long lease in Joshua Tree in Septem-ber, so I'll be here for another six months. After that, I'll likely return to Los Angeles, though not as your neighbor. I'd love to get coffee then. But I by no means expect you to wait around.

Penelope

I fold the letter and put it back into its envelope and put it on my bedside table. Then I put my laptop on my belly and begin typing a response.

Hi Penelope,

I finally stopped thinking of you every day, then Zev showed up with your letter. I'm a little pissed you saw him and not me, but whatever. I'm pissed at you for a lot of reasons. I've been putting it all into my writing. I stopped drinking and smoking and my skin looks fantastic—I'm frequently mistaken for a girl in her mid-20s. Sorry, "woman." I stopped eating microwave food too. I do yoga every day and walk 4–7 miles. I completed a new manuscript. It's a rough draft, but still a draft. I wrote it in just a few months. My agent seems to like me again and says I'm ready to "get my queer writer girl on." Sophie has become a good friend. She knows every remotely intelligent dyke in Southern California and told me she likes you but thinks Laura is kind of a dud. She's also met your Russian distraction and told me she got a perfect score on her GREs, so nice work.

I don't know why you're insecure about your letter-writing abilities. I liked the paragraph about us falling in and out of love. I don't agree with it at all, but it was well written. Also you have very sexy handwriting—feminine but also authoritative. Reminds me of . . . well, never mind.

Oh and congrats on the residency!!! You were absolutely correct to take it, and for the record I would not have gone if you tried to take me: the desert does not agree with me. I hope you make lots of beautiful art featuring high-IQ blonde women that ends up in some prestigious biennial.

Six months is nothing. I'll have to edit this book. It's about a girl in her mid-30s figuring out what to do when her coping mechanisms stop working. I don't know where I got the idea. You might be in it. Or a version of you. Don't worry, you look good. (I look bad. Or the version of me in it does.)

Astrid

nine

For a few weeks I await a response to my letter to Penelope, checking the mailbox every day, a chore I typically avoid as I'm on a self-imposed spending freeze and the mailbox is now filled exclusively with bills I pay electronically and then must recycle. A very unsexy chore.

After two weeks, I stop checking, and my mailbox fills up again, I assume, with papers I don't need.

With Sapphic Scribes' assurance that it's ready—by which I mean mostly Sophie's assurance because I'm sure Charli and Pia halfheartedly skimmed my work in the same way I halfheartedly skim theirs—I send my new book to Agent Allison, and suddenly it's time to go to San Francisco again for my parents' birthday. Felix picks me up, which is great because I don't have to drive that terrifying stretch of the 5 alone. He's been living in his van in Arizona near some "dope climbing," where he teaches outdoor education to kids, so I'm on his way.

Felix seems happier and lighter than normal.

He says the same about me.

I greet him with a bottle of fancy body wash and cologne from an Oregon company that uses sustainable harvested plants to make craft fragrances, and he seems surprised, but touched. I hope he uses them. His van smells of BO.

During the drive, Felix drinks coffee from a thermos and talks nonstop. I'm reminded that we are related. He's mostly talking about his new crush, which is unusual for him. He normally doesn't have much romantic interest. I always assumed he formed his identity in reaction to me, as most siblings do. I was obsessed with getting good grades and winning, so Felix was unmotivated and chill, more focused on "hanging out" and engaging in non-competitive outdoor activities like rock climbing. I always had a crush; Felix was a lone wolf. But now he's crushing hard. Maybe my brief period of celibacy has encouraged him to react against me once again by getting high on limerence.

As he talks, I zone in and out, occasionally looking at the hazy mountains in the distance, the avocado and strawberry fields, and taking sips from my big bottle of San Pellegrino. When I zone back in, he's talking about this woman he met climbing. Molly? Lily? I've never totally understood Felix's taste in women—his type could be best described as "YouTube yoga teacher"—and Molly/Lily seems like no exception. When I ask what he likes about her, Felix says she's "nice and happy and athletic." Sounds positively sexless, but I don't say that. Instead, I say, "I'm happy you're happy" as we pass Harris Cattle Ranch, California's largest beef producer.

We plug our noses.

:::

For dinner we eat Swedish food—pickled herring and crawfish and kalops stew—in my parents' icy dining room. I hate Swedish food, and I normally hate this dinner, resent having to be here, but I feel slightly less bitchy than usual. Without coming down constantly, I'm not as angry. I'm uncomfortable most of the time, prickly and sensitive to life after years of numbing into oblivion. Everything hurts more but somehow feels less bleak.

And here in my childhood home, I realize that what I once identified as hostility might actually just be painful awkwardness. My family wants to get along, but we all have different interests and are similarly uncomfortable in our own skin. Watching my parents sip their vodka sodas and smelling the faint hint of marijuana on Felix's sweater, I realize we're each medicating away our discomfort, trying to be pleasant.

I guess we're all a bit slow to warm.

Felix tells my parents about his crush, who it turns out is named Molly, and my parents respond with questions about money, about Felix considering grad school, about his picking a vocation. Previously, I'd have read this line of questioning to mean my parents don't care about Felix or his desires, but now I'm realizing the opposite is true. If my parents didn't care, they'd just be polite and say what Felix wants to hear. They care, so they're concerned. They just want their children to be safe and financially secure when they're gone.

"I don't care about money," Felix says. "I'm happy in my van."

My mom stabs a piece of beef with what I once would have interpreted as aggression, but now see as efficiency, the most practical way to get the beef onto her fork and into her mouth, where it will be converted into energy used to write briefs, earn money to care for her financially irresponsible children.

"Molly won't want to marry a man who lives in his car," my mom says. "Does she know you went to private school? Does she know we spent over a hundred thousand dollars on your education?"

I sip my LaCroix and look at Felix, who looks wounded.

"Let him be himself," I say, then realize this statement is meaningless to my parents, boomers who weren't socialized to be easily wounded individualists. "Felix knows what he's doing,"

I say. "He'll be okay." I don't have much evidence that this is true, but I'm nonetheless confident that Felix will figure it out. We both will. My parents nod, and I feel like I said the right thing for once.

.:.:.

After dinner, Felix and I wander the neighborhood. Under a tall cypress tree, he offers me his Pax pen.

I wave the pen away. "I'm off the sauce."

"Good for you." He hits and exhales toward the tree. Smoke gathers, then fades before dark green leaves, disperses up toward a cobalt sky. "Thanks for standing up for me," he says, watching the smoke.

I shrug, look at my shoes. "Of course."

"Are you seeing anyone?" Felix asks. He never normally asks this question, I suppose because I offer romantic updates unsolicited.

I consider telling Felix about my fling with Penelope. He seemed to like her, probably because she looks like a YouTube yoga teacher. But I'm off that sauce, too, talking about women to avoid . . . whatever I'm trying to avoid.

"I'm focused on my writing," I tell him.

"That's good," he says, and we keep walking. "You seem better."

"Better than?" I don't like that he's making me feel sick.

He takes a big drag of his Pax pen. "You used to be kind of a bitch," Felix says.

Felix often makes a big deal about how I "traumatized him" by bullying him when he was a kid, but there is insignificant airtime given to the plight of the older sibling, of having 100 percent of your parents' love, then suddenly and without warning having 50 percent snatched away, then fighting your whole life to get that other 50 percent back, but never getting it back, because you're competing with a tall and handsome boy, the salt of the earth. And also Felix was fucking irritating, always bothering me when I was just trying to watch *Saved by the Bell* in peace.

"Well, you were annoying," I say, annoyed right now.

"You were really mean," he says. "You'd make fun of my clothes and the way I talked, you'd call me stupid and say I smelled bad."

I take a deep breath, try very hard not to say what I want to say, something along the lines of: *you got something against honesty?*

"I'm sorry," I say instead. "I was just really fucking insecure."

The moon lights up the cross at the top of Mount Davidson in the distance.

ten

Felix is knocking on my door, asking if I'm ready to "hit the road." My parents are already at work, but they left a note.

> *Astrid and Felix,*
> *Thanks for coming home for our birthdays. Wonderful to see you.*
>
> *Love, Mom & Dad.*

It's cold as ever, but for the very first time I feel a little touched, grateful to have a family who wants to be around me. They may not tell me I'm pretty or smart or talented, but they show their love in other ways. They're doing the best they can. We all are.

On the drive, Felix and I drink coffee and then water and listen to *Tha Carter*, *Tha Carter II*, and *Tha Carter III*—which we agree is Lil Wayne's best album.

"Oh, Astrid," Felix says as we pass Harris Cattle Ranch, "I really like that body wash and cologne you got me."

I smile, and realize once we pass the cattle ranch that the usual BO smell that accompanies Felix has dissipated somewhat.

"Good," I say. "I hope Molly likes it."

Soon we're winding down the grapevine.

When Felix drives up my street, a shocking sight catches my eye: a baby pink Fiat parked beside my driveway.

Could it be a coincidence?

"You okay?" Felix asks.

"That car." My heart skips. How do people live without consuming massive amounts of alcohol all the time? My cells are jumping out of my skin and on fire. I feel everything and I don't like it at all.

"Dope, right?" Felix says, tilting his head at the car.

"No," I say. "It, um, belonged to an ex," I say. "A kind of scary ex."

"Devon?" Felix asks. I'm mildly charmed that Felix remembers my crazy ex, but also saddened that I've been dating the same crazy woman over and over again for most of my adult life.

That I'm that crazy woman too.

"No," I say. "But basically."

Felix looks confused.

"Similar vibe," I say.

"You want me to come up with you?" he asks.

I consider this. Felix likely can't stop Ivy from being crazy, but he is strong and the beard makes him look a little unhinged and therefore intimidating. "Actually," I say. "That would be great." I grab my bag from the back seat. "Hopefully it's just a strange coincidence."

"I don't know, Astrid," he says, helping me with my bag. "It's a pretty unusual car."

Walking up the stairs, I'm on edge—I've been extra nervous on these stairs since my big tumble, but this time it's a little different. I'm not scared of falling, but I keep waiting for Poison Ivy to pop out, for a flash of pink fabric or a high-pitched angry voice, the smell of tangy orchids, but I only see and smell the eucalyptus tree. My front door is locked and the lights are off, as they should be. Felix looks in the bushes around my bungalow with the flashlight on his phone. Inside, he looks in my closets and even under the sofa.

"I think the coast is clear," Felix says finally.

"I guess it was a coincidence," I say.

"I guess." Felix shrugs.

"Thanks for helping me," I say to Felix. "With everything."

We hug, and I get oddly emotional.

"Love you, sis," Felix says.

"Love you too," I say, and I mean it.

eleven

I awake with a general sense of doom. My body is adjusting to its new normal—raw, unmedicated, "feeling things." But today it's a little worse than usual. Compounding my unease, I have a text from Kat Gold that says, *girl we need to powwow because I'm pretty sure Kristen Stewart is trying to fuck me???*

I silence my phone and take *Perfume and Pain* outside with my coffee. Plopping in the shade, I flip to a random page. Gail is first developing a crush on Wanda with her golden hair and creamy skin. "So dainty. So sweet. So childlike. So innocent."

It hits differently knowing that Gail kills herself in the end.

From the stairs, I hear voices. Deedee's voice and another voice too. She's been interviewing new potential tenants for Penelope's old bungalow. Deedee told me Penelope finished paying out the lease, so Deedee was in no rush to find someone new, but suddenly it seems she needs the money because she's had a bunch of people here in the past few weeks.

In my periphery, two bodies come up the stairs, a blur of yellow and pink. The second voice, not Deedee's, sounds familiar.

I know this voice, and a familiar scent hits.

Looking up from my book, my eyes meet Poison Ivy's. In a pink dress. Cartoonish fake eyelashes. Beside Deedee in her standard floral muumuu.

"Oh, wonderful," Deedee says. "Astrid is here."

My heart throbs unpleasantly.

Ivy smiles at me with eerily vacant eyes, as though she's seeing me for the first time.

"Astrid will be your neighbor if you're approved," Deedee says to Ivy.

My brain spins. Ivy is here, and this time it doesn't seem to be a dream. For the first time, she isn't an apparition. She's here, and I'm here, and she keeps looking at me like she doesn't know me, and I guess she doesn't, at least not this version of me—present, sober, not behind a screen.

"Astrid, this is Ivy, your potential new neighbor," Deedee tells me. I worry I'm going to vomit or lose consciousness.

"Nice to meet you," Ivy says with a wide and terrifying smile. The women walk off across the yard to look at the bungalow. I gulp my water and think of who to text. I want to text Penelope, but I assume my number is still blocked. I text Sophie, then remember she's on a writing retreat without cellphones. Fucking lesbians and their wireless writing retreats. I text Otto, and he doesn't respond. I text Felix, and he calls me.

"You okay?" Felix asks. His voice soothes me. I remember how he drove me to and from San Francisco and looked in my bushes and under my furniture to protect me.

"Yeah," I say. "Stay on the phone with me for a bit?"

"Okay," he says.

I ask him about Molly and he tells me that yesterday they went on a hike and saw a mountain lion sleeping in a tree. At least Ivy isn't a mountain lion.

Soon Ivy and Deedee are back in the yard, chatting, walking toward me. If I didn't know any better, I'd think Ivy looked totally normal, a perfect tenant.

Deedee's about to say something to me, and then I point to my phone to signal I'm busy. Deedee nods in understanding. When they've disappeared, I tell Felix thanks and I love him and I'll call him soon and we hang up.

Looking back at the page, it shakes slightly in my hand. "Innocent? The girl was a she-devil!" I linger over the words for a few seconds, letting the breeze flap the page. I zone out until a presence hovers over me.

My gaze lifts.

"Hi, stranger," Ivy says and I blink. She taps the *Perfume and Pain* cover with a glittery pink nail. "You knew I was coming?"

I put the book on my lap. "Definitely not," I say.

"Don't look so scared," Ivy says. She sits beside me, and I feel like I'm choking on her aldehydic perfume.

I swallow, slide my amethyst along its chain.

"You love that fugly necklace, don't you?" Ivy says, grabbing the crystal pendant from my hand. When our skin briefly touches, it's like an electrical shock. I say nothing, just wait for her to let go.

When she finally does, the pendant is cold on my chest.

"Cat got your tongue?" she asks.

"I'm just a little surprised," I say. "Given our last few interactions."

"You seemed to like me just fine at your little party!" Ivy says.

Oh. My post-Penelope bender. So, she was there. And then she was gone.

"You disappeared," I say.

"I went camping," she says.

"You went camping," I repeat. Peering at Ivy with sober eyes, I wonder how I felt safe with someone so unstable and dishonest.

There is absolutely no way this woman blinking her fake eye-lashes and reeking of noxious chemicals went camping. Ivy didn't go camping just like her mom isn't dead.

"You burned your neck," Ivy says. "It was sexy." Ivy shifts a lock of my hair to reveal the side of my neck and I shiver. "Too bad," she says. "Almost healed." Her finger grazes over my now-faint scar.

I jump back.

"Oh, don't be so dramatic," Ivy says, squeezing my forearm. "We're lesbians! We're theatrical. We have to be. Otherwise, people would forget we exist."

"Right," I say, removing my arm from her grasp. "Your thesis."

"Exactly!" Ivy yelps. "We've experienced normal lesbian courtship patterns. We're ready to move in together. We should have a baby." She winks at me like a creepy doll. "A baby would solve everything."

I inhale sharply, hold my fugly amethyst for protection. "You told me your mom was dead," I say. "Joey said she was alive."

Ivy looks toward the trees, then back at me. Surprising me, she laughs. "I thought we were playing a game," she says.

A breeze hits and the metallic orchids float through my nose, something shifts, and I'm hit with a not unpleasant memory of Ivy telling me she loved me at Johnny Rockets.

"I've missed you, Astrid," Ivy says. She reaches into her purse and retrieves a tiny pillbox, pops it open. Inside are four bright blue 20 mg Adderall pills. And while I haven't craved the Patricia Highsmith in months, something about Ivy being here, smelling her perfume, the surreal nature of this experience, plus the ball of dread in my stomach, makes me want to throw it all out the window and hop on a speedball. Part of getting better is getting worse! As Ivy said, I've healed well. I've been detoxing and now it's time to retox. Forget everything. Be loose. Be bad. Feel good. Dread be gone!

I reach toward the pillbox and I'm about to take a pill when my phone starts vibrating. It's Felix.

"Ignore it," Ivy demands.

I answer it.

"Hey," I say.

"I had a feeling she would be back," Felix says. "This energy healer I recently saw told me I'm clairvoyant, and I had a vision of Ivy coming back. Spirit says you need to get rid of her. I can help you."

"Hang up," Ivy says.

"Is that her?" Felix asks.

"Yeah," I say.

"Tell her to leave," Felix says. "Do you have sage?"

I take a deep breath, torn, between wanting to take a pill and disappear, and wanting to do the right thing, listen to my brother, who is trustworthy and cares for me.

"Of course I have sage," I say into the phone. "I live in Los Angeles." I laugh and head inside.

"Where are you going?" Ivy asks.

"This is serious, Astrid," Felix says. "This person is dangerous. At least to you."

"You aren't going to offer me a drink?" Ivy asks, trailing after me.

"I hear her following you," Felix says. "Light the sage immediately."

I go into my bedroom to get the sage, find it by my window and look for a lighter, hearing Ivy stomping around in the other room, saying things to me I can't make out.

"Light it fast," Felix says.

I find a lighter and flick it, but it isn't lighting.

"What the fuck are you doing in there?" Ivy yells. "The drugs are out here, little miss sketchball."

I keep flicking the lighter, but no flame comes.

"It isn't lighting," I tell Felix.

"Find another one," he says.

"I'm not you," I say. "I don't smoke spliffs. I don't have a billion lighters lying around." I keep flicking—rhythmically, robotically, rapidly. With my free hand, I clutch my amethyst, which begins to warm. Finally, a flame appears and the sage lights, a gift from God, Spirit, whatever.

"It's lit," I say.

I blow on it hard. Embers hiss and turn neon orange, and smoke trails out of my bedroom, toward Ivy. The smoke knows exactly where to go. I blow again, and the other room seems to quiet. I blow again and slowly follow the smoke, nervous to see Ivy in the other room. But I don't see her. She isn't in the living room. She isn't in the kitchen. I check the closets and under the couch.

"I don't see her," I tell Felix.

I go outside and look at the grass, which glints in the sunlight, resembling plastic.

And once again, Ivy is gone.

twelve

I gaze at Penelope's bungalow longingly, wishing it were several months ago, wishing she were still here and she could come and tell me I'm not a bad person.

Pacing the yard, I scroll my iPhone contacts.

And I call Deedee.

"Hi, Astrid," Deedee says. "How are you?"

I move to a patch of sun that energizes me.

"I'm okay," I say. "I'm calling about the potential tenant you brought over today."

"Ivy," Deedee says. "She's great, isn't she? She's not Penelope, but I think she'll be a suitable replacement."

I look up at a eucalyptus tree, watch the leaves ripple in the wind.

"So," I say, swallowing. "This is kind of awkward, but I briefly dated Ivy."

Deedee says nothing for a few seconds. "Oh?" she says finally. "I didn't realize, she didn't say anything. When I introduced you, it seemed like you'd never met."

"I was really caught off guard," I say. "I get that she makes a good first impression, but"—I swallow again, watch the leaves sway—"she's kind of, like, been . . . stalking me?" I phrase it as a question because I'm not sure if it's true. Joey said I was using

Ivy. Ivy said we were playing a game. Maybe we were. Maybe I'm a bad sport.

"Oh no, Astrid," Deedee says, sounding legitimately concerned. "That's horrible. I feel awful for bringing her over and forcing you to interact with her."

I'm surprised Deedee is responding this way, so nurturing and parental. When I was younger and would get unwanted attention from men, I'd complain to my mom and she'd tell me I was ungrateful or weak. So I'd try to stomach it, try to see the good: I was wanted, I should be grateful, I should get high on the attention. But Deedee seems to think having a stalker is not something I should be grateful for.

"Don't feel bad," I say, still unsure of whether I am a victim or just a bad sport. "You didn't know. It's my own weird situation. And I'm sorry I dragged you into it."

"Astrid, please don't apologize," Deedee says. "It's not your fault. I've been there. Before Don. It's easy to feel like it's your fault, but it isn't."

"Thanks, Deedee," I say, and wonder who was stalking her.

"Of course, Astrid," Deedee says. "I'll reject her right now. And please let me know if she becomes a problem for you again. Don was in the military, you know. She can't fuck around with us."

I unleash a laugh. Strange feelings swirl inside of me. Deedee is protecting me. She is prepared to wield her military husband to keep me safe. She's saying "us," like we're a family.

"Thank you so much, Deedee," I say, my eyes wet with both laughter and, I suppose, emotion.

We hang up, and I'm alone in the yard, but I don't feel lonely. I have this whole yard on the hill to myself, and I can see the skyscrapers of downtown LA glinting in the distance. It's winter now, so it's going to get dark soon. I fetch my headphones and lie on the grass, listen to music, and watch the sky change colors until it's dark and cold.

Opening my front door, I hear a rustling in the yard and my heart starts to race. I try to calm myself down. If it's Ivy, I can call Felix. What if it's Joey, looking for Ivy once again? I can call Deedee. She can bring her military husband to protect me. I turn around, slowly, and see a bobcat on the other side of the yard. It looks healthy and majestic, its thick fur glinting in the low moonlight.

We make eye contact, briefly, me and the bobcat.

Then the bobcat slinks away, and I go back inside.

thirteen

When Sophie's back from her wireless writing retreat, she calls and asks me if I want to go to a Lesbian LitCrawl reading.

"Fuck no," I say.

"Come on," Sophie says. "Michelle Tea will be there. I heard she's a fan of yours."

"Really?" I can't help myself.

"Well, no," Sophie says. "But just come. It's not like you have anything better to do. Doesn't it seem like a fun excuse to wear an outfit and ogle the who's who of the lesbian literati?"

"No," I say. "That sounds terrible." I sip some water and think about what perfume I would wear. Probably something off-putting and a little scary, although I haven't strayed from the moon milk in a while. "And what if Ivy is there?"

"I'm a really amazing friend," Sophie says, "and I checked her Instagram and she's in Greenwich Village—probably living her pulp fantasies—with some girl who looks like you, so you're safe."

How the hell is Ivy already in New York with another girl? She was in my yard saying she wanted to have a baby with me just four days ago.

"Is she prettier than me?" I sip again. "Actually, never mind."

::::

Before the reading, Kat Gold texts me. *What are you doing, bitch?* I tell her I'm going to a reading against my will but Michelle Tea will be there and Kat says *Omg I love that chica* and suddenly Kat Gold is sitting with Sophie and me in the bar beside the bookstore and everyone is staring at us.

The bar is decorated with glass brick and palm trees, very '80s Miami. Sophie is wearing a high ponytail held up by a hunter green ribbon and she seems happy, lighter, glowing a little. I can't tell if her newfound radiance is due to her proximity to Kat Gold—who is wearing a baby tank that says Abuse of Power Comes As No Surprise—or something else.

"How have you bitches been?" Kat Gold asks us once we get our drinks.

Sophie is flushed and seems to have trouble putting words together.

"Sophie just got back from a wireless writing retreat," I say, speaking for Sophie.

"How was it, my little scholar?" Kat asks Sophie.

"It was nice," she says. "Actually, it was hell . . . But I finished my draft!"

"Cheers!" I hold up my glass and Kat follows. "I'm proud of you," I say, oddly the truth, odd because I'm excited about the accomplishment of someone other than myself.

We all clink glasses.

"Thanks," Sophie says. "I'm proud of me too."

As we sip, I consider whether to tell Sophie and Kat about Ivy's strange visit to my yard with Deedee, about blowing Ivy away with sage smoke based on my clairvoyant brother's instructions.

I feel the entire bar's eyes on us, and I'm so glad I'm a writer and not an actress, that no one aside from the occasional poolside twink recognizes me in public.

"Is there something wrong with me?" I ask them.

Sophie tilts her head, causing the ribbon to fall down the side of her neck.

"There's a lot wrong with you," Sophie says.

"But it's mostly cute." Kat winks.

Sophie laughs. "What's bringing this up for you?" She's an excellent emotional support pup.

"Ivy is not an outlier," I say. "I've dated Ivy over and over again. Obviously, this is a me problem."

"Slow down," Sophie says.

"Ivy is the chick who wrote the blog post?" Kat asks.

Sophie nods, and I spill the beans about Ivy's strange visit.

"Holy unhinged," Kat says. "I kind of love her?"

"The girl is deranged, Astrid," Sophie says. "It has nothing to do with you. She's like this with everyone. And, wow, your brother is an angel."

I make a mental note to send my brother more products from the sustainable scent company he likes. They sell incense that might go with his new prophetic persona.

"It must have something to do with me," I say. "You all have never dated anyone like Ivy."

"Um, I have," says Kat. "You didn't know me in my twenties— sorry, I mean my early twenties." I conceal a smile. I knew Kat was lying about her age. "I dated like twelve Ivys. I dated men—*and* women, thank you very much—who went through my phone and lied and accused me of things I hadn't done. Do you know how many times I've had to change my locks? I had a woman hack into my email and write my own mother telling her I had a cocaine problem, which I really didn't—I was just having fun!"

"We've all dated toxic people," Sophie says, seeming a bit looser. Kat has a way of putting people at ease. She smirks. "All lesbians have had to banish a woman with sage smoke. You aren't special, Astrid."

I smile. Being special or unique used to be something I wanted. But recently nothing brings me comfort like a reminder of my own insignificance.

I exhale and some sadness reappears in my gut.

"What about Penelope?" I say. "She ditched me."

"Oh my god," Sophie says. "Get over yourself. Every person— gay or straight or pan whatever—has been ditched by an older person who thinks they know better." Sophie smirks again. "It's literally the plot of *The Price of Salt*—which I just reread by the way, and Carol is kind of evil?"

I consider this. I always found Carol hot, aspirational, an ice queen, a dream woman. And in certain particularly delusional moments, I saw Penelope as the Carol to my Therese.

"I love Carol," Kat says. "Evil maybe, but definitely sexy."

"Evil how?" I ask.

"So, I've been seeing this woman," Sophie says.

"Bury the lede much!" My voice comes out high-pitched and squeaky. Am I jealous? Maybe a little bit. I want Sophie to my-self, but I also want her to be happy. So, this is why she's glowing.

"You go, girl," Kat says. "Make us jealous." She's speaking what I'm thinking, but Kat is merely performing, and I guess this is the point of actors—to perform what everyone else is thinking.

Sophie grins. "It's too early, I don't want to jinx it." She's red-dening a little and it's adorable. "I met her at the retreat."

"So anyway, I reread the book, and then I asked her if she

wanted to rewatch *Carol* with me, and she was all 'Hell no, *Carol* sucks.'"

I laugh. "Love her vibe."

"A firecracker," Kat says.

"And she made an interesting point," Sophie continues. "She teaches at UCLA—"

"Hot!" I interject. "A professor. Perfect for you."

"Beyond perfect," Kat adds. "Can I be the flower girl at your wedding?"

Sophie smiles. "Don't jinx it!" She sips her drink. "Anyway, she said her students—Zoomers—hate Carol. They think she's a bad person, a bad mother. They think she's mean as fuck to Therese and Abby and even her husband." Sophie's really animated, bathing in the sweet euphoria of lesbian limerence. "She says her Gen X friends also hate Carol for similar reasons. Zoomers are moralistic and Gen Xers are earnest, they like nice people. But us millennials are so psychotic and heartless, we're just like 'Carol is so hot, I want her to run me over with a car.'"

I laugh. It's true. "I've said that before," I say.

"Me too," Kat says.

"Same," says Sophie, then shakes her head. "But I've seen the light and I can't go back."

"I guess Carol is sort of negging Therese the entire book," I say. "I mean, 'flung out of space' is nothing if not a neg."

"Aw, I think it's sweet," Kat says, and I'm now certain Kat has a T-shirt that says Flung Out of Space.

"It's really not," Sophie says. "Like 'you're so strange, flung out of space!' Therese is probably terrified of Carol. She's probably dissociated and having a trauma response and that's why she seems spacy."

I laugh. Kat seems distracted by her phone.

"Everyone says it's romantic because they get together in the end," Sophie says. "But there is no way in hell they stay together. Carol will cheat on her as soon as Therese gets a lick of agency, then move on to the next traumatized shopgirl."

Sophie is right. Maybe it's time I outgrow *Carol* like I outgrew the Patricia Highsmith, like I outgrew Didion and nihilism, like I outgrew dating twenty-seven-year-old hysterics, like Penelope outgrew me and moved to the desert. Maybe Penelope really is my Carol, the older woman who met me at my most vulnerable, seduced me, then left me in the dust for the next tragic blonde.

"She could move on to me next," Kat says, putting her phone down and looking at me with feverish eyes.

Ignoring Kat, I say to Sophie, "Well, I'm doubly happy for you." I mostly mean it and am only a tiny bit jealous. "For your dissertation and for—wait, what's her name?"

"Carmen." Sophie smiles.

"Oh my god," I say. "Like the Lana Del Rey song!"

"Love that bop," Kat says, and I have a feeling she's never heard it.

I'm glad Sophie found a fun and smart woman who shares a name with a Lana Del Rey song. I sip and try to manifest the same thing for myself.

Kat's phone dings. "Oh my god," she says, examining the screen.

"What?" I ask.

She's staring at her phone like it's a million-dollar bill.

"K Stew texted me," she says. "I have to go."

Sophie gasps. "You must!"

I wonder if Kat Gold has read Kristen Stewart's poetry, whether she owns a T-shirt that says I'll Suck the Bones Pretty.

"Bye, my little Carols," Kat says, and air kisses us both. "Stay sexy."

The whole bar watches her leave.

When Kat's gone, Sophie says, "I love her" and I say, "She did not remotely get the thesis of your Carol argument," and Sophie says, "Not at all, but with that face? I'm just happy she showed up."

Sophie tightens her bow and then shows me a photo of Carmen.

I'm devastated to learn she is extremely hot.

fourteen

Waiting for Agent Allison to read and either like or not like my book is torture. I keep refreshing my Gmail and when I get bored of that, I text Otto. *There is a character based on you in my new book*, I write. He responds quickly, *If this book turns into a movie I get to pick who plays me*. I ask, *Who do you want to play you?* He says, *Nicki Minaj*. I write *LOL*. Otto is still typing. *Mischa Barton should play you*, he says. *Like OC-era Mischa Barton*, I say. *No*, he says, *Like Mischa Barton in The Hills New Beginnings when she auditions to play Ruth the Southern hooker in a Lifetime movie and doesn't get the role*. I'm about to tell Otto to fuck himself when Kat Gold texts me.

Cum outside, she writes.

I shut my laptop and obey my boss. I expect Kat to be in her car, her divorce vehicle, but instead she's standing on the street chewing gum and tapping a Yeezy sneaker on the pavement. She spits her gum on the ground and then kisses my cheek. The teal wad of gum is stuck to the sidewalk, where someone will surely step on it. Couldn't she have the decency to spit it in a bush?

"Hi, my little Carol," she says. "Love your friend by the way. Her name is escaping me."

Kat Gold claims to love so many people and it's increasingly clear to me that Kat Gold only loves herself.

"She loves you," I say and at least I'm not lying. "Sophie is her name."

Kat's already ahead of me, not listening. "Let's walk and talk," she says, pumping her limbs down the hill. The air is balmy, and I swear I can taste the ocean, even though it's twenty-five miles away. "So, K Stew. I'm wearing her down."

"Wearing her down?"

"Yes, bitch," she says. "I'm growing on her, I can tell."

"How?"

Kat Gold stops, smirks at me. I look away and keep walking. We can't stop every time she wants a reaction from me. I need to get my steps in.

"I can tell when someone's into me, Astrid, can't you?"

"Not really," I say. I walk toward my typical route and Kat grabs my arm.

"The paps," she says, and I remember our last walk, the photographs ending up in the *Daily Mail*. I obey Kat and switch course.

"God, Astrid," she says. "You're so clueless." Then, "I love you."

Today I'm feeling less amused by Kat Gold, more annoyed. I'm not clueless, I just put my mental energy into things other than discerning whether people want to fuck me. Well, that isn't entirely true, but the point is Kat claims to love me, but she really just wants her starring role. And for some reason she's fabricating a romance with Kristen Stewart, who is engaged, and who either way would have no interest in Kat Gold, who is too petite for her. I've paid enough attention to Kristen Stewart's dating history to know she exclusively dates Amazons. Kat is tall enough to model, sure, but she has the type of body that looks like it could crumble in a strong wind. K Stew wants to be dominated. And who can blame her?

"Does that word mean nothing to you?" I say.

"What word?" asks Kat.

"Love," I say. "You use it a lot."

A lizard darts in front of me and I try not to step on it.

"I have infinite love to give," Kat says to the sky.

"Right," I say to my shoes.

Kat and I continue to walk and she continues to talk, analyzing Kristen Stewart's last text message to her in the manner of a forensic psychologist on one of the true crime shows I'm trying not to watch. I begin to zone out, watch the light dip through the leaves, creating patterns on the pavement. I'm seeing a mermaid in the shadows when I interrupt Kat, the way she frequently interrupts me, to ask if Satchels of Gold hired Rye as a writer on the adaptation.

Kat shakes her head. "Rye wants nothing to do with us or you." I prepare for her to elaborate, but instead she looks at a black SUV rolling up and says, "Ride's here!" The car's windows are tinted, but when she gets in, I see the car is driven by a man, a man I know is not her driver because Kat gets in the front seat and also: she kisses him.

At home I open my manuscript and convince myself it's horrible, banal, corny, algorithmic, that Agent Allison will inevitably hate it and drop me, even though I'm no longer canceled, but because I'm just a bad writer, like Ivy said in her Tumblr post. Glancing at a scene starring the character based on Penelope, I start to worry I used Penelope for material the same way Kat is using me for a starring role. And then I worry that I used Ivy to get my heart rate up the same way Kat Gold is using K Stew to seem relevant. Rye is right to want nothing to do with us.

I google *who is Kat Gold dating now?* I click Images. I scroll through the results until I find him. The man I saw Kat kissing this afternoon. The man, it turns out, is a Republican senator.

I tweet: *hypocrisy is trending.*

Several people text me thinking my tweet is about them, assuring me that they know that Amazon is evil, but they have an autoimmune disease that makes it difficult to get to the grocery store, that they know cancel culture is an arm of the prison industrial complex, that they love Marx but they also love luxury and is there a fucking problem with that?

I put my phone in my underwear drawer and go on a walk.

While I'm walking, I think: Did I ever love Ivy or Penelope or do I, like Kat Gold, only love myself?

fifteen

When Penelope texts me that she's back in LA, I've nearly forgotten who she is. I'm thirty-six now, and the age of my neighbor-enemy-turned-lover feels worlds away. I have a new neighbor, an engineer named George. We've only exchanged a few words. We both mind our own business, sitting quietly in our respective sides of the yard without acknowledging one another, and we both drive Subarus.

The day I hear from Penelope, I drive my Subaru to Malibu to have lunch with Agent Allison on the roof of her hotel, which overlooks the water. She's in town for a wedding and said she'd come to the East Side, but I wanted to see the ocean for health purposes. Scientists say the negative ions are good for the brain, or at least one scientist I follow on Twitter said that. Although my brain has been behaving lately. Agent Allison and I have been busy going back and forth trying to perfect my new book until we submit it to publishers. I spend all my time editing, exercising, reading, walking with Zev, getting coffee with Sophie, and hanging out by water features with Otto when he comes to town to dress a celebrity.

Today is only my second time meeting Agent Allison in person. The first time I met her was on my first book tour, for which the publisher insisted I fly to New York. The Patricia Highsmith hadn't turned on me yet, and online culture wasn't quite so savage, so I coasted through the trip—buzzing from event to event, strutting through the streets and saying things like *I love the energy of this city!*

Agent Allison and I order chicken Caesar salads and a side of fries to split. She drinks a glass of sauvignon blanc and I drink an IPA, which I allow myself as long as it's just one. It turns out I'm not a legitimate alcoholic, but I knew that. I was just insecure and bored. As long as I'm busy working on a project, I can keep my impulse control issues in check. I just can't let my brain go idle, that's when the demons take hold, the demons that tempt me, et cetera.

"How was going to set?" Agent Allison asks after the waiter leaves with our order. The TV show based on my astrology novel is filming, and Kat Gold convinced me to go to set. *It'll be so fun, babe!* So I went, and it was not fun. But Kat Gold remains convinced she's going to break up Kristen Stewart's engagement, which is amusing to hear about in a sort of repulsive way. I told Kat Gold that if she really wants to cosplay as a dyke, she should date someone older and less conventionally attractive, like Eileen Myles or even Ilene Chaiken.

"It was interesting," I say, not a lie. I don't need to blurt everything that comes to mind, like that being on set made me very stressed out, that there were too many people blowing hot air in my face, and I didn't know what to do with my hands and kept feeling painfully aware of my tongue's position in my mouth, and Kat Gold's rendition of my mannerisms caused me to contemplate jumping off the tallest building I could find.

"Good," Agent Allison says, her big blue eyes made bluer by our proximity to the ocean. "I'm glad it's been a good learning experience for you."

"Kat's been a great mentor," I say, and Astrid of three years ago would have found this to be a very corny thing to say, but it's true—I don't necessarily admire or even like Kat Gold, but she's paying my bills and she laughs extremely hard at my jokes—and, well, I can't bite the hand that feeds me.

I want to ask about my new book but decide to wait. The waiter brings our fries and salads and we talk about other peoples' books. What we're reading. Which writers are crazy. Which writers slept with their editors' husbands. (Believe it or not, there's more than one.) We talk about the Housewives and the Kardashians, how it's strange that actresses are seen as more high-brow than reality TV stars when Bethenny Frankel clearly has a higher IQ than 99.9 percent of actresses, including Kat Gold.

When we're done with our salads and most of our drinks, Agent Allison tells me she thinks my book is ready to put on submission.

"I still can't believe you wrote a love story," she says, picking up a fry.

I shrug. I guess I didn't realize I was writing a love story. I thought I was just writing a book. Maybe every book is a love story. And I'm definitely in love with writing books, which elicits in me the same feelings as a crush and is often accompanied by the same crushing disappointment when things don't work out. But I'm grateful for Agent Allison. Good writing doesn't exist in a vacuum; it requires a nurturing and motivating community. Sophie and Agent Allison helped me get from twenty-six, being a cocky little provocateur, to thirty-six, realizing I just want to write something entertaining and sweet, that love is beyond politics, that it's cosmic and universal, and that's all people want from a book.

Just after we get the check, my phone lights up on the table with a text from Penelope Paladino.

Agent Allison must clock something on my face because she says, "Someone exciting?"

"Just an old friend," I say.

.....

I'm awaiting my car at the valet and watching waves crash in the distance when a high-pitched cackle pierces the air. Two drunk girls, women, whatever, tumble out of the back of a black car, arms wrapped around each other in a way that makes it unclear to me whether they're sisters or dykes. When they start making out, I'm relatively convinced it's the latter. I try not to stare and shift my gaze back to the ocean. Out of my periphery, their heads part and I am surprised to hear my name.

"Astrid?" one of the women says, and she instantly looks familiar. She has ash blonde hair and wide-set eyes. It's Nadia the Russian knot scholar. How does she remember my name?

"Hi," I say uncomfortably. It's hard to establish small talk with someone you met for twelve seconds, but whose pretentious esoteric website you've visited dozens of times. "You're Penelope's friend?"

Nadia snickers and so does her friend-slash-lover. A realization appears to dawn on the friend-slash-lover's face. "Oh my god," she says. "It's Astrid the Swedish novelist."

Nadia jabs her friend's rib cage, and I'm frozen by the realization that Nadia was perhaps obsessing about me in the precise way I was obsessing about her.

"Penelope and I aren't really friends," Nadia says. "She sort of ghosted me."

I shoot the valet attendant a threatening look, hoping he'll make my car appear quicker, like now, so I can escape.

"Are you still with Penelope?" Nadia asks.

"We were never really together," I say. I don't say that she sort of ghosted me too.

Nadia cocks her head and I can't believe this woman staring at me blankly got a perfect score on her GREs. She's wearing a bodycon dress and a cloying floral perfume, and I wonder if Sophie was confusing her with a different Nadia. This woman can't be an academic studying Slavic knots. Maybe she can. Ivy's an academic and she was always wearing pink cowboy boots. Maybe they're all aesthetically questionable.

"Oh," Nadia says. "She really liked you."

I shrug. I don't know why Nadia is still talking to me. But I guess I've cornered unwilling participants into similar conversations on the Patricia Highsmith.

"She's very compelling, Penelope," Nadia says, seeming suddenly more sober and like she might actually have a brain. "The way she alternates between making you feel safe and cared for and then pulling away, like she's completely forgotten about you and you wonder if you imagined her attention. It's a powerful elixir." Nadia giggles. "Like a drug."

Saving me, the drunker friend-slash-lover tugs Nadia's arm. "Let's go, babe," she whispers in Nadia's ear.

"Nice seeing you, Astrid," Nadia says.

My car arrives as the girls stumble off.

· · · ·

I decide not to open Penelope's text until I'm home.

On the drive, I watch the turquoise water give way to winding canyons and obsess over my conversation with Nadia. I keep thinking of the scene in *Carol* where Therese wakes up to find Carol gone and Abby, Carol's ex played by Sarah Paulson, in her place. Therese is all silent and disturbed, and Abby is just chatting at her, sort of like I was staring at the water while Nadia chatted at me. Just two women left in the lonely wake of an inscrutable older woman's affection.

Once I'm deposited from the canyon onto the 101, and there is nothing pretty to stare at, I call Sophie.

"Guess who I just ran into?" I say when she answers.

"Oh no, not Ivy again," Sophie says, then forces a yawn. Even in my nervy state, I appreciate Sophie's performative boredom.

"Nope," I say.

"Penelope?" she says.

"Nope," I say. "Although she did text me."

"*Pardon?*" Sophie says. "Bury the lede much? Is she back in LA?"

"I don't know," I say. "I haven't opened the text."

"You're so strange, Astrid," Sophie says.

Kat Gold said my strangeness was a gift.

"Well then, who?" Sophie asks, seeming less taken with my strangeness. "I give up. You have too many complicated relationships with too many women for me to run through them all."

I frown at the freeway.

"Nadia Kotov."

"Oh yeah, she's hot," Sophie says. "Did you date her too? Jesus, how do you even find the time?"

"No, no, I didn't date her," I say. "But she just stopped me at this random hotel in Malibu. She told me Penelope ghosted her and said she's very compelling, like a drug," I say. "Oh, and her friend said, 'That's Astrid the Swedish novelist' like in the same way I was calling her 'Nadia the Russian knot scholar.'"

"God, dykes are so unhinged," Sophie says, and I can't tell if she's talking about Nadia or her friend or me or all three of us.

"I thought about what Carmen said." Carmen is now Sophie's

girlfriend, and in fact they just moved in together, and I'm happy for Sophie and only a little envious, only occasionally wondering *why her and not me.* "About Carol being evil, and I thought about that scene when Carol ditches Therese and sends Abby to fetch her, and Abby is chatting while Therese is just staring, and in Malibu I felt like I was Therese and Nadia was Abby."

"I think Nadia is more of a Rooney Mara," Sophie says, and I'm a little hurt, even though she's totally right from a purely aesthetic perspective.

"Okay, okay," I say. "No one is arguing that I'm anywhere near as pretty as Nadia Kotov."

"Oh, that's so not what I meant," says Sophie. "I actually prefer Sarah Paulson. Rooney seems dead inside. You used to seem dead inside, but less so now." I hear another woman's voice in the background. "Carmen's here."

"Hi, Carmen," I say. "Put her on speaker."

"Hi, Astrid," Carmen says, her voice a little tinny.

"I have a question regarding Patricia Highsmith," I say, and for once I'm talking about the actual author and not my former drug cocktail.

Carmen groans theatrically and I really do love her for Sophie, and I really am only a little jealous.

"Did Penelope Carol me?" I ask. "Did she fling me into space and am I stuck here for good?" I'm annoyed at the realization that I've been thrust back into Penelope's dumb orbit, that all my work trying to get over her seems to have evaporated with one encounter with one Russian knot scholar, and one text I haven't read yet.

"Penelope texted Astrid today," Sophie pipes in. "Astrid never provides context. Oh, and she also ran into this other woman Penelope briefly dated and the woman sort of cornered her and Astrid thinks she's in *The Price of Salt.*"

Carmen sighs. "Every dyke thinks she's in *The Price of Salt*," she says.

"Thanks for nothing," I say.

"Just tell Astrid what she wants to hear," Sophie says. "It's easier for everyone."

I'm pretty sure I hear them kiss and it's cute and disgusting.

"Look," says Carmen. "I don't know Penelope well, but I've met her a few times and she seems decent. Carol is a straight-up sociopath. I don't get that vibe from Penelope."

"Other people Astrid have dated have that vibe," Sophie says.

"Shush," I say to Sophie, then to Carmen, "Nadia the ex-lover said Penelope is like a drug."

"All women are like drugs," Carmen says, and I think I hear them kiss again.

"Okay," I say. "I'll let you all go."

"Thank god," Sophie says. I hear shuffling in the background. "Penelope is compelling, but so are you. Don't forget it."

She hangs up.

I consider this word, *compelling*, that keeps being thrown around with respect to Penelope and now, according to Sophie, me. What does it even mean? I ask Siri, "What is the definition of compelling?" My little robot responds, "Compelling, adjective, means evoking interest, attention, or admiration in a powerfully irresistible way." Okay, it's essentially witchcraft.

Exiting the freeway, I experience a brief moment of gratitude that I'm a lesbian. That I don't have to get Botox or filler or a ponytail facelift because to do so would invite the male gaze, and it's the female gaze I'm after, and we just want *compelling*, which is energetic and cannot be reduced to a visual. How a year ago I was so crushed to be thirty-five, I thought it indicated that my youth was over, that my life was over, that I'd aged out of being a party twink and therefore had nothing to look forward to but death and decay. But now I realize my life is just starting. I've stopped being a dumb little provocateur, I keep my rude thoughts to myself, I've just written a love story, and men have finally stopped looking at me.

I never believed Dan Savage when he said "It gets better," but maybe I just hadn't waited long enough.

: : :

Back home, when I finally open Penelope's text, it's very anti-climactic. *Astrid, I'm back in LA. Would love to buy you a coffee this week if you're free.—Penelope.*

I consider telling her I just ran into her friend, but like Nadia said, they aren't friends. Penelope ghosted Nadia and probably doesn't want to hear about her. I'm surprised she even wants to see me, Astrid the Swedish novelist, who she also ghosted.

Fingering my green amethyst, I respond that I'm free Thursday.

sixteen

Penelope is living in Eagle Rock again, but on the other side of the hill from Deedee's. We meet at a coffee shop between us.

When I arrive, Penelope is already seated at a table, looking at her phone. She's wearing that red dress, and I start to wonder if she owns any other dresses. She's wearing lipstick and eyeliner. I'm wearing Sambas.

Penelope lights up when she sees me. She hugs me and I smell patchouli that briefly jolts me back in time. While obsessing over her absence, I ordered samples of nearly every patchouli-forward scent I could find on the internet. But nothing smelled like her. I could ask her right now and solve the mystery, but I worry the answer will be disappointing, and besides: I've moved on.

"You look incredible," she says.

"Thanks," I say. "You too." She looks the same, still very pretty, but a little older, which I suppose is natural given that time has passed. There are more gray hairs around her ears. I like that she doesn't bother to color them. In Los Angeles, it's very rare to see a woman who allows herself to age naturally, and I must admit: it's compelling.

Her nipples peek through her dress, and I look away.

"How was the desert?" I ask.

"Oh, it was fantastic," she says, then gets up. "Let me buy you something."

I let her get me a cappuccino, and while she's gone, I steal a quick sniff of my wrist. Privately whiffing my own arm is the closest thing I have to the Patricia Highsmith these days, sniffing secretly the way I used to covertly take drugs in bathrooms. I'm wearing the moon milk, have been wearing it since that romantic bender in Penelope's bungalow. For a few months, I associated it with her, with her bungalow, with safety and warmth and red and green, velvet and paint, and I even smelled patchouli even though that's not a note in the perfume. But eventually, it started to smell like me. A Swedish girl. Spicy and moody but secretly sweet. I spritz it every morning, the tiniest amount, and the scent keeps me company throughout the day. I even bought a whole bottle, which has a rounded cream-colored cap that resembles a breast. I guess I finally have a signature scent. And what is that if not maturity?

Penelope returns with my cappuccino and a matcha for herself. Lesbians and their matcha, I swear to God.

"I was really taken with your letter," she says.

"Is that why you didn't reply?" I say.

"I didn't want to start something."

"Then why are we here?"

"I made a promise," she says.

I sip my drink. It's a dumb answer, which she maybe senses because she keeps talking.

"I was going to feel it out."

"What are you feeling?" I ask.

"That you're annoyed at me." She looks down at her matcha. "Rightfully so."

"Not annoyed," I say, and it's true. "Just sort of . . . awkward?

Like not nervous, but we have no precedent for our relationship outside of this hyper-particular context."

"You're right," Penelope says. She laughs, and I start to see a flash of what I saw before, a rosy warmth brightening her features, lighting up her eyes. "You're completely right."

"Do we have anything in common?" I ask. "Other than Cat Power."

"We both like Zev," Penelope says. "And Otto. And Felix."

"You like Felix more than I do," I say, then remember how Felix saved me from Poison Ivy and feel guilty. I guess I like Felix too. I guess I love him.

"I met his girlfriend," Penelope says.

"Huh?" How did Penelope meet my brother's girlfriend before I did?

"They were climbing in Joshua Tree and stopped by," she says. "She was sweet. Pretty."

"A pretty outdoorswoman," I say. "He should marry her."

Penelope laughs. "He told me he's thinking about it."

And—poof—I'm back in the dream state. Not real life, but reality adjacent. Familiar characters acting uncharacteristically.

"Does she look like a YouTube yoga teacher?" I ask Penelope.

"You know," she says. "I've never done YouTube yoga, but if I picture it—" She closes her eyes and I get a better look at her, the smudged eyeliner, dark red lips, her pronounced eye sockets, more pronounced than last time, and just when my gaze moves down to her nipples, she opens her eyes. "Yep," she says, and my eyes dart back up. She definitely caught me looking, and smiles deviously, and I'm so deep in the dream. "YouTube yoga teacher for sure."

Penelope sips her matcha. A tiny bit of green remains on her upper lip and I fantasize, briefly, about licking it off.

"I assume you're seeing someone?" Penelope asks as I stare at her upper lip.

My heart rate quickens and I don't think it's the caffeine, or at least not just the caffeine. "Nope," I say. "Totally celibate." A bead of sweat drips down my arm.

Penelope looks surprised, maybe happy.

"I assume you're over me now that I no longer need saving?" I know she isn't seeing someone. I can tell by the way her nipples are screaming at me.

I expect her to laugh, but she doesn't. She's silent for a moment. "Not at all," she says finally. "I'm under you."

"Oh, no," I say.

Penelope looks hurt for a second.

"I prefer you on top." I smile, and Penelope nearly chokes on her matcha. We both laugh.

"Hey," I say when a silence falls between us. "Can I ask you something?"

Penelope nods.

"The patchouli," I say. "Your scent. What is it?"

"Oh." Penelope laughs. "I make it myself. I use this aged patchouli oil I found at an Italian pharmacy near Portofino. And I mix it with a little vetiver and rose. And jojoba oil as a carrier."

"Of course," I say, "I tried to find it online."

"That's adorable," she says, and I think she's going to say something else, but instead she just looks down and grabs her purse. She's obviously going to bolt because I've been too extra and thrown myself at her like a fool. I'm typing *SLAA meeting near me* on my phone under the table when Penelope places something between us. I look up from my phone. A translucent green stone sits on the table.

"I bought a green amethyst," she tells me.

Mildly possessed, I pull my chain out from under my T-shirt. Penelope leans over and touches the gem. I shiver. The stone throbs on my chest.

I sip my drink. "Do you have it on you?"

Penelope raises an eyebrow.

"The patchouli," I say.

She picks up the stone. "No," she says. "It's at my house."

"Can I spray it on you?" I ask.

She smirks, rubs the stone with her thumb. "You're a strange one, Astrid Dahl."

"That's a yes?"

:::::

Penelope's new living room is decorated with the same blood-red rugs and velvet furniture and dead roses, and the scent hits me like a ton of bricks: palo santo and paint and musk and, of course, patchouli. The space is less homey than Deedee's—angular with newer fixtures—and the yard is smaller. There's a rusty metal table under a lemon tree, where I sit while Penelope retrieves the perfume.

While I wait, I pull out my phone. I have a text from Sophie. *How is it??* I'm not sure how I could possibly answer that. I also have two texts from Kat Gold. *Guess where I am, bitch??* Then, *K Stew's bed baby!!!* I write back, *suck her bones pretty!!* then turn off my phone.

When I look up, Penelope appears in the door frame in just a bra and her underwear—both black lace. Pinched in between two dark green fingernails is the perfume bottle.

"Come," Penelope says.

I get up, go to her, and she grabs my hand like she did at the Cat Power show, and I'm just so deep in the dream. She pulls me through the kitchen and into her bedroom. Eyeing the cloud lamp above the bed, I start to feel afraid. Nadia the Russian knot scholar said Penelope is compelling because she gives you warmth and then yanks it away, like a drug, like Carol did to Therese. But Carmen said I'm not actually in *The Price of Salt*, that I'm not in any novel, that this is, in fact, my life.

Penelope hands me the perfume.

I spritz it once into the air and inhale deeply, feel my thoughts slow down. Penelope lies on the bed and motions with a green fingernail for me to come closer, a come-hither motion like she did in my dream. I take off my shoes and, for the sake of equality, my shirt and my jeans as well. Then I straddle her. First, I spray her neck, and when I do, she tilts her head back and moans quietly. I spray her collarbone, her decolletage, shoulders, biceps, forearms, and fingers. I spray her abdomen, still toned and freckled, her belly button. I spray her hips, her bikini line, her thighs. I spray her calves and her feet and her toes. Then she turns over, and I spray her shoulder blades, the arch of her lower back, her ass cheeks.

I spray and I spray and I spray and my mind disappears. I don't think, I just spray. And Penelope continues to moan softly, and soon I'm moaning, and then we're kissing, and she tries to put her fingers inside me, but I push them away. "Not yet," I say. I keep spraying. Orange light splashes on the wall.

I spray her until the bottle is empty.

Acknowledgments

Infinite thanks to my agent, Sarah Phair, who worked tirelessly with me on this book and many others. Massive thanks to my dream editor, Olivia Taylor Smith, with whom I've been blessed to work on three books, and the whole Simon & Schuster team. Big thanks to Sarah Fonseca for her early insight and lesbian pulp history lesson. Major thanks to early readers: Diana Clarke, Crissy Milazzo, Vanessa Roveto, and Ariel Courage. And to my writing group, SFD—KK Wootton, Catie Disabato, Maggie Murray, Ana Reyes, Adam D'Alba, and Jon Doyle—who helped immensely on this draft and thankfully is nothing like Sapphic Scribes. Thank you to my family for their support. And thank you Patricia Highsmith, who said, "Obsessions are the only things that matter."

About the Author

Anna Dorn is the author of three books: *Vagablonde, Bad Lawyer*, and *Exalted. Exalted* was nominated for a Los Angeles Times Book Prize. Anna lives in Los Angeles.